THE COURTESAN'S JEWEL BOX

Chinese Stories of the Xth-XVIItb Centuries

TRANSLATED BY
YANG XIANYI and GLADYS YANG

Fredonia Books
Amsterdams. The Netherlands

The Courtesan's Jewel Box

Translated by
Yang Xianyi and Gladys Yang

ISBN: 1-58963-433-0

Reprinted from the 1981 edition

Fredonia Books
Amsterdam, the Netherlands
http://www.fredoniabooks.com

CONTENTS

Introduction

YAN DUNYI[1]

The development in China of short stories written in the language of everyday speech was closely related to a form of folk literature deeply rooted among the people — the art of story-telling.

Professional story-tellers in the market-places would improve on historical or traditional tales until these came to possess a high literary value. Later these stories were transcribed and these texts, known as *hua ben* 话本, were the scripts used and handed down by story-tellers. As time went on they became more and more widely known, found their way into the hands of men outside the profession, and were compiled as written stories. But in China they are usually referred to as *hua ben* or "story-tellers' scripts," to indicate their origin.

Stories written in the vernacular during the Song (960-1279) and Yuan (1279-1368) Dynasties developed from these early story-tellers' scripts. This accounts for their popularity among the common people of that time, and for the fact that both in form and content they differ from the earlier stories in the classical language.

The classical tales of the third to tenth centuries deal for the most part with supernatural beings, ghosts and miraculous events, or with love and separation; but since they were written in the classical language, they could not be widely read and were known to a limited circle only. From the Tang Dynasty (618-907) onwards there was a great development of mercantile

---

[1] A deceased editor of classical literature in the People's Literature Publishing House, Beijing

economy in China, large towns grew up, handicraft industries prospered, and a considerable urban population appeared. Since few townsmen were well versed in the literary language and the contents of the classical stories were remote from their everyday life, they were greatly attracted by the tales of the story-tellers which developed to meet their demands.

After the establishment of the Song Dynasty there was a further expansion of agriculture, commerce and handicrafts, and the towns became increasingly prosperous. The two great cities of Bianliang (present-day Kaifeng) and Lin'an (present-day Hangzhou) were centres for the development of the story-tellers' art. These stories have a characteristic form. They usually open with quotations from poems which have little or nothing to do with the plot; and the main story is often preceded by an anecdote known as the introductory story, which has a similar theme or some relationship to the main topic. These features developed to meet specific needs, to fill up the time while the listeners gathered round and settled down, or to lengthen the duration of the recital. Often the story itself is also interspersed with verses and concludes with a verse or certain set phrases. The language is lively and fluent, being the vivid, highly expressive vernacular of that time, and comments and questions are frequently addressed directly to the readers. All these characteristics of the oral narrative have been retained in the written scripts.

The contents of these tales were also enriched by the use of material from many sources. Thus we find love stories challenging the feudal conventions, accounts of the revolts of peasants and townsfolk against the ruling class, tales of the supernatural, satires which ridicule not only the ruling class but even kings and emperors, as well as stories of trials and detection which demonstrate the people's wisdom, and chronicles of happenings in real life. During the troubled years of the Southern Song Dynasty (1127-1279) these stories also described the people's sufferings and the cruelty of the invaders, laying stress on certain victories against the aggressors in order to inspire and encourage the people. Almost all these tales without exception were created by folk artists, who produced these written scripts on the basis of their own experience and artistic gifts from stories approved by many listeners and revised by a succession of story-tellers. Hence this was truly anonymous folk literature. Of course, these stories may have been improved upon by members of the writers' groups organized by educated men of the time to transcribe and polish scripts for folk artists; but undoubtedly the oral versions were kept substantially unchanged, these scripts being in fact the written records of this oral literature. They enjoyed a much greater popularity than general accounts of past history, for they gave a fuller picture of real society and real life, and the listeners could understand clearly the events described and sympathize completely with the characters in the stories.

Another characteristic of the Song Dynasty tales was the extent to which they reflected contemporary life and expressed the ideas, interests and wishes of the urban class. Since the makers of these stories were townsfolk themselves, their likes and dislikes, joys and sorrows, were the same as those of the urban class as a whole, as can be seen in their development of plots and characterization.

During the Mongol invasion of China little progress was made in this form of literature, which did not recover till after the establishment of the Ming Dynasty (1368-1644), when production and agriculture were restored, mercantile capital expanded, many large and small towns sprang up, and a brisk trade was carried on with other countries. By the middle of the sixteenth century, therefore, these stories had revived to meet the needs and demands of a greater urban population, and similar short stories were being written by the literati themselves. Such stories, which existed as literature to be read instead of transcriptions of oral narrations, are known as "stories modelled on *hua ben*." Composed by writers, they may in a sense be considered as modern short stories, though they retain the form and distinctive style of the earlier story-tellers' scripts.

During the Ming Dynasty, stories modelled on *hua ben* took the place of the old scripts transcribed from oral narrations; and this fact naturally led to changes in content. Although the stories written during the Ming Dynasty continue to reflect contemporary life, sometimes even more penetratingly than the earlier *hua ben,* while the construction of the plot and the language also show a certain improvement, these tales are often moralistic and attach undue importance to outward form and strange incidents. Such tendencies were inevitable in the transformation of these stories from pure folk art to the work of the literati, and they are most marked towards the end of the dynasty. Later these tales declined, becoming lifeless, decadent and unrealistic. Thus when we speak of this form of literature, we refer to the stories written before the end of the Ming Dynasty.

Probably even in the Song and Yuan Dynasties there were printed texts recorded from early oral narratives, which were doubtless polished and revised at the time; but hitherto we have found no text which we can affirm with certainty was first printed in the Song Dynasty. The earliest existing collections are Song stories edited and compiled in the Ming Dynasty. Ming scholars collected, edited and published old stories while writing new ones themselves, taking the opportunity of including in the collections of old tales certain new ones which had never been used as scripts by story-tellers.

The most important collection is the well-known one edited by Feng Menglong, which is divided into three books of forty stories each: *Stories to Teach Men* 喻世明言, *Stories to Warn Men* 警世通言, and *Stories to Awaken Men* 醒世恒言. Feng Menglong was a dramatist, collector of folk literature, and writer of stories and novels who lived at the end of the sixteenth and beginning of the seventeenth century. Some of the stories in his collection can be assigned definitely to the Song and Yuan Dynasties, others to the middle of the Ming Dynasty, and some are by Feng himself. He must also have polished or rewritten some of the old stories, for in certain places one can detect his style. These three books provide our most important material for the study of this type of literature.

After Feng Menglong another dramatist, Lin Mengchu, published another collection of stories modelled on the *hua ben* known as *Astonishing and Miraculous Tales* 拍案惊奇, containing seventy-nine stories in all, forty in the first volume, thirty-nine in the second. But whereas Feng's are mainly earlier tales re-edited and published with some of the editor's own stories, the *Astonishing and Miraculous Tales* are entirely the work of Lin Mengchu.

At the beginning of the Qing Dynasty (1644-1911) there appeared a popular collection containing forty stories, known as *Strange Stories Past and Present* 今古奇观. Nearly all the tales in this come from Feng and Lin's works. A number of them are somewhat moralistic, others are excellent stories. Since there were very few printed editions of Feng's works, for a time this later book became the most popular collection.

The twenty stories presented in this selection have been chosen from Feng and Lin's collections. Written between the tenth and seventeenth centuries, they are some of the most representative tales of the heyday of *hua ben* literature and the period of its revival. Of these, "The Jade Worker," "Fifteen Strings of Cash," "The Monk's Billet-Doux," "The Foxes' Revenge" and "The Honest Clerk" probably date from the Song Dynasty. The dates of "The Oil Vendor and the Courtesan" and "The Old Gardener" are uncertain. The remaining thirteen belong to the Ming Dynasty.

These stories are of different types and have different themes. Most of the categories of short stories mentioned earlier can be found here. These tales were selected for their positive message, their high artistic qualities, and their truthfulness to life. With great realism they reflect the social conditions of the time and the people's ideals and struggles. While portraying what was progressive in the outlook of the townsmen of those days, they satirize feudal morality and feudal society.

These tales are far removed, of course, from modern short stories; but if we compare them with earlier tales and anecdotes in our classical literature, they seem relatively close to us. And they form an important part of our literary heritage.

In this English edition some of the verses and introductory anecdotes, which are unrelated to the main story or would require copious footnotes, have been cut.

The twenty-two illustrations in this book are reproduced from Ming Dynasty editions of the early seventeenth century. These photographs were supplied by the deceased Professor Wang Gulu of Beijing Normal University.

盛滿五樓不下烈火
性卸惟望妙乎佳閣
椿子

The Jade Worker

During the Shao Xing period (1131-1162) there lived in Hang-zhou, the southern capital, a certain Prince of Xian'an, who was a native of Yan'an and the military governor of three garrison areas. One day, seeing that spring was nearly over, he took some of his womenfolk out to enjoy the scenery. On their way back in the evening, they had passed through Qiantang Gate and the women's sedan-chairs had just crossed Carriage Bridge when the prince, whose chair brought up the rear, heard some-one call from a shop by the bridge:

"Come out, lass, and look at the prince."

A girl came out, at sight of whom the prince exclaimed to his bodyguard: "This is just the girl I have been looking for! See that you bring her to the palace tomorrow."

The bodyguard assented, and immediately set about carrying out the prince's orders. There was a house beside the bridge with a signboard on which was written: The House of Qu, Ancient and Modern Paintings Mounted. And it was out of this shop that an old man had come, leading a girl.

What was she like, this girl?

Her cloudlike hair was lighter than cicada's wing;
Her mothlike eyebrows fairer than hills in spring;
Her lips were cherry-red, her teeth like jade,
And sweeter than an oriole she could sing.

Such was the girl who had come out to see the prince's sedan-chair.

The bodyguard sat down in a tea-house opposite, and when an old woman brought him tea he said: "May I trouble you

1

to ask Mr. Qu from the mounting shop across the street to step over to have a word with me?"

The woman fetched Old Qu; and after the men had exchanged greetings they sat down.

"What can I do for you?" asked Old Qu.

"It is nothing — just an idle question. Is the girl you called out to watch the prince's sedan-chair your daughter?"

"She is. We have only the one child."

"How old is she?"

"Eighteen."

"Do you intend to marry her to someone or to present her to some official?"

"I'm a poor man. Where would I get the money to marry her off? I shall have to send her to serve in some official's house."

"What accomplishments has your daughter?"

Then Old Qu told him, in the words of the song:

> As days grow longer, in her quiet room
> The girl embroiders many a flower in bloom,
> And rivals Nature with her needle now
> To stitch bright blossoms on a slanting bough,
> With tender leaves, soft buds and tendrils rife,
> In all but scent completely true to life;
> So many a roving butterfly and bee
> Fly in to light on her embroidery.

"Just now," said the bodyguard, "the prince noticed from his sedan-chair the embroidered apron your daughter is wearing. We are looking for a girl to do embroidery in the palace. Why don't you present your daughter to the prince?"

The old man went home and talked it over with his wife; and the next day he drew up a petition and took the girl to the palace. The prince paid for the girl, and gave her the name Xiuxiu.

Some time later, when the emperor presented the prince with a flower-embroidered battle dress, Xiuxiu immediately made another exactly like it. The prince was pleased, and said: "His Majesty has given me this embroidered battle dress. What rare gift can I give him in return?"

He found a piece of fine, translucent white jade in his treasury, and calling for his jade workers asked them: "What can you make out of this piece of jade?"

"A set of wine cups," said one.

"That would be a pity," said the prince. "How can we use such a fine piece of jade to make wine cups!"

"This piece is pointed on top and round at the bottom," said another. "It can be made into the kind of doll women use when they pray for children."

"That type of figurine is only used on the seventh of the seventh month," objected the prince. "It would be useless at other times."

There was a young craftsman in the group whose name was Cui Ning, a native of Jiankang in Shengzhou. He was twenty-five years old and had served the prince for several years. Now he stepped forward with clasped hands and said: "Your Highness, this pear shape is no good. All it can be carved into is a Guanyin."

"Good!" exclaimed the prince. "The very thing!" He ordered Cui to start on the job.

In less than two months, the jade Guanyin was finished; and when the prince sent it with a petition to the imperial palace, the emperor was delighted with it. Cui's pay was increased, and he continued to serve the prince.

Time passed, until it was spring again. One day, on his way back from a pleasure trip, Cui went with three or four friends into a wineshop just inside Qiantang Gate. They had drunk a few cups only when he heard a great hubbub in the street, and throwing open the window to look out he heard people shouting: "There's a fire at Jingting Bridge!"

Not stopping to finish his wine, he and his companions ran downstairs and out into the street, where they saw a great fire:

First smouldering like glowworm's light,
It soon flared up like torches bright,
Outshone a thousand candles' glare
And made a blaze that filled the air,
As if whole mountains had been burned,
Or Heaven's furnace overturned!

So fierce was the fire!

"That's not far from our palace!" exclaimed Cui.

He ran back to the palace, only to find that everything had been moved out and the whole place was deserted. Unable to find a soul, he was heading down the left corridor in the bright glare of the fire, when a woman reeled out from the hall, muttering to herself, and collided with him. Recognizing Xiuxiu, Cui stepped back and murmured an apology.

The prince had formerly promised Cui: "When Xiuxiu has served her term, I shall marry her to you." The attendants had urged him on several times, saying: "You will make a fine couple!" And Cui had thanked them for their encouragement. He was a bachelor and had taken a fancy to the girl, while he was such a fine young man that Xiuxiu wanted him for her husband too.

Now, during this confusion, here was Xiuxiu coming down the left corridor with a handkerchief full of gold and jewels in her hand. When she bumped into Cui, she said: "Master Cui, I've been left behind! All the maids have run off, so there is no one to look after me. You must find me some place to stay."

Cui accompanied her out of the palace, and they walked along the river bank until they came to Lime Bridge. Then the girl said: "Oh, Master Cui, my feet do hurt so! I can't go any further."

Cui pointed to a nearby house and said: "My home is only a few steps from here. You can rest there." So they went into his house and sat down.

"I am ever so hungry," said Xiuxiu again. "Do buy me

some cakes to eat. And, after the fright I've had, a little wine would do me a world of good."

Cui thereupon bought some wine, and they drank a few cups together. And:

After the girl three cups of wine had drained,
Her downy cheeks two crimson blossoms stained.

As the proverb says: Spring is the time for flowers, and wine is the handmaid of love!

Xiuxiu asked Cui: "Do you remember that day when we were watching the moon on the tower, when the prince promised to marry me to you, and you thanked him. Do you remember that?"

Cui put his hands together respectfully and muttered: "Yes."

"That day," said Xiuxiu, "everybody cheered you and said what a fine couple we would make. How could you have forgotten?"

Once more, Cui simply mumbled: "Yes."

"Why should we go on waiting? Why not become husband and wife tonight? What do you think?"

"I dare not."

"If you refuse," she threatened, "I shall call out and get you into trouble. What did you bring me to your house for, anyway? I shall go and tell them at the palace tomorrow."

"Very well, miss," said Cui. "We can be husband and wife if you like. But on one condition: we must go away. We can take advantage of this fire and confusion to slip away tonight."

"Since I am your wife now," said Xiuxiu, "I'll do as you think best."

That night they became husband and wife; and before dawn they left, carrying their money and possessions with them. Stopping for meals on the way, resting at night and travelling by day, they finally came to Quzhou.

"There are five highways out of this town," said Cui. "Which way shall we take? Suppose we go to Xinzhou? I am a jade worker and I have friends in that city, so we may be able to settle down there." Accordingly they took the road to Xinzhou.

After they had been a few days in Xinzhou, however, Cui said: "Many people travel to and fro between here and the capital, and if anyone tells the prince that we are here, he will certainly send men to arrest us. We aren't safe here. We had better go somewhere else." Then they set out again for Tanzhou.

After some time they reached Tanzhou, which was a long way from the capital. They rented a house in the marketplace, and put up a signboard on which was written: Cui, the Jade Worker from the Capital.

"We are nearly a thousand miles from the capital now," Cui told Xiuxiu. "I think we should be all right. We can set our minds at ease and live the rest of our lives as husband and wife."

There were some officials in Tanzhou, and, when they found that Cui was a skilled worker from the capital, they gave him work from time to time.

Cui made secret inquiries about the Prince of Xian'an, and learned from someone who had been to the capital that during the fire that night a maid had disappeared from the palace; a reward had been offered for her discovery and a search had been made for several days, but she had never been found. No one knew that Cui had gone off with her, nor that they were living in Tanzhou.

Time sped as swiftly as an arrow, until more than a year had passed.

One morning when Cui opened his shop, two men in footmen's black liveries came in, sat down and told him: "Our master has heard that there is a worker named Cui here from the capital, and he wants you to come to do some work for him."

Telling his wife where he was going, Cui left with the two men for Xiangtan County. They took him to a house where he met the official, agreed to undertake the work and then started home again. On his way home he passed a traveller. This man was wearing a bamboo fibre hat, a cloth jacket with a white collar, black and white puttees and sandals, and he was carrying two bundles hanging from a long shoulder pole. When they came face to face, the traveller looked closely at Cui. Cui paid no attention to him, but this stranger had recognized the jade worker and he proceeded to walk briskly after him.

Well might we say:

What mischievous boy sounds the clapper today,
To make the love-birds fly away?

II

On bamboo fence the morning glories bloom,
The moon casts chequered shade on my thatched room;
My crystal goblets filled with country wine,
And country dainties in jade dishes fine,
I should at last have cast all cares away,
To spend my time in mirth and laughter gay;
Though all my friends are far away or dead,
A hundred thousand soldiers I once led.

This poem was written by General Liu Qi of the Xiongwu Army Area in Qinzhou. After the Battle of Shunchang in 1140, General Liu had retired to live in Xiangtan County in Tanzhou. A famous general who had never attempted to amass wealth, he was in fact very poor. He often went to village inns to drink, and the villagers who did not know him sometimes made rowdy jokes at his expense. "I held a million barbarian troops as nothing," remarked the general once. "But now these country folk treat me with contempt!"

So he wrote this poem which became known in the capital. When the Prince of Yanghe, then Commander of the Imperial Guards, saw this poem he was very moved. "To think that General Liu should become so poor!" he exclaimed. He ordered officers to send money to him. And when Cui's former master, the Prince of Xian'an, heard of the general's poverty, he also sent a messenger with money to him. This messenger, who passed through Tanzhou, was the man who saw Cui on the road from Xiangtan and followed him all the way home.

He saw Xiuxiu sitting at the counter of the shop, and called out: "Master Cui! I haven't seen you for a long time. How does Xiuxiu come to be here too? I have been delivering a letter for the prince to Tanzhou; that is how I happen to be here. So Xiuxiu has married you. Well, well!"

Cui and his wife were nearly scared to death now that they had been recognized. This newcomer was a sergeant in the palace who had served the prince since he was a boy. Because he was trustworthy, he had been chosen to take the money to General Liu. His name was Guo Li, and he was also known as Sergeant Guo.

Cui and Xiuxiu entertained Sergeant Guo to a feast, and begged him: "When you go back to the palace, for Heaven's sake don't breathe a word about us to the prince!"

"The prince will never know," replied Guo. "I hope I can mind my own business." Then he thanked them and left.

When he reached the palace, he gave the prince the general's reply; then, looking at his master he reported: "On my way back, as I came through Tanzhou, I saw two people."

"Who were they?"

"That girl Xiuxiu and the jade worker Cui. They gave me a meal and wine, and told me to say nothing."

"So that's what they have been up to!" exclaimed the prince. "How did they get all that way?"

"I don't know," said Guo. "I only know that he is living there now. He has a signboard up and is doing business."

The prince ordered his attendants to go to the city government and have an officer sent immediately with a warrant to Tanzhou. This officer took assistants and money for the road and, when he arrived at Tanzhou, requested the authorities there to help him to find Cui and Xiuxiu. It was like —

> *Swift hawks that on weak sparrows fall,*
> *Or tigers slaying lambkins small!*

In less than two months Cui and Xiuxiu were caught and sent to the palace. And as soon as the prince heard of their arrival, he took his seat in the court.

During his campaign against the Tartars, the prince had wielded a "small blue" sword in his left hand and a "big blue" sword in his right hand. And many were the Tartars those two swords had killed! They were now sheathed and hung on the wall of the court. When the prince had taken his seat and all had bowed to him, Cui and Xiuxiu were brought in and made to kneel before him. Fuming with rage, with his left hand the prince grasped the small blue sword and swung his right arm to draw it from the sheath, glaring as if he were killing Tartars again and gnashing his teeth in fury.

The prince's wife felt very nervous. "Your Highness!" she whispered to her husband from behind the screen. "We are right under the emperor's eye here! This is not the frontier. If they have done wrong, let the city authorities deal with them. Don't go slicing off heads at random."

The prince answered his wife: "How dare these two wretches run away! Now they are caught and I am angry, why shouldn't I kill them? But since you advise against it, I'll have the maid taken to the back garden and Cui sent to be tried by the city court." The prince also ordered that the officers who had arrested the runaways be rewarded with money and wine.

Haled before the city court, Cui confessed: "After the fire that night, when I went to the palace and found everything had been taken away, I met Xiuxiu in the corridor and she took hold of me and said: 'Why have you put your hand in my breast? Unless you do as I say, I shall make trouble for you.' She wanted to run away, and I had to go with her. This is the truth I'm telling."

The city authorities sent the record of the case to the Prince of Xian'an, who was a stern but just man. "Since this is the case," he said, "let Cui's punishment be light." To punish him for running away, Cui was beaten and banished to Jiankang.

Cui was sent off under armed escort. He had just left the North Gate and reached Gooseneck Bend, when he saw a sedan-chair behind him carried by two men and heard someone shouting: "Wait for me, Master Cui!" Cui thought he recognized Xiuxiu's voice, but could not understand how she came to be running after him. Once bitten, twice shy: bending his head, he kept on his way. Presently, however, the sedan-chair caught up with him and a woman got out who proved to be none other but Xiuxiu.

"You are going to Jiankang, but what about me?" she demanded.

"What do you want?"

"After you were sent to the city court for trial, I was taken to the back garden and given thirty strokes with a bamboo stick, then driven out. When I heard that you were going to Jiankang, I hurried after you to join you."

"Good," said Cui.

So they hired a boat and went straight to Jiankang, after which Cui's escort returned to the capital. If that escort had been a talkative fellow, Cui would have been in trouble again; but the man knew that the Prince of Xian'an had a fiery temper and that people who offended him did not escape lightly. Since he did not serve the prince, it was none of his business. Besides, Cui had treated him well on the way, buying him wine and food. So he held his tongue.

Cui and his wife settled down in Jiankang. And since he had already been sentenced, he was no longer afraid to meet people, but went on plying his trade as a jade worker.

"We are doing well here," said Xiuxiu one day, "but my two old parents must have had a hard time of it since I ran away with you to Tanzhou. And when we were arrested, they tried to commit suicide. Let us send someone to the capital to fetch them here to live with us."

"Very well," said Cui. He told a man where his wife's parents lived, and sent him to the capital to fetch them.

When the man reached the capital, he found the quarter

where Xiuxiu's parents lived and asked the people there to direct him to their house.

"There it is." Someone pointed it out to him.

He went to the gate but found it closed, locked and bolted with a bamboo bar. "Where have the old couple gone?" he asked a neighbour.

The neighbour said: "It's a sad story. They had a daughter as pretty as a flower, whom they presented to a noble family. But the girl was not content with her good fortune, and ran away with a jade worker. Some time ago, she and her lover were caught and sent back from Tanzhou for trial here. The girl was taken to the prince's back garden for punishment, and when that happened the old couple tried to take their own lives. They have since disappeared: that is why their house is locked up." This being so, the messenger went back to Jiankang.

One day, before his messenger had come back, Cui heard someone outside his shop saying, "You want Cui's shop? Here it is." When he called to Xiuxiu to see who it was, she found it was no other than her parents. They greeted each other, delighted to meet again. The next day, the messenger returned and reported how he had failed to find them, and journeyed in vain; but the two old folk had come of their own accord.

"Thank you for going to so much trouble," said Xiuxiu's parents to the messenger. "We didn't know where you were," they told Xiuxiu. "We had to search far and wide before we could find you." So they all settled down together.

Now one day the emperor went to his treasury to look at his treasures, and when he picked up the jade Guanyin Cui had made, one of the jade bells on the figure fell off.

"How can this be repaired?" he asked an officer in attendance.

The officer examined the carving and remarked: "What a fine figurine! It is a pity the bell is gone." When he looked at the base, he found the inscription: Made by Cui Ning. "It is quite simple!" he cried. "Since we know who carved this, all we have to do is call him here to repair it." Accordingly,

the emperor ordered the Prince of Xian'an to send Cui Ning to the palace.

When the prince reported that Cui was living at Jiankang because he had committed a crime, messengers were immediately despatched to summon him to the capital. The emperor gave Cui the jade figurine and told him to repair it carefully. Cui thanked the emperor, then found jade of the same colour as the original piece, made a new bell and fixed it to the Guanyin. When he returned the figurine to the emperor, he received a handsome reward and was ordered to move back to the capital.

"Now I am in the emperor's good books, I am in luck again!" said Cui. "I shall find another house by the river where I can set up my workshop; and I shan't care who sees me!"

As it happened, he had opened shop only a couple of days when Sergeant Guo passed by. When he saw Cui, he said: "Congratulations, Mr. Cui! So this is where you live!" But when he looked up and saw Xiuxiu standing behind the counter, he gave a start and turned to go.

"Call back that sergeant!" said Xiuxiu to Cui. "I want to ask him something."

A man who does not cause his friends to mourn
Will never feel their hatred and their scorn!

Cui laid hold of Sergeant Guo, who was shaking his head and muttering: "Strange! Strange!" And he had to go back with Cui to the shop.

After Xiuxiu had greeted Guo, she said: "Sergeant Guo, in Tanzhou we were good to you and kept you to a feast; but when you came back you told the prince and broke up our marriage. Now we have won the emperor's favour: we are not afraid of anything you may say!"

The sergeant had nothing to answer, and could only mutter an apology as he slunk off.

When he got back to the palace, he told the prince: "I have seen a ghost!"

"Is this fellow raving?" demanded the prince.

"Your Highness, I've seen a ghost!"

"What ghost?"

"Just now I passed the riverside and saw Cui's jade shop. Then I saw a woman behind the counter, and it was that maid Xiuxiu."

"Nonsense!" thundered the prince. "I had Xiuxiu beaten to death and buried in the back garden. You saw it yourself. How could she be there again? Are you trying to make a fool of me?"

"I wouldn't dare, Your Highness!" protested Guo. "Just now she called me to stop and spoke to me. If Your Highness doesn't believe me, I'm prepared to bet my life on it."

"All right," said the prince. "Write that down and sign it."

Guo was fated to get into trouble: he actually signed a wager, which the prince kept. Then the prince ordered two bearers who were on duty to take a sedan-chair to Cui's shop, and told Guo: "Fetch that woman here! If it is really Xiuxiu, I shall cut her head off! If it isn't, you shall take the punishment instead." Then Guo and the two bearers went to fetch Xiuxiu.

Guo was from the northwest. He was a simple fellow, and did not realize that one cannot sign documents like that. He went with the two bearers straight to Cui's shop, and found Xiuxiu sitting behind the counter. She saw Guo burst in, but did not know that he had bet his life that she was a ghost and come to arrest her.

"Madam!" cried Guo. "The prince has ordered us to take you to the palace."

"Wait a minute, then," said Xiuxiu, "while I have a wash and comb my hair." Having washed and changed her clothes she came out, mounted the sedan-chair and said goodbye to her husband.

When the bearers had carried her to the palace, Sergeant Guo went in first to the prince who was waiting in the hall. With a salute, Guo said: "I have brought Xiuxiu here."

"Fetch her in!" ordered the prince.

Guo went out and said: "Madam, the prince asks you to go in."

But when he lifted the chair curtain, he felt as if doused with a barrel of icy water. His jaw dropped and he stood there gaping, for Xiuxiu had vanished!

"We don't know what can have happened," said the two bearers when questioned. "We saw her get into the chair, we carried her here, and we haven't left the chair."

The sergeant was called back into the palace.

"Your Highness!" he shouted. "It really was a ghost!"

The prince swore: "This is too much!" and ordered: "Seize this fellow! Let me fetch that wager, and I shall cut off his head." He took down the small blue sword from the wall.

Sergeant Guo had served the prince for many years, during which period the prince had been promoted a dozen times: but because Guo was a rough fellow he had never risen higher than the rank of sergeant. Now he was panic-stricken, and said: "I have two bearers as witnesses. Please call them in and question them."

Immediately the two chair-bearers were sent for, and they said: "We saw her get into the sedan-chair, and we carried her here. But then she disappeared." Since their stories tallied, it seemed that Xiuxiu really must have been a ghost. Then the prince sent for Cui, who told him all that had happened.

"Apparently Cui is not to blame," said the prince. "Let him go." But when Cui had left, the enraged prince gave the sergeant fifty strokes on the back.

When Cui learned that his wife was a ghost, he went home to question her parents; but the two old people just looked at each other, then walked out of the door and jumped with a splash into the river. He immediately called for help and tried to rescue them, but they had vanished. The fact is that when Xiuxiu's parents knew that she had been beaten to death, they had drowned themselves in the river. They were ghosts too.

Cui went home in low spirits. When he reached his room, there was Xiuxiu sitting on the bed.

"My love!" begged Cui. "Spare me!"

"For your sake," answered Xiuxiu, "I was beaten to death by the prince and buried in the back garden. But it was all Sergeant Guo's fault — he talked too much. Today I have got my own back, because the prince has given him fifty strokes on the back; but now that everybody knows I am a ghost, I can't stay here any longer."

Having said this, she got up and seized Cui with both hands. He uttered a cry, and fell to the ground; and when the neighbours came in to look, they found that:

His pulse had stopped, his spirit fled,
And the unhappy man was dead!

So he was carried off to join his ghostly wife and parents.

The Honest Clerk

How can we judge today and yesterday?
Pomp is but vanity; so is decay.
Without my knowledge, time is slipping by
Like geese that to the far horizon fly.
My eyebrows now have turned as white as snow,
Faded my ruddy cheeks of long ago;
And sad at heart I gaze back at the glades
Where wild winds bluster as the daylight fades.

These lines were written by Wang Chuhou of Huayang County in the prefecture of Chengdu, when he was nearing sixty and saw in the mirror that his hair was turning white. Everything in the world must pass from youth through maturity to old age: this is a natural law to which there can be no exception. And, in the general way, everything turns from white to black: only beards turn from black to white. When a commissioner named Liu who wore flowers in his hair saw in the glass how white his hair had grown, he composed the following verses:

Mine has been a life of pleasure,
Drunk in spring I used to lie;
Old in years, my heart is young still,
Flowers tip my cap awry.
Now my hair and beard are white,
White as snow: it makes me sigh!
All in vain my friends have urged me
My white hair and beard to dye;
Once I dreaded dying beardless,
Now, long past my fifties, I

16

Do not care how white my hair is;
I shall sport it till I die!

This story is about a white-headed old man of Kaifeng, who was over sixty. He would not reconcile himself to being old, however, and his passion for the fair sex resulted in his losing all his money and nearly becoming a homeless ghost. What was his name and what did he do? For, as the poet says:

Though dust will always rise from trampling feet,
Too soon the human heart must cease to beat.

In Kaifeng, the eastern capital, lived a gentleman named Zhang Shilian who owned a thread shop. A widower of over sixty, he lived all alone, for he had no children; but with a fortune of a hundred thousand strings of cash he was able to employ two clerks to manage his business.

One day Mr. Zhang beat his breast and sighed.

"I am getting on in years," he told his two clerks, "but I have neither son nor daughter; so what use are my hundred thousand strings of cash?"

"Sir," replied the clerks, "why don't you marry again, so that you may have children who can continue to sacrifice to your ancestors?"

In raptures, Mr. Zhang sent immediately for the matchmakers Mrs. Zhang and Mrs. Li. What were they like, these two matchmakers?

All single folk they could lure to wed,
All loneliness cure on the marriage bed;
With ceaseless pressure and cunning wiles,
With sly enticements and tempting smiles,
They could make a goddess pine and sigh
And leave her heavenly court on high.

Mr. Zhang told the matchmakers: "I am worried, ladies, because I have no son. So I am going to trouble you to find a wife for me."

Mrs. Zhang said nothing.

"This old fellow has already got one foot in the grave," she was thinking. "Who would consent to marry him? What answer can I make?"

Mrs. Li nudged her, though, and said: "This is easy."

As the matchmakers were leaving, Mr. Zhang called them back to announce: "I have three conditions."

The words he uttered nearly sealed his doom,
To end a homeless ghost without a tomb!

"What are your three conditions?" asked the matchmakers.

"I'll tell you," said Mr. Zhang. "First, I want no ordinary woman: she must be a beauty. Secondly, her family status must equal mine. Thirdly, since I have a hundred thousand strings of cash, she must bring an equal amount as her dowry."

Laughing up their sleeves, the two matchmakers answered: "These three things can easily be managed." Then they took their leave.

On their way back, Mrs. Zhang said to Mrs. Li: "If we succeed in bringing this off, we shall make about a hundred strings of cash. But did you ever hear of anything like his conditions! A woman of the kind he wants — wouldn't she rather marry a young gentleman instead of an old man like him? Does he think that white beard of his is made of sugar?"

"I know of someone suitable," said Mrs. Li. "She is a beauty and her family status is as good as his."

"Who is she?"

"She used to be Minister Wang's concubine. When the minister first got her he doted on her; but she let fall some careless remarks which offended him, and now he is quite willing to give her away provided some respectable family wants her. She must have a few tens of thousands of strings of cash at the very least. I'm only afraid she is too young for him."

"We don't have to worry about her being too young, but about his being too old. Of course, Mr. Zhang will be satisfied with her; she's the one who won't feel too happy. But if we take twenty years off his age when we propose the match to her, then it should be all right."

"Tomorrow is a lucky day for matchmaking. I'll go with you first to Mr. Zhang's house to arrange the settlement; then we'll go on to fix it up with Minister Wang's side." This agreed, they went home.

The next day the two matchmakers met as arranged and went together to Mr. Zhang's house.

"Yesterday you laid down three conditions, sir, and we have been lucky enough to find just the woman for you," they told him. "First, she is very good-looking. Secondly, she comes from a respectable family — Minister Wang's. Thirdly, she has one hundred thousand strings of cash as dowry. We are just afraid you may consider her too young."

"How old is she?"

"She is nearly forty years younger than you."

Mr. Zhang was overjoyed and beamed with smiles.

"I am counting on you to bring this off!" he cried.

To tell the story briefly, both sides agreed; and after the usual exchange of presents and the gift of a swan, amid flowers and red candles the couple married. The next morning the sacrifice to the ancestors took place. Mr. Zhang wore a purple silk gown, new cap, new boots and socks; and the bride put on a wide-sleeved red silk dress with golden flower designs, a cape and a veil also embroidered with golden thread.

> With arching eyebrows like a crescent moon,
> With downy cheeks most like a peach in bloom,
> Lovely as jade and as a flower fair,
> Her charms were numberless, beyond compare;
> Her grace was infinite, her spirit high,
> She seemed, in short, a goddess from the sky!

As Mr. Zhang looked her over from head to foot, he silently congratulated himself; but when the bride lifted her veil and saw her husband's white beard and hair, she silently cursed her fate.   After the wedding night Mr. Zhang was happy, but his young wife was in despair.

One day more than a month later, a priest came to the house, bowed to Mr. Zhang and said: "Today your star is in the ascendant, so I have brought you your horoscope."   Indeed on the first and fifteenth of each month and on his birthday, Mr. Zhang always had his fortune told.

But after one look at the horoscope young Mrs. Zhang burst into tears; for she saw her husband's age there, and he was over sixty!   As she mentally cursed the two matchmakers for ruining her life, she realized that the old man had recently grown more infirm.

> *He had grown quite hard of hearing,*
> *And his kidneys ached all day;*
> *With a nose that ran, and rheumy eyes,*
> *He was in a shocking way!*

One day Mr. Zhang said to her: "I have to go out on business, my dear. I'm sorry to leave you by yourself."

"I hope you will come back early," the young wife forced herself to say.   But as he left she thought: "With my good looks and rich dowry, to be married to a white-bearded old man — it's too bad!"

Her maid, who was standing by, suggested: "Why not go out for a little while, madam, to pass the time?"   So the young wife went out with her maid.

Now outside the house was Mr. Zhang's shop, where rouge and thread were sold.   On both sides in the shop were shelves, while in the middle was a door-curtain with a purple silk fringe. There were two clerks in the shop.   One of them, Li Qing, was over fifty; the other, Zhang Sheng, was about thirty.   When the maid unhooked and lowered the curtain, the two clerks asked the reason, and she told them: "The mistress is coming out to look at the street."

When the two clerks stepped outside to bow to their mistress, the young woman parted her rouged lips to disclose dazzling white teeth, while the words she uttered pierced Zhang Sheng to the heart. She first called Li Qing to her and asked: "How long have you been with Mr. Zhang?"

"I have been here more than thirty years."

"Does he look after you well?"

"All that I possess I have received from the master," answered Li Qing.

When she put the same question to Zhang Sheng, he answered: "My father came here to work more than twenty years ago, and I came with my father to serve the master. I have been working for over ten years too."

"Does the master treat you well?"

"The food and clothes for all my family come from the master."

"Wait a minute," said the young mistress.

She turned and went inside, to come out again presently and offer something to Li Qing, who put his sleeve over his palm to take the gift and bowed to express his thanks. Then she called Zhang Sheng to her and said: "I must give you something too. This is not much, but you may find it useful."

Zhang Sheng, too, bowed to thank her for her gift. Then the young woman watched the street scene for some time before going in, while the two clerks went out on business. Now Li Qing had been given ten pieces of silver, whereas Zhang Sheng had been given ten pieces of gold. Zhang did not know, however, that Li had only received silver; neither did Li know that young Zhang had been given gold. The day was now growing late.

> *Birds fly back to the woods in gathering gloom;*
> *Candle in hand, the good wife seeks her room;*
> *Now travellers a roadside hostel choose,*
> *While fishermen walk home through the bamboos;*
> *And, riding on their plodding oxen slow,*
> *Back to the lonely village cowherds go.*

The clerks made up the accounts and handed in the account

books to their master. The record of all that had been bought and sold, including the amount of credit given, was then duly signed.

These two clerks were on duty in the shop on alternate nights, and this evening it was Zhang Sheng's turn. Outside the shop was a small room lit by a lamp, and here Zhang sat until he was ready to go to bed, when he heard a knock at the door.

"Who is it?" he asked.

"Open quickly," came the answer. "Then I'll tell you."

When he opened the door, someone slipped in and hid in the shadows. It was a woman.

Much surprised, Zhang demanded: "What brings you here so late, madam?"

"I have not come on private business," she answered. "The lady who gave you a present earlier in the day sent me."

"The mistress gave me ten pieces of gold. I suppose she has sent you to ask for them back."

"No, no, you don't understand. Li Qing was given only silver; but now the mistress has told me to bring you yet another present." She set down a bundle of clothes which had been fastened to her back, opened the bundle, and said: "These are for you, and these are for your mother." Then she took her leave of him and went out. She turned back, however, to say: "I forgot the most important thing!" She took from her sleeve a lump of silver weighing fifty taels, and leaving this with him went away.

Zhang Sheng was so bewildered by all these unexpected gifts that he could not sleep all night. Early the next morning, he opened the shop and attended the customers as usual; but as soon as Li Qing arrived Zhang turned the work over to him and went home. There he showed the clothes and silver to his mother.

"Where did you get these?" she asked.

When he told her all that had happened the previous day, she said: "Son, what does your young mistress mean by giving you all these gold coins, clothes and silver? I am over sixty, and since your father died I have only you to depend on. If you get into trouble, to whom can I turn? You mustn't go there tomorrow."

Since Zhang Sheng was a respectable young man, who had always deferred to his mother, he took her advice and stopped going to the shop. When Mr. Zhang noticed that his younger clerk was absent, he sent to ask the reason and Zhang's mother told the messenger: "My son has caught a chill and is not well: that's why he can't go. Tell Mr. Zhang that he will go back to work as soon as he is better."

A few days later, when Zhang Sheng still did not come to the shop, Li Qing called at their house and asked: "Why doesn't he come? I need help in the shop." But the young man's mother still alleged that he was unwell and had, in fact, taken a turn for the worse during the last few days; thus Li had to go back without obtaining any satisfaction. Mr. Zhang sent four or five other messengers, but each time Zhang Sheng's mother maintained that her son was ill; and when Mr. Zhang found that he still stayed away, he concluded that he must have found another job.

Time passed swiftly, until soon Zhang Sheng had been more than a month at home. As they say: If a man only eats and does no work, he can eat through a mountain. Though he had been given so much by the young mistress, he dared not produce the lump of silver, neither dared he sell the clothes. But since he was remaining idle day after day, soon he had no money left, and he said to his mother: "You wouldn't let me go to Mr. Zhang's house, so that I have lost my job. Now, staying at home, how can I meet expenses?"

When the old woman heard this, she pointed at the ceiling and said: "Son, do you see that?"

Looking up, Zhang saw a bundle hanging from the crossbeam. His mother took it down and told him: "It was with this that your father brought you up." The bundle when opened proved to be a work-basket. "Stick to this line," said the old lady. "You can learn your father's trade, and sell rouge and thread."

When the Lantern Festival came round, Zhang Sheng thought: "Tonight is the Lantern Festival, and there will be a display of lanterns by the palace gate." He asked his mother: "May I go to see the lanterns?"

"Son," said his mother, "you haven't been that way for a long time. If you go to watch the lanterns, you'll be passing Mr. Zhang's house again and you may get into trouble."

"Everybody's going," said Zhang. "They say the lanterns this year are magnificent. I'll come back early, and I needn't pass Mr. Zhang's house."

"Very well," said his mother. "But you mustn't go alone. Find some friend to go with you."

"I'll go with young Wang."

"All right. Only you must promise me not to drink and to come back together."

So it was arranged, and the two young men went together to the palace gate to watch the lanterns, arriving just in time to see the presentation of imperial wine and gold coins. All was bustle and excitement, and Wang said: "We can't see from here: we aren't tall or hefty enough. Why should we let ourselves be jostled and knocked about? Let's go somewhere else to watch. I know where they have another sea-monster-and-mountain lantern."

"Where's that?"

"Don't you know? Minister Wang has a small sea-monster-and-mountain lantern, and it will be on show tonight."

They retraced their steps until they reached the mansion of Minister Wang, but it was just as crowded there as before the palace gate. Then Zhang lost sight of Wang, and he was worried. "How shall I go back?" he wondered. "My mother insisted that we must keep together; but now I can't find him. If I go back first, my mother will be worried about him; if he goes back first, she will wonder what has happened to me." Losing all interest in the lanterns, he was wandering round forlornly when it occurred to him: "My old master's house isn't far from here. Every year on the Lantern Festival he closes the shop and has a fireworks display. It must be still on."

He strolled aimlessly towards Mr. Zhang's house. Great was his surprise, however, when he found the gate closed and made fast by two bamboo poles fastened crosswise, while an oil lamp hanging there shed light on a notice posted on the gate. Dumbfounded, the young man was at a loss to understand what had happened. Going up closer to the notice he read: "The Kaifeng Constabulary has found citizen Zhang Shilian guilty of...." But before he had time to read the actual charges, someone near by shouted: "Who the devil are you? What do you mean by hanging around here?"

The startled Zhang Sheng took to his heels, but the man who had called out ran after him, shouting: "Who is it? How dare you! Why are you looking at that notice at this time of the night?" Young Zhang fled in terror to the corner of the alley, where he turned and headed home. It was nearly midnight now, and the moon was bright in the sky. As he was walking along, someone else overtook him and called out: "Mr. Zhang, you're wanted!"

Zhang turned and saw that it was a serving-man from some inn. "I suppose young Wang is waiting for me at the corner," he thought. "We may as well have a drink before we go back."

He went with the serving-man to an inn, and followed him upstairs to the door of a room.

"Here you are," said the man.

When the curtain was raised, Zhang Sheng saw a woman, carelessly dressed and with dishevelled hair.

Her cloudlike tresses were in disarray,
And tears had flowed to stain her powdered face;
Her former wealth and splendour passed away,
She seemed a moon which sullen clouds efface,
Or blossom trampled by the dusty way.

"Mr. Zhang!" she exclaimed. "It was I who asked you to come here."

The woman looked familiar, yet he could not place her.

"Don't say you don't recognize me, Mr. Zhang!" she cried. "I am old Mr. Zhang's wife."

"How do you come to be here?"

"It's a long story."

"What happened?"

"I should never have trusted those matchmakers and married Mr. Zhang. He forged silver, and when it was found out he was arrested and taken to the court, and I haven't heard of him since. All his property has been confiscated, so that now I have nowhere to go and can only throw myself on your mercy. Do let me stay in your house for a while, for old times' sake!"

"That would never do, madam!" replied Zhang. "In the first place, my mother is very strict; and in the second, we should never do anything which might lay us open to suspicion. It's quite out of the question."

"I suppose," said she, "you are thinking of the proverb: It's easy to summon a snake but difficult to dismiss it. You are afraid that I may stay on and prove a burden to you. But let me show you this." She took from her pocket a string of pearls. There were one hundred and eight of them altogether, bright and glittering and as big as peas.

Zhang could not suppress an exclamation of wonder. "I have never seen such beauties!" he cried.

"Most of my possessions were confiscated," she told him. "But this I managed to hide. If you will let me stay in your house, you can sell them pearl by pearl, and that should keep us for some time."

> A traveller homeward finds the day too short,
> A prey to worry finds his horse too slow;
> Wine in the tavern, loveliness or wealth —
> How many men will these three things forgo?

"If you really want to come," said Zhang, "let me ask my mother's permission first."

"I will go with you," she rejoined. "I'll wait on the other side of the street while you ask her."

Zhang Sheng went home and told his mother all that had happened. His mother was a kindly old soul, and when she heard of the young woman's plight she exclaimed: "Poor thing! Poor thing! Where is she?"

"She is waiting across the street."

"Let her come."

The young woman came in, and when they had greeted each other she told the old lady all her story, concluding: "Now I have no relations to turn to, so I have come to you. Please let me stay."

"It's quite all right for you to stay here for a few days," said Zhang's mother. "It's just that we are poor, so we are afraid our house is not good enough for you. But you may think of some relatives later to whom you can go."

Then the young woman took the pearls from her pocket and showed them to Zhang's mother, who admired them under the lamplight and repeated her invitation to the young woman to stay. The latter said: "Tomorrow you can sell one pearl and start a rouge and thread shop, hanging the work-basket over the door as your sign."

"Now that we have this," said Zhang, "even if we sell it cheaply we shall raise a large sum and we haven't yet touched the fifty taels of silver: with that we can buy stock."

After this, Zhang Sheng took over old Mr. Zhang's business, and people called him the young Mr. Zhang. Although his former mistress tempted him repeatedly, he persisted in treating her as his superior and did not succumb to her charms. Then the Spring Festival came round —

When smoke curls up from every hill and dale,
And paper coins are fluttering in the breeze,
When country people mourn their dead or sing,
The time of sudden showers and blooming trees;
Then orioles on the cherry branches cry,
Beneath the willows sleeping drunkards lie,

And pretty girls enjoy themselves in spring
Swinging on coloured ropes like nymphs on high.

All the citizens of Kaifeng went out to visit Jinming Pool, young Mr. Zhang among them. On his way back that evening, he had just entered Wansheng Gate when he heard someone calling: "Zhang Sheng! Zhang Sheng!"

"Everybody calls me young Mr. Zhang nowadays," he thought. "Who can this be calling Zhang Sheng?" Turning round, he found it was his former master, old Mr. Zhang. The old man's face was tattooed with four golden characters, his hair was unkempt, his face unwashed, and he was very shabbily dressed. Zhang Sheng took him to a quiet room in a tavern, and when they had sat down he asked him: "How did you come to this, sir?"

"I should never have married that woman from Minister Wang's house," replied the old man. "On New Year's Day she was watching the street from behind the door-curtain, when a page walked past carrying a hamper. She called to him to stop, and asked: 'What news is there in the minister's house?' 'Nothing much,' said the boy. 'But the other day our master missed a string of one hundred and eight pearls, and the whole household was blamed.' When she heard this she changed colour, turning first white, then red; and the boy left. Soon after, two dozen men came to my house, seized all her property and mine and took me to the court for investigation and torture. They demanded the pearls; but I had never set eyes on them, and I told them so. Then I was cruelly beaten and thrown into gaol. Luckily, that same day she went to her room and hanged herself; and since they could not find anything, the case was closed. Right up to this moment, though, no trace has been found of those hundred and eight pearls."

"Both the woman and the pearls are in my house now!" thought Zhang. "And we have sold a few of the pearls!" Thoroughly bewildered and alarmed, after treating the old man to food and drink he took his leave.

All the way home, he was thinking: "I can't make head or tail of this." When he reached home and saw the young woman, he fell back several steps and implored her: "Madam, spare me!"

"What do you mean?" she demanded.

When he repeated all that old Mr. Zhang had told him, she declared: "The idea! Just look at me! My clothes are hand-sewn and my voice is clear, not hollow. Can't you see for yourself? He knows I am here and has made up this tale so that you won't keep me."

"There may be something in that," Zhang admitted.

A few days later someone called from the street: "You are wanted, young Mr. Zhang!" Zhang Sheng went out and found old Mr. Zhang there. "I'll get the woman to come out to see him," he thought. "Then I can decide whether she is woman or ghost." He ordered a maid to invite the young woman out; but when the girl went to the inner chamber she could not find her — the woman had vanished!

Realizing then that she had been a ghost all the time, Zhang Sheng told everything to old Mr. Zhang, who asked: "Where are the pearls?"

Zhang Sheng brought them from his room. Old Mr. Zhang asked him to accompany him to the minister's house to return the necklace, and the pearls that had been detached and sold he redeemed. Minister Wang then pardoned old Mr. Zhang and restored his property so that he was able to open shop again; and the old man summoned priests from the Tianqing Taoist Monastery to sacrifice to the spirit of his wife so that she might rest in peace.

It was because the young woman had become enamoured of Zhang Sheng in her lifetime that even after death she had sought him out; but fortunately he was an honest man, who did not yield to temptation, thus he was able to keep clear of trouble. All too many people nowadays, however, are ensnared by wealth or lust: not one in ten thousand is equal to Zhang Sheng.

Though most men worship wealth and beauty too,
A good man will not stoop for all their charm;
And if one is as honest as Zhang Sheng,
Then neither ghost nor man can do him harm!

Fifteen Strings of Cash

Now some are born intelligent,
Some hide the gifts that Heav'n has sent;
The merest glance may make you foes,
And laughing chat may end in blows.
Men's hearts are devious as a stream,
And stern as mail their faces seem;
Women and wine make kingdoms fall,
But study does no harm at all.

This verse points out how difficult it is for a man to behave correctly; for life is fraught with danger and human hearts are hard to fathom. Since the ancient way of life was lost, men have taken many paths in their pursuit of gain and often brought trouble on their own heads; many, too, are the accidents which may befall a man or his family. Thus, as the ancients say: There is meaning in every frown and meaning in every smile, and a man should be very careful how he frowns or smiles.

My story is about a gentleman who lost his own life, ruined his family and caused the death of several others through some remarks made in jest after drinking. First, however, I shall tell you another tale by way of introduction.

During the Yuan Feng period (1078-1085) there lived a young scholar named Wei Pengju. He was just eighteen and had been married to a very lovely girl for not quite one month, when the spring examination was announced and he had to leave his wife, pack up and go to the capital. When they were taking leave of each other his wife urged him, whether he received an official post or not, to come back as soon as he could and not to forget their love.

31

"Fame and fortune are within my grasp," replied Wei. "Don't worry about me." Then he left for the capital.

Sure enough, he passed the examination, winning ninth place in the first rank, and took up his post in the capital with great pomp. Wei then wrote a letter home and sent a servant to bring his wife to the capital. In his letter, after the usual greetings and the news of his official post, he wrote: "Because I have no one to look after me in the capital, I have found myself a concubine; but we are waiting for you to come and enjoy our wealth and splendour together."

Wei's servant took this letter and went straight home. When he saw the young mistress, he congratulated her and handed her the letter; but when she opened and read it, she exclaimed: "How could your master be so heartless! He has only just been appointed to an official post, yet he has already taken a concubine!"

"I didn't hear anything of the kind when I was in the capital," the servant reassured her. "It must be a joke, ma'am. You'll see that when you get there. There is no need to worry."

"Very well," said the wife, "if you say so."

While waiting for a boat, she packed her belongings and sent a letter by another messenger to the capital. This messenger reached the capital, asked for Wei's hostel, gave him the letter and left after accepting a meal. When Wei opened the letter and read it, he found it was very brief. All his wife had written was: "Since you have married a concubine in the capital, I have found a male concubine at home, and we shall be coming to the capital together soon."

Wei realized that his wife was joking, and thought no more of it; but before he had put the letter away, his servant announced another successful candidate. Now in the hostels at the capital one does not have as many rooms as at home, and this caller was a good friend who knew that Wei's wife was not with him, so he walked straight into the living room and sat down. After talking for a little about the weather, Wei went out for a wash, whereupon his visitor, happening to look at the papers on the desk, saw this letter. Greatly amused, he read it aloud; and Wei, who could not hide it now, turned very red. "This is sheer nonsense," he protested. "I played a trick on her, so she wrote this back as a joke."

His friend roared with laughter, and said: "This is hardly a joking matter!" Then he left.

That friend was a young fellow who liked to gossip, so in no time this story about Mrs. Wei's letter was known in all the hostels. Some scholars, who envied Wei for winning distinction while still so young, made much of the incident and one of them reported it to the court, claiming that Wei was too young and frivolous to hold an important government post. The result was that Wei was demoted to a provincial post; and though he bitterly repented his folly, it was too late. After this incident he never gained promotion and his career, which had promised so well, was ruined.

After this tale of how one joke cost a man a fine official post, I shall tell you another about a gentleman who was cut off in his prime and responsible for the death of two or three other innocent people, just because of a joke he made after drinking. How did it happen? As this verse says:

> Our life on earth with danger is beset,
> While others laugh and gossip as they please;
> The white cloud is not master of its fate,
> Since it must drift with every giddy breeze.

During the reign of Emperor Gao Zong (1127-1162) the capital was moved south to Hangzhou, where it vied in wealth and splendour with the former capital in the north. On the left of Arrow Bridge in Hangzhou lived a gentleman named Liu Gui. He came from a well-to-do family, but after he inherited the property luck was against him; and although he studied at first, later he saw little hope of an official career and had to go into trade. As he was no professional, however, he had no head for business and soon lost his capital. He had to sell his big house to buy a small one and live in two or three rooms with his wife, a Miss Wang whom he had married in his youth, and a concubine whom he had married later because his wife had no son. The concubine's family name was Chen, and she was the daughter of a cake-vendor. They called her Second Sister, and Liu had married her in the days when he was still comfortably off. His family consisted of just the three of them. Liu himself was a most agreeable man whom all his neighbours liked. They used to say to him:

"You are having a spell of bad luck, Mr. Liu. But better times are sure to be ahead."

This was what they all predicted, yet nothing of the sort happened; and Liu just stayed at home feeling thoroughly depressed, unable to find any way out of his difficulties.

One day he was sitting idly at home when Old Wang, his father-in-law's seventy-year-old servant, came in.

"This is our master's birthday, sir," said Old Wang. "He has sent me to invite you and the mistress over."

"So it is!" exclaimed Liu. "I've been so taken up with my own troubles that I actually forgot the old man's birthday."

He and his wife got out some clothes which they made up into a bundle and gave the servant to carry. Leaving the concubine in charge of the house, and telling her that they would not be able to come back that night but would return the next evening, they set out. Seven or eight miles from the city they came to Mr. Wang's house. Liu greeted his father-in-law; but as there were many other guests present, he could not talk about his poverty. When the guests had left, however, Liu's father-in-law asked him to stay in the guest room, and the next morning he had a talk with his son-in-law.

"You can't go on like this," he said. "You know the proverbs: A man who does nothing but eat can eat up a mountain, and a man's gullet is as deep as the sea, but time passes as quickly as a shuttle! You must think of some way of making a living. When my daughter married you, she expected you to provide her with food and clothing. This really won't do, you know."

Liu heaved a sigh and said: "You are right, sir. But it is easier to catch a tiger in the mountain than it is to find a friend in need. Who in the world will sympathize with me as you do, sir? We must resign ourselves to poverty: to beg for help would be labour wasted."

"There is something in what you say," agreed his father-in-law. "But I can't let things go on like this. Today I mean to lend you some money to start a grocery shop, so that you can make enough to live on. What do you say to that?"

"I am more grateful than I can say," replied Liu. "That will be the very thing for us!"

After the midday meal, Mr. Wang got out fifteen strings of cash and gave them to Liu, saying: "Take these now to start a shop. When it is ready, I shall let you have another ten strings. Let your wife stay here for a few days; and when you have settled on a day to open shop, I shall take her home myself to offer my congratulations, if you are agreeable."

After thanking his father-in-law again and again, Liu shouldered the money and left. It was already late when he reached the city; but, happening to pass the house of an acquaintance who wanted to go into business too, he thought he might as well stop to discuss the matter with him. He knocked at the door, someone answered within and his friend came out, greeted him and asked the reason for his call.

When Liu explained his plan, the other said: "I have nothing to do at present. If you can use me in your shop, I should be glad to help."

"Good," said Liu.

After they had talked business for some time, Liu's friend kept him to dinner; and, since wine and food were ready, he had a few cups. But Liu was not a good drinker, so presently, feeling the wine go to his head, he took his leave saying: "I've trespassed on your hospitality today. Please come to our humble house tomorrow to talk things over further." His friend saw him to the street corner where he said goodbye to him.

With his money on his back, Liu staggered home and knocked

at the door. It was past the time to light the lamps and his concubine, left alone at home with nothing to do, after waiting for them till dark had closed the door and dozed off before the lamp; so she did not hear him knocking. He had to knock for a long time before she woke up and answered: "I'm coming." Then she got up and opened the door to let him in.

As she took the bag of money from him and put it on the table, the concubine asked: "Where did you get so much money? What are you going to do with it?"

Now Liu was slightly drunk, and he was also annoyed with her for taking so long to open the door; so he decided to frighten her.

"If I tell you, you will be angry," he said. "But I can't keep it from you: you will have to know. I'm so hard put to it now, that I've had to pawn you to somebody. I don't want to let you go for good, though; so I've only asked him for fifteen strings of cash; and if I come into luck, I shall redeem you with interest. But if I remain as hard up as ever, I'll have to let you go."

When the concubine heard this, she could scarcely believe her ears; yet there were the fifteen strings of cash confronting her! Liu had never said an angry word to her in his life, and her relationship with his wife was good too — what could have made him so cruel all of a sudden?

"Well," she said doubtfully, "you should at least have told my father and mother."

"If I had informed your parents, they would certainly have raised objections. Tomorrow when you've gone to that man's house, I'll send someone to convince your parents of the necessity for this. They won't be able to blame me."

"Where were you drinking today?"

"With the man to whom I pawned you. After drawing up the contract, I drank a few cups with him before coming back."

"Why is Elder Sister not back?"

"She couldn't bear the thought of parting with you like this; so she will come back after you have left tomorrow. This was the only way out for me, and it's all settled now." As he spoke, he was secretly laughing to himself. Then, without undressing, he lay down on the bed and fell asleep.

The young woman was very upset. "What kind of man has he sold me to?" she wondered. "I must go home first and tell my father and mother. If he's told that other man to fetch me tomorrow, they can go to my home to settle matters there."

After turning things over in her mind, she piled the fifteen strings of cash by Liu's feet and, taking advantage of the fact that he was drunk, quietly put together some clothes, softly opened the door and tiptoed out, closing the door behind her. She went to the house of a neighbour on their left whose name was Zhu; and she slept that night with Mrs. Zhu, whom she told:

"Today, for no reason at all, my husband has sold me; so I must go home to tell my parents about it. I'll trouble you to tell my husband tomorrow where I've gone. The man who's bought me can come with my husband to my parents' house to discuss the matter and arrange a proper settlement."

"That's right," said Mrs. Zhu. "I'll give Mr. Liu your message after you've gone."

The next morning the concubine set off for home.

Just like a fish escaping from a hook,
She flourished off without one backward look.

Mr. Liu slept till midnight, when he woke to find the lamp still lit and his concubine no longer at his side. Thinking she was in the kitchen clearing up, he called out to her to bring him tea; but though he called several times, there was no answer. He made an effort to get up, but because he was still befuddled he dropped off again.

Just then a bad man happened to come along. Having lost all his money through gambling, this rogue had slunk out at night to steal something, and he came to Liu's house. Since the concubine had only pulled the door to when she went out, the thief was able to open it at a push and slip inside unobserved. When he reached the bedroom, he found the lamp still lit but could see nothing worth taking. As he groped about the bed, however, he saw a man sleeping with his face to the wall and a pile of cash at his feet. He was taking a few strings, when Liu woke up and shouted:

"Hey! You can't do that! I have just borrowed that cash from my father-in-law to live on! What shall we do if you steal it?"

Without troubling to reply, the thief lunged out at Liu's face; but Liu dodged the blow and leapt out of bed to grapple with him. When the thief saw how active his opponent was, he fled from the room. Liu would not let him go, however, and followed him to the kitchen where he was about to shout to rouse the neighbours. The thief, hard pressed and at a loss what to do, suddenly caught sight of a bright axe lying close at hand. In desperation, he seized the axe and swung it at Liu's face, felling him to the ground. He followed up with another blow, and so the unhappy man was killed!

"There was no drawing back once you forced my hand," panted the thief. "It was you who chased me, not I who wanted your life." Going back to the bedroom he took the fifteen strings of cash, tore up a sheet to wrap them in, fastened this loot on himself, and made off, pulling the door to behind him.

The next morning when the neighbours got up, Liu's door was still closed and there was not a sound from his room.

"Mr. Liu!" they called. "You've overslept!" But no one answered. Then they pushed open the door and went in, only to find Liu dead on the ground. His wife had gone home two days previously; but where was the concubine? There was a great uproar until Old Zhu, the neighbour in whose house the young woman had stayed the night before, said: "Yesterday evening the concubine stayed in my house. She told us Mr. Liu had sold her for no reason, so she was going back to her parents; and she asked me to tell Mr. Liu to take her new master there to settle matters with her parents. If we send to fetch her back, we should be able to get to the bottom of this.

We must also fetch Mrs. Liu back before we decide on anything."

"You are right," they all agreed.

They first sent a messenger to Mr. Wang's house to break the bad news. The old man and his daughter wept bitterly, and Liu's father-in-law said:

"He was all right when he left yesterday, and I had given him fifteen strings of cash to start a business. How did he come to be murdered?"

"It was like this," said the messenger. "When Mr. Liu came home it was already dark and he was tipsy. None of us knew about his money, and we are not sure what time exactly he got back; but this morning we found his door ajar, and when we went in there he lay murdered on the ground, while the fifteen strings of cash were nowhere to be seen and the concubine had disappeared too. We made such a noise that Old Zhu from the house on the left came out. He told us that the concubine had stayed in his house yesterday, because she claimed Mr. Liu had sold her for no reason and she wanted to go and tell her parents. She spent the night there and left early this morning. We decided that we should let you know what has happened, and men have been sent, too, to catch up with the concubine. If they don't overtake her on the road, they will go all the way to her parents' house; but they must bring her back to find out the truth. You and your daughter had better come back now to avenge Mr. Liu." Old Mr. Wang and his daughter hastily made ready and, when the messenger had been given wine and food, hurried to the city.

Now the concubine had left Old Zhu's house early that morning to start home. She had walked only half a mile, though, when her feet started aching and she sat down by the roadside to rest. Presently a young man came down the road, wearing a cap with zigzag designs and a loose gown, clean socks and silk shoes. Over his shoulder he was carrying a bag containing cash. When he came up with the concubine he saw that, while no beauty, she had pretty eyebrows and good teeth, her face was rosy and her eyes inviting. In a word, he found her quite attractive.

Men may be dazzled by a country flower,
And country wine weak heads may overpower.

He put down his bag, came up to her, made a low bow and said: "Are you all alone, ma'am? May I ask where you are going?"

With a curtsey, she answered: "I am going home to my parents. I felt tired, so I am taking a rest. Where are you from, sir, and where may you be going?"

Clasping his hands before him, the young man answered respectfully: "I come from the country. I have just sold silk in the city and got some cash which I am taking to Chujiatang."

"Why, my parents live near Chujiatang! I would like it so much if you could walk with me for part of the way."

"Certainly, if you wish it," replied the young man. "I shall be delighted to accompany you."

They went on together; but they had gone less than a mile when two men came running after them, sweating and panting, with the fronts of their jackets open. "Stop, madam!" they shouted. "We've something to say to you."

Startled, the concubine and the young man came to a halt. When the two men caught up, they seized them both without a word of explanation, crying: "A fine thing you've done! Where do you think you are going?"

The concubine was taken aback, but she saw now that these were neighbours, one of them being the master of the house in which she had stayed the previous night.

"Didn't I tell you last night," she said, "that my husband had suddenly taken it into his head to sell me, so I was going home to tell my parents? Why have you come after me?"

"Never mind that story of yours," retorted Old Zhu. "Murder has been done in your house, and you must come back to clear yourself."

"My husband has sold me: he took home the money yesterday. What is this about murder? I'm not going back."

"So you're being stubborn, eh?" roared Old Zhu. "Well, if you won't come with us — here, officers! These are murderers! Arrest them! Otherwise we'll find ourselves involved and you won't have any peace here either."

Seeing that things had taken an ugly turn, the young man said to her: "It looks as if you had better go back, ma'am. I'll leave you here."

But the two neighbours shouted: "If you hadn't been here, that would have been all right. But since you are travelling together, we can't let you go either."

"How ridiculous!" protested the young man. "I just happened to meet this young lady on the road and walked a short distance with her. This can have nothing to do with me. What do you want me for?"

"Murder has been done," said Old Zhu. "Do you expect us to let you go, and involve ourselves in a lawsuit with the accused absent?"

They ignored all the protests of the concubine and the young man.

By now a crowd had gathered, and people advised the young man: "You can't just make off. A man with a clear conscience needn't fear a midnight knock on his door. You'd better go along."

"If you refuse to go," said Old Zhu's neighbour, "that shows you have a guilty conscience. But we won't let you escape." They seized the young man and the concubine and hustled them off.

When they reached Liu's door, they found the house in a great hubbub. And when the concubine went in and saw Liu dead on the floor, killed by an axe, and realized that the fifteen strings of cash on the bed had vanished, her jaw dropped and she was too frightened to speak.

The young man was appalled, too, and exclaimed: "How

unlucky I am! By happening to accompany this young lady, I've got myself mixed up with murder!''

In the midst of all this confusion, old Mr. Wang and his daughter limped in. They wailed over the corpse, then turned to the concubine and demanded: "Why did you kill your husband, steal the cash and fly? Heaven is just, and you have been caught. But what have you to say for yourself?"

"It's true that there were fifteen strings of cash," said the concubine. "But when he came back last night he told me that he was so pressed for money he had pawned me for fifteen strings of cash and that today I should have to go to that other man's house. Because I didn't know what sort of family he had pawned me to, I decided to tell my parents first; and late last night I put the fifteen strings of cash in one pile by his feet, then closed the door and went to stay in old Mr. Zhu's house, so that I could go home first thing this morning. When I left, I asked Mr. Zhu to tell my husband that since he had found me a new master they should go together to my family to settle the business. I've no idea how he got murdered."

"Well!" cried the wife. "Yesterday my father gave him fifteen strings of cash to bring home as capital to support us all. Why should he deceive you by saying it was money raised by pawning you? In the two days when you were alone at home you must have had an affair with a man. Seeing how poor we were, you didn't want to stick it out; and when you saw the fifteen strings of cash that put an idea into your head, so you killed my husband and stole the money. Then you deliberately stayed one night with the neighbours, after planning to run off with your lover. You were walking with a man today. What have you to say to that? Can you deny it?"

All agreed: "Mrs. Liu is right."

Then they asked the young man: "Didn't you plot Mr. Liu's death with his concubine, and secretly arrange to meet at some deserted place and escape together? What have you to say?"

"My name is Cui Ning," replied the young man. "I have never set eyes on this young lady before. Last night I came into town to sell silk — I have the money from the sale on me — and today on my way back I happened to meet this lady. When I asked her where she was going and why she was alone, she mentioned that she was walking my way; so I accompanied her. I know nothing of what has happened here."

Do you think they would listen to him? They searched his bag; and when they found there exactly fifteen strings of cash, not a coin more, not a coin less, they cried: "The guilty can never escape Heaven's justice! You murdered him, stole his money and his concubine and tried to make off, involving us in a lawsuit in which the accused has fled."

Then the wife seized the concubine and old Mr. Wang seized Cui Ning. With all the neighbours as witnesses, they marched straight to the city magistrate's office. When the city magistrate heard that it was a murder case, he took his seat in the court and ordered the plaintiffs to state their case from the beginning. Old Mr. Wang was the first to speak.

"Your Honour," he said, "I am a native of this district, living in the country. I am nearly sixty and have only one daughter whom I married some years ago to Liu Gui who lived in this city. Later, as they had no son, Liu took a concubine from the Chen family. They called the concubine Second Sister, and the three of them got on quite well together and never quarrelled. The day before yesterday, since it was my birthday, I sent a man to fetch my daughter and son-in-law to stay for one night; and the next day, realizing that my son-in-law had no means of supporting his family, I gave him fifteen strings of cash to set up a business which would bring them in enough to live on. The concubine had stayed at home to look after the house. Last night when my son-in-law went home, she seems to have killed him with an axe and fled with a young man named Cui Ning; but they have both been caught. I beg Your Honour to take pity on my son-in-law's strange death. Here are the wicked man and the adulteress, with the stolen money as evidence. May it please Your Honour, in your wisdom, to pass sentence!"

Then the city magistrate called to the concubine: "Come here! How did you plot with your lover to murder your husband, steal the money and escape? What have you to say?"

"Though I was only Liu Gui's concubine," she replied, "he treated me well and his wife was good to me. Why should I want to harm them? But last night my husband came home half drunk, with fifteen strings of cash. When I asked him where the money came from, he said he had pawned me for fifteen strings of cash, because he couldn't support the family; and he hadn't let my parents know about it, but wanted me to go to the other man the next day. I was so upset that I slipped out that night to stay with a neighbour, and I set off early this morning for my parents' home. I had asked my neighbour to tell my husband to go with my new master to my parents' home to settle the business. I was on my way home when the neighbour I had stayed with caught up with me and dragged me back. I know nothing about my husband's murder."

"Nonsense!" shouted the city magistrate. "The fifteen strings of cash were given him by his father-in-law, yet you claim that he raised the money by pawning you: that is obviously a lie. And why should a woman slip out at the dead of night? You must have been planning to run away. You couldn't have done this alone: some man must have abetted you in this murder and robbery. Out with the truth now!"

Before the young woman could speak again, several neighbours stepped forward, knelt down and said: "Your Honour is as all-seeing as Heaven. The concubine did spend the night in the second house to the left of their house, going off this morning. When we discovered that her husband had been murdered, we sent men after her who overtook her on the road. She was walking with that young man and they refused to come back; they had to be dragged back by force. We also sent for Mrs. Liu and her father, and when they arrived Liu's father-in-law said he had given the dead man fifteen strings of cash yesterday to set him up in business; but now Liu was dead and the money gone! When we questioned the concubine, she said she had left the money piled on the bed; but we found the fifteen strings of cash on the young man. This proves that the concubine and the young man must have plotted the murder together. How can they deny it, with such clear evidence against them?"

The city magistrate believed all they said and, calling the young man forward, demanded: "Here, in the seat of the imperial government, how dare you act so lawlessly? Confess now how you made off with Liu's concubine, stole his fifteen strings of cash and murdered him, and where you were going together."

"My name is Cui Ning," said the young man, "and I live in the country. Yesterday I came into town and sold some silk: that's how I got these fifteen strings of cash. This morning I fell in with this young lady on the road; but I didn't even know her name, to say nothing of the murder."

In a towering rage, the city magistrate thundered: "Nonsense! How could there be such a coincidence: they lost fifteen strings of cash, and you got fifteen strings for your silk! You are obviously lying. Besides, a man shouldn't covet his neighbour's wife or horse: if she was nothing to you, why were you walking together and putting up together? No doubt a cunning knave like you will never confess unless I have you tortured."

The city magistrate had Cui Ning and the concubine tortured until they fainted away again and again. Old Mr. Wang, his daughter and the neighbours insisted that the couple were guilty, and the city magistrate wanted to close the case, so the unfortunate concubine and Cui Ning were tortured until they broke down and agreed that they had been tempted by the money and killed Liu, then had taken the fifteen strings of cash and fled. The neighbours, acting as witnesses in the case, put their crosses to the confessions; Cui Ning and the concubine were pilloried and sent to the prison for those condemned to death; and the fifteen strings of cash were returned to Mr. Wang — who found they were not enough to pay the men in the yamen!

The city magistrate drew up a report of the case which he

submitted to the imperial court; and after due consideration an imperial edict was issued to the effect that since Cui Ning was guilty of adultery, robbery and murder, he should lose his head according to the law; while the concubine, who had plotted with her lover to kill her own husband, was guilty of the worst crime and should be sliced to death. The confessions were then read out in court, after which Cui Ning and the concubine were brought from the gaol to be sentenced — he to decapitation and she to be cut into pieces. Taken to the public square for execution as a public example, they had no way to protest.

When dumb men eat wormwood, how great their distress!
Their dread of its sharpness they cannot express.

Now, worthy readers, if the concubine and Cui Ning had really committed robbery and murder, would they not have fled the same night? Why should she allow herself to be caught by spending one night with a neighbour and setting off to see her parents the next day? Anyone who thought twice could see that injustice had been done; but the city magistrate was a fool who, in his impatience to close the case, did not stop to think that anybody will confess under torture. And when a man commits injustice, either he or his descendants will suffer; for the wronged ghosts will not rest till they are avenged. Thus a judge must not condemn people as the whim takes him, nor torture prisoners as he pleases: justice and wisdom are required. For the dead can never come to life again, and the broken can never again be made whole.

Mrs. Liu stayed on in her husband's house, where she had set up a shrine for him before which she mourned every day; and when her father advised her to marry again, she said: "Even if I don't mourn for the required three years, I ought at least to mourn for one."

Her father agreed and let her be. But time passed quickly, and when she had eked out a miserable existence alone for nearly a year, Mr. Wang saw that she could not carry on much longer and sent Old Wang to fetch her, saying: "Ask the mistress to pack up and come home. As soon as she has observed the anniversary of her husband's death, she may marry again."

Since Mrs. Liu was in difficulties, after careful thought she agreed with her father. Accordingly she made a bundle of her belongings which she gave to Old Wang to carry, and having said goodbye to her neighbours left the city. It was autumn and, caught in a sudden squall on their way home, they had to leave the road to find shelter in the forest. They took the wrong path, however.

> *Like pigs or sheep that near the butcher's knife,*
> *Each step they took was shortening their life!*

For as Mrs. Liu and her servant were walking through the forest, someone shouted from behind them: "I am the king of the mountain! Stop and pay toll!"

As the travellers stood there trembling, a man leapt out, wearing a red cap and a tattered old battle dress with a red silk sash and a pair of dark boots. He had a sword in his hand which he brandished as he advanced. Old Wang was fated to die, for he said: "Bandit! Skunk! I know your sort. I don't mind risking my old life to have it out with you." The old fellow charged at him, head down; but the bandit dodged and the old man fell flat on the ground.

In a rage, the bandit swore: "Surly old bull!" He ran the old man through and through with his sword, until Old Wang's blood was spilt on the ground and it was clear he was dead.

When Mrs. Liu saw how fierce this man was, she feared that all was up with her; but hitting on a desperate plan to save herself she clapped her hands and cried: "Bravo!"   .

Glaring at her, the bandit stayed his hand to shout: "Who was he to you?"

"Unhappy that I am," she lied, "when my husband died I was tricked by the matchmakers into marrying this old man who was good for nothing but eating. Now you have killed him for me and rid me of a plague."

When the bandit saw that she was submissive and not bad looking, he asked: "Will you stay and be my wife?"

Knowing that she had no choice, she answered: "I would like to serve Your Highness."

Smiling now, the bandit sheathed his sword; and when he had thrown the servant's corpse into a gully, he led Mrs. Liu towards a mean-looking cottage. He picked up a clod of earth and threw it at the roof, whereupon a man came out to open the gate and they went into the hall. The bandit had a sheep killed and wine heated, then married Mrs. Liu. Indeed, they got on quite well together, for —

> *Although they were not meant for man and wife,*
> *Necessity inured them to the life.*

Curiously enough, in less than half a year after gaining Mrs. Liu, the bandit made several big hauls and became quite rich. Mrs. Liu, who was very intelligent, kept giving him good advice and told him: "The proverb says: An earthen pitcher will sooner or later be broken over the well, and a general is likely to die in battle. We have enough now to keep us in comfort for the rest of our life; but if you go on flouting the will of Heaven, you are bound to come to a bad end. Though an outlaw's life is good, it is not like having a home. Why don't you turn over a new leaf and start a small business to make an honest living?"

She pleaded with the bandit day and night, until she prevailed on him to abandon his wicked ways and rent a house in the city where he opened a grocery shop. During his leisure hours he would often go to monasteries to worship Buddha and observe fasts.

One day when he was resting at home, he told his wife: "Though I started life as a bandit, I knew that a man has to pay for his crimes, so it was just to make a living that I frightened people into handing over their money. Later, after I got you, I never did much; and now I have changed my ways. But it worries me sometimes to think how I killed two men wrongly in the past and ruined two other innocent people. I've never told you about this before; but I would like to atone for my sins by having sutras chanted for their spirits, to get them out of hell."

"How did you kill two men wrongly?" she asked.

"One was your husband. You remember how he charged at me in the forest, and I killed him. He was an old man and I had no grudge against him, but I killed him and took his wife. He can't be resting easy in his grave."

"But if not for that," she said, "we wouldn't be together now. Don't worry over what's past and done with. Who was the other?"

"It was even more wrong of me to kill the other man," he said. "And two innocent people were involved who had to pay with their lives. It happened over a year ago. I had lost money in gambling and hadn't a cent left, so I slipped out one night to see what I could pick up. I noticed a door that was not locked, and when I pushed in there was not a soul there; but in the inner room I found a man drunk in bed with a pile of cash by his feet. I took some of the money and was leaving, when the fellow woke up and started crying: 'That cash was given me by my father-in-law to start a business. If you steal it, my whole family will starve.' Then he rushed to the door and was about to shout for help. Things were looking bad for me, when I saw an axe for chopping wood by my feet. In desperation, I picked up the axe, shouting: 'It's either you or me!' I cut him down with two strokes, then went back to his room and took all the fifteen strings of cash. Later I heard that his concubine and a young man named Cui Ning were wrongly accused of the robbery and murder and executed. Though I have been a bandit all my life, these two cases are the only ones that neither Heaven nor men could forgive; and I ought to sacrifice to the spirits of my victims."

When Mrs. Liu heard this, she moaned to herself: "So my

husband was killed by this beast too! And Second Sister and
that young man were innocent after all! Come to think of it,
I was wrong to insist that they pay with their lives: they will
never forgive me in the nether regions." She pretended,
however, to be in the best of spirits, and said nothing.

The next day, she seized an opportunity to slip out, and went
straight to the city magistrate's office to inform against her
husband's murderer. A new city magistrate, who had taken
up office only a fortnight before, was presiding over the court
when the attendants took her in. When she came to the steps,
she cried aloud. Then she denounced the bandit, describing
how he had killed her husband Liu Gui, how the former city
magistrate had not investigated carefully because he was eager
to close the case, how the concubine and Cui Ning had forfeited
their lives though they were innocent, and how later the bandit
had killed her father's old servant and made her his mistress.
Now that justice had prevailed and the criminal had confessed
his guilt, she begged the city magistrate to pass judgement and
right the past wrong. After she had spoken she wept again.

Moved by her words, the city magistrate sent men to arrest
the bandit, and when he was tortured they found that his confession tallied in every point with her statement; accordingly
he was condemned to death. The case was reported to the
imperial court and, when the usual sixty days had passed, the
emperor decreed that since the bandit had committed robbery
and murder and caused the ruin of innocent people, he should
be executed on the spot according to the law; the former city
magistrate, who had passed a wrong sentence, should be dismissed from his post and struck off from the official list; the families
of Cui Ning and the concubine who had died unjustly should
receive pensions from the authorities; and since Mrs. Liu had
been forced by the bandit to become his wife and had avenged
her husband's death, half of the bandit's property should be
confiscated but half should be left to her to live on.

Mrs. Liu went to the execution ground to watch the sentence
being carried out; and when the bandit's head had been cut off

she took it and offered it as sacrifice before the shrines of her
dead husband, the concubine and Cui Ning. After lamenting
bitterly over them, she gave the property she had received to
a nunnery, and she herself every morning and evening chanted
Buddhist sutras for the souls of the dead until she died of old
age. As the verse says:

> Guilty or innocent, they died unblessed,
> Their ruin caused by careless words in jest;
> Then learn to speak the truth while you are young;
> The root of every evil is the tongue!

The Monk's Billet-Doux

In Lancers Lane in Kaifeng, the eastern capital, lived a captain of the imperial guards named Huangfu Song. Twenty-six years old, he had a wife of twenty-four and a maidservant of thirteen named Yinger. The three of them lived alone without any other relatives.

Then Captain Huangfu was sent to deliver winter uniforms to the frontier, and he did not come back till after New Year. Towards noon on the day of his return, after the morning customers had left, a man entered the small tea-house owned by Wang Er at the top of Lancers Lane. What did he look like, this man? He had big eyes under bushy eyebrows, a snub nose and thick lips, a turban like a bucket, a broad-sleeved coat, neat trousers, and clean shoes and socks.

When this man came in and sat down, Wang Er served him a bowl of tea and greeted him. As the customer sipped his tea, he glanced at Wang Er.

"I would like to wait for someone here," he said.

"Certainly," replied Wang Er.

After some time a boy came down the road carrying a tray and crying: "Quail fritters! Who'll buy my quail fritters?"

The customer beckoned to him.

"Here!" he called.

The boy carried his tray into the shop, put it on a table, strung a few fritters on a bamboo skewer and added a pinch of salt.

"Here you are, sir." He set them before the customer.

"Right," said the man. "But will you do something for me?"

"What is it, sir?"

The man pointed to the fourth house in the lane.

"Do you know that house?" he asked.

"Yes," said the boy. "That is Captain Huangfu's house. He has just come back from delivering uniforms to the frontier."

"How many people are there in his family?"

"Just him, his wife and a maid."

"Do you know his wife?"

"His wife usually stays behind the bamboo curtain; but I often go there to sell them fritters, so I know her. Why do you ask?"

The man took from his belt a pouch embroidered with gold thread, and drew from this fifty coins which he put on the boy's tray. The boy was very, very pleased.

"What can I do for you, sir?" he asked, his hands clasped respectfully before him.

"I'll tell you," said the man.

Taking from his sleeve a white paper packet containing a pair of ear-rings, two short gold hairpins and a letter, he gave them to the boy.

"I'll trouble you to give these to the lady I just inquired about," he said. "Don't give them to the captain. But when you see his wife tell her that I asked you to be sure to give them to her, and beg her to accept them. Go now. I shall wait for you here."

Leaving his tray on the counter of the tea-house, the boy took the package down the lane; and when he reached Captain Huangfu's house he lifted the bamboo curtain over the door and peeped in. The captain was sitting in an armchair by the door, so he saw the young vendor raise the curtain, peer furtively in and shrink back.

"Hey!" he shouted. "What do you want?"

When the boy did not answer but took to his heels, the captain leapt up, overtook him in a couple of strides and pulled him back.

"What's the idea?" he demanded. "Why look at me and make off?"

"A gentleman told me to bring three things to your wife," said the boy, "but not to give them to you."

"What three things?"

"You mustn't ask. They're not for you."

Captain Huangfu punched the boy hard on the head.

"Come on! Let me see them!" he ordered.

Smarting from the blow, the boy produced the package from his pocket.

"I was told to give these to the mistress," he grumbled, "not to you."

The captain grabbed the packet and opened it to find a pair of ear-rings, two short gold hairpins and a note, which he unfolded.

"Greetings to my lady!" he read. "Now that spring is here, I hope you are well. The other day I was fortunate enough to be able to drink with you, and I have been thinking of you ever since. The press of affairs prevents my calling in person, so I have written a little poem instead to express my longing for you."

The poem was as follows:

> *Your husband must be back now;*
> *I rage the whole night through!*
> *Then take these golden trinkets,*
> *And take this billet-doux.*
> *Take these and do not doubt me;*
> *Be merry, sweet, instead;*
> *Though I, since last I left you,*
> *Have mourned my lonely bed!*

After reading this, the captain glared ferociously and gnashed his teeth.

"Who gave you these?" he demanded.

The boy pointed to Wang Er's tea-house at the top of the lane.

"A gentleman with bushy eyebrows, big eyes, a snub nose

and thick lips asked me to give them to your wife," he said. "He told me not to give them to you."

Seizing the wretched boy by the hair, the captain marched straight up the lane to Wang Er's tea-house.

"The gentleman was here just now on the couch," said the boy, pointing inside the shop. "He told me to give that package to your wife, but not to you. Why should you beat me?"

But seizing the boy by the hair again and turning a deaf ear to Wang Er's remonstrances, the captain marched back home. In a towering rage he shut and barred the gate, while the fritter vendor trembled for fear. Then the captain called for his twenty-four-year-old wife, who was lovely as a flower.

"Take a look at these!" he cried.

Not knowing what had happened, she sat in the armchair while her husband showed her the letter and trinkets. She was completely bewildered by the billet-doux.

"Who has been drinking with you here these three months that I've been away at the frontier?" demanded the captain.

"We became husband and wife when little more than children," she protested. "How could I drink with another man while you were away?"

"Where did these trinkets come from then?"

"How should I know?"

Pointing an accusing finger at her with his left hand, the captain slapped her hard with his right. She screamed, hid her face in her hands, and fled sobbing to her room.

Then the captain called thirteen-year-old Yinger. He took down from the wall some bamboos for making arrows, set them on the ground, and ordered her to step forward. What was she like, this Yinger?

With plump, thick legs and arms yet shorter,
She chopped the wood and drew the water;
She ate and drank enough for three;
A proper, lusty maid was she.

Taking a rope from the dresser, the captain tied the maidservant's hands behind her back, looped the rope over a rafter, and strung her up. This done, he picked up a bamboo.

"Who has been drinking here with your mistress these three months that I've been away?" he demanded.

"No one," she replied.

The captain slashed at her legs with the bamboo until she screamed like a pig being slaughtered. Then he repeated his question, received the same answer and beat her again. At last Yinger could bear it no longer.

"These three months that you've been away," she said, "the mistress has not slept alone for a single night."

"Aha!" snorted the captain.

He let the maid down and unfastened her.

"Come over here," he ordered. "Tell me now, with whom did she sleep?"

"I dare not lie to you, master," said Yinger, wiping her eyes. "After you went away, the mistress never slept alone for a single night. She slept with me."

"Curse you!" swore the captain. "Are you making fun of me?"

He sent her angrily away.

After this he found a lock, went out, closed the gate and locked it from outside; then hurried to the corner to fetch four local police sergeants. With them he returned to his house, unlocked the gate, pushed it open and seized the fritters boy.

"I'll trouble you, officers, to arrest this rogue," he said.

"Certainly, sir!" responded the sergeants.

"Don't go yet," said the captain. "There are more of them."

He called out thirteen-year-old Yinger and his twenty-four-yead-old wife, who was lovely as a flower.

"Take them away too!" he cried.

"Sir," said one of the sergeants apologetically, "we dare not take your good lady."

"You dare not take her, eh?" roared the captain. "I tell you, this is a murder case!"

So he frightened the four sergeants into taking his wife, Yinger and the fritters boy to City Magistrate Qian's yamen.

Upon reaching the yamen, Captain Huangfu saluted the city magistrate and handed in the billet-doux. City Magistrate Qian ordered the accused to be sent to the detention house, and summoned Police Inspector Shan Ding to put him in charge of the case. First Shan Ding questioned the boy who sold fritters.

"It was a man in the tea-shop with big eyes, bushy eyebrows, a snub nose and thick lips, who told me to give the package to the lady," said the boy. And even after many beatings he stuck to his story.

Then the police inspector questioned Yinger.

"Nobody came to drink with the mistress," she said. "And I don't know who wrote the letter."

Even after many beatings she stuck to her story.

Then the police inspector questioned the captain's wife.

"We became husband and wife when little more than children," she said, "and there are just the two of us. We have no relatives to call on us. I don't know who can have written that letter."

The inspector saw that she was too delicate to stand torture, and he did not know how to bring pressure to bear on her; but presently he ordered two gaolers to bring a bandit from his cell.

> With sunken cheeks and hairy chin,
> That gaol-bird was as foul as sin!

The young woman covered her face with both hands, and dared not look at this wretch. Then the inspector ordered the gaolers to mete out punishment. They pulled the criminal's cangue forward; and, having tugged the bandit's head down, they seized bamboos and beat him till he screamed like a pig being slaughtered.

"Have you killed?" asked the inspector.

"I have! I have!"

"Have you committed arson?"

"I have!"

After ordering the two gaolers to take the bandit back to his cell, the inspector turned to the captain's wife.

"You saw that felon," he said. "After a few strokes he confessed to murder and arson. So if you are guilty, ma'am, you had better confess at once; for how could you stand such a beating?"

Tears streamed down the young woman's cheeks.

"Inspector," she said, "I can hide nothing from you."

They fetched her paper and brush to write her confession, and this is what she wrote:

We became husband and wife when little more than children, and we receive no visits even from relatives; so I don't know who can have sent the letter. It is for Your Honour to declare what I have done wrong.

After four or five interrogations, her answer was still the same.

In this way three days passed, and the inspector was baffled. He was standing outside the yamen on the fourth day when the captain came up and greeted him.

"How is it that after three days you still haven't settled this case?" demanded Captain Huangfu. "I shall soon be suspecting that you have accepted bribes from the man who wrote the letter, and are deliberately holding matters up."

"Well, sir," said the inspector, "what is it you want?"

"All I want is a divorce," was the reply.

The inspector went into the yamen and, when the time came for the evening session, reported the captain's request to the city magistrate. City Magistrate Qian then called for the young man.

"To sentence a thief we must find the stolen goods, and to sentence guilty lovers we must catch them together," he said. "With no evidence, how can we bring in a verdict?"

"I don't want to take my wife back," said the captain. "I would rather divorce her here in this court."

"Let it be as the husband wishes," decreed City Magistrate Qian.

So the captain went home alone.

The fritters boy and Yinger were released and told to go home. But the captain's wife, having learned that her husband did not want her and had divorced her, wept as she left the yamen.

"My husband does not want me, and I have no relatives to whom to turn," she thought. "What can I do? I had better make an end of myself."

She walked up Tianhanzhou Bridge and was about to throw herself into Bian River when someone gripped her clothes from behind. Turning round, she saw an old woman.

Her eyebrows were as white as snow,
Her form was bent and spare.
Her eyes were dim as autumn pools,
And white as clouds her hair.

"Child," said the old woman, "why are you trying to make away with yourself? Do you know me?"

"No, ma'am," replied the young woman. "I don't recognize you."

"I am your aunt. After your marriage, because my family is poor and I was afraid you might despise me, I never called on you. But the other day I heard that you and your husband had quarrelled; and I have been waiting all this time to see you. Now I understand you are divorced. But why do you want to jump into the river?"

"I have no roof above my head and no ground beneath my feet," replied the captain's wife. "My husband no longer wants me, and I have no relatives to whom to turn. What can I do but die?"

"Why not come and stay with me till you can think of something better?" asked the old woman.

"Who knows whether she is my aunt or not?" thought

the girl. "But I have nowhere to stay. I may as well go with her and see what happens."

So she went to the old woman's house, which was bare of any means of sustenance, being merely a lodging with simple furniture and some green cloth for curtains. Here she stayed for a couple of days.

One day they had just finished their meal when they heard a man shouting outside.

"Old woman!" he called. "You've sold my things. Why don't you pay me for them?"

Looking quite flustered, the old woman went out to welcome this unwelcome guest.

"Please come in and take a seat," she said.

Then the young woman saw a man with big eyes under bushy eyebrows, a snub nose and thick lips, a turban like a bucket, a broad-sleeved coat, neat trousers, and clean shoes and socks.

"Why!" she thought. "He looks just like the boy's description of the man who sent that letter."

The stranger came in and sat down on a stool.

"Old woman," he said with a haughty air, "you've sold stuff of mine worth three hundred strings of cash; but now a month has passed and not a cent have you paid me."

"Though I've found a customer, the money hasn't been paid yet," said the old woman. "As soon as it comes, I'll bring it to you, sir."

"You never delayed so long in previous transactions," protested the man. "Be sure to bring me the money the moment you get it."

When the old woman came back from seeing him off, she looked at the young captain's wife, and tears poured down her cheeks.

"What can I do?" she cried.

"What is the matter?" asked the other.

"This gentleman used to be a secretary in Caizhou Prefecture, and his name is Hong," said the old woman. "He is not an official any more now, but he sells trinkets. The other day he gave me something to sell for him, but someone cheated me; so I haven't got the money to pay him. Of course he is annoyed. He gave me another commission too, which I haven't been able to carry out either."

"What was that?"

"He asked me to find him a good-looking woman. If I could find someone like you, he would be pleased. Now here are you: your husband has given you up, and you can't go on like this. Why not let me introduce you to this gentleman? For then you'll find a home, and your aunty will have someone to rely on too. What do you think?"

After careful reflection the young woman decided there was nothing for it but to agree, and she moved to the man's house.

Soon a year passed, and once more it was New Year's Day. Ever since Captain Huangfu divorced his wife, he had been very unhappy.

"Each New Year's Day," he thought, "my wife and I used to go to Taxiangkuo Temple to burn incense; but this year I shall have to go alone. I don't even know where my wife is."

Tears streamed down his cheeks and he was in despair; but he forced himself to put on a purple silk gown and take the silver censer to the temple to offer incense.

He was just leaving the temple when he saw a man walk in with a woman. The man had big eyes under bushy eyebrows, a snub nose and thick lips; and the woman with him was the captain's former wife. Captain Huangfu gazed at his wife, and she gazed at him; but although their eyes met they dared not speak. Then the other man took her into the temple.

Standing outside the gate wondering what to do, the captain saw a mendicant collecting alms there.

"You got me into this fix!" exclaimed the mendicant at

the sight of the man with the captain's wife. "And now you're here!"

He was striding after them, when the captain called to him to stop.

"Are you trying to overtake them?" he asked.

"Yes," replied the mendicant. "I've suffered a lot because of him. It's his fault that I can't hold up my head."

"Do you know the woman?"

"No, I don't."

"She was my wife."

"In that case, what is she doing with him?"

Then the captain told him about the billet-doux and the divorce.

"So that's it," said the mendicant. "Do you know who he is?"

"No," said the captain.

"This scoundrel was a monk in Fantai Monastery east of this prefecture when I was there. My master was the abbot of that monastery, and he spent over a hundred coins to initiate this fellow into the order as his assistant. But a year ago this scoundrel disappeared with two hundred taels' worth of our master's silver utensils, and I was blamed for the theft. After being beaten and driven out of the monastery, I have had to beg for food. This is all owing to him. I know the priest here, so they let me stay in this temple to collect alms. But now that I've seen that rogue again, I'm not going to let him go."

Just at this moment the man he was speaking of came down the corridor with the captain's wife. The mendicant would have rushed forward to seize him had not the captain stopped him and pulled him aside by the temple gate.

"Don't lay hands on him yet," he said. "Let us follow to see where they go, then bring a suit against him."

So they followed the man.

After seeing her husband, tears had welled into the young woman's eyes as she entered the temple and offered incense.

"Why did you shed tears at the sight of your former husband, madam?" asked the monk when they left the temple. "I had a hard time getting you. When first I passed your door and saw you standing by the curtain, I lost my heart to you because you were so lovely. I've been to a lot of trouble to win you."

By now they had reached their house.

"I wonder who could have sent me that letter," said the woman as they entered.

"If you want to know," he answered, "it was I who told the fritters boy to deliver it to you. Your husband was taken in by my trick and divorced you."

When the woman heard that, she seized the man and screamed for help; but her cries threw him into such a panic that he tried to throttle her. Meanwhile the captain and the mendicant had followed them to the door and seen them going in. Hearing cries for help, they dashed in and found the monk strangling the captain's wife. Captain Huangfu and the mendicant promptly seized the wicked man and carried him before the city magistrate.

When City Magistrate Qian took his seat in court to deal with this case, the captain and his wife explained all that had happened. The city magistrate was angry and ordered his officers to put the villain in a cangue and give him one hundred strokes, then send him to the police station for a thorough investigation.

After the trial, Captain Huangfu was told to take his wife back, and they became husband and wife again. The mendicant was rewarded. The wicked monk made a full confession; and since he had carried out this dastardly plot, seduced another man's wife and attempted to murder her, he was sentenced to be beaten to death. As for the old crone who had abetted him by pretending to be the young woman's aunt, she was condemned to penal servitude in another district.

A story-teller who was present when they led the seducer out to execution composed this impromptu poem:

Behold now where the guilty monk is led!
He shall be whipped and flogged till he is dead.
But all along the road, as he proceeds,
The people stare to hear him tell his beads;
And when this scene the guardian angels scan,
They surely praise him as a holy man!

The Foxes' Revenge

All living creatures share a common nature,
Whether they are mammals or hatched out from eggs;
If you are good to them they won't forget it —
Just think of the bird who repaid its protector with rings!

This verse refers to a scholar of the Han Dynasty named Yang Bao, a native of Huaxi, who was a learned and brilliant youth at twenty. During the festival of the Double Ninth[1] one year he went for a walk outside the city, sitting down in a wood to rest when he was tired. Luxuriant trees cast a cool shade and the birds were singing, but suddenly amid all this loveliness a bird fell with a thud at his feet. Cheeping pitifully it tried to fly, but could only flutter helplessly about the ground.

"How odd!" thought Yang Bao. "What can have happened to this bird?"

Upon picking it up he saw that it was a golden oriole somebody had injured, which was crying piteously.

"I'll take you home and look after you till you can fly again," said Yang Bao, pitying the little creature with all his heart.

Just then a young man with a catapult came up from behind him.

"I brought that oriole down, sir," he said. "May I have it?"

"I can easily give it to you," replied Yang Bao, "but though

---

[1] The ninth day of the ninth month by the lunar calendar was a festival on which people often went to the country, climbing hills or enjoying the scenery.

a bird is not like a man, life is equally precious to it. Why should you kill it? If you kill a hundred, you still won't have enough for one meal; and if you sell ten thousand, you still won't make a fortune. Why don't you make your living some other way? I would like to buy this bird from you to save its life."

He took some money from his pocket.

"I don't catch birds for food or money, but for the fun of it," said the young man. "If you want this oriole, sir, you can have it."

"Why should you have fun at the expense of innocent creatures?" asked Yang Bao.

"It was wrong of me," admitted the other, throwing away his catapult as he left.

Yang Bao took the golden oriole home and kept it in a hat box, feeding it on yellow petals until its wing healed. After a hundred days it could fly again. It would fly off, then fly back, and Yang Bao became most attached to it. One day, however, it did not return. Yang Bao was worrying over its disappearance when a lad in a yellow jacket with delicate eyebrows and fine eyes came in and kowtowed to him. Yang Bao hastily helped him to his feet, and the lad produced a pair of jade rings which he gave to him.

"You saved my life, sir," he said, "but I have only these trifles to show my gratitude. With these rings your descendants will become great ministers."

"I have never met you before," replied Yang Bao. "When did I save your life?"

"Don't you know me?" asked the lad with a smile. "After I was shot down in the wood, you fed me with yellow petals in your hat box."

This said, he changed into a golden oriole and flew off. And later Yang Bao's descendants did indeed distinguish themselves in each successive generation.

"Why, story-teller," I hear someone protest, "everybody

knows that story about the oriole and the jade rings. Why waste time repeating it?"

Well, readers, it is because I am going to tell you now about another youth who wounded wild animals. But this man did not repent like the fellow who hurt the oriole, and so he lost nearly all he had and became the talk of the town I used the story about the golden oriole as an introduction; and I advise you all to do good deeds like Yang Bao and not to ask for trouble like the other young man.

> *You'd better keep your mouth shut when required,*
> *You'd better give things up when so desired;*
> *If you will do these things, free from strife,*
> *You will enjoy a long and peaceful life.*

During the reign of Emperor Xuan Zong (712-756) of the Tang Dynasty, there lived a young man named Wang Chen, who was a native of Changan. He had a smattering of classical knowledge, could write passable compositions, and enjoyed drinking and fencing. What he liked best of all, however, was riding and shooting with the catapult. Having lost his father when a child, he lived with his mother and wife, a daughter of the Yu clan, and his unmarried brother Wang Zai, who had great physical strength, excelled in the military arts, and served in the imperial guard. Their family was wealthy, with many servants; and they were living happily together when An Lushan revolted, stormed the Tongguan Pass and made the emperor fly westwards. Wang Zai left with the imperial train. And Wang Chen, afraid to remain in the capital, packed up his valuables and left home too, taking his mother, wife and whole household to the Changjiang Valley for safety. They bought some land and property in Little Bay near Hangzhou, and settled down there.

When news came that the capital had been retaken and the roads were safe once more, Wang Chen decided to return to Changan to look up old friends and relatives and set his estates there in order before moving his family back. Having told his mother of his plan, he lost no time in packing his baggage; then taking only one servant — Wang Fu — with him, he said goodbye to his mother and wife and went by boat to Yangzhou. This was a most prosperous city. An important centre in the Changjiang and Huai River area, through which travellers from both north and south had to pass, its harbour was filled with junks, its shore was thronged with people, and its markets were crowded with merchants and customers. Leaving the boat here, Wang Chen dressed himself as an army officer and hired a man to carry his baggage, then proceeded on horseback, enjoying the mountain and river scenery as he travelled. In a few days he reached a place called Fanchuan, not far from the capital; but as there had been fighting in this area all the villagers had fled, the houses along the road were deserted, and few travellers passed this way.

> *With mountains all around, and cool, dim woods,*
> *And lofty peaks that towered to the sky,*
> *The waterfalls made bright cascades of silver,*
> *And creepers hung like a thousand silken streamers.*
> *Few climbed the winding paths through these misty*
>   *mountains,*
> *Few lived in the lonely depths of these shadowy forests;*
> *But lovely mountain flowers laughed in the breeze,*
> *And nameless birds poured out their songs together.*

Feasting his eyes on the mountain scenery, Wang Chen rode slowly along. It was late afternoon when he heard voices in the forest, and drawing nearer saw not men but two foxes! Leaning against an old tree, one of them holding a book in its paws, they were laughing and chatting as they pointed at the pages as if they understood what was written there.

"What are those silly beasts up to?" wondered Wang. "I'd like to know what they're reading. I'll give them a taste of my catapult."

Reining in his horse he took his polished horn bow, reached into his pocket for some shot and took aim.

"There!"

The bow arched like a full moon, and the missile flew like a shooting star.

Little did the foxes enjoying themselves there suspect that they had been seen. As the bow-string twanged they looked up, and the shot flew straight into the left eye of the fox holding the book. Dropping the volume, it howled in pain and made quickly off; and as the other fox bent to pick up the book Wang Chen shot again, hitting the beast on the left cheek so that it too fled with a howl of pain. When Wang Chen led his horse forward and bid Wang Fu pick up the book for him, he found it filled with strange hieroglyphs not one of which could he understand.

"What language can this be?" he wondered. "I must ask some antiquarian later."

Putting the book in his sleeve he rode out of the forest and down the highway towards the capital. At that time a strict watch was kept at the city gates, and everyone going in or out was questioned; moreover the gates were closed as soon as it grew dark. By the time Wang Chen reached the city dusk had fallen, and finding the gate shut he decided to spend the night in an inn outside the city wall. He alighted at the door, and when the innkeeper saw that he carried sword and bow and was dressed like an army officer, he hurried forward respectfully.

"Please take a seat, sir," he said, and told a pot-boy to fetch a cup of tea.

Meanwhile Wang Fu had unstrapped the baggage and carried it inside.

"If you have good rooms, landlord," said Wang Chen, "please give me one."

"I have plenty of rooms," replied the innkeeper. "Just take your pick, sir."

He lit a lamp to show him round, and when Wang Chen had chosen a clean room the innkeeper moved his baggage in, then stabled his horse for him. This done, the pot-boy came in.

"Will you have a drink, sir?" he asked.

"If you have good wine, bring me two measures with a plateful of beef," said Wang Chen. "And give my man the same."

When the pot-boy had gone Wang Chen went out too, closing his door behind him. Presently the pot-boy returned with the wine and the meat.

"Will you drink in your room or here in the hall, sir?" he asked.

"Out here," replied Wang Chen.

Then the pot-boy set the wine on a table and Wang Chen sat down. Wang Fu poured out the wine for him, and when he had drunk a few cups the innkeeper came over.

"May I ask where you come from, sir?" he inquired.

"From the Changjiang Valley."

"You don't talk like a southerner, sir."

"As a matter of fact, I used to live in the capital. But after An Lushan revolted and the emperor went to Sichuan I took my family south to avoid trouble. When I heard that the rebels had been beaten and His Imperial Majesty had returned to the capital, I decided to come back to set my affairs here in order before bringing my family home. Because the road was said to be unsafe, I dressed as an army officer."

"So we are from the same district!" exclaimed the innkeeper. "I hid in the country too, and came back less than a year ago."

As fellow-provincials, they immediately became very friendly and started exchanging reminiscences about the hardships of exile.

The landscape is as lovely as before,
But half the citizens are here no more.

They were in the middle of an animated conversation when someone called out from behind them: "Have you an empty room, innkeeper?"

"I have rooms all right," replied the landlord. "How many of you are there?"

"Just myself."

He was indeed alone, with no baggage.

"In that case, I'm sorry, but I can't take you," said the innkeeper.

"Why not?" demanded the newcomer angrily. "Are you afraid I won't pay you?"

"Certainly not, sir. But Lord Guo, the Garrison Commander, has forbidden all innkeepers to take in strangers. Anyone who does so on the sly is liable to be severely punished. You have no baggage, sir, and we don't know you, how can I keep you?"

"So you don't know me, eh? I am Hu Er, Lord Guo's steward. I have been to Fanchuan on business and come back too late to get into the city: that's why I want to spend the night in your inn and why I have no baggage. If you don't believe me, come with me tomorrow morning to the city gate to ask the guards there. They all know me."

Impressed by the stranger's connection with Lord Guo, the innkeeper believed him.

"No offence meant, sir," he said. "I didn't recognize you at first. Please step inside and rest."

"Later," replied the other. "I am hungry. Bring me some wine and food. I am fasting," he added, "so don't bring me any meat."

He walked over to Wang Chen's table and sat down opposite him, while the pot-boy went for wine and food. Wang Chen observed that he hid his left eye with his sleeve as if it were hurting him.

"I had bad luck today, landlord," said the stranger. "I met two wild beasts and hurt my eye through a fall."

"What beasts did you meet?"

"On my way back from Fanchuan I saw two foxes rolling on the ground and howling with pain in the forest. When I tried to catch them, though, I slipped and fell. So the foxes got away, while I nearly blinded myself in one eye."

"No wonder you are keeping it covered," said the innkeeper.

"Today I came past Fanchuan too," put in Wang Chen. "I also met two foxes."

"Did you catch them?" asked the stranger eagerly.

"They were reading a book in the forest," replied Wang Chen. "With my catapult I shot the fox holding the book in the left eye, so that it dropped the book and fled. And when the other fox tried to pick up the book I hit it on the left cheek, making it run for dear life too. I got the book but not the foxes."

"Foxes reading a book!" exclaimed the stranger and the innkeeper. "How extraordinary!"

"I'd like to know what's written in that book," said the stranger. "May I have a look at it?"

"It's full of strange hieroglyphs," said Wang Chen. "I can't make out a single word."

Putting down his wine cup, he prepared to take the book from his sleeve. Before he had time to do so, however, the innkeeper's five-year-old grandson came into the yard and saw that one of the guests was a fox, although he did not know what such an animal should be called.

"Grandpa!" he cried, running forward and pointing at the fox. "Why is this big cat sitting here? Why don't you chase it away?"

At once Wang Chen realized that this was the fox whose eye he had injured, and hastily drawing his sword he struck at its head. The fox dodged backwards, revealing its true form as it rolled on the ground, then dashed out. Sword in hand Wang Chen chased it past several doors until it leapt over a wall; and then, unable to find the gate, he had to turn back. He was met by the innkeeper, carrying a lighted lamp, and Wang Fu.

"You had better let it go," said the innkeeper.

"If your grandson hadn't seen it," replied Wang Chen, "it would have got away with the book."

"Foxes are tricky beasts," said the innkeeper. "It may come back later."

"The next time a stranger mentions those beasts to me, I'll know it's the fox again," replied Wang Chen. "I shall have my sword ready."

While speaking they had reached the inn where the other lodgers, who had heard this story with amazement, gathered round to question Wang Chen. After talking till his mouth was dry, he supped and retired to his room for the night. Since the fox had tried to recover the book by a trick in spite of its pain, Wang was sure that the volume must be valuable and prized it more highly than ever.

At midnight there came a knocking at the gate.

"Hurry up and return us that book!" shouted the foxes. "If you do, we shall repay you well! If you don't, you will be sorry for it."

When Wang heard this he was very angry. Throwing on his clothes and seizing his sword, he left his room on tiptoe for fear of waking the others. But when he reached the gate, he found the innkeeper had locked it.

"By the time I call the landlord to open the gate the foxes will have disappeared and I shan't be able to get at them," he thought. "I shall only be disturbing people for nothing. I had better let it go till the morning."

So he went back to bed. But the foxes shouted at the gate for a long time, waking everybody in the inn; and the next morning the other guests reasoned with Wang Chen.

"Since you can't make out what's in the book, what's the use of keeping it?" they asked. "You had better return it. Otherwise the foxes may really cause trouble, and you'll be sorry·when it's too late."

Now if Wang had been sensible enough to take their advice, all would have been well. But since he was too obstinate to listen to them, later the foxes practically ruined him.

For a man who neglects the advice of a friend
Will repent and shed tears of regret in the end.

When Wang had breakfasted and settled his bill he packed up and rode into the city, seeing houses in ruins, streets half deserted, and far fewer passers-by than in the good old days. He was cut to the quick to find his old home nothing but a heap of rubble; and since he could not stay here he found a lodging where he could leave his baggage, then went to look for his relatives, not many of whom were left. They told each other all that had befallen since last they met, and at the saddest parts of their stories shed tears of grief.

"Many, many families were separated during the rebellion," said his relatives, "to be captured, killed or suffer endless hardships. We ourselves barely escaped with our lives. You should count yourself very lucky that all your family are safe and sound and you have lost only your house. Besides, we have looked after your landed property, so that none of your estates have been seized; and you will still be a wealthy family when you come back."

Wang Chen thanked them, then bought a house, furnished it with all that was needful, and got his farms back into good working order. He had been occupied in this way for two months when one day, as he left his house, a man in mourning with a bundle on his back approached rapidly from the east. Wang Chen saw with a shock that this was none other than his servant Liuer.

"Where have you come from, Liuer?" he called. "Why are you dressed like that?"

"So this is where you live, master," said Liuer. "I have had a hard time finding you."

"Tell me," repeated Wang, "why are you dressed in mourning?"

"Here is a letter, master. You will see from this."

He carried his bundle into the house and took from it a letter which he handed to his master. Wang saw that it was in his mother's handwriting.

"Son," he read, "after you left us we heard that there was more trouble in the north, and I worried day and night till I fell ill. All drugs have proved useless, and I shall soon be dead; but since I am over sixty I am not dying before my time. I regret only that there have been all these disturbances during my last years, and that I am dying far from home with neither of my sons at my side: this does distress me. As I come from the northwest, I do not want to be buried in a strange land; but the rebels are still strong and as long as the capital may fall into their hands again you should not stay there. After careful thought I believe your best course will be to dispose of all the property in the capital and use the money for my funeral; then, when you have buried me, come back here to the Changjiang Valley, where the soil is rich and the people good. Of course, an estate is not built up easily, so you must not dispose of our Changjiang Valley property carelessly. When the war is over, you can make plans to go back to the north. If you disobey me and are killed by the rebels, so that there is no one to continue our family sacrifices, I shall not recognize you as my son even when you join me in the nether regions. Mark well what I have said!"

When Wang had read this letter he fell weeping to the ground.

"I came to set my estates here in order so that we might come home," he said. "I never dreamed that anxiety for me would cause my mother's death. Had I known, I would not have come. But it is no use regretting that now."

After weeping for some time he asked, "Did my mother say anything else before she died?"

"No," replied Liuer, "only that your houses and farms in the north must be ruined, and that even if you recovered and restored them you shouldn't stay here, because there may be another revolt in the capital any time. She wanted you to make arrangements for the funeral as quickly as possible and to settle down safely in Hangzhou after bringing her coffin north. She said that if you didn't carry out her wishes, she would not rest easy in her grave."

"Of course I cannot disobey my mother's last wishes," said Wang Chen. "And there is reason in her proposal that we should live in the south, because the fighting is not over here yet. Hence there is much to be said for leaving."

He made haste to procure mourning clothes and set up a shrine, then sent men to prepare the ancestral graveyard, at the same time begging friends to help him sell his property.

"You will need a month at least to build the sepulchre, master," said Liuer two days later, "and the family will be worrying. Shall I go back first to tell them that all is well?"

"That is a good idea," replied Wang.

He wrote a letter to his wife and gave the servant travelling money to go back first.

"I'm going on ahead, master," said Liuer when he was leaving. "I hope you will settle things here and come on as quickly as you can."

"You don't have to remind me of that," retorted Wang Chen. "I only wish I could fly home this moment."

Then Liuer left the house with a well satisfied air.

When Wang Chen's relatives heard what had happened, they came to offer condolences and advised him not to give up his northern estates. However, since this was his mother's last wish, Wang Chen would not listen to them. In his haste he sold his good land for half its value; and in little over twenty days, when a grave had been dug in the ancestral graveyard and all things made ready, he packed up and left the capital with Wang Fu, to travel post-haste to Hangzhou to fetch his mother's coffin.

We will go back now to Wang's family. When his mother and wife heard that rebellion had broken out again in the north, they worried day and night about Wang Chen, regretting that they had ever let him go. So two or three months later, when the gateman announced that the master's servant, Wang Fu, had arrived with a letter from the capital, they ordered him to be admitted immediately. Wang Fu kowtowed to his mistresses, then presented the letter; and although they noticed that his left eye was badly hurt, in their haste to read the letter they did not stop to question him. The letter ran as follows:

"After leaving you, mother, I travelled safely to the capital, where I found all our property safe and have now carried out all the necessary repairs. I was lucky to meet my old friend Secretary Hu here, for he introduced me to the prime minister, who has graciously given me an official post in the northeast. Since I have already received my credentials and must shortly leave, I am sending Wang Fu to invite you to accompany me to my new post. As soon as you receive this letter you should sell all our property in the south and come to the capital as fast as you can. Sell at a loss rather than delay. As we shall soon meet, I will say no more now. Your dutiful son, Chen."

When Wang Chen's mother and wife read this letter, they could hardly contain themselves for joy.

"How did you hurt your eye, Wang Fu?" they asked.

"I'm ashamed to tell you!" replied Wang Fu. "I dozed off in the saddle and fell off my horse, nearly knocking out this eye."

"Has the capital changed much? Are all our relatives still there?"

"The whole city was more than half destroyed," he told them. "It is quite different from the old days. Most of our relatives were killed or captured or else fled. There are only a few families left now, and they all had their property stolen, their houses burnt down or their land seized. Ours is the only family not to have lost a single house or field."

When the women heard this they were even more overjoyed.

"Our property is safe and he has been given an official post!" they cried. "We must thank Heaven and our ancestral spirits which have protected us. When we are ready to leave, let us sacrifice to them and pray for a bright future and continued prosperity."

Then they asked: "Who is this Secretary Hu?"

"An old friend of our master," replied Wang Fu.

"I have never heard him speak of a friend named Hu who is an official," said the old lady.

"Perhaps this is a new friend," suggested his wife.

"That's right," assented Wang Fu. "He only met this man recently."

"Wang Fu, you've had a hard journey," said the old lady after further questions. "Go and have some wine and food now, then rest."

The following day Wang Fu said: "It will take you several

days to prepare for the journey, ma'am, and there is no one to look after our master in the capital. Hadn't I better go back first to give him your reply and get everything ready, so that as soon as you arrive we can start for his new post?"

To this the old lady agreed. She gave Wang Fu a letter and some travelling money; and after he had left she sold all their land, houses, furniture and utensils, keeping only some clothes and valuables. Because she was anxious to lose no time she did not bargain about the price, and much of the property was practically given away. Finally she called in monks to perform sacrifices, hired a junk, and chose an auspicious day to start the journey. Some friendly neighbours' wives came to see them off, and so they set sail, travelling from Hangzhou to Suzhou, then went up the Changjiang River and made for Yangzhou. Because their master had received an official post, the servants were in the highest spirits and could hardly keep still for excitement.

After leaving the capital, Wang Chen travelled as fast as he could until he reached Yangzhou. There he set down his baggage in an inn by the harbour and disposed of his horse, after which he had a meal and ordered Wang Fu to hire a boat while he sat outside the inn keeping an eye on his baggage and watching the passing vessels. Presently he noticed a large junk coming upstream, with four or five men laughing and singing in the prow. As the boat drew nearer he saw to his surprise that these were his own retainers.

"Why are they not at home?" he wondered. "What are they doing on this boat?"

Then it occurred to him: "Perhaps after my mother's death they have gone to work in another family."

He was speculating in this way when the cabin curtain was lifted, and he recognized the girl who looked out as one of their maidservants.

"How extraordinary!" he exclaimed to himself.

He was about to hail the junk when the servants saw him.

"What brings you here, sir?" they cried. "Why are you in mourning?"

They immediately ordered the boatmen to bring the boat to the shore.

Meanwhile, roused by this commotion, Wang Chen's mother and wife lifted the cabin curtain to look out; and when Wang Chen saw that his mother was not dead he hastily took off his mourning, unpacked his baggage and changed into ordinary dress. By this time the servants had come ashore to meet him; and, ordering them to pick up his baggage, he boarded the junk to greet his mother. When he saw Liuer at the prow, however, he seized him and started beating him.

"He hasn't done anything wrong," declared the old lady, coming out of the cabin. "Why are you beating him?"

When Wang Chen saw his mother, he let go of Liuer and bowed.

"By bringing your letter to the capital and raising a false alarm," he said, "this dog has made me act in an unfilial way!"

"But he has been at home all this time," they exclaimed in surprise. "He never took any letter to the capital."

"Only a month ago he brought me my mother's letter," protested Wang Chen. "And I sent him back after two days to reassure the family. Then I sold our property and started back myself post-haste. How can you say he never went to the capital?"

"What can have happened?" they demanded incredulously. "Does Liuer have a double?"

Even Liuer laughed.

"I never went to the capital, not even in a dream," he declared.

"Show me the letter," said Wang Chen's mother. "Let me see whether it is in my writing."

"If it hadn't looked like your writing," replied Wang, "I would never have believed it."

But when he undid his baggage and took out the letter, he found a sheet of white paper without a word on it. Gaping in consternation, he turned this over and over in his hands.

"Where is the letter?" demanded his mother. "Show it to me."

"This is amazing," muttered Wang Chen. "How could all that writing have disappeared?"

"I can't believe it!" said his mother. "The only letters we've exchanged since you left are the one you wrote when you sent Wang Fu to fetch me, and the reply I sent you by him. How could there be a false Liuer to deceive you with a false letter? And now you say it has changed into a blank sheet — I never heard such nonsense in my life!"

When Wang Chen heard that Wang Fu had been home, it was his turn to be astounded.

"Wang Fu has been with me all the time in the capital," he assured them. "He has come here with me now. I never sent him with any letter to you."

"That makes even less sense," objected his mother and wife. "A month ago Wang Fu brought us a letter from you, saying that all our property in the capital was safe and that Secretary Hu had introduced you to the prime minister, who gave you an official post. You told us to sell all our houses and land in the south and come straight to the capital to accompany you to your new post. So we disposed of all our property and hired this boat for the journey. How can you say Wang Fu never came back?"

"This is becoming more and more fantastic!" exclaimed Wang Chen. "No Secretary Hu ever introduced me to the prime minister or got me a job. And I never wrote to invite you to the capital."

"Can Wang Fu be an impostor too?" demanded the old lady. "Fetch him here at once."

"He went to hire a boat," replied Wang Chen. "He will be back presently."

The servants gathered at the prow to keep a lookout, and soon saw Wang Fu in the distance running towards the wharf. He was dressed in mourning too. They waved to him frantically, and Wang Fu recognized them.

"What are they doing here?" he wondered.

When he drew near they saw that he had changed. When he brought the letter, he had been blind in his left eye; but now both his eyes were as round and bright as brass bells.

"Wang Fu!" they called. "When you came home the other day you were blind in the left eye. How is it that you're all right again now?"

Wang Fu spat at them.

"You're the ones who are blind," he retorted. "When did I go home? And why accuse me of being blind?"

"This is an odd business!" they laughed. "Our mistress wants to see you in the cabin. Take off that mourning and go in."

Wang Fu looked flabbergasted.

"Is the old lady still alive?" he demanded.

"Of course she is," they replied.

Wang Fu did not believe them, though, so without removing his mourning he dashed straight into the cabin.

"Fool!" shouted Wang Chen. "Your mistress is here. Go and change your clothes at once."

Then Wang Fu hurried out, removed his mourning and went back to the cabin to kowtow to the old lady, who rubbed her eyes as she stared at him.

"Well, I never!" she declared again and again. "When he came the other day his left eye was blind, but today it is perfectly all right. I suppose it couldn't have been him after all."

She hastily took out her son's letter to have a look at it, only to find that it was a sheet of blank paper too, without an ink mark on it.

The whole family was staggered. They were at a loss to understand who could have masqueraded as Liuer and Wang Fu, or why anyone should trick Wang Chen in Changan and his mother in Hangzhou in order to ruin the family. Fearing worse might follow, they were filled with doubts and forebodings. But after thinking hard, Wang Chen recollected that the false Wang Fu had been blind in the left eye, and then he saw light.

"I have it!" he cried. "This is the work of those accursed beasts!"

His mother immediately asked what he meant, and he told her how he had shot the foxes at Fanchuan and taken their book, how one of them had masqueraded as a man in the inn to recover the book, and how they had hammered on the inn gate all night.

"I thought they changed into men simply to get the book," he said. "Little did I dream they had such cunning."

The others shook their heads and shot out their tongues in amazement.

"These fox fairies are fearfully cunning," they declared. "In two places so far apart they were able to fool us by imitating men's handwriting and appearance so well. If you had known this, you should have returned them the book."

"A plague on these wicked beasts!" swore Wang Chen. "I shall certainly not return the book. If they trouble me again, I'll burn the accursed thing."

"We had better keep to the point and discuss our main problem," said Wang Chen's wife. "Here we are — neither north nor south — what shall we do?"

"All the property in the capital has been sold," said Wang Chen. "If we go there, we shall have nowhere to stay. Besides, it's a long way to travel. We had better go back south."

"But we have nothing left in the south either," objected his mother. "Where shall we live?"

"We shall have to rent a place for the time being," said Wang, "and make plans later."

As they headed the boat back south, the servants who had been all fire and spirit before were as cold and dull as puppets whose strings have been snapped — silent and limp. They had set off exultantly, but returned in despair. Upon reaching Hangzhou, Wang Chen and the servants went ashore first to rent a house in the quarter where they had lived before and buy the necessary furniture and utensils. Then they carried over their baggage and fetched Wang Chen's mother and wife. When they reckoned how much money they had left, it was less than half their original capital; so between anger and despair they stayed at home fuming, unwilling to go out. The neighbours who had seen Wang Chen's mother leave and then return came to inquire, and when Wang told them his story they marvelled and spread the tale till half Hangzhou knew it.

One day Wang Chen was watching his servants clean the hall when a dignified, well-dressed stranger walked in.

> *He had a black gauze cap and green silk gown,*
> *A jasper ring on his cap and a purple belt;*
> *His socks were white as snow,*
> *His shoes like rosy clouds;*
> *He'd a lordly look and natural dignity.*
> *A man like that, if not a god,*
> *Must at least be a high official or ruler of men.*

Wang Chen saw that this stranger was no other than his brother, Wang Zai, who came up to him and bowed.

"How have you been, brother," he asked, "since we parted?"

Wang Chen returned his bow.

"To think of your finding us here!" he exclaimed.

"When I went to the capital and looked for our old home," said Wang Zai, "I found it had been razed to the ground; and the thought of all you must have suffered in the war made me very sad. Then I was relieved to learn from our relatives that the family had taken refuge in the south. They told me too that you had been to the capital to set our property to rights, but left again after hearing of our mother's death. I came here posthaste and found the house where you used to live; but when the neighbours told me that you had moved and that our mother was well, I went back to the boat to take off my mourning before coming here. Where is our mother now? And why have you moved to such a shabby place?"

"It is a long story," replied Wang Chen. "I will tell you after you've seen mother."

He led Wang Zai inside, and servants announced his arrival to the old lady. The knowledge that her second son had come home made her very happy, and she hurried out to meet them as they were going in. Then Wang Zai kowtowed to her.

"Son!" she cried. "I have been thinking of you day and night. Have you been well?"

"Yes, thank you, mother. When I have greeted my sister-in-law, I'll tell you all I've been doing."

After Wang Chen's wife and the maids and servants had greeted him, Wang Zai took his brother by the sleeve and led him to the hall. Their mother came with them, and they sat down together.

"You start first, brother," said Wang Zai. "How did you get into this state?"

Wang Chen told him in detail how he had shot the foxes at Fanchuan and how the foxes had tricked him and his mother into selling all their property.

"So that's the reason!" exclaimed Wang Zai. "Well, it's your own fault; you can't blame the foxes. They were just reading in the forest, while you were passing by on the public highway. They hadn't interfered with you, so why did you have to shoot them and take their book? If one of them went to the inn in spite of its pain to recover the book, that shows they must have needed it desperately. Yet you not only refused to return it, but chased them angrily with drawn sword; and that night when they begged you to let them have it, you refused again. You can't read the book yourself, so it is useless to you. Why should you keep it? You've only yourself to blame for the plight you're in now."

"That's just what I say," agreed their mother. "What's the use of keeping the book? It's only asking for trouble."

Wang Chen made no reply, but this lecture left him thoroughly irritated.

"How big is the book?" inquired Wang Zai. "What is the writing like?"

"It's a slender volume," replied Wang Chen. "I don't know what language it is, because I can't decipher a word."

"Let me have a look at it," said Wang Zai.

"That's right," put in the old lady. "Show it to your brother. He may be able to read it."

"I don't suppose I shall," said Wang Zai. "I'm curious to see it though."

Wang Chen fetched the book and gave it to his brother, who turned the pages from beginning to end.

"This is certainly strange writing," he said.

Then he stood up and walked to the middle of the hall.

"I was Liuer the other day," he announced. "Now that you've returned our magic book, I won't worry you any more. You can set your mind at rest."

This said, he rushed outside.

Wang Chen chased furiously after him.

"How dare you, detestable beast!" he cried. "You shan't get away!"

Seizing the fox by its garments, he pulled so hard that the silk gown was torn. Then the fox shook itself, slipped out of its clothes, reverted to its true form and streaked out as swiftly as the wind. Wang Chen and his servants hurried to the street, but though they hunted in all directions not a trace of the beast could they find. Because the foxes had ruined his family, chided him and now taken the book, Wang Chen was gnashing his teeth in rage. As he was gazing round, he saw a blind priest standing under the eaves of the house opposite.

"Have you seen a fox pass by?" asked Wang Chen.

The blind priest pointed eastward.

"It went that way," he said.

Wang Chen and his men started racing down the street, but when they had passed five or six houses they heard a shout behind them.

"Wang Chen!" called the blind priest. "I was Wang Fu the other day. Your brother is here too!"

They wheeled round to see the two foxes gambolling mischievously with the book between their paws. But when they rushed forward to catch them, the beasts made off like wind.

As Wang Chen was racing past his own door, his mother called
out to stop him.

"I'm glad that source of trouble has gone!" she cried. "Why
should you chase them? Come home now."

Though nearly bursting with anger, in deference to his mother
Wang Chen had to call his men back. When they picked up the
clothes the fox had worn to look at them, the garments changed
in their hands.

> The silk gown changed to banana leaves,
> The black gauze cap to a lotus leaf,
> The jasper ring was a willow twig,
> The purple belt a creeper;
> The socks were two sheets of white paper,
> And the red shoes pine tree bark.

At this sight they were all amazed.

"What magic arts those foxes have!" declared the servants.
"Where can our second master be now? Fancy the fox imitating him so well!"

The more Wang Chen brooded over this, the angrier he grew.
Finally he had to take to his bed, and his mother called in
doctors to attend him.

A few days later some of the servants were in the hall when
Wang Zai walked in again, in the same gauze cap and silk robe.
They naturally thought this must be the fox disguised as before.

"That fox is back again!" they shouted.

After running for clubs and sticks, they rushed forward to
beat him.

"You fools!" shouted Wang Zai. "How dare you? Go and
tell your mistress I am here."

They paid no attention, however, but went on belabouring
Wang Zai until he lost his temper, seized one of their sticks and
laid so lustily about him that they dared not come near, but hid
in adjoining rooms.

"You cursed beast!" they swore, pointing at him. "Now
that you've got the book, what have you come back for?"

Bewildered but angry, Wang Zai forced his way in. And as the servants bolted towards the back quarters, the old lady heard the noise and came out to ask what this confusion meant.

"That fox has changed into our second master again," they told her. "He is forcing his way in."

While she was uttering cries of dismay, Wang Zai entered her presence. At the sight of his mother he put down his stick and stepped forward to kowtow.

"Mother," he asked, "why did those fools call me a fox and beat me?"

"Are you really my son?" she demanded.

"You bore me," he replied. "Of course I am your son."

While they were talking seven or eight men came in carrying Wang Zai's baggage. Then the servants knew that this was indeed their master and kowtowed to him in apology. And when he asked the reason for what had happened, his mother told him all about the foxes.

"Your brother was so angry that he fell ill," she said. "He is not well yet."

Wang Zai was aghast.

"In that case," he said, "I suppose that letter Wang Fu brought me in Sichuan was false too?"

"What did the letter say?"

"I went in the imperial train to Sichuan, where I was assigned work under Governor Yan Wu of Jiannan and later promoted to be a lieutenant. That is why when His Imperial Majesty returned to the capital I did not follow him. Two months ago Wang Fu brought me a letter from my brother saying that he had moved to the Changjiang Valley during the revolt, and that you had just died, so that I must come at once to help take your coffin north to our ancestral graveyard. Wang Fu said he had to go to the capital to prepare the graveyard, and left the next day. Then I resigned from my post, disposed of all my property and travelled here as fast as I could. When I reached your old house the neighbours directed me here; and learning that you were alive and well I went back to the boat to change my clothes, meaning to ask my brother what made him send me such false news. Who could imagine an extraordinary thing like this?"

When he took the letter from his baggage and they found it had changed into a blank sheet of paper too, they did not know whether to laugh or swear.

After Wang Zai went in with his mother to greet his brother and sister-in-law and tell them his story, Wang Chen nearly had an apoplectic fit.

"Though these foxes caused us so much trouble," said the old lady, "they *did* go to Sichuan to fetch Zai back, and it's thanks to them that we are united again. Let's count this to their credit and stop complaining."

After two months Wang Chen recovered, and they settled down permanently in Hangzhou.

And even to this day, readers, in the Changjiang River Valley, an impostor is called a fox.

The Hidden Will

Now although the classics of Confucianism, Taoism and Buddhism teach men to strive after virtue, in my view their lengthy exhortations are quite superfluous, as to be a good man all that is necessary is filial piety and brotherly love. And of these two, the more important is filial piety. A good son, who loves what his parents love and respects what they respect, will naturally live in perfect accord with his brothers who are his own flesh and blood, if he wants to please his father and mother. Since all the family property has been acquired by the parents, why should brothers distinguish between "yours" and "mine," between valuable and worthless? Sons in a poor family, who inherit nothing, have to build up an estate by their own sweat and toil. So when those who have land and property still quarrel over their portions and accuse their parents of favouritism or injustice, their father and mother will not rest happy in their graves. This is not the behaviour of filial sons.

Well did the ancients say: Brothers are more to be prized than property. No one is closer to a man than his parents; but they are already grown by the time he is born, and must die before him; so he can spend only half his life with them. No one is dearer to a man than his wife, who can live with him till their hair is white; but before their marriage they belong to different families and spend their childhood apart. Brothers, however, are born in one family and remain together from childhood till old age. They settle problems together, help each other out when times are hard, and are as intimate as hands and feet. For such is brotherly love. If you lost a handsome property today, you may acquire another tomorrow; but losing a brother is like losing one of your limbs — you will never be whole again as long as you live. Thus we see the truth of the saying "Brothers are more to be prized than property." And it is better to be a beggar with nothing to inherit than to destroy such brotherly love for the sake of land; for in this way you can avoid trouble.

I will now tell you about a certain Magistrate Teng of our Ming Dynasty, who settled a property dispute between two brothers. This tale should help all who hear it to prize virtue, set little store by wealth, and hold fast to filial piety and brotherly love. It does not matter, readers, whether you have brothers or not. Let each examine his heart, and learn to live better.

> *The good will hear; their hearts will bleed;*
> *But wicked men will pay no heed.*

In the reign of Emperor Yong Le (1403-1425) there lived a prefect named Ni Shouqian in Xianghe County of Shuntian Prefecture, who had amassed great wealth, a rich estate and fine houses. His wife, a daughter of the Chen family, had given birth to a son named Shanji but died since her son's marriage. After her death Prefect Ni resigned from office to live alone; but he was a vigorous old man who collected rents and made loans in person, being unwilling to take his ease.

"Not many people live to be seventy," said Shanji to his father. "But you are seventy-nine, sir, and next year will reach the venerable age of eighty. Wouldn't it be better if you entrusted the management of the estate to me, and took it easy?"

But the old man shook his head, and recited the following verse:

> *For as long as I live I'll control my estate;*
> *I don't want you to worry or labour till late;*
> *I will keep you from cold and from hunger and thirst,*
> *Till they carry me over the threshold feet first!*

For the whole of the tenth month every year Prefect Ni used to make the rounds of the farms on his estate to collect rents, when his tenants entertained him with their plumpest fowls and choicest wine. And this year he went out as usual. One day after noon he was strolling round the village to enjoy the scenery, when he came upon a girl and a white-haired old woman, who were washing clothes on a rock by the brook. Though the girl was dressed in the simple country fashion, she was strikingly beautiful.

Her glossy hair was black as jet,
Her limpid eyes as clear as rills,
Her fingers fine as onion shoots,
Her eyebrows arched as distant hills;
Her homespun clothes became her well
As silk or fine embroidery,
And lovely as a wild flower
She had no need of finery.
A daintier girl was never seen.
And she had barely turned sixteen.

Then and there Prefect Ni lost his heart to the girl, and when she finished washing her clothes and left with the old woman he watched them as they walked past several houses and entered a small gate in a fence. Then he turned back at once to summon the village headman, and bade him ask the girl's companion whether she was betrothed or not.

"If not," said Prefect Ni, "I would like to take her as my concubine. I don't know whether she is willing or not."

Only too anxious to please his master, the headman immediately went off to carry out his instructions. He discovered that the girl's name was Mei. Her father had passed the prefectural examination; but both he and the girl's mother had died while she was a child, and she had been living ever since with her grandmother. She was seventeen, and not yet engaged.

"Our master likes the look of your granddaughter," said the headman to the girl's grandmother when he had ascertained these facts. "He would like to marry her. And although she will only be a second wife, the old mistress has been dead for

a long time, so there will be no one to order her about. She will
naturally have the best of everything, and you will be supplied
with all the clothes, tea and rice you need, to say nothing of a
fine funeral at the last. I only hope you will not let this good
chance slip."

Dazzled by such glittering prospects, the old woman gave her
consent at once. The marriage arrangements were made without
difficulty, and the headman went back to report his success to
Prefect Ni, who was overjoyed. After settling the amount of
the wedding gifts and choosing an auspicious day, he decided
to send the presents and go through the wedding ceremony in
the village to avoid any objections his son might raise. So they
were married, and a striking couple they made too — one so old
and the other so young!

Three days later the prefect called for a sedan-chair and had
his young wife carried home to meet his son and daughter-in-law.
The entire household kowtowed to their new mistress, and were
delighted when the prefect made them all gifts of cloth. Ni
Shanji was the only one who was not pleased; and although he
said nothing to his father, he had plenty to say to his wife when
they were alone.

"The old man has made a proper fool of himself!" he declared. "A man of his age is like a candle in a draught. He ought
to think what he is about. He knows he has only five or ten years
at the most to live, yet he does a ridiculous thing like this, marrying a slip of a girl who can only be his wife in name! Think
of all the cases we know of old men who can't satisfy their young
brides, but force them to run wild; and when some scandal of
the sort comes to light, what a disgrace it will be for our family!

"There's another thing too. Young women who marry old
husbands are like refugees in a famine — when times are better
they mean to go home again. Such a woman will steal everything she can lay her hands on, hiding a little here and a little
there, and making up to her old husband all the time in order to
get clothes and jewels out of him. But when the tree falls, the
bird takes flight. She will marry again, carrying off her booty

to keep her in comfort. There's the canker in the tree and the maggot in the grain! Nothing can be more harmful for a family than having a woman like this in it!"

"This woman has such seductive ways," he went on, "she's more like a prostitute than a girl from a good family. She's the type who knows how to assert herself, and she'll take advantage of the fact that father is in his second childhood to keep him under her thumb. Since she's half concubine and half slave-girl, we oughtn't to have to address her respectfully; so that later on we can control her. Yet father has such ridiculous ideas; he insists on everybody calling her the mistress, or even madam. Does that mean we have to call her mother? We can't let her get away with that! If we're too polite to her she'll give herself airs and make our life quite unbearable."

So the two of them grumbled all the time; but when some busybody told Prefect Ni what they were saying, the old man kept his displeasure to himself. Fortunately his bride had a sweet disposition and treated everybody so politely that she managed to get on with the whole household. Two months later she conceived, but kept this a secret from everyone but her husband. One day became three, and three nine, until ten months[1] had passed; and then, to the amazement of all, she gave birth to a son. Since this happened to be the ninth day of the ninth month, the boy was given the milk name[2] of Chongyang. The eleventh was the prefect's eightieth birthday, and guests thronged the house to congratulate him. Prefect Ni entertained them to a feast to celebrate his own birthday and the birth of his infant son at the same time; and the little boy was given the ceremonial bath customary on the third day.

"Sir," said the guests, "the birth of another son shows that your vital energies are undiminished in spite of your advanced years."

---

[1] The Chinese reckoned that pregnancy lasted for ten months.

[2] Chinese children were often given pet names or "milk names" when very small

Prefect Ni was highly gratified by such compliments; but Shanji started complaining again behind his back.

"Men are impotent by sixty, not to say eighty," he muttered. "How can a withered tree bear flowers? Heaven knows whose bastard this child is; but my father certainly never sired him, and I'm not going to recognize him as my brother."

When his father learned of this, once again he concealed his disappointment.

Time sped like an arrow, till another year had passed and Chongyang was one year old. Close and distant relatives gathered for the traditional ceremony of the Year Tray,[1] and offered their congratulations again; but Shanji went out instead of keeping the guests company. And though his father knew what was in his heart he did not call him back, but entertained the relatives himself for the whole day. Though he said nothing, however, he was very much displeased. The proverb says: A good son gladdens his father's heart. But Shanji was so grasping and vindictive that he could not bear to think of his younger brother growing up to divide the estate with him; so instead of recognizing him as a brother, he was spreading wicked rumours in order that he might later do the child and his mother an injury.

Prefect Ni, as a scholar and a former official, understood this perfectly well. He was sorry that he was too old to see Chongyang grow up, and that soon the boy would be left to the tender mercies of his elder brother; but in order not to arouse Shanji's resentment, he forced himself to show forbearance. His heart ached for his little son, however, and he pitied his young wife too. Thus he often brooded mournfully over the matter, and regretted what he had done.

Soon four years passed, and the little boy was five. Since he was clever and lively, his father decided to choose a school-name for him and let him start his education; and because his

---

[1] On a child's first birthday, a trayful of different objects was placed before it; and whatever it picked up was thought to indicate its future fortune.

elder brother was named Shanji (Virtue Maintained) the prefect called him Shanshu (Virtue Manifested). Then, choosing an auspicious day, he prepared wine and sweetmeats and took the lad to pay his respects to his teacher. This man was the tutor the prefect had engaged for his grandson, and he now intended the young uncle and nephew to study together and profit from the same instruction. But Shanji had quite different ideas. He resented his younger brother being given a name like his own; and feared that if Shanshu studied with his son, the latter would grow used to calling him uncle and might later be bullied by him. He preferred to take his son away and find another teacher for him. That very day he called his son out from the classroom, and would not let him go back on the pretext of illness. At first Prefect Ni really believed the lad was unwell; but a few days later the tutor enlightened him.

"Your worthy son has found another instructor for your grandson, and wishes him to be taught alone," he said. "I am at a loss to understand this."

Then Prefect Ni became very angry, and decided to summon Shanji and demand an explanation from him. But presently he thought better of it.

"He was born disobedient, and it's no use talking to him," he reflected. "Let him do as he pleases."

Pacing sadly back to his room, he tripped over the threshold and measured his length on the ground where he lay unconscious. His concubine hastily carried him to the couch and called a doctor, who declared that the prefect had had a stroke, and lost no time in reviving him with a decoction of ginger and putting him to bed. Although his mind was quite clear, Prefect Ni was completely paralysed. His concubine sat by his bed, preparing soup and medicine for him and waiting on him hand and foot; but several drugs were tried to no avail.

"It is only a matter of time now," said the doctor, after feeling the patient's pulse. "A complete cure is out of the question."

Upon hearing this, Shanji came several times to the sick room; and when he saw that his father's illness looked mortal, he began giving orders right and left and beating and cursing the servants as if he were already the master of the house. This upset the prefect even more. His concubine could not stop sobbing, and the little scholar asked leave from the classroom to stay with his father.

When Prefect Ni knew that his end was near, he sent for Shanji and gave him a book containing the inventory of all his land, houses and retainers.

"Shanshu is only five," said the prefect, "and still needs someone to provide for him. However, his mother is still too young to manage an estate; so it would be risky to give him a share of the property now, and I am making over the whole to you. When Shanshu grows up, for my sake please find him a wife and give him a small house and about ten acres of land, so that he need not go cold or hungry. I have written this down in this book, so that you will have something to go by when the time comes to divide the property. If my concubine wishes to marry again, let her do so; but if she prefers to remain a widow and live with her son, don't put any pressure on her. If you carry out all my instructions after I am dead like a good son, I shall rest in peace in the nether world."

When Shanji opened the book, he saw everything written there clearly and in detail.

"Don't worry, father! Don't you worry!" he said, smiling broadly. "I'll carry out your instructions to the letter."

Then, hugging the inventory of property, he left in high glee. As soon as he was out of hearing, the prefect's concubine pointed to her son with tears in her eyes.

"Isn't this poor child your own flesh and blood?" she asked. "Why should you disown him and give everything to your elder son? What are we to live on in future?"

"You don't understand," said Prefect Ni. "I know that Shanji is not to be trusted. If I were to divide the property equally, this child's very life would be in danger. It is better to please Shanji by giving him the whole estate, in order not to arouse his jealousy."

"That is all very well," she sobbed. "But the saying goes: No difference should be made between the son of a first wife and the son of a concubine. It looks ridiculous to give so much to one and so little to the other."

"I cannot help it," replied Prefect Ni. "As you are still young, I have entrusted the child to Shanji, so that half a year or a year after my death you can choose a good husband to support you in comfort for the rest of your life. Don't stay here to be badly treated."

"How can you suggest such a thing?" cried his concubine. "I come from a line of scholars too, and I know that no woman should marry twice. Besides, I have this boy. How could I bear to leave him? No, no, for better or for worse, I am going to stay with him!"

"Do you really mean that?" demanded Prefect Ni. "Are you sure you won't regret such a decision afterwards?"

Then she swore a great oath that she would remain true to his memory.

"Since you are so determined," said Prefect Ni, "I shall see that you and your son want for nothing."

Thereupon he took something from under his pillow and gave it to her. At first she thought it was another inventory of property; but it turned out to be a scroll one foot wide and three feet long.

"What is this?" she asked.

"This is a portrait of myself, which holds a secret meaning," replied the prefect. "Keep it safely hidden and don't show it to anyone. But if Shanji refuses to do anything for our son when the boy grows up, remember what I am telling you. Wait till an upright and intelligent official comes to this district, then take this scroll to him and lodge your complaint, telling him my last words. When he has studied the picture carefully, he will see that you and your son are able to live in comfort."

The concubine put the scroll away carefully. Prefect Ni lingered on for a few more days; but one night his breath failed,

he did not answer when they called him, for he was dead. He
was then in his eighty-fourth year.

> *All's possible to men while they have breath,*
> *But everything is ended by their death;*
> *Since wealth cannot be taken to the grave,*
> *Why should men work so hard, or skimp and save?*

After Ni Shanji received the inventory of the property and
the keys to all the granaries and storehouses, he was so busy
every day counting his money and possessions that he had no
time to inquire after his father's health. Indeed, when the old
man breathed his last, the concubine had to send a slave-girl to
inform Shanji of the unhappy news. Only then did he and his
wife hurry over to wail and call their father's name; but in less
than an hour they were off, leaving the concubine to watch by
the dead. Fortunately the funeral clothes and coffin were ready,
and all necessary preparations had been made; so there was no
need for Shanji to exert himself in any way. After the corpse
was laid out, the concubine and her child kept watch beside it,
crying morning and evening, and not stirring a step from the
coffin. Shanji, however, did nothing but entertain guests,
without the least sign of sorrow. Before the customary seven
weeks were over, he chose a day for the interment; and the very
evening after this ceremony he ransacked the concubine's room
to see if his father had left any silver there. Afraid that he
might take away the scroll, the concubine hit upon a clever plan.
She opened the two cases she had brought with her at her marriage, having filed them with old clothes, and invited Shanji
and his wife to inspect them. When Shanji saw that she was
willing for these cases to be inspected, he did not trouble to
look at them; and after he and his wife had turned the room
upside-down, they left. Then the concubine gave way to grief
and began to sob bitterly, while her little son started crying in
sympathy.

> *Why, an image of clay would have wept at the sight,*
> *And a statue of bronze shed a tear for their plight!*

The next morning Shanji called in a builder to inspect their rooms in order to have them redecorated for his son's marriage; and ordered Shanshu and his mother to move to three rooms in a back courtyard, where they were given only one small bed and a few rough tables and stools. Not a single piece of handsome furniture did they have. As for the two maids who had been waiting on them, the elder was taken away, leaving them with only one girl of barely twelve. Every day their rice had to be brought from Shanji's kitchen, and no one cared whether there were vegetable or meat for them or not; so the young mother finally asked for some rice and made an earthen stove to cook for herself. And morning and evening she plied her needle to make enough to buy vegetables and daily necessities and send her son to a neighbour's house to study.

Shanji made his wife walk over several times to urge the young widow to marry again, and sent go-betweens to propose matches to her; but when she swore that she would rather die than remarry, they had to leave her alone. And because she was so meek and uncomplaining, although Shanji had a violent temper, he finally dismissed both mother and son from his mind.

The years sped by, and soon Shanshu was fourteen. His mother had been careful not to let fall a word of all that had passed before his father's death, for fear that the boy might make some careless remark which would cause trouble. But by now he was able to understand matters for himself, and it was impossible to keep him in the dark any more. One day he asked his mother for a silk gown, and was told that she had no money to buy one.

"My father was a prefect," protested Shanshu, "and he had only two sons. Why should my elder brother be living in luxury, while I can't even have a new gown? If you have no money, mother, I'll ask my brother for some."

He was turning to go, when his mother caught hold of him.

"Son!" she cried. "Why should you ask a favour for a small matter like a gown? The proverb says: He who does not waste his luck will have it by and by. If you wear cotton while you're young, you'll wear silk when you grow up; but if you wear silk while you're young, you may not even have cotton later. Wait for a year or two, till you have made more progress in your studies, and I shan't mind selling myself into slavery to buy you a gown. Your brother is not a man to be trifled with."

"Very well, mother," said Shanshu.

But he was not convinced.

"My father was a very rich man, so there should be enough for both his sons," he thought. "And it's not as though I were a step-son or an illegitimate child. Why doesn't my brother do anything for me? In spite of what mother says, I don't believe he'd grudge me one length of silk. How can she talk of selling herself to buy me a gown? My brother isn't a man-eating tiger — why should I be afraid of him?"

So, without telling his mother, he went to the big house where his brother lived, and greeted him. Shanji started when he saw him, and asked what he had come for.

"My father was a gentleman," said Shanshu, "but I am so shabbily dressed that people laugh at me. I come to ask you for some silk, brother, to make a gown."

"If you need clothes," replied Shanji, "ask your mother."

"But mother is not in charge of our father's estate, brother, and you are."

At this mention of the estate, Shanji flushed angrily.

"Who put you up to this?" he shouted. "Did you come to ask for a gown or to demand part of my property?"

"The property will have to be divided some day," replied Shanshu. "But I come today to ask for a gown so that I can keep up appearances."

"You bastard!" raged Shanji. "What appearances do you have to keep up? My father's fortune is for his wife's son and grandsons, not for an outsider like you. Someone must have put you up to this, and sent you here to make trouble. But you'd better not make me lose my temper, or you and your mother will find yourselves with no roof over your heads."

"We are equally our father's sons," protested Shanshu. "Why should you call me a bastard? And who cares if you do lose your temper? I suppose you want to kill my mother and me so that you can have the whole estate yourself!"

"You miserable wretch!" bellowed Shanji. "How dare you pit yourself against me?"

He seized the boy by the sleeve, and punched him six or seven times till his head was bruised and swollen. Then Shanshu wrenched himself free and ran off like a streak of smoke. He came crying to his mother, and told her all that had happened.

"I warned you not to go looking for trouble, but you wouldn't listen to me," she scolded him. "I'm glad he beat you."

But even as she said this she rubbed his head with her skirt and mingled her tears with his.

A widow, still of tender years, consoles her orphaned son;
Their food and clothes are scanty, and comforts they have
none.
The lack of filial piety makes brothers disagree;
So one branch blooms while one is bare upon the selfsame
tree.

The more the widow thought over the matter, the more she dreaded Shanji's rage; so she sent the maid to apologize.

"The boy is ignorant," she said. "He is very sorry if he offended his brother."

This was not enough to assuage Shanji's anger, however. Early the next morning he summoned several of his kinsmen, produced the will written in his father's own hand, then sent for Shanshu and his mother to show it to them.

"Respected elders," he said, "it is not that I am unwilling to support Shanshu and his mother or am trying to drive them out. But yesterday Shanshu came to pick a quarrel with me about the estate. If he has so much to say now, I'm afraid that when he grows up there will be no end to his complaints. So today I intend to give them their share of the property: a house in the East Village in which they can live, and fifty-eight *mu* of land. This is in accordance with my late father's will, from which I dare not deviate in the slightest. I beg you to be my witnesses in this."

The assembled relatives knew Shanji's violent temper, and these instructions were in the prefect's handwriting; so none of them dared protest for fear of offending Shanji. They simply voiced approval.

"A thousand taels of gold cannot buy a dead man's pen," said some flatterers. "Since you are acting on your father's instructions, there is no more to be said."

Even a few who were sorry for Shanshu and his mother, could only say: "Sensible men don't live solely on their patrimony; sensible women don't wear merely the clothes they brought with them as brides. Many people who begin with nothing acquire considerable wealth, and now you have a house and land of your own, so that is a good start. You must work hard and not think you have too little. Every man's fortune depends on his own efforts."

The widow reflected that she could not stay for ever in the back courtyard, so she was willing to take her son to live on their own. She and Shanshu thanked the relatives, bowed before the ancestral shrine, and took their leave of Shanji and his wife. She found someone to carry their few sticks of old furniture and the two cases which she had brought with her as a bride; then hired a beast and rode to their house in the East Village. The land was overgrown with weeds, and the house had obviously not been repaired for years, for many tiles were missing from the roof, which leaked, and the floors were damp. She did not see how they were to live there; but she swept out one or two rooms and moved their beds and beddings in. When she called one of the farm-hands in to question him, he told her that these fifty-eight *mu* were the worst soil you could find. In good years the harvest amounted to half a crop only, while in bad years even the seed would be lost. But as the widow was lamenting their misfortune, her son proved his intelligence.

"My brother and I are equally my father's sons," he said.

"There must be some reason for this unfair division. That will couldn't have been a forgery, could it? The adage says: A patrimony should be shared by old and young alike. Why don't you bring a lawsuit against Shanji, mother? Let the magistrate decide what's a fair division; then I shan't complain any more."

This came as a reminder to his mother, and at last she told the boy the secret she had kept for nearly ten years.

"I can assure you that the will is in your father's handwriting, son," she said. "He was afraid your brother might injure you because you were only a child, so he left the whole estate to him in order to appease him. But just before he died he gave me a portrait of himself, and impressed on me that there was a secret concealed in it, saying that when an upright and intelligent official came to this district I should send it to him to study carefully. For then, he promised, we should have our rights and want for nothing."

"Why didn't you tell me this earlier!" cried Shanshu. "Where is the portrait, mother? Do let me see it at once!"

His mother opened a case and took out a cloth package which she opened to disclose another package in oiled paper; and when she broke the seals, she took out a small scroll one foot wide and three feet long. They hung this on a chair, and mother and son knelt down together before it.

"We cannot buy incense and candles in this village to burn before you," said the widow respectfully to the portrait. "Please forgive our lack of respect."

When Shanshu had done reverence before his father's picture, he stood up to examine it carefully. It was a wonderfully life-like painting, showing the prefect sitting on a chair and wearing his official cap on his white hair. He held his infant son in his left arm, and was pointing to the ground with his right hand. They studied this picture for some time, but could make nothing of it, and finally rolled and wrapped it up and put it away again feeling as much in the dark as ever.

A few days later Shanshu was passing the temple of the god of war on his way to a neighbouring village to see if he could find anyone to help him solve his problem, when he came upon a group of villagers carrying a pig, a sheep and other sacrifices to offer at the shrine. As Shanshu stopped to watch, an old man crossed the road and leaned on his bamboo staff to gaze at the crowd too.

"Why are you offering sacrifice today?" this old man asked one of the villagers.

"We were falsely accused," was the answer. "Luckily our new magistrate is very wise and saw that justice was done. We had asked the god's aid, and are coming today to offer thanks."

"How did justice miscarry? And how was the case settled?"

"I am the headman of a ward of ten families," said one man. "My name is Cheng Da. In my ward lived a tailor named Zhao, who was very clever with his needle. Sometimes he worked all night in the houses of customers, or didn't go home for days at a time. One day he went out and never came back. After a month, his wife sent out everywhere to search for him; but he was nowhere to be found. Some days later, though, the body of a man with his head smashed in was found in the river. The local people reported this to the authorities, and at the inquest somebody recognized Zhao by his clothes.

"Now the day before Zhao left home he and I had words after drinking; and it is a fact that I lost my temper and chased him home, then smashed some of his furniture. But I never dreamed his wife would accuse me of murder! The former magistrate, Mr. Qi, believed her, and condemned me to death; and when the people of my ward would not inform against me, he accused them of being accomplices. There was no one to whom I could appeal, and I had to spend three years in gaol. Fortunately, our new magistrate, Mr. Teng, is a very intelligent man although he only passed the provincial examination. When he went into the case again, I told him what an injustice had been done, and he inclined to believe me.

" 'A quarrel after drinking doesn't mean that men are mortal enemies,' he said. 'What reason did you have to murder him?'

"He granted my request for another hearing, and summoned

the witnesses. And the first thing he asked the tailor's widow was whether she had married again or not.

" 'Why, yes,' she said. 'I was too poor to carry on alone.'

" 'Whom did you marry?'

" 'Another tailor. His name is Shen Bahan.'

"Magistrate Teng sent at once for Shen Bahan.

" 'When did you marry this woman?' he asked.

" 'Over a month after her husband died.'

" 'Who was your go-between? What presents did you send her?'

" 'Zhao had borrowed nearly eight taels from me; so when I heard he was dead I went to ask for my money. The widow said she couldn't pay, but she was willing to marry me to settle the debt. So we had no go-between.'

" 'How could a workingman like you afford to lend him seven or eight taels of silver?'

" 'I lent it in instalments, Your Honour.'

"The magistrate handed him paper and a brush and told him to write down the exact amount of each loan. Then Shen Bahan made out a statement declaring that on thirteen occasions he had lent Zhao rice or silver, amounting to seven taels and eighty silver cents in all.

" 'You murdered Zhao!' shouted the magistrate the moment he set eyes on this statement. 'How could you allow an innocent man be accused?'

"Magistrate Teng had Shen put to torture, but he would not confess.

" 'I will give you a proof of your crime,' said Magistrate Teng, 'to show you it is no use denying it. A real usurer would have lent to other people as well as Zhao. You must have been carrying on with his wife, and Zhao knew it but was willing to keep quiet as long as you paid him. Later on, when you decided you would like to marry the woman, you murdered Zhao and told his wife to accuse Cheng Da of the crime. Your statement today is in the same writing as the accusation she handed in then. You must be the murderer!'

"Then he ordered the woman to be tortured with the thumb racks to make her confess. After hearing the magistrate describe all that had happened as if he had seen it with his own eyes, she was too frightened to deny his charges any longer. As soon as the thumb racks were fitted on her, she confessed; and Shen Bahan had to admit his guilt too.

"The fact is, Shen Bahan had been carrying on with Zhao's wife for some time on the sly; but when he started hanging about the house, Zhao tried to put a stop to the affair for fear it become known. Then Shen asked Zhao's wife to help him kill her husband so that she could marry him; but she refused. One day he invited Zhao to a tavern on his way home, and made him drunk; then took him to the river bank, knocked him down, bashed his face in with a stone, and threw his body into the river. Then, after waiting for some time in order not to attract attention, he married the woman and took her home. By the time the corpse floated up and was recognized, he knew that I had quarrelled with Zhao, so he made the woman accuse me. She did not know he was the murderer till after her marriage to him; but by then, of course, she was his wife and could not say anything.

"After the magistrate discovered the truth, he passed sentence on them and released me. Now my good kinsmen and neighbours have collected money for this sacrifice to the gods. Tell me, old man, did you ever hear of a case like this?"

"Such honest, intelligent magistrates are rare," said the old man. "You are lucky to have him in your district."

This was enough for Shanshu, who immediately went home to tell his mother all he had heard.

"Now that we have found such a good official, why not take the portrait and appeal to him at once?" he demanded. "What are we waiting for?"

So they found out the date for the magistrate to accept complaints; then, rising before it was light, set out with the scroll for the yamen. When they cried out that they had been wronged, the magistrate was surprised to see that instead of

filing a petition all they had brought was a small scroll.   In
answer to his questions, the widow told him of all Shanji's mis-
deeds and her husband's last words to her.   Then Magistrate
Teng took the scroll and dismissed them, promising to study the
portrait carefully at his leisure.

A secret in the portrait was concealed;
They would be rich if once it was revealed.
To save her and her son from indigence,
The magistrate showed great intelligence.

When Magistrate Teng had no further cases to hear, he repaired to his own quarters to make a careful examination of
this scroll one foot by three feet, which showed Prefect Ni carrying a child and pointing to the ground.

"The child is obviously Shanshu," thought the magistrate.
"But does that finger pointing to the ground mean that the prefect hopes I will carry out his wishes although he is under the
earth? . . . Since he left a will in his own writing, it is difficult
to take any action.   No, if he said the portrait holds the key to
a mystery, there must be more to it than that.   And if I can't
get to the bottom of this, my reputation will suffer."

Every day when he finished work, he unrolled the portrait
to examine it; but though he pored over it for days, he could
make nothing of it.   However, since the problem was fated to
be solved, it is not surprising that a way out was found.

One day the magistrate was studying the portrait after his
midday meal when a maid brought him tea, and in reaching out
for the cup, he spilled some tea over the scroll.   Putting down
the cup he went out to the verandah to dry the scroll in the sun,
when to his astonishment he saw faint writing beneath the
picture.   He immediately separated the painting from the mount,
and drew out a sheet of paper which had been slipped between
the two.   It was Prefect Ni's will, and these were its terms:

This is the will of an aged prefect now over eighty and
likely to die at any time, I have no regrets except that —
Shanshu, the son of my concubine, is only one year old and

will not come of age for a long time. Shanji, the son of my wife, is utterly lacking in filial piety, and I fear he may injure his younger brother.

I leave all my land and the two large houses which I have recently purchased to Shanji. Only the small house on the left is to go to Shanshu. Though this cottage is not large, there are five jars containing five thousand taels of silver buried under the left wall, and six jars containing five thousand taels of silver and one thousand taels of gold under the right wall. This will make up for the lack of land.

Let Shanshu reward the astute official who settles this matter with three hundred taels of silver.

> Written by Ni Shouqian
> in his eighty-first year

The date and the prefect's seal were appended.

This portrait and will, then, had been prepared with considerable foresight by Prefect Ni when he was eighty-one and Shanshu one. Well did the ancients say: None knows the son better than his father.

Magistrate Teng knew how to make the most of every opportunity, and the mention of all this gold and silver made his mouth water. With a thoughtful frown, he devised a plan and sent a runner to summon Ni Shanji to the yamen.

Now Shanji had been revelling in his sole possession of the estate. When a runner arrived with the summons, calling out that Shanji must go at once to the yamen, he had to set out without delay. He found the magistrate presiding over the court.

"Ni Shanji is here," reported the runner.

The magistrate bade him approach.

"Are you Prefect Ni's elder son?" he asked.

"I am, Your Honour."

"Your step-mother has lodged a complaint against you. She says that you have driven her and your younger brother out, and taken possession of all your father's land and property. Is this true?"

"I have brought up my step-brother Shanshu since he was a child," replied Shanji. "Recently he and his mother said they would like to live by themselves; I didn't drive them out. As for the property, it was divided according to the will my father wrote himself just before his death. I dared not disobey his wishes."

"Where is the will?"

"I have it at home, and can bring it to show you."

"According to the complaint, the estate is worth ten thousand strings of cash, which is no trifling sum. This being so, the authenticity of the will has yet to be proved. Since you are the son of an official, I do not wish to cause you any unnecessary unpleasantness. Tomorrow I will send for your step-mother and her son, and go to your house to inspect the estate for myself. If there has been an unfair division, we must not allow personal considerations to interfere with the administration of justice."

The magistrate then ordered his runners to escort Shanji out and summon Shanshu and his mother for a hearing the next morning.

Since the runners had been bribed by Shanji, they let him go without further ado, then went to the East Village as they had been instructed.

Now Shanji had been thrown into a panic by the intimidating tone adopted by the magistrate. It was true that there had been no division of the estate; but father's will alone was not enough — he still needed his kinsmen to vouch for him. He was busy late into the night sending presents of silver to the heads of all the branches of the family, and requested them all to come to his house the next morning to speak up for him if the magistrate questioned his father's will. None of these relatives had received a single gift from Shanji since the prefect's death, nor had he invited any of them to drink so much as a cup of wine at festivals; yet here he was now sending them lumps of silver. He was like the men who burn no incense when all goes well, but embrace Buddha's feet in time of trouble. Chuckling to themselves they pocketed the silver, but made up their minds to see what the magistrate's attitude was the next day before committing themselves. As a contemporary wrote:

> *Don't blame your father's widow for the action she has*
> *brought;*
> *It's for your own unkindness you must pay.*
> *Had you allowed your brother silk when first he asked your*
> *aid,*
> *You'd not be handing silver out today!*

When Shanshu's mother received a summons from the district runners, she knew that the magistrate was intervening on their behalf; so the next morning she got up early and took her son to the yamen.

"I sympathize with you, madam, and your fatherless son," said Magistrate Teng. "Naturally I would like to help you. But I understand that Shanji has been acting according to a will in his father's handwriting. What, then, can I do?"

"Although his father wrote such a will, he did so to protect my son," replied the widow. "It doesn't represent his real wishes. If you could see the account books, Your Honour, and the figures connected with the estate, this would be quite clear."

"You know the proverb: It is hard for an honest official to settle family disputes," said Magistrate Teng. "I shall be able to see that you and your son have enough to live on; but you must not expect too much."

"We shall be satisfied if you can save us from cold and hunger," she replied. "We don't expect to become wealthy folk like Shanji."

The magistrate then bade them go to Shanji's house to wait for him there.

Meantime Shanji swept and tidied his reception hall, and placed a chair draped with a tiger-skin in the place of honour. Then, having lit some of his best incense, he sent messengers to urge his kinsmen to come in good time.

When Shanshu and his mother arrived, they greeted the assembled relatives one by one, and asked them to put in a good word for them. Although Shanji was infuriated by this, he had to control his rage, while each thought what he would say to the magistrate. Before long they heard the shouting in the distance which heralded an official's approach; and Shanji adjusted his clothes and went out to meet Magistrate Teng. The elder relatives, who had some knowledge of society, followed him out; while the younger and more timid took cover behind the screen in front of the gate, and craned their necks to watch.

They saw a double procession of yamen attendants bearing signs and banners, followed by a blue canopy shading the sedan-chair of this talented and intelligent official. When Magistrate Teng reached Shanji's gate, his attendants knelt down and raised a shout; while the two brothers and the widow fell to their knees to welcome him. Then the chief runner called out to them to rise, the chair-bearers set down the great sedan-chair, and the magistrate alighted slowly and with dignity.

Just as he was about to cross the threshold, however, he suddenly bowed repeatedly to the empty air, and appeared to be making rejoinders to an invisible host who was greeting him. The whole company watched in amazement. They saw him bowing all the way to the hall as he kept up a stream of polite conversation. Once in the hall, he inclined his head towards the chair covered with a tiger-skin, as if someone had invited him to be seated there; then turned and picked up another chair, which he placed in position for the host. Only after several more polite disclaimers did he take his seat.

Suspecting that the magistrate had seen a ghost, nobody dared approach him. They stood transfixed with surprise on either side and stared. Sitting there and clasping his hands, the magistrate spoke.

"Your wife lodged a complaint with me, sir, in connection with the property. How do you think the matter should be settled?"

Having said this he assumed the attitude of one listening. After a long time he shook his head and shot his tongue out in horror.

"Your elder son's conduct has really been disgraceful!" he exclaimed.

He listened again for a while, then asked:

"What provision have you made for your younger son?"

And after another short interval he said:

"The smaller house to the east? But how will he support himself? . . . Ah, yes, yes. I shall see that this is done. . . . This is for your younger son too? I shall carry out all your instructions."

Then there was another silence, after which the magistrate clasped his hands again.

"How dare I accept such a handsome gift?" he demurred, and declined repeatedly.

"Well, sir, if you absolutely insist," he said at last, "I shall have to accept it. I will certainly make out a deed of property for your younger son."

After this he rose and bowed several times, saying that he must take his leave. Then the onlookers, who had been watching in amazement, saw him look round.

"Where is Prefect Ni?" he asked.

"We haven't seen any Prefect Ni," replied the runners.

"How extraordinary!" exclaimed Magistrate Teng.

He called Shanji.

"Just now your respected father greeted me in person at the gate, and has sat there talking to me all this time. Surely you heard what he said?"

"I did *not*, Your Honour," replied Shanji.

"He was a tall gentleman," continued the magistrate, "with a thin face, high cheekbones, almond-shaped eyes, long eyebrows, large ears and a sparse silver beard. He wore an official hat, black boots and a red gown with a gold belt. Wasn't that Prefect Ni?"

All present broke into a cold sweat and fell to their knees.

"That is exactly how he looked when he was alive," they declared.

"I wondered why he disappeared so suddenly," mused the

magistrate. "Well, he told me there are two large houses on this estate, as well as a smaller house to their east. Is that true?"

"It is," replied Shanji, who dared conceal nothing.

"Let us go and have a look at this small house," said the magistrate. "I have something more to say to you there."

After hearing the magistrate talking away so long to himself and describing Prefect Ni so accurately, they all believed that the prefect's ghost had appeared, and shot out their tongues in consternation. Little did they know that the crafty magistrate had simply been describing the portrait he had seen, and that not a word he said was true!

> A sage's words will not be heard,
> But men from ghosts will run;
> So by this trick the magistrate
> Convinced the elder son.

Ni Shanji led the way and the others followed, and so they came to the small house to the east of the large houses. This had been the prefect's home before he passed the examination; but since he built the large houses it had been used as a granary and left in charge of a caretaker. After making a tour of the premises, Magistrate Teng sat down in the middle room.

"That must have been your father's spirit," he said to Shanji, "for he told me all your family business and asked me to carry out his instructions. This old cottage is to go to Shanshu. Are you agreeable to that?"

Shanji kowtowed.

"I shall abide by Your Honour's decision," he said.

The magistrate then went through the inventory of the property.

"A fine estate!" he remarked more than once as he read it. And when he reached the instructions as to the division of property at the end, he smiled.

"It is true that the prefect left these instructions in writing," he said to himself. "But just now he told me that Shanji had not been a good son. The old gentleman seems to have been rather changeable."

He called Shanji forward.

"Since the instructions are here in black and white, all the landed property is still to go to you," he said. "And Shanshu cannot dispute this."

The widow moaned, and was about to step forward to appeal against this decision, when the magistrate went on:

"This old cottage is left to Shanshu, and Shanji must not dispute his possession of anything in it."

"The ramshackle furnishings here are not worth anything," thought Shanji. "As for the grain that was stored here, I moved about three quarters of it away a month ago; so there's very little left. I shan't lose anything."

He therefore answered promptly: "This is a most discerning judgement, Your Honour."

"Now that you have both agreed to this," continued the magistrate, "you must neither of you go back on your word. Your kinsmen are here as witnesses. Just now the aged prefect told me that there are five jars containing five thousand taels of silver under the left wall of this house; and these are for his younger son."

Shanji did not believe this, so he said: "Even if there were ten thousand taels, they would belong to my brother and I would not dispute his possession."

"If you attempted to," retorted the magistrate, "I would not allow it."

He ordered his attendants to take picks and mattocks, while the widow and her son led the men to the east wall of the cottage, where, sure enough, they found five big jars buried, each filled to the brim with glittering silver. And when they weighed the contents of one jar it came to sixty-two and a half catties, or exactly one thousand taels.

All who saw this were amazed, and even Shanji was convinced now that the magistrate had been speaking the truth.

"If my father's ghost hadn't appeared to the magistrate and

told him this, how could he have known where the silver was hidden?" he said to himself. "We didn't know ourselves."

The magistrate had the five jars placed in a row before him, and addressed the widow.

"There are five more jars containing five thousand taels of silver under the right wall," he said, "as well as one jar of gold. Just now Prefect Ni decreed that this gold should be given me as a reward. When I declined he insisted until I was forced to accept."

The widow and Shanshu kowtowed.

"The five thousand taels below the left wall already surpass our greatest expectations," they said. "If there are more jars under the right wall, how dare we question the magistrate's wishes?"

"I am only repeating what Prefect Ni told me," said the magistrate. "I do not think he was deceiving me."

He then bade his men dig under the western wall, where to be sure another six jars were found, five containing silver and one gold. Shanji's eyes gleamed covetously at the sight, and he longed to seize just one ingot; but he dared not go back on his word.

Magistrate Teng wrote out a certificate of ownership for Shanshu and made over the caretaker to them too. The widow and her son were overjoyed. Together they kowtowed their thanks. And Shanji, though nearly bursting with rage, had to kowtow once or twice too and mutter a formal expression of thanks.

Then the magistrate wrote his name on some strips of paper, and with these sealed the jar of gold which had fallen into his clutches, before having it loaded on his sedan-chair to be taken to the yamen. Moreover, everyone said that Prefect Ni had wanted him to have this, and it was only right that he should take it. No one dared utter a word of protest. Truly, as the ancient fable says, when the clam and curlew are locked in strife, the fisherman has his chance.

If Shanji had been more generous to his brother and agreed to divide the estate up fairly, he and Shanshu could have shared this one thousand taels of gold and it would never have ended up in the hands of a stranger. As things were, Shanji raged inwardly, and got himself a bad name as a heartless son and brother. His endless scheming to deprive Shanshu of his birthright only recoiled upon his own head.

As for the widow and her son, they went to the yamen the next day to thank Magistrate Teng, and he returned them the portrait, which he had remounted after extracting the will. Only now did Shanshu and his mother understand that the finger pointing down in the portrait was to indicate the presence of buried gold and silver.

With their ten jars of silver, they bought fields and orchards, and became rich. Later Shanshu married and had three sons, all of whom distinguished themselves in their studies. But Shanshu's was the only branch of the Ni family to prosper. Shanji's two sons grew up to be loafers and wastrels, who sold their two big houses to their uncle after their father's death. And all round who knew the story said the two Ni brothers were justly dealt with by Heaven.

> *The ways of Heaven are always strictly just,*
> *And Ni Shanji was by his greed undone;*
> *Because he wronged his father's second wife,*
> *The prefect had to guard against this son.*
> *A will was left concealed within a scroll;*
> *A stranger took the gold beneath the wall;*
> *Disputes can only end in costly suits,*
> *So let this be a warning to us all!*

The Two Brothers

This story happened during the Xuan De period (1426-1435) of our dynasty, when an old man named Liu De lived at Hexiwu on the bank of the Grand Canal nearly seventy miles from Beijing. This was an important stage on the road to the capital, boats swarmed like ants in the harbour, while the creak of carts and the hoof-beats of horses never ceased from dawn till dusk. Several hundred families lived here, and by the river was a prosperous market town. Both Liu De and his wife were over sixty, but they had neither brothers nor children. The old man owned a house and a few acres of land, and at his gate he had a little tavern. He was a kindly man, who liked to help people out of difficulties. If customers came to drink wine in his tavern but did not bring enough money, he would not argue with them. If anyone paid him too much, he would always return what was over, not accepting an extra cent.

"That fellow made a mistake," said a friend who learned of such a case. "You should count this your good luck; why return the money?"

"The reason I have no son," replied Liu, "must be because I did not do enough good in my last life, so in this life I shall be punished by dying without a son to sacrifice to me. How can I go on doing wrong? If I take a cent more than I deserve, some accident may happen or I may fall ill, in which case I shall have to spend more instead. Would it not be better to return the extra money and worry no more about it?"

Because he was so fair, all the townsfolk respected him and considered him as an elder.

One day in the coldest part of winter a bitter north wind

117

blew, the sky grew dark with clouds, and there was a heavy snowstorm.

> *Though curtains hang in heavy folds the snow comes drift-*
> *ing through,*
> *And penetrates through lattices and screens of fine bamboo;*
> *Now softly as light willow seeds the sparkling snowflakes*
> *fly,*
> *Now swirling like white petals that the wind has whirled*
> *on high.*
> *From leaves within a bamboo grove their muted voices*
> *come,*
> *They bring with them the fragrance of the golden winter*
> *plum;*
> *The soldiers at the frontier freeze as soon as they stand*
> *guard,*
> *The hermits shiver in the hills on pallets cold and hard;*
> *Young nobles fill gold goblets now and feast till late at*
> *night,*
> *While pretty girls add charcoal to the embers burning*
> *bright.*

Because it was cold, Liu De warmed a pot of wine and drank with his wife before the brazier, then rose and went to the door to watch the snow. He saw in the distance a man with a bundle on his back battling against the wind and snow, accompanied by a boy. As they drew nearer, the man suddenly fell down in the snow and could not get up again; and though the boy hurried to his assistance, because he was young and weak he was pulled down as well, and the two of them rolled on the ground. It took them some time to struggle to their feet.

Liu De rubbed his old eyes and saw that the elder traveller, who was about sixty, was wearing puttees and hempen shoes, and his clothes were very ragged. The other was a delicate-featured lad in small cloth shoes. The old man brushed the snow off his clothes and turned to the boy.

"The storm is too fierce and we are too numbed with cold

to go on, child," he said. "There's a tavern. Let's buy a pot of wine to warm ourselves before we go further."

So they entered the tavern, put their bundle on the table and took seats, the boy sitting beside the old man. Liu De warmed a pot of wine, cut a plateful of beef, and brought these on one tray with two cold dishes and two sets of cups and chopsticks to the table. The boy took the pot and filled a cup, which he presented to his father with both hands, then poured a cup for himself.

"Is this your son?" asked Liu, seeing how well-mannered the lad was although so young.

"He is," said the old man.

Liu asked how old he was, and the father replied that the boy's name was Shenger, and he was twelve.

"May I ask your name, sir, and where you may be going?" inquired Liu. "Why should you travel in a snowstorm like this?"

"My name is Fang Yong, I am a soldier of the imperial garrison at the capital. Since my home is Jining in the province of Shandong, I am going back there to collect my pay. I did not expect this snow." He asked Liu his name.

"My name is Liu — that is it written on the sign. Jining is a long way from here: why don't you hire some beast to carry you, instead of travelling the hard way?"

"I am a poor soldier; how can I afford it? We must make our way along slowly."

Liu noticed that he was eating the cold vegetable dishes only, not touching the beef.

"Are you both observing a fast?" he asked.

"What fasts do we soldiers observe?" retorted the other.

"Then why don't you eat some meat?"

"To tell you the truth, we have not much money with us. Even if we stick to vegetables, we may not have enough to see us home. If we eat meat, it will cost us several days' rations, and then how can we get back?"

Seeing how poor they were, Liu felt sorry for them.

"In a snowstorm like this," he said, "wine and meat in your belly will help keep out the cold. Go on and have some. I won't charge you for it."

"You must be making fun of us. How can we eat without paying?"

"The fact is, this is not like other taverns. If passers-by happen to be short of money, I treat them to a meal. Since you are short, let me stand host."

"It is very kind of you," said the old soldier seeing that Liu was in earnest. "But it is not right to accept undeserved favours. When I come back this way, I shall repay you."

"Within the four seas all men are brothers," said Liu. "These trifles are not worth anything. Why speak of paying me back?"

Then the old soldier helped himself to meat while Liu filled two bowls with rice.

"You may as well eat your fill before going on," he said.

The old soldier thanked him again. Since father and son were famished, they fell to like hungry wolves and ate their fill.

All men should rescue creatures in distress,
And save the starving first;
All food tastes good to those that faint for meat,
All drink to those that thirst.

As they finished their meal, Liu told his wife to bring them two cups of hot tea; but when the old soldier took silver from his wallet, Liu hastily stopped him.

"I just told you that I was inviting you," he protested. "How can I accept your money? If I accept, it will mean that I tricked you into buying my meat. Keep your money for your journey."

At that the old soldier put his money away, thanked Liu again and again, then shouldered his baggage and said goodbye. By the time they left the tavern, the snow was so heavy that you could not see a man just in front of you. Buffeted by the bitter wind, they staggered back a few steps.

"Dad," said the boy, "how can we go on when it is snowing so hard?"

"What else can we do?" replied the old soldier. "We must struggle on till we find some lodging for the night."

Tears ran down the boy's cheeks, and Liu pitied them with all his heart.

"Why must you suffer such hardships and press on through this blizzard?" he asked. "I have a spare room and plenty of bedding. Why not stay here till the weather clears?"

"Nothing could suit us better," replied the old soldier. "But we shouldn't give you so much trouble."

"Say no more! No man travels with his house on his back. Come in quickly now, and don't let yourselves get wet."

Then the old soldier came in again with the boy, and Liu led them to a room where they put down their baggage. Though the bed was complete with matting and straw, Liu feared they might still be cold and piled on more straw. Then the old soldier unpacked his baggage and laid out his bedding. It was early still by the time he and the boy had made the bed, so they came out of the room. Liu had closed the tavern door and was sitting near the fire with his wife.

"Mr. Fang!" he called. "If you're cold, we have a brazier here and you can warm yourself."

"I would like to," replied the soldier. "But with your good lady there it would not be fitting."

"We are all old folk," countered Liu. "You need not have any scruples."

Then the soldier came over with the boy to sit near the fire. By this time they were on more familiar terms, so calling Liu by his name the old soldier asked: "Why is it that you and your wife are alone at home? Do your sons live somewhere else?"

"To tell you the truth," replied Liu, "though we are both sixty-four this year, we have always been childless, so we have no son."

"Why don't you adopt a son? It would be good to have someone to look after you when you are old."

"I did mean to adopt one; but then I saw how often adopted

sons refuse to look after family affairs, but cause more trouble instead. It is simpler to have none; for if you look for one in a hurry, you won't find a lad to suit you. That is why we gave up the idea. If I found one as good as your son, that would be fine, but how is that possible?"

They chatted in this way until it was late, when the old soldier asked for a lamp, said goodnight to Liu, and went with his son to bed.

"Child," he said, "we are lucky today to have met such a good man. If not for him, we would have been frozen to death. Tomorrow, whether it snows or shines, we'd better start out early. I don't want to give more trouble."

"Yes, father," said the boy.

Then they lay down to sleep. The old soldier had caught cold, though, and by the small hours of the morning he had a raging fever and was panting for water. At night and in a strange place the boy could not fetch him water, but had to wait till dawn, when he got up, opened the door and looked out. Old Liu and his wife were still asleep, however. Not daring to disturb them, the boy closed the door again and waited by the bed till he heard Liu coughing outside.

"Why are you up so early, young master?" asked Liu.

"The fact is, sir, that my father suddenly ran up a fever last night and is panting now for water. That's why I'm up so early."

"Ah!" cried Liu. "He must have caught a chill yesterday. He can't drink cold water in his state; let me boil some hot for you."

"I'm afraid we're troubling you too much," said the boy.

Liu told his wife to boil a big kettle of water, and took it himself to the room; then the boy helped the old man sit up and drink two bowls. When the old soldier opened his eyes and looked round, he saw Liu.

"You are too good to us, sir," he said. "How can we ever repay you?"

"Don't talk like that," protested Liu. "Just rest and cover yourself well. Once you perspire, you'll be all right."

The boy helped his father to lie down again; and Liu, as he pulled the bedding over him, noticed how thin it was.

"This bedding is not enough for a man with a chill," he said. "How can you sweat like this?"

When his wife who was outside the door heard this, she fetched a thicker quilt.

"Here's an extra quilt, young master," she said. "See that you cover him well. In this bitter weather, to have a chill is no joke."

The boy accepted the bedding, and Liu saw the old soldier well covered before he left. After washing and dressing he came back again.

"Is he sweating yet?" he asked.

"I've just felt him," said the boy. "There's no sign of sweat."

"That means his case is serious. We must call in a doctor to prescribe medicine to make him sweat. Otherwise how can we cure him?"

"We've no money with us, sir. How can we call in a doctor and buy medicine?"

"Don't worry. I'll see to that."

Then the boy kowtowed to Liu.

"Since you are so good as to try to save my father, sir, if I can't pay you back in this life, in my next I will serve you as your dog or horse."

Liu hastily helped him up.

"No more of this," he said. "Since you are staying here, I'm responsible for you. How can I stand by and do nothing? Go and look after your father while I go for a doctor."

By then the snow had stopped and the weather had cleared; but carriages and horses had churned the snow on the street into slush more than one foot deep. Having put on his wooden clogs, Liu looked out, then came back inside. Believing the old man had changed his mind, tears started to the boy's eyes; but just as he was about to question him, Liu came out from the back leading a donkey. Only when he rode off did the boy feel reassured. Luckily the doctor lived near by, so very soon he arrived on another donkey, followed by a servant carrying his medicine box. He alighted at the gate, and Liu asked him into the hall to have some tea, then led him to the sick room. By this time the old soldier had lost consciousness. The doctor felt his pulses.

"This is a double chill," he said. "Cold humours have entered his innermost organs. As the book on such ailments says:

> *A double chill no cure can mend;*
> *In seven days his life must end.*

This is incurable. Other doctors might say they could save him, but I am an honest man and won't deceive you. It is no use prescribing medicine."

The boy was so terrified, his tears fell like rain as he kowtowed to the doctor.

"Take pity on us so far from home!" he cried between his sobs. "If you will prescribe some medicine to save him, we shall never forget your kindness."

The doctor helped him up.

"I am not making difficulties," he said, "but this disease is mortal. There is nothing I can do."

"Sir," pleaded Liu, "the proverb says: Drugs can cure only those who are fated to live, Buddha helps only those who are fated to reach sainthood. Please don't feel bound by the ancient rules, but prescribe boldly as you think best. It is possible that he may not be destined to die and may recover after taking your medicine. But should he die, we will certainly not hold you responsible."

"Very well," said the doctor. "I will give you a prescription. If it makes him sweat, he may have a chance. In that case come at once to let me know, and I'll prescribe something else. But if he does not sweat his sickness is incurable, and there's no need to come back to me."

He bade his servant open the medicine box, and took from it some medicine which he gave to Liu.

"Boil this quickly with ginger for him," he said. "There is only one chance in ten thousand; don't count on it too much."

Liu brought out a packet of a hundred coins for the doctor. "Please accept this trifle for your fare," he said.

But the doctor declined most emphatically, and left. Liu and his wife prepared the medicine themselves, took it to the sick room, helped the boy raise the old soldier up to drink it, then covered him well with the quilt. The boy kept watch at his side. This trouble had kept Old Liu so busy all morning, he had not attended to his tavern nor even breakfasted. He did not break his fast till noon, when he called the boy to eat; but because his father was so gravely ill, the boy had no appetite. When he was pressed he ate half a bowl of rice. That evening they felt the invalid again, but there was still no sign of perspiration, and Liu was worried too. The doctor when asked to come once more refused. And on the seventh day, sure enough, the old soldier breathed his last.

We ply a thousand tasks while we have breath;
But everything is ended at our death.

The unhappy boy fell weeping to the ground, and the old couple shed tears to see his bitter grief. They helped him up and tried to reason with him.

"You cannot bring the dead back to life, Master Fang. It's no use crying so much. You must think of your health."

Kneeling before them again, the boy wept.

"I am so unfortunate!" he said. "The year before last my mother died, and because we had no money to bury her, my father and I started home to fetch some silver. We didn't expect to run into such a snowstorm or that travelling would be so hard. When we met you, our benefactors, and you gave us wine and food and let us stay in your house, we thought ourselves more than lucky. When Heaven did not protect us and my father was suddenly taken ill, you were kind enough to find a doctor and buy medicine, looking after my father day and night and treating us better than your own family. I thought when my father recovered we could repay you; but now he has died and all your kindness has proved vain. Since I have no kinsman here and no money in my pocket, I shall not be able to bury him. So I beg you to lend me a few feet of ground for his grave; then I will serve you all my life as your slave to repay your kindness. I don't know whether you agree to this."

He prostrated himself before Liu.

"Don't worry, young master." The old man helped him up. "You can leave the funeral to me. We can't just bury the body without a coffin."

The boy wept and kowtowed again.

"A plot of ground for burial is more than I dare expect. How can I trouble you to spend more money? How can I ever repay you?"

"This is what I want to do," retorted Liu. "I don't expect any return."

He hastily took some silver to buy the clothes and coffin, and hired two workers to put the body in the coffin, then prepared a sacrifice and burned paper coins. Needless to say, the boy broke down again and again as the coffin was interred in a vacant plot behind the house and a tombstone erected saying that this was the grave of Fang Yong, a soldier of the imperial garrison. When all had been done, the boy thanked Liu and his wife.

Two days later Liu said to the boy: "I would like to send you home to find some kinsman to take your father's coffin back; but I fear you are too young to travel alone; so you had better stay here for the time being. When someone you know passes by, he can take you with him, and you can plan to carry your father's coffin home later. What do you say?"

The boy knelt on the ground.

"You are as bountiful as the earth and as generous as high heaven," he declared. "Before I have done anything to repay you, how can I think of leaving you? Besides, you have no son.

Though I am not talented, if you will keep me as your slave I can wait on you morning and evening as if you were my father. And when you pass away I can at least sweep clean your grave. Then I shall fetch my mother's coffin from the capital and bury both my parents beside your grave, so that their spirits can always stand guard over it. This is my humble wish."

The old couple were delighted.

"If you will stay," said Liu, "it means that Heaven is giving me a son. How can I look on you as a servant? From now on let us be as father and son."

"Since you consent," said the boy, "let me kowtow to you now."

He set two chairs in the middle of the hall and asked Liu and his wife to be seated, then paid his respects to them as a son and changed his surname too. But Liu, not wanting him to give up his former surname completely, made Fang his personal name, and henceforth he was called Liu Fang. The boy worked hard every day, helped look after household affairs, and treated the old couple very respectfully, so that they looked upon him as their own child.

> *A loving father Liu Fang found,*
> *Liu De a filial son;*
> *The boy served both his fathers well,*
> *The dead and living one.*

Time sped like an arrow, till Liu Fang had been there for two years. It was late autumn; there was heavy wind and rain for more than a fortnight, the water in the canal rose to about a hundred feet, seething, turbulent and swift, and many boats passing were wrecked. One afternoon Liu Fang was clearing up the tavern when he heard a great hubbub. Thinking there was a fire, he hastened out to look, and saw a crowd on the canal bank staring into the water. He ran forward to see what was happening, and found a great junk carrying passengers upstream had been wrecked and was drifting downstream. More than half of those aboard had been drowned, while the survivors were

clinging to the rudder or the mast, sobbing, swearing, and crying
for help. Though the men on the bank wanted to go to their
aid, the storm was so fierce that it would mean risking their
own lives; thus they stood and watched as the poor wretches
fell into the water, and could only exclaim in sympathy. But
suddenly there was a great gust of wind and the junk was swept
towards the shore; then the men on the bank raised a cheer, and
in no time more than twenty poles with hooks had grappled the
boat, and some dozen men were rescued, who were lodged in
different houses. There was one lad of less than twenty who,
wounded in several places by the hooks, lay swooning on the
ground, clutching a bamboo case. Liu Fang pitied him, and shed
tears as he remembered what had happened to himself two
winters before.

"This man is in the same sorry plight," he thought. "If not
for Mr. Liu, my father and I would have perished far from
home. Now there is no one to help him. I'll go home to tell
my parents, and save his life."

He ran home to report this to Liu and his wife, and proposed
that they take the young man in and nurse him back to health.

"This will be a good deed," said Liu, "and it is our duty."

"Why didn't you bring him with you?" asked Mrs. Liu.

"I dared not without first asking your permission."

"Nonsense," said Old Liu. "I'll go with you."

They went together to the bank and found a crowd surround-
ing the young man. Old Liu pushed his way through the crowd.

"Young master!" he called. "See if you can stand up, and
I'll help you to my home to rest."

The young man opened his eyes, looked up, and nodded. Old
Liu and Liu Fang tried to help him up; but one was too young
and weak, the other too old and feeble — they could not move
him.

"Move aside, sir," said a hefty young fellow beside them.
"Let me do it."

He put his arms round the young man and raised him easily.
Then, one on each side, he and Old Liu took the young man's

arms and led him away. Though too weak to talk, the lad was conscious, and he nodded towards the bamboo case.

"I'll carry your case for you," said Liu Fang.

He lifted it on his shoulder and went in front, while the crowd parted to let them pass, then followed behind.

"This is very good of Mr. Liu," said some men who knew him. "This unfortunate fellow is far from home with no one kind enough to take him in. Only Mr. Liu, hearing this, would help him to his house. Such good men are very rare. What a pity he has no son of his own. Heaven is really unjust."

"Though Mr. Liu has no son of his own," rejoined another, "Liu Fang whom he adopted is very filial — better than a real son. This must be Heaven's way of rewarding him."

Some people who did not know Liu, seeing the old man coming himself to help the young man and carry his case, assumed he must be a relative. When they learned the truth, they marvelled. Other heartless men argued only about how much money the bamboo case contained. Thus though men look alike they have different hearts. Enough, however, of this.

When Old Liu and the stranger had helped the young man home into a guest room, Old Liu thanked the stranger and the latter left, while Liu Fang put the bamboo case down beside the young man. Old Mrs. Liu hastily fetched dry clothes, helped him to change, then put him to bed. Liu knew that a man who has nearly drowned should not take hot wine; so he bade his wife just take the chill off some wine, made the young man drink his fill, then covered him with Liu Fang's quilt. That night Liu Fang shared one bed with him. The next morning Old Liu came to ask after him, and the young man, feeling better, struggled to get off the bed and express his thanks; but Old Liu quickly stopped him.

"Don't tire yourself," he said. "Your health must come first."

The young man kowtowed to him from the bed.

"I would have died, but you saved my life," he said. "You are a second father to me; but I have not yet asked your name."

Old Liu told him what it was.

"That is my name too," said the young man.

"Where do you come from?"

"My name is Liu Qi and I come from Zhangqiu in Shandong. Two years ago I went to the capital with my father to take the examination. Unfortunately there was a plague, and within a few days both my father and mother died. I had no money to take their coffins home; so I had to cremate them." He pointed to the bamboo case. "I was taking their ashes back for burial, little thinking I would run into further trouble. I would surely have died if you had not saved my life. Yet now I have lost all I had and am empty-handed. How am I going to repay you for all your kindness?"

"Don't say that," replied Old Liu. "All men have feelings of compassion, and to save one life is better than building a pagoda. If I expected repayment, it would mean I was out for profit. That is not my way."

At this Liu Qi felt even more grateful. After resting for two days he was able to get up, and kowtowed his thanks with tears to Liu and his wife. Since this young man was gentle, well-mannered and very respectful, the old couple took a great fancy to him and gave him good wine and food every morning and evening. This kind treatment made Liu Qi rather embarrassed, and he felt he ought to leave; but since his wounds had festered so that he could not travel, and he had no money, he had to stay there. Being about the same age Liu Fang and Liu Qi took to each other at once. Each described all the troubles he had seen and sympathized with the other. Thus they became sworn brothers, and loved each other as if they were one flesh and blood.

One day Liu Qi said to Liu Fang: "You are so intelligent, why don't you study the classics and history?"

"I would like to study," replied Liu Fang, "but I have no one to teach me."

"As a matter of fact, I have studied the classics since childhood and learned not a little. for I meant to have an official career; but unfortunately my parents died, and now I have no more ambition. If you would like to study, just get some books and I will teach you."

"How fortunate I am!" exclaimed Liu Fang.

He hastened to tell Old Liu, and when the old man heard that Liu Qi was a scholar and was willing to teach Liu Fang, he was very pleased indeed and bought them a great many books. Then Liu Qi taught all he knew; and since Liu Fang was more intelligent than most men, he did not have to have anything explained twice. In the daytime he worked in the tavern, at night he read under the lamp; and in a few months he became well-versed in the classics and literature. Liu Qi by then had stayed six months in Old Liu's house, and they loved each other more than actual kinsmen; but though he had found a home here, it upset him to think he was not earning his keep. And since his wounds had now healed, he decided to go home.

"I am most grateful to you and Mrs. Liu for saving my life," he told the old man. "I have troubled you for half a year, and you have been kinder than words can express. Now I must leave you while I take my parents' ashes back for burial. After the mourning I shall try to repay you."

"This is pious of you," said Liu, "so I must not stop you. When do you mean to start?"

"I will bid you goodbye now, and start tomorrow morning."

"In that case, let me hire you a boat."

"Travelling by water is dangerous, and besides I have no money. I mean to go by road."

"Travelling by road with a beast costs several times what it does to go by boat. It is also much more tiring."

"I shall not hire a beast, but walk."

"You are too weak to walk so far."

"The proverb says, sir, that a man who has silver can use his silver; a man who has none must use his strength. How can a poor fellow like myself be afraid of hardships?"

"This can easily be settled," said Old Liu after a moment's thought.

He bade his wife prepare a farewell feast for Liu Qi, and
in the middle of the feast the old man shed tears.

"Like floating duckweed we came together by chance," he
said, "and during these six months we have been like one flesh
and blood. Of course we are sorry now to let you go. But to
bury your parents is of prime importance; so we must not press
you to stay. I wonder whether after you have gone we shall
ever meet again?"

He was overcome with grief, and both Mrs. Liu and Liu Fang
shed tears as well.

"I am forced to leave you now," said Liu Qi, who was also
weeping. "Once the period of mourning is over I shall hasten
back to serve you. Please do not be too sad."

"My wife and I are nearing seventy. Like candles in the
wind, we may be blown out any day. How can we tell whether
we shall still be alive by the time you finish mourning? If you
have any feeling for us, come back as soon as you have seen to
the burial; for that will be a comfort to your old friends."

To this Liu Qi agreed. The next morning Mrs. Liu rose early
to make breakfast for him; then Old Liu produced a bundle
which he placed on the table, and told Liu Fang to go to the
back to fetch the donkey.

"I have kept this donkey for a long time," he told Liu Qi.
"But since I never travel far it is no use to me; you had better
take it, then you won't have to hire another. In this bundle are
a quilt and some rough cotton clothes, so that you won't catch
cold on the road."

From his sleeve he produced a packet of silver, and this he
gave to him too.

"These three taels for the road should see you home," he
said. "But as soon as your business is done, be sure to come
back. Don't forget now."

At the sight of these generous gifts Liu Qi shed tears.

"You have been so kind to me, I shall never be able to repay
you in this life," he said. "In my next life I shall be your dog
or horse to show my gratitude."

"What a thing to say!" said Old Liu.

Then the bundle and bamboo case were loaded on the donkey, and Liu Qi took his leave. Old Liu and his wife saw him to the door and bade him farewell with tears. Liu Fang, reluctant to see his friend go, walked with him for three or four miles before leaving him.

After travelling for some days, Liu Qi reached his old home in Shandong. But the previous year there had been high winds and heavy rain, the Yellow River flooded, the district of Zhangqiu was inundated, and people, cattle and houses were swept away. Now for many miles at a stretch there was nothing but desolation. Having nowhere to go, Liu Qi put up at a hostel. He wanted to bury his parents, but having no family and no means of livelihood he had first to find somewhere to stay. He searched all the nearby towns and villages for friends and relatives, but not one could he find; and after staying in the hostel for more than a month, his three taels were nearly spent and he was worried. Once this money was finished it would be hard to move; so he decided to go back to Hexiwu to his benefactor to ask Liu for a small plot of ground to bury his parents' bones, after which he could stay there. His mind made up, he settled his bill at the hostel, then rode back on the donkey as fast as he could to Liu's house. Upon alighting he saw Liu Fang reading in the tavern.

"Have your parents been keeping well?" Liu Qi called out.

Liu Fang looked up and saw it was Liu Qi. He put down his book and led the donkey inside, unstrapped the luggage and bowed.

"My father and mother have been thinking of you day and night," he said. "Your coming is very welcome."

They went together to the hall, and when the old couple saw who it was they were overjoyed.

"We have been longing to see you!" they exclaimed.

Liu Qi came forward to kowtow, and Old Liu bowed in return.

"I suppose you have buried your parents," said Old Liu.

Weeping, Liu Qi told him all that had happened.

"I have nowhere to stay in my old home," he said, "so I have brought the ashes back to beg for a plot of ground to bury them. Then I would like to be your son and remain here to serve you every day if you agree."

"There is plenty of vacant land. Choose what you like. As for becoming my son, that would be doing me too much honour."

"If you will not take me as your son, it means you do not agree to my request."

He asked Old Liu and his wife to take the seats of honour and kowtowed to them; then he buried his parents' ashes behind the house. After that Liu Fang and Liu Qi became brothers and worked together, going so diligently about their tasks that the tavern prospered more and more. They also served their parents well as befitted true sons, until all the townsfolk envied Old Liu and declared Heaven was rewarding him for his virtue.

Time flew by until another year had passed, during which the four of them lived happily together. But now the old couple's health failed through old age. Though the young men waited on them day and night, all prayers to the gods and all prescriptions proved vain — the old people were dying before their eyes. The two young men were very sad; but, fearing their grief might upset the old couple, they comforted them and shed tears behind their backs. Then Old Liu knew he was dying, and called his sons to his bedside.

"We were childless in our old age, and thought at our death there would be no one to offer sacrifice," he said. "Little did we know that Heaven would take pity on us and give us both of you as our sons. Though you are adopted, we love each other more than real parents and sons; and therefore I can die now without regret. If after my death you will go on working together and keep up this small property, I shall close my eyes in content in the nether regions."

They wept and kowtowed and promised to do as he said. In two more days the old man and his wife died. The two brothers lamented bitterly, wishing they could have died in their parents' stead; then they prepared the best funeral clothes and coffins and invited monks to say mass for nine days and nine nights. After the funeral, they decided to build a large grave in which the parents of the three families should be buried together, and Liu Fang went to the capital to fetch his mother's coffin. On an auspicious day, Liu and his wife were buried in the middle, Liu Qi's parents on the left, and Liu Fang's parents on the right — the three tombs like a string of pearls. All the villagers admired this filial piety, and attended the interment to show their respect for Old Liu's goodness.

Now after Old Liu's death Liu Fang and Liu Qi stayed together all the time, sharing their meals and their bed and becoming even more devoted to each other. They gave up the tavern to start a cloth shop instead. And when the travelling merchants who bought their cloth found that they were honest and their prices fair they spread their fame, so that people flocked to buy from them and within a couple of years they had acquired an excellent property worth several times more than Old Liu's. They had two houses complete with servants and two pages, and abundance of furniture and utensils. Thus they cut a very respectable figure.

There were several wealthy families in this district and, when they saw these two youths growing daily more prosperous and knew they were unmarried, they sent matchmakers to call on them. Liu Qi was willing to marry, but Liu Fang insisted on remaining single.

"You are nineteen this year," urged Liu Qi, "and I am twenty-two. It is time for us to take wives and to have children, so that our three families may have successors. Why are you unwilling?"

"We are both in our prime," replied Liu Fang, "and should give all our minds to our business. What time do we have for marriage? Besides, we are the best of friends and very happy together. If we take bad wives, they will prove a burden to us. It is better not to marry."

"No," said Liu Qi. "The proverb says: Without a wife there can be no family. While we look after our business in the shop, there is no one to mind our household. Besides, we are making more friends now; but if guests come and we have no wives to prepare the food, it will look rather bad. These are little things; but when our father adopted us, he hoped we would have descendants to continue his line and watch over the ancestral graveyard. If we do not marry and have no descendants, won't we be wronging him? How can we face him in the nether regions?"

But though he pleaded again and again, Liu Fang made excuses and would not agree. Since his brother would not marry, Liu Qi felt he could not take a wife himself. One day he called on a good friend named Qing, who happened to mention marriage. Liu Qi told him about Liu Fang's refusal to take a wife.

"I can't understand what's in his mind," he said.

"This is obvious," replied Qing with a laugh. "You and he are partners; but he came into the family before you, and will be jealous if you marry first. That's why he keeps refusing."

"My brother is very honest and straightforward," protested Liu Qi. "This cannot be the reason."

"He is in the first flush of youth," retorted Qing, "and must understand the joys of a marriage bed. Why else should he refuse? If you don't believe me, send a matchmaker to him privately, to propose that he marries first. I assure you that will work."

Filled with misgivings, Liu Qi left him. On his way home he happened to meet two matchmakers who were going to see him to propose a match with the daughter of Mr. Cui who owned a silk shop in the town. And when Liu Qi asked the girl's age, he found that she suited Liu Fang very well.

"This match would do excellently for my younger brother," he told them. "But he is rather odd and shy in company. You had better go to discuss it privately with him. If you succeed, we shall certainly reward you well. I won't go home now, but wait in the oil shop at the entrance to the lane to hear your news."

The two matchmakers assented and left him. Soon they came back to report: "Your brother is certainly odd. However much we urged him, he would not agree. When we persisted he grew angry and spoke to us very sharply." |

Then Liu Qi knew that Liu Fang was genuinely unwilling to marry, though he still could not understand why.

One day he saw two swallows making a nest in the beams, and wrote a poem on the wall to sound his brother out. His verse ran:

> *Two cock swallows are building a nest in the beams,*
> *And together they toil all day long without rest;*
> *But unless they can find a she-bird to lay eggs*
> *They'll be left, at the last, with a bare, empty nest.*

When Liu Fang saw this, he smiled and read it through several times, then took up the brush and wrote the following verse beneath it:

> *Two swallows fly together now to nest;*
> *Heaven has seen to it that they're a pair;*
> *The female is content to have her mate;*
> *Why does the male not know a female's there?*

Liu Qi was quite staggered.

"This poem seems to indicate that my brother is a woman," he thought. "No wonder she looks so delicate and has such a gentle voice. That must be why she won't take off her underclothes at night, not even her socks; and even in the hottest part of the summer she always wears two layers of clothes. Apparently she has been imitating Mulan[1] of old."

Even so, he could not be certain, and dared not speak out too soon. He went to Qing's house and recited the poem to him.

"The meaning of this is clear," said Qing. "Your brother

---

[1] Mulan is a popular heroine. To save her father from serving as a conscript, she dressed as a man and joined the army in his stead.

can't be a man. But you have been sleeping together all these years; how is it you never found out?"

Liu Qi told him how she never took off her clothes.

"That clinches it," said Qing. "Now ask her to tell you the truth, and see what she says."

"We are as devoted to each other as real brothers. How can I mention such a thing?"

"If she is really a woman she can marry you, in which case you can both show your gratitude to your parents and preserve your brotherly love. What objection can there be?"

Since they discussed this at some length, Qing prepared a meal and wine, and they feasted together till late. By the time Liu Qi reached home it was dusk; and when Liu Fang saw that he was slightly tipsy, she helped him into their room.

"Where have you been drinking?" she asked. "Why are you back so late?"

"I was drinking with Qing, and we forgot the time as we were talking."

While speaking he was looking hard at Liu Fang. Formerly, he had never suspected she was a woman; but now that he wanted to find out the truth, the more he looked the more like a woman she seemed. Though he had no evil intentions, he was eager to satisfy his curiosity, but he could not bring himself to ask outright.

"The poem you wrote today after me was very good," he said, "much better than mine. Will you write another one?"

Liu Fang smiled and said nothing, but taking paper and brush at once wrote another verse:

> *Two swallows cry together as they nest,*
> *And you while young should find a helpmate too;*
> *How came it that He's fair and flawless jade*
> *Was not accepted by the King of Chu?*[1]

Liu Qi took the verse and read it.

---

[1] He owned a rare piece of uncut jade, which he offered to the King of Chu; but the latter refused to accept it, not recognizing it as a treasure.

"So you are a woman after all!" he said.

Liu Fang coloured up with shame, and was too confused to reply.

"We are like true brothers," continued Liu Qi. "Why shouldn't we discuss this? May I ask why you dressed up as a man in the first place?"

"When my mother died and I was going home with my father, we thought it would be more convenient on the journey if I dressed as a boy. Then my father died but had no permanent resting place, for I could not bury him with my mother; so I dared not change back my costume, but wanted to settle down somewhere and look after my parents' grave. Luckily our adopted father gave us the property and my parents could be reburied. I would have told you then, but we had just started our cloth shop and I feared you could not handle all the business yourself. That is why I delayed. But now that you keep asking me to marry, I have had to make it clear."

"What pains you took to see your parents well buried!" exclaimed Liu Qi. "We have shared one bed all these years, yet you never revealed your secret in the least. You are really a heroine, both pious and chaste! How I admire you! But in your poem you hinted that you might accept me; so I certainly will not marry any one else. We met by chance, and have been together several years; we were brothers before, but shall now be husband and wife. This is not the work of men but the doing of Heaven. And if you will give your consent, we can pledge everlasting love. What do you say?"

"I have been thinking of this for a long time. All our ancestral graves are here, and if I marry anybody else it will not be easy for me to pay my respects at my parents' grave. Besides, our adopted parents treated us like their own children; it would not be right to leave this place. If you do not despise me, then I will be your slave and look after the graves of our three families. This is what I would like. To marry secretly, though, without a proper go-between, would not be proper.

I hope you will consider this carefully, to avoid all gossip. That would be best."

"We will act on your excellent suggestion," agreed Liu Qi.

That night they slept in different rooms. And the next morning Liu Qi asked Qing to send his wife as go-between to propose the match to Liu Fang, who by this time had changed back into woman's dress. Liu Qi prepared costumes and trinkets and chose an auspicious date; then after sacrificing before the three graves they married with due ceremony, inviting all the neighbours to a great feast. This threw the whole of Hexiwu into a hubbub, and everybody marvelled and praised the virtue of the Liu family. After Liu Qi married Liu Fang, husband and wife respected and loved each other and together they acquired a great property, and had five sons and two daughters. Their descendants are still prosperous today, and have now become a large clan, while their town is called the town of the Three Just Ones, as the following verse testifies:

The lack of love makes brothers foes,
While love makes stranger friend;
And so their fame has spread afar,
Well-known throughout the land.

The Beggar Chief's Daughter

During the Shao Xing period (1131-1162) of the Song Dynasty, though Hangzhou was the capital of the empire and a wealthy city it abounded in beggars. The beggars had a chief whom they addressed as "Master," who controlled all their activities and levied a daily tribute on all the alms they received. If rain or snow prevented them from begging, he would prepare gruel to feed them; he also provided them with tattered clothing. So, like slaves who dared not offend their lord, the beggars obeyed their chief implicitly.

With the regular tribute the chief received from his followers, he practised usury; and if he did not gamble or squander his money on singsong girls, it was easy for him to become a man of substance. The post was such a reliable source of income that no man in his senses would think of relinquishing it. But it had one drawback. The title did not sound well. No matter how much property a beggar chief might acquire or how many generations of wealthy forbears he could boast, he was king solely among beggars and beyond the pale for ordinary citizens. No one outside his family would respect him. He could act the great man only in his own home.

But although this was the case, society, as we know, is divided into two great classes, the respectable and the low; and only prostitutes, actors, bondservants and official underlings belong to the second category, not beggars. Beggars may have no money, but no stigma attaches to them. You have only to think of Wu Zixu of the Spring-and-Autumn Period (722-481 B.C.), who fled from his country and played his flute for food in a market-place in the Kingdom of Wu. Or Zheng Yuanhe of the Tang Dynasty, who at one time sang and begged for a living but later prospered and slept under silk coverlets. Such men reflect credit on the profession. So although this class of citizens is generally looked down upon, it is unquestionably superior to prostitutes, actors, bondservants and official underlings. Enough, however, of this digression.

Our story is about a beggar chief in Hangzhou named Jin Laoda, whose forefathers had followed the same profession for seven generations. A man of property, Jin had fine houses, fertile fields, handsome clothes, good food, grain to fill his granaries, money to fill his pockets, and a troop of servants and maids to wait on him. Though not the richest, he was one of the wealthiest men in the capital. And because Jin aspired to respectability, he ceded his title to a fellow clansman named Scabby in order to retire and live in comfort, severing his disreputable connection with all the beggar tribe. Such is the force of habit, however, that people in that district persisted in referring to him as the beggar chief. He could not rid himself of the name. Jin was now over fifty and his wife had died leaving him no son but an only daughter named Yunu, a girl of remarkable beauty.

> The maid was rare as flawless jade,
> And fair as any flower in May;
> Attired in palace robes she seemed
> Some beauty of a bygone day!

Jin prized his daughter above jewels. He had her taught to read while yet a child, and at fifteen or sixteen she could write poems in various metres or dash off impromptu verses. She was a fine needlewoman too, and a skilled performer on many musical instruments; for she excelled in everything she did. And Jin had set his heart on marrying this paragon to a gentleman. But though it was not easy to find a girl like this even in famous old families, because she was the daughter of a beggar chief she was not approached by eligible suitors.

And as her father would not marry her to a common trades-man, at eighteen she was not yet betrothed.

One day a neighbour called and told Jin: "By Taiping Bridge there lives a handsome, learned young scholar of twenty named Mo Ji. Because both his parents have died and his family is poor, he is still unmarried; but recently he passed the examination qualifying him to join the Imperial College, and he would be willing to live with his wife's family after marriage. Why don't you ask him to be your son-in-law?"

"That is a very good suggestion," said Jin. "May I trouble you to be the matchmaker?"

The neighbour consented, and went straight to Taiping Bridge to find the young scholar.

"I'll be frank with you," he told Mo Ji. "Their ancestors were beggar chiefs, but Mr. Jin gave that up long ago. She's a good girl, and the family is rich. So if you don't think it beneath your dignity, I'll help to arrange a match between you."

Mo Ji was silent.

"I can neither support myself nor find a wife," he was thinking. "If I stoop to marry this girl and live with her family, I shall be killing two birds with one stone. I am in no position to care if others laugh at me."

"Yours is an excellent proposal, sir," he said to the match-maker. "But I am too poor to buy presents for the bride. What can I do?"

"You won't have to buy so much as a sheet of paper," replied the other. "Leave it all to me."

When the neighbour took Mo Ji's reply to Jin, an auspicious day was chosen for the wedding; and, instead of sending gifts to the bride, Mo Ji actually received new clothes for his marriage from his father-in-law. When he discovered that Yunu was both lovely and talented, he was overjoyed; for without spending a cent he had got a beautiful wife and a comfortable home. He felt he was in heaven! As for his friends, knowing his poverty they forgave him for marrying into such a family. None of them laughed at him.

When the young couple had been married for a month, Jin prepared a sumptuous banquet and bid his son-in-law invite all his scholar friends to honour them with their presence. But after they had been feasting for six or seven days in succession, Jin's clansman Scabby heard about it and was offended — with good reason too.

"He's a beggar chief, so am I," fumed Scabby. "The only difference between us is that his family had the job for several generations and piled up a lot of money. As one of his kin I should be invited to drink at my niece's wedding; but he has invited outsiders to celebrate instead and they have already been feasting for six or seven days, while I have not even received an invitation card! His son-in-law is only a scholar, not a minister or councillor of state. Am I not Yunu's uncle? Am I not good enough to sit at the same table? Why should he look down on me like this? I'll go and cause trouble to spoil their feast!"

He called together some fifty or sixty beggars to go with him to Jin's house. This is how the beggars looked:

> *In filthy knotted rags and broken hats,*
> *They carry threadbare rugs and tattered mats;*
>   *With batons of bamboo,*
>   *And battered rice bowls too,*
> *They swarm the rich man's gate and raise*
>   *A frightful how-d'ye-do.*

When Jin opened the gate to find out the reason for this din, in rushed Scabby with all his beggars to raise pandemonium. Striding straight up to the feasters Scabby helped himself to the good wine and food, shouting as he did so:

"Call the young couple to pay their respects to their uncle!"

The scholars took to their heels in alarm, followed by Mo Ji. Old Jin could do nothing but apologize profusely to the beggars.

"Today my son-in-law was the host," he told Scabby. "I

had no say in this. I shall prepare a special feast some other time to show how sorry I am."

He distributed largesse to all the beggars and asked them to take two jars of his best wine as well as some chicken and geese to Scabby's house for a feast there. The confusion lasted till dark, when finally the trouble-makers dispersed. Yunu was crying with rage in her room; and that night Mo Ji stayed with a friend, returning only the next morning. At the sight of his son-in-law Jin blushed for shame, for he had lost face completely; and Mo Ji was considerably upset too, but like his father-in-law he said nothing of his feelings.

> *When dumb men take wormwood, though great their distress,*
> *Their dread of its sharpness they cannot express.*

Yunu, ashamed of belonging to such a low-class family, determined to encourage her husband to make his way in the world. She urged him to study hard, and spared no expense to buy all the books, ancient and modern, which he might need. Neither did she begrudge money to invite scholars to practise essay writing and study the classics with him. She also gave him a generous entertainment allowance so that he might enlarge his circle of acquaintances and thereby increase his reputation. In this way Mo Ji's scholarship improved daily and his fame spread, until at the age of twenty-three he passed the provincial examination and the highest examination in the capital and became a member of the Hanlin Academy. After the feast to welcome the new academicians, he started riding home triumphantly in his new black gauze cap and palace robes; but as he drew near Jin's house, all the people on the street gathered round to stare and the children pointed their fingers at him.

"Look!" they cried. "The beggar chief's son-in-law has become an official!"

Mo Ji had to put up with such comments as he rode along, for he could not very well create a scene in the street. And

when he arrived home and saw Jin, he still paid his father
in-law every outward respect, although he was thinking re
sentfully:

"If I'd know how successful I was going to be, I could hav
waited to marry into a noble family; but now I've got a begga
chief as my father-in-law. I shall never be able to live thi
down! Even when we have children, they will be descendee
from a beggar chief and people will point the finger of scor
at them. Well, what's done is done, and my wife's behaviou
is exemplary; she hasn't committed any of the seven sins fo
which I could divorce her. How true the saying is: Marry ii
haste, repent too late!"

He went about looking thoroughly depressed; and althoug.
Yunu asked several times why he was so sad, he would no
tell her. The truth was that Mo Ji's good fortune had mad
him forget all his wife had done for him when he was poor
Indeed, his utter disregard for all her assistance shows tha
his heart was not in the right place.

Some days later, Mo Ji was appointed the Census Office
in the Wuwei Prefecture. His father-in-law prepared a fare
well feast for him, and this time the beggars dared not com
to make trouble. Since Wuwei was not far from the capita
and could be reached by river, Mo Ji decided to take Yun
with him to his post; and after travelling for a few days b
junk they reached Caishi Rock and moored by the north bank
That night a full moon made all as bright as day; So Mo J
unable to sleep, dressed and went out to enjoy the moonligh
from the bow of the boat. There was no one in sight and, a
he brooded bitterly over the disgrace of having a beggar chie
for his father-in-law, a wicked thought flashed through hi
mind.

"If this woman were dead, I could marry another and ri
myself of that everlasting shame."

Immediately he went to the cabin to call his wife up to watc
the moon.

Yunu was fast asleep, but Mo Ji woke her and insiste

on her getting up. Unwilling to refuse her husband, she threw some clothes over her shoulders and stepped to the cabin door to look up at the moon. Then Mo Ji, taking her by surprise, dragged her to the bow and threw her into the river. This done, he quietly woke the boatmen.

"Row on at once!" he ordered. "If you make good time, I shall reward you well."

Unaware of all that had passed, the boatmen hastily cast off and rowed rapidly away, not pausing until they had gone nearly four miles. After they had moored again, Mo Ji told them that while watching the moon his wife had fallen into the river, and he had been powerless to save her. Since he gave the men three taels of silver as a tip, they understood very well what had happened but dared say nothing. There were some foolish maids on board who believed that their mistress had really fallen into the river by accident, but after crying for some time they thought no more of the matter.

> *Because he scorned the name of beggar chief,*
> *The heartless husband spurned his loving wife;*
> *But one who severs sacred marriage ties*
> *Will be esteemed a scoundrel all his life.*

When Yunu was thrown into the river, she was utterly terrified and feared her last moment had come. But she felt something support her feet beneath the water and carry her to the shore, where she struggled up the bank. Upon looking round, however, she could see nothing but a vast expanse of water. The boat had gone. Then she realized that her husband despised her now that he was great, and wanted to drown her so that he could marry into some respectable family; so, although she had escaped with her life she had nowhere to go, and the consciousness of her plight made her weep bitterly.

As chance would have it, soon after Mo Ji's boat cast off, the newly appointed Transport Commissioner of Huaixi, Xu Dehou, moored his boat just where Mo Ji had pushed Yunu into the water. Chatting and sipping wine before going to bed,

Xu and his wife were looking at the moon through their cabin window when they heard a woman crying on the bank. She was weeping so pitifully that Xu immediately ordered his boatmen to investigate, and they found a woman sitting alone on the shore. Invited aboard and asked whence she came, she told Xu that she was the wife of the Census Officer of the Wuwei Prefecture. At the commissioner's request she told him her whole story from beginning to end, weeping as she spoke. And Xu and his wife, moved to tears, comforted her.

"Don't cry now," they urged. "We will adopt you as our daughter and think of some way to help you."

Yunu bowed in thanks. Then Xu told his wife to give her dry clothes into which to change, and bade her rest in the back cabin. He made the servants address her as their young mistress, and forbade the boatmen to breathe a word of that night's happenings.

After some days Xu arrived at his post. And since the Wuwei Prefecture was within his jurisdiction and he was the census officer's superior, Mo Ji was among the many subordinate officials who came to pay their respects to the new transport commissioner.

"He is a handsome fellow," thought Xu, upon first seeing Mo Ji. "What a pity that he should stoop to such a dastardly deed!"

A few months later Xu told his subordinates: "I have a daughter who has her share of talent and beauty; and since she has reached the marriageable age, I would like to find a good husband for her who would be willing to live in our family. Can you suggest anyone suitable?"

All the officials had heard that young Mo Ji had lost his wife, so they recommended him, declaring that with his unusual talents he would make an ideal son-in-law for Commissioner Xu.

"I thought of him too," said Xu. "But a man who has won success so early in life may be ambitious. He probably won't want to live as part of our household."

"He comes from a poor family," rejoined Xu's subordinates. "With you as his father-in-law, sir, he will be as lucky as a reed protected by a fine tree. What objection could he have?"

"If you think it possible, will you suggest the match to Mo Ji?" asked Xu. "Propose it as your own idea, to see what his reaction is. Don't say that I wish it, for fear of embarrassing him."

Accordingly, Mo Ji's colleagues spoke to the young man, offering to be his matchmakers. Mo Ji was only too eager to get on good terms with high-ranking officials, but an alliance by marriage with his superior had been beyond his wildest dreams.

"If you can arrange this," he answered joyfully, "I shall be eternally grateful."

"Just leave it to us," they assured him, and went back to report to the commissioner.

"It is very kind of Mo Ji to consent," said Xu. "We are so fond of this daughter that I fear we have spoiled her; that is why we don't want her to leave our house when she marries. Since Mo Ji is young and has a will of his own, we are afraid they may have occasional disagreements which would distress us very much. We must make this clear beforehand, and hope he will bear with her. Only on this understanding dare we invite him to our home."

When this was announced to Mo Ji, he agreed unconditionally. He was no longer a poor scholar now, so he sent gilt paper flowers and coloured silk to the bride's house. The auspicious day was fixed, and he was positively itching in his eagerness to become the commissioner's son-in-law.

Meanwhile Xu asked his wife to tell Yunu: "The commissioner does not think a girl of your age should remain single, so he wants you to marry a young scholar who has passed the palace examination. Please don't refuse!"

"Though I come from a low family," replied Yunu, "I know how I should act. As I married Mo Ji I should be true to him all my life. Even though he forsook me because we were too low for him, and acted so cruelly and wickedly, I must do what is right. It would be wrong to marry anyone else" After saying this she burst into tears.

Then Mrs. Xu, realizing that she was sincere, told her the truth.

"This young palace graduate is no other than Mo Ji. My husband is angry with him for his callousness, but wants to bring you together again; so he has pretended that you are his own daughter and asked his colleagues to arrange this match. Mo Ji has agreed readily, and tonight he is to become our son-in-law. You can have your revenge when he enters the bridal chamber."

Then Yunu dried her tears, powdered her face and adorned herself for the wedding. When evening came, Mo Ji dressed himself smartly with a gilt paper flower in his cap and a red sash over his shoulders, and rode to the commissioner's house on a fine horse with a decorated saddle and two groups of musicians in front. All the officials escorted the bridegroom to his new home, and the road was lined with cheering spectators.

> *On fine white horse, with cymbals and with drums,*
> *See where the handsome, lordly bridegroom comes!*
> *His last ties broken with the beggar chief,*
> *For his ill-fated wife he feels no grief.*

That night carpets were spread and coloured silk hung in the transport commissioner's house, and trumpets and drums sounded to herald the bridegroom's arrival. Upon reaching the gate Mo Ji alighted from his horse, and Xu in robe and belt of state came out to welcome him. Then all the other officials took their leave, and Mo Ji entered the inner quarters. The bride, with a red silk veil over her face, was helped in by two maids; then the master of ceremonies outside the balustrade called upon the young couple to bow to heaven and earth, to the bride's father and mother, and finally to each other. After this, the newly-wed pair were escorted to the bridal chamber for their wedding feast.

By this time Mo Ji felt he was in heaven, and his happiness defied description. With his head in the air he swaggered to the bridal chamber. But no sooner had he entered it when from behind the doors on both sides darted seven or eight maidservants, some young, some old, armed with sticks and bamboos. Strokes rained down on his shoulders and back until even his gauze cap fell off; but though he cried out with pain he could not escape. At last, in desperation, he fell to the ground and shouted:

"Father-in-law! Mother-in-law! Save me!"

Then he heard a girl's voice order: "Don't beat the brute to death. Bring him to me."

At that the blows stopped. Tweaking his ears, tugging at his arms, and turning a deaf ear to all his protests, the maids lifted him almost off the ground to carry him to his bride.

"What have I done to deserve this?" Mo Ji cried.

But when he looked up, whom should he see seated calmly under the bright candlelight but his former wife, Yunu!

"Ghosts! Ghosts!" shrieked Mo Ji, frightened almost out of his wits.

The maids burst out laughing, and Xu came in.

"Don't worry," said the commissioner. "This is no ghost but the adopted daughter I found at Caishi Rock."

Then Mo Ji's heart stopped pounding so fast, and he made haste to kneel down and kowtow.

"I admit my guilt," he acknowledged. "Please pardon me!"

"This has nothing to do with me," replied Xu. "It is my daughter's forgiveness you should ask."

But Yunu spat in her husband's face and cursed him.

"You heartless brute!" she cried, "don't you remember the ancient saying? A man should not forget the friends he made when he was poor; a prosperous man should never forsake the wife who shared his poverty! You came to my family empty-handed, and it was thanks to our help that you were able to study and win fame. That is how you gained your present success. I was looking forward to sharing your splendour, little knowing you would be so ungrateful as to think no more of all that had passed. But forgetting our love and repaying kindness with cruelty you threw me into the river! Luckily Heaven took pity on me and Commissioner Xu rescued me and made me his goddaughter; for otherwise I should certainly have been drowned and my body devoured by the fish. How could you be so heartless as to murder me in order to marry again? How dare you look me in the face today?"

Then breaking down and sobbing bitterly, she heaped curses on him for his ingratitude and cruelty. Covered with shame, Mo Ji had nothing to say. He could only kowtow and beg to be forgiven. When Xu felt that Yunu had reviled her husband enough, he helped Mo Ji to his feet.

"Don't be angry now, daughter," he said to Yunu. "Your husband has repented, and I fancy he will always treat you respectfully in future. Though you were married before, you are making a fresh start today. Please spare him further reproaches for my sake."

To Mo Ji he said: "You brought this on yourself, son, and you can't blame anyone else for it. Tonight you must just accept your punishment. But I shall ask your mother-in-law to put in a word for you." So saying, he left the chamber.

After a short time the commissioner's wife arrived, and reasoned with Yunu until she persuaded her to forgive Mo Ji. The next day Xu prepared a feast for his son-in-law, and returned him all his wedding presents.

"A girl can accept wedding presents once only," he said. "You must have sent gifts to the Jin family, so I cannot accept any more."

When Mo Ji bowed his head and said nothing, Xu went on: "Your contempt for your father-in-law so poisoned your relationship with your wife that you nearly committed a fearful crime. Now I am only a transport commissioner, I fear my official status is too low for you."

Mo Ji blushed scarlet and bowed again and again to apologize.

He dreamed of an alliance with the great,
And little thought to meet his wife again;
But beaten, cursed, and covered with disgrace,
The wicked man's ambitions proved but vain!

From this time onwards Mo Ji and Yunu lived together more happily than before. Xu and his wife treated Yunu as their own daughter and Mo Ji as if he were indeed their son-in-law, while Yunu looked on the old couple as her own parents. Then Mo Ji, moved by their example, invited Jin to live with them for the remainder of his days. When eventually Xu and his wife died, Yunu mourned for them like a daughter to repay their kindness. And for generations after this the Mo family and the Xu family remained on intimate terms.

A loyal man wins praise throughout his life,
But cursed be he who spurns a loving wife!
A murdered wife may come to life again:
So all attempts to thwart the gods are vain!

A Just Man Avenged

At leisure in my study, reading history,
I came upon a strange and moving tale
Of a good official crushed by an evil lord;
And my gown is stained with tears for the gallant man.
But do not spurn office because of such injustice,
For the sun and moon cannot be dimmed for ever,
And retribution is bound to come at last,
When justice is meted out to good and evil.

During the Jia Qing period (1522-1566) a wise emperor was on the throne, the elements were propitious, the country prospered and the people were at peace. But then the appointment of one evil minister corrupted the entire government and endangered the security of the state. Who was this evil minister? He was Yan Song, a native of Fenyi in Jiangxi Province. Having won favour by flattery and ingratiating himself with the eunuchs, he sacrificed as a Taoist and made a great show of writing invocations and fasting to please the emperor. So he was rapidly promoted to a position of authority. A circumspect manner cloaked his vindictive nature; and after slandering and ruining the prime minister, Xia Yan, he stepped into his shoes. Then, exalted and powerful, he was feared by officials and common citizens alike.

Yan Song's son, Yan Shifan, who rose gradually from the rank of a college student to be vice-minister of the Board of Works, was even craftier than his father. Since he combined talent with extensive knowledge, a good memory and a cool, calculating brain, the prime minister listened readily to his advice and consulted him whenever he was in doubt. Thus

they were known at court as the Old Prime Minister and the Young Prime Minister.

Working hand in glove, these evil men seized power, accepted bribes and sold government posts and titles. Any official who wished for promotion had only to bribe the prime minister well and beg to become his godson to be appointed to an important post. So the most despicable hangers-on flocked to them, until all ministries and offices were filled with their men; while all who opposed them came to grief, being beaten, banished or killed. The result was that only those prepared to sacrifice their lives dared to protest against the Yans' injustice, and all but the most devoted patriots preferred to see the country ruined rather than offend the prime minister. As an anonymous poet of the period wrote:

> *Why study hard in your youth,*
> *When gold will carry you to a high position?*
> *Look at Prime Minister Yan:*
> *He always appoints the rich to official posts.*

Another verse ran:

> *The Son of Heaven trusts the powerful,*
> *And any remonstrance will only lead to trouble;*
> *Thus everything else today takes second place,*
> *But flattery is the thing.*

Yan Song and his son took advantage of the emperor's favour to fleece and oppress the people, until their sins were mountain-high. Then a loyal subject did a remarkable deed and left a stirring tale behind him. Though he died, his name will live for ever.

> *Where there are dutiful sons, the parents know happiness;*
> *Where there are loyal officials, the land is at peace.*

This man was called Shen Lian, and he was a native of Shaoxing in Zhejiang Province. Well versed in all the arts of peace and war, his ambition was to serve his country and people, and from boyhood he had the greatest admiration for Zhuge Liang,[1] and especially for the two memorials his hero had written while on his way to the front. He made several hundred copies of these to paste over his walls, and after drinking would recite them at the top of his voice. Moreover, when he reached the line, "I devote myself heart and soul to affairs of state, and shall do till I die!" he would sigh and shed tears. He did this so often that everyone considered him eccentric.

In 1538, Shen Lian passed the palace examination and was made a county magistrate. He served three terms as a magistrate, acquitting himself so well that:

> *His subordinates obeyed the law*
> *And he would take no bribes;*
> *The local despots ceased their crimes,*
> *And the common folk had peace.*

Because of his integrity and refusal to fawn on his superiors, Shen Lian was transferred to the capital as secretary of the Imperial Constabulary and there he saw with indignation the crooked ways and ill-gotten wealth of the Yan family. One day at an official banquet he was disgusted by Yan Shifan's arrogance. In the middle of the feast Yan began to shout in the most ill-mannered way, and calling for a big goblet, penalized those who would not drain this when he proposed a toast. This goblet contained over a pint, yet the other guests dared not cross Yan. There was a Censor Ma present, however, who was physically incapable of drinking. When Yan deliberately sent the goblet to him, he begged repeatedly to be excused; but Yan would not let him off. After one sip, the censor flushed crimson and showed signs of acute discomfort. Then Yan strode over to his table, seized the unhappy man by one ear and poured the contents of the goblet down his throat. After forcing himself to gulp down the wine, Censor Ma felt dizzy and the walls began to revolve around him. His

---

[1] A famous statesman of the Three Kingdoms Period (220-280).

head was heavy, his feet light; and as he staggered and fell, Yan clapped his hands and roared with laughter.

Shen Lian could contain himself no longer. Rolling up his sleeves, he seized the goblet, filled it to the brim, and carried it to Yan.

"You did Censor Ma the honour of inviting him to drink," he said. "Since he is too drunk to return your courtesy, let me invite you in his stead!"

Taken aback, Yan was raising his hand to decline, when Shen Lian bent an angry look on him.

"If others can drink this, so can you!" he thundered. "Others may be afraid of you, but I am not!"

Seizing Yan by one ear he poured the wine down his throat, then threw the goblet on the table, clapped his hands and roared with laughter. All the officials present turned ashen pale, and lowered their heads in terrified silence. But when Yan left on the pretext that he had drunk too much, Shen did not rise to see him off.

"Loyal men and traitors cannot work together," he sighed. "They cannot work together."

He repeated this sentence, which was another quotation from Zhuge Liang, seven or eight times, likening Yan Song and Yan Shifan to Cao Cao[1] and his son. And though the others sweated for fear Yan Shifan should hear him, Shen ignored them completely. After draining several cups of wine in swift succession, he went home and slept soundly till dawn.

When he awoke he remembered what he had done.

"In a fit of temper I forced that accursed Yan Shifan to drink," he reflected. "He will certainly try to get even with me; and since I have offended him anyway, I may as well get in first if I can. Their crimes are hated by both gods and men; but they are high favourites at court, and my position is too low for my words to carry any weight. I meant to look for

---

[1] Cao Cao (155-220), one of the ablest generals at the end of the Han Dynasty, was generally considered a usurper. His son became the first king of Wei.

a suitable occasion to denounce them, but now I cannot wait. . . ."

His head on the pillow, he mentally drafted a memorial to the emperor until it was light; then got up, burned incense, washed his hands and wrote a memorandum describing the many evil deeds of Yan Song and Yan Shifan, and how they were seizing power and accepting bribes. He enumerated ten great crimes whereby they had deceived their sovereign and endangered the realm, and begged the emperor to have them executed in the interests of the state.

Then the following edict was issued: "Shen Lian has been found guilty of slandering high officials in order to increase his own reputation. Let him be given a hundred strokes in the Imperial Constabulary, deprived of his official rank, and banished to the northern frontier."

Yan Shifan sent men to urge the constables to beat Shen Lian to death; but fortunately Lu Ping, the officer in charge, had a sense of justice. He had always admired Shen Lian's integrity and been on good terms with him; therefore he did what he could for his superior by pretending to beat him hard while actually giving him light strokes.

The Ministry of Civil Affairs then registered Shen Lian as a common citizen of Bao'an, and with his wounds still unhealed he was forced to pack up immediately, hire a carriage and set out with his wife and children on a long, hard journey. He had four sons, the eldest of whom, Shen Xiang, was a stipendiary scholar who had remained in Shaoxing; but the three others had accompanied their father to Beijing. Shen Gun and Shen Bao had studied in the capital, while Shen Qiu was only one year old; and these three left now with their parents. But for fear of the Yan family, none of the government officials dared see them off.

> *With one memorial he offended the mighty;*
> *Now, lonely, he sets off for the desolate frontier;*
> *And none dare see him off or cling to his saddle,*
> *Lest they too offend the great and are made to suffer.*

After many hardships on the road, at last they reached Bao'an in the Xuanfu Military Area, a frontier outpost with none of the luxuries of the cities of the interior. The unfamiliar landscape depressed them; for after several days' rain the place looked unusually dark and gloomy. Shen Lian wanted to rent a house, but having no acquaintances there did not know how to set about it. As he was wondering what to do, a passer-by carrying a small umbrella stopped at the sight of the baggage by the roadside, struck by Shen's distinguished air.

"May I ask your name, sir, and where you come from?" he asked.

"My name is Shen, and I come from the capital."

"I hear there was a Secretary Shen in the capital who memorialized the throne requesting the execution of Yan Song and his son. Could you be he?"

"I am."

"I have long admired you and am most fortunate to have met you, but we cannot talk here. My humble home is not far away. Will you condescend to bring your honourable family to stay with me for a while before you make other plans?"

Impressed by such sincerity, Shen Lian agreed. And they soon reached the stranger's house which, though no mansion, was clean and pleasant. The stranger invited Shen into the hall, then kowtowed to him, and Shen hastily returned his greeting.

"Who are you?" he asked. "Why are you so good to us?"

"My name is Jia Shi," replied the other. "I am a guard in the local garrison. My brother was a lieutenant here, and when he died leaving no son I stepped into his position. But as soon as that traitor Yan seized power, all those with inherited ranks had to pay heavy bribes. I had no desire to be an official, and luckily my ancestors have left me a few acres of land, so I live as a peasant. Some days ago, I learned that you had impeached the Yans, and knew you must be a just man and a loyal minister. When I heard that you would be coming here, I longed to meet you. And now that Heaven has granted me my wish, I count myself most fortunate."

After this speech he prostrated himself.

Shen Lian helped him to rise, then called Shen Gun and Shen Bao forward to greet their host. Jia Shi told his wife to take Mrs. Shen to an inner chamber to rest; and when the luggage had been brought in and the coachman paid and dismissed, he ordered his men to kill a pig and prepared wine for the guests.

"It is raining hard, and I don't suppose you have found lodgings yet," said Jia. "You had better stay in my humble house. Please make yourselves at home and have some wine to refresh yourselves after your hard journey."

"Meeting by chance, how can I impose on your hospitality?" rejoined Shen after thanking him.

"Our country ways are rough," replied Jia. "Please do not think us remiss."

After toasting each other they fell to deploring current events, and found so much in common that they regretted not having met earlier.

The next morning Shen said to his host: "May I trouble you to help me find a house for my family?"

"What kind of house?" asked Jia.

"If I could find one like yours, I should be very satisfied. As for the rent, I leave that entirely to you."

Jia went out to look for a house, and returned some time later.

"There are plenty of houses for rent," he announced, "but they are all damp and dirty. It will be hard to find anything suitable at short notice. Your best course will be to stay here for the time being, while I take my family to live with relatives until you return to the capital. What do you say?"

"You are too good," replied Shen Lian. "But how can we turn you out of your house? That is quite out of the question."

"Though I am only a peasant I know right from wrong," protested Jia. "I admire you as a true gentleman, sir, and have been longing to serve you; and at last Heaven has given me this chance. By lending you these few poor rooms I am simply showing my respect. You mustn't refuse them!"

Then and there he ordered his men to bring out the cart, horse and donkey, to move away his family's personal belongings, leaving the furniture and household utensils for Shen Lian. Deeply moved by such generosity, Shen asked Jia to become his sworn brother.

"I am a common peasant," demurred Jia. "And you are a gentleman."

"When a true man finds a friend after his own heart, there is no distinction between high and low," replied Shen.

Since Jia was the younger by five years, he addressed Shen as his elder brother, and Shen bade his sons address Jia as their uncle. Then Jia presented his wife, and they feasted together as relatives, after which Jia moved out to live with his brother-in-law, while Shen Lian stayed on in his house. A contemporary wrote the following verse in praise of this:

> In a chance encounter he showed his sincerity,
> And lent his house to his friend to prove his love.
> How shameful that so many kinsmen and friends
> Should fight over property and contend for wealth!

When the elders of Bao'an heard that Secretary Shen had been banished to their district for impeaching Prime Minister Yan, they admired him so much that they all wanted to meet him. Some sent him rice and fuel, others wine and dishes, yet others sent their sons and younger brothers to be his pupils. Every day Shen would discuss loyalty and piety with the local people, or tell stories of just and true men in history, pounding the table indignantly as he described their misfortunes. At other times he would sing tragic songs, sigh or shed tears. The old and young of Bao'an listened spellbound, and joined in when he cursed the Yan family. In fact, anyone who remained silent during these tirades was abused for his lack of humanity and justice. They took such pleasure in his company that, when they learned that Shen Lian also excelled in military arts, they asked him to join in their archery contests.

Then Shen Lian bade them make three men of straw. On

one he wrote Li Lingfu, the Tang Dynasty traitor; on another Qin Hui, the Song Dynasty traitor; and on the third Yan Song, the Ming Dynasty traitor; and he used these three straw figures as targets.

"You traitor!" he would cry, when shooting at these figures. "Here comes my arrow!"

The honest northerners enjoyed this sport with him, not caring whether the Yan family heard of it or not. But as the proverb says: All powerful men have their informers. When someone reported to Yan Song and his son what was happening, they racked their brains furiously for some excuse to have Shen Lian killed.

There was then a vacancy for a military governor in Xuanfu and Datong, and Yan Song made the Ministry of Civil Affairs appoint his godson, Yang Shun. When Yang Shun went to take his leave of his patrons, Yan Shifan entertained him to a feast, during which he dismissed the attendants and privately directed Yang to find some way to put Shen Lian publicly in the wrong. After assenting readily, Yang left.

> *The poison is ready to mix in the wine,*
> *The sword is drawn ready to strike;*
> *So pity the loyal man, Shen Lian,*
> *Still boasting before his figures of straw!*

Soon after Yang Shun reached his post, Altan Khan, the Tartar chief at Datong, invaded China. He took over forty strongholds in Yinzhou by storm and captured many prisoners; but Governor Yang dared not resist him. Only after the enemy had left were Chinese troops sent in pursuit, who beat gongs and drums, waved flags, fired guns and raised pandemonium, without seeing so much as the shadow of a Tartar! Then, realizing that he had blundered and might be punished, Governor Yang secretly ordered his men to seize the common people who were fleeing before the soldiery, shave and cut off their heads, and send them to the Ministry of War as Tartars' heads, for which a reward was given. Thus many innocent people were massacred.

As soon as Shen Lian learned of this he blazed with indignation, and wrote a letter which he asked a lieutenant to hand to Governor Yang. Regarding Shen as a trouble-maker who was capable of writing anything, the lieutenant refused to accept the letter, whereupon Shen put on dark clothes and a private citizen's cap and waited outside the yamen for Governor Yang, then handed him the letter himself.

"Personal achievement and fame mean little," read the governor, "but the people's lives are of paramount importance. How could you have the heart to kill common citizens to gain false credit? The Tartars merely rob our people and carry them off captive, whereas our own troops kill them. Thus our officers are more to be feared than the Tartars."

And the following verse was appended to the letter:

> *Did you kill to report your achievements to your sovereign,*
> *To win credit at the price of ten thousand lives?*
> *Listen, some stormy night on the battlefield:*
> *The unjustly slain are calling for their heads!*

The governor tore up this letter in fury.

Then Shen Lian wrote a dirge and went with his young men to sacrifice to the spirits of those unjustly killed. He also wrote these two verses on frontier warfare:

> *As the enemy's beacon fires flare high at the frontier,*
> *How hard the Chinese general exerts himself!*
> *He kills not the khan but our people,*
> *Staining his sword with the blood of the wrongly slain.*

And:

> *They fled from the Tartars, hoping to save their lives;*
> *But instead they met their death.*
> *Had they known that their heads would be sent in as*
> *   enemy heads,*
> *They would surely have chosen surrender to the khan.*

When the governor's trusted lieutenant made copies of these poems and the dirge and sent them secretly to Yang Shun, the latter's rage knew no bounds. He altered the first verse to read:

> *As the enemy's beacon fires flare high at the frontier,*
> *The Chinese general exerts himself in vain.*
> *Would that the khan would k·ll this flattering minister;*
> *For then there would be no need for the emperor's sword!*

He wrote a letter enclosing these verses, sealed it, marked it confidential, and sent it to Yan Shifan. In this letter he declared that Shen Lian was secretly gathering assassins to kill Yan Song and his son in order to wreak his hatred; and during the Tartar invasion he had written these poems urging the khan to kill the prime minister — in other words, he was guilty of treason.

When Yan Shifan read this, he was startled and consulted his trusted censor, Lu Kai.

"If I am sent to inspect that district," said Lu, "I can settle this for you."

Yan Shifan was delighted and ordered the Court of Censors to despatch Lu to that area; then, on the eve of the censor's departure, invited him to a farewell feast.

"Convey my regards to Yang Shun," he said. "I hope you will co-operate with him. If you can rid me of this thorn in my flesh, I shall certainly not let either of you down, but reward you with some noble rank."

Lu assented. A day or two later he left with his credentials for Xuanfu, where he met Governor Yang and told him of Yan Shifan's instructions.

"This has been rankling with me day and night, so that I have not been able to sleep or eat," said Yang. "But I have not yet hit on a good plan for killing him."

"We should both keep our eyes open," said Lu. "We must not disappoint the prime minister, and it would never do to let slip this chance of advancing ourselves."

"You are right," agreed Yang. "If either of us finds an opportunity, he should let the other know."

After they parted, preoccupation with what Lu Kai had said kept Governor Yang awake all night. The next morning when he went to his yamen his lieutenant reported:

"Two rebels caught in Weizhou have been sent here for Your Excellency to sentence."

"Bring them in," ordered Yang.

The escort came in, paid his respects and presented an official document. When Governor Yang opened and read it he laughed for joy; for these two rebels, Yan Hao and Yang Yinkui, were followers of the sorcerer Xiao Qin, leader of the White Lotus Sect, who travelled constantly into Tartar territory and deceived people with his superstitious rites. He had assured Altan Khan that he had magic means to kill men and cause city walls to crumble; and the khan, foolish enough to believe him, had given him the title of Great Master. Xiao Qin had several hundred followers, who formed a separate unit in the Tartar army and acted as guides each time Altan Khan raided the border; thus they had done China great harm. Yang's predecessor, Governor Shi, had sent envoys with gifts to the Tartar chief, Tuotuo, to inform him:

"The Son of Heaven is willing to make peace with you and establish a system of barter whereby we exchange cloth and grain for your horses. A cessation of hostilities and a period of peace would be beneficial for both our countries; but we fear Xiao Qin may attempt to obstruct a settlement and stir up strife. This Xiao Qin is a rogue and a charlatan, who has no magic powers but has been tricking you into carrying out raids for his own selfish ends. If you doubt this, ask him for some proof of his boasted arts. If he can indeed make walls crumble and kill men by witchcraft, by all means treat him well. If he cannot, then he has deceived you, and you had better deliver him to us in chains. Then our celestial court, pleased with your help, will reward you handsomely; and once the horse barter is established you will reap endless profit year after year. Would that not be much more advantageous than pillage?"

Tuotuo approved of this proposal and reported it to Altan Khan, who was also favourably impressed, and told Xiao Qin that a thousand horsemen would follow him across the frontier to test his skill in causing walls to crumble. Then Xiao, knowing that he was doomed to exposure, disguised himself and fled by night. He was challenged and seized by the garrison at Juyong Pass, then taken to Governor Shi; and when he confessed that he had many followers in the west and south, orders were given for their arrest. Since the names of the rebels Yan Hao and Yang Yinkui were on Xiao Qin's list, Governor Yang was delighted that they had been arrested, for he felt their capture reflected credit on him and he could make use of them to trap Shen Lian. That same evening he invited Censor Lu to discuss the matter in one of his inner chambers.

"We cannot get Shen on any other charge," said Yang, "but there is nothing the emperor dislikes more than this treasonous alliance between the Tartars and the White Lotus Sect. Now we can make these two men write in their confession that they were Shen Lian's pupils, and that after he lost his post he became discontented and incited them to practise sorcery and ally with the Tartars to overthrow their own country. Since Heaven has decreed their capture, we can ask His Majesty's permission to execute Shen Lian in order to avoid further trouble, after first writing privately to the Yans urging them to order the Ministry of Justice to report this promptly to the imperial court. Then Shen Lian will not escape."

Lu clapped his hands in approval. Then and there, the two of them decided on the contents of the reports and arranged to send them in together. When Yan Song received these reports, he told his son to inform the Ministry of Justice. The minister, Xu Lun, was a cowardly, incompetent old man, who after receiving the prime minister's order lost no time in addressing a memorial to the throne along the lines proposed by Yang and Lu. Then an imperial edict was issued ordering the immediate execution of the sorcerer Shen Lian by the local authorities; Yang's son was appointed a lieutenant, and Lu was promoted three ranks and promised a new post in the capital as soon as there was a vacancy.

Once Governor Yang had sent in his report, he ordered his men to seize Shen Lian and throw him into gaol. Shen's wife and sons were frightened out of their wits, and the two lads took counsel with Jia Shi.

"Those scoundrels Yang Shun and Lu Kai must have done this to please the prime minister," said Jia. "And the fact that your father has been thrown into gaol means they have certainly charged him with some serious crime. You two young gentlemen had better go as far away as you can and remain in hiding until the Yans have fallen from power. If you stay here, they will kill you too."

"How can we leave without waiting to see what becomes of our father?" asked Shen Gun.

"Now that your father has fallen into his enemies' hands, he is beyond help," replied Jia. "It is more important to continue your family line than to throw away your lives for the sake of filial piety, and you had better advise your mother to save herself too. As for your father, I shall see that he is properly looked after. You needn't worry on that score."

When the two brothers went in to tell their mother this, however, she raised objections.

"Your father is innocent," she said. "How can we abandon him now that he is in gaol? Though Uncle Jia has been so good to us, he is not a kinsman after all. I am sure those two scoundrels Yang and Lu are angry only with your father; they can't possibly involve us in this. If you run away because you are afraid, and your father dies, there will be no one to bury him and you will be condemned for ever as unfilial sons. How could you hold up your heads again?"

After saying this she wept bitterly, and her sons shed tears too. As for Jia Shi, when he heard that Mrs. Shen would not listen to reason, he sighed and left. A few days later he received reliable information that Shen Lian had been condemned to death as a member of the White Lotus Sect. Shen Lian kept cursing his enemies loudly in gaol, and Governor Yang, who knew that injustice had been done and feared that he might lose face if the prisoner denounced him publicly on the way to the execution ground, ordered the gaoler to report that Shen Lian had died of illness, then had him murdered.

When Jia Shi broke this news to Mrs. Shen, it goes without saying that she and her sons lamented bitterly. Jia, who had many connections, succeeded in buying Shen's corpse by persuading the gaoler to produce a false corpse if the head had to be publicly exhibited. Then, unknown to the Shen brothers, he buried his old friend's body with due rites in a spare plot of ground.

"I have saved your father's body and shall show you his grave when the trouble is over," he told them. "For the present, though, I must keep it a secret."

The young men thanked him again and again, while Jia urged them once more to leave that district.

"We know that we have occupied your house for a long time, uncle," said Shen Gun, "and we feel very bad about it. But our mother wants to remain here till our father's name is cleared, then move his coffin to our ancestral graveyard. That is why we want to stay on."

"I always advise people for their own good," replied Jia angrily. "I urged you to move for your own sake, not because I want my house back. Since your respected mother has made up her mind, I cannot insist. But I myself find it necessary to leave home for a year or so. Stay here by all means as long as you please."

Just then he caught sight of two of Zhuge Liang's memorials in Shen Lian's handwriting on the wall.

"May I have these two scrolls as a memento?" he asked. "Then, when we meet again, we shall know each other by them."

Shen Gun took down the scrolls, rolled them up and gave them to Jia Shi, who put them in his sleeves and left, shedding tears. Jia knew that Governor Yang and Censor Lu were wicked men, who would not rest content with murdering Shen Lian, and that as Shen's friend he was likely to be involved. So he fled to Henan to stay with a kinsman there.

When Censor Lu received the imperial edict based on the report from the Ministry of Justice, he had the rebels Yan Hao and Yang Yinkui executed, and gave orders for Shen Lian's head to be displayed with theirs. By this time, however, Shen's corpse had been bought by Jia Shi, and the censor did not realize that another corpse had been substituted for it. But when Governor Yang saw that his sole reward was an official rank for his son, he felt resentful.

"Yan Shifan promised to make me a noble," he told Lu. "I wonder why he has not kept his word?"

"Shen Lian was the Yans' arch enemy," replied Lu after some thought. "Though he is dead, his sons are still alive. It is no use cutting grass unless you pull out its roots. No doubt the prime minister is not completely satisfied."

"That is easy," replied Yang. "We can send in another memorial reporting that Shen Lian has been executed, but it appears his sons are in the plot too, and they ought to be punished and their property confiscated as an example to all evil-doers. We should also arrest those wild young men who practised archery with Shen Lian, as well as the fellow who lent Shen his house, and have them all punished. Then the prime minister's vengeance will be complete, and he can hardly fail to keep his promise."

"That is an excellent plan," approved Lu. "But there is no time to be lost. If we can seize them all while his family is still here, so much the better. I am only afraid Shen's sons may scent danger and fly, in which case we shall have trouble."

Yang Shun agreed. They sent a memorial to the throne and a letter to the Yan family pledging their loyalty. At the same time they ordered the prefect of Bao'an to watch the culprits well and not allow them to run away, for as soon as an edict was issued they would have to be arrested.

Few eggs remain whole when the nest is broken;
When grass is cut its roots are torn out;
And sons of good men unjustly killed
Are sacrificed to please the mighty.

Within a few days the imperial edict arrived and the local
authorities issued warrants for the arrest of Shen Lian's family
and all his friends. Jia Shi alone had left home, and they had
to report that he had escaped. A contemporary wrote in praise
of Jia's foresight:

Rare indeed is a loyal friend like Jia,
Whose escape displays his foresight.
Though the net was flung to catch all those near by,
This bird had flown far away beyond the horizon.

Governor Yang tried Shen's sons himself, ordering them to
confess that they had worked for the enemy. And when they
protested that they were innocent, he had them tortured until
their bones were broken, their flesh torn, and they died in
agony under the rods, their spirits taking flight to the nether
regions. Dozens of others who had been arrested with them
were also executed as their accomplices. Shen Lian's youngest
son, Shen Qiu, was spared because he was still a child; but he
and his mother were banished to the outpost of Yunzhou.

Then Censor Lu said to Governor Yang: "Shen's eldest son,
Shen Xiang, is a well-known scholar in Shaoxing. Once he
passes the official examinations he will try to pay us back. We
had better get rid of him now, to avoid trouble in future. The
prime minister will approve of our caution."

Yang agreed, and wrote to the authorities in Zhejiang Province asking to have Shen Xiang sent to his district for trial.
Then he bade his trusted secretary, Jin Shao, select able runners who would take the letter to Shaoxing and murder Shen
Xiang on the way back. If they could procure a certificate from
the local authorities stating that Shen had died of illness, to
close the affair, he promised to reward them well and to recommend Jin for promotion. The secretary was delighted. He made

a careful choice of two experienced runners, Zhang Qian and
Li Wan, invited them to his quarters for a good meal, and
presented them with twenty taels of silver from his own pocket.

"How can we accept this when we have done nothing for
you?" protested Zhang and Li.

"This silver is not from me but from Governor Yang," replied Jin. "He wants you to take a summons to Shaoxing to
arrest Shen Xiang. Be very strict with him on the way; and
if you see that he does not reach here alive, you will be well
rewarded. If you fail, you will find that the governor is no
person to trifle with. You will be held fully responsible."

"How dare we disobey the governor's wishes?" replied
Zhang and Li. "Your instructions shall be faithfully carried
out."

They pocketed the silver, thanked Jin, took the summons
from the prefecture, and travelled with all speed southwards.

Now Shen Xiang was a stipendiary scholar of Shaoxing
Prefecture. When he heard that his father had been deprived
of his official rank and banished to the frontier, he was very
worried and wanted to go to Bao'an. He could not leave,
however, because he had no one to whom to entrust his family.
Now suddenly men from the prefect's yamen loaded him with
chains and took him without a word of explanation to court,
where the prefect showed him the summons and handed him
over with the official reply to the runners from Bao'an, charg-
ing them to be careful on the way. Realizing that his father
and two younger brothers had been killed and his mother
exiled to a lonely outpost, Shen Xiang cried aloud all the way
out of the court, and at the gate he found his whole family
waiting in tears. The authorities had ordered the confiscation
of his property, and the prefect had sent constables to seal up
his house and drive out the inmates. This so added to Shen
Xiang's grief that he wailed till he was out of breath. Then
his relatives came to bid him farewell, proffering a few words
of comfort though they knew they would probably never see
him again. His father-in-law, Meng Chunyuan, offered a

packet of silver to the runners and begged them to look after Shen Xiang well on the road; but they refused to accept the money until his wife added two pairs of gold hairpins.

"The odds are that I shall be killed," Shen Xiang told his wife with tears. "Don't grieve for me, but consider yourself a widow and go back to live with your parents. You come from a good family, so there need be no question of your re-marrying and I can set my mind at rest."

Then he pointed to Shunü, his concubine.

"She is very young," he told his wife, "and has no family to which to return. I should bid her marry again, but I am thirty now and have no son, and she is two months pregnant. If she gives birth to a son our ancestral sacrifices can be con-tinued. So for my sake, wife, will you take her to your home for a while? You can send her away after she has given birth if you wish."

"How can you suggest such a thing, husband?" put in Shunü before he had finished. "If we let you go hundreds of miles away with no one to look after you, we can never rest easy in our minds. Our mistress may go back to her own family, but I shall go with you, shabby as I am. Then you will have someone to keep you company, and our mistress need not worry so much."

"Of course I would like to have a companion," rejoined Shen Xiang, "but this journey is not likely to end well. Why should I involve you and perhaps cause your death in a strange province?"

"Everyone knows that you were at home all the time your father was in the capital," said Shunü. "Even if they slander your father, they can hardly accuse you of being his accomplice when you were so far away. I shall go with you to the capital to plead your innocence, and I am sure you will not be con-demned to death. And if they throw you into gaol, I shall be near enough to look after you."

Shen Xiang's wife was concerned for him too, so because there was reason in what Shunü said she urged him to take the concubine with him. And since Shen Xiang had always liked Shunü for her talent and wit, now that his wife supported her proposal he agreed to take her. That night they stayed with his father-in-law, and the next morning when the two runners Zhang Qian and Li Wan pressed him to set out at once, Shunü changed into cloth garments and a black kerchief, said goodbye to Shen Xiang's wife, shouldered her baggage and walked out behind her husband. The family's grief at parting can be imagined.

During the journey Shen Xiang's concubine stirred not a step from his side, and served him his food and drink herself. At first Zhang and Li treated them well; but once they had crossed the Yangzi River and were continuing on foot from Xuzhou, far from Shen's home, the runners began to grow rough, shouting curses and making things more difficult for their prisoner. Shunü noticed this.

"Those wicked men mean mischief," she whispered to her husband. "I am only a woman, and I don't know the way. But if we pass through wild, lonely country, you must be on your guard."

Shen Xiang nodded, although he was confident that all would be well. When a few more days had passed, however, and he noticed that the two runners kept laying their heads together in a suspicious manner and that they had a glittering Japanese sword in their baggage, he began to be afraid.

"You said these runners are plotting mischief," he told Shunü, "and I am inclined to agree with you. After crossing the boundary of Jining Prefecture tomorrow we shall reach the Taihang and Liang Mountains, and that is wild, bandit-infested country. If they attack us there, we shall have no means of defending ourselves. What shall we do?"

"If you know of a way to escape, please take it and leave me to shift for myself," begged Shunü. "They can't eat me."

"Inside the East Gate of Jining lives a certain Secretary Feng, who has retired from office because he is in mourning for his father," said Shen Xiang. "He is a gallant man, and my father's classmate and good friend. If I call on him tomorrow, he will certainly take me in. But how can a woman deal with these two ruffians? I'm afraid they will hold you responsible for my escape, and I don't like the idea of that. If you feel confident that you can deal with them, I shall go with an easy mind. Otherwise, let us live or die together as fate decrees. I shall meet death without regret."

"You must escape if you can," replied Shunü. "I shall be able to cope with them. Don't worry."

Thus husband and concubine deliberated in secret, while the two runners snored away after a hard day's journey capped by heavy drinking. The next morning when they set out again, Shen Xiang asked Zhang Qian: "How far are we from Jining?"

"Only twelve or thirteen miles," replied Zhang. "We shall be there before noon."

"Inside the East Gate of that town lives a Secretary Feng who used to be my father's friend," said Shen. "While in the capital he borrowed two hundred taels of silver from my father, and I have his note of hand with me. He used to be in charge of the Beixin Customs, so he has plenty of money, and I am sure he will repay me now that I am in trouble if I ask him. This money would give us ample to spend on the road, and we could travel in comfort."

While Zhang Qian hesitated, Li Wan immediately approved of this scheme.

"Shen seems an honest man," he whispered to Zhang. "Besides, his baggage and concubine are here — what can go wrong? Let him go and get the money, I say. It will all be ours, won't it?"

"Very well," replied Zhang. "But wait till we've put down our baggage in an inn. Then I can keep an eye on the woman there while you follow Shen. That should be safe enough."

By ten o'clock that morning they reached Jining, and deposited their baggage in a clean inn outside the city.

"Which of you will come with me to the East Gate?" asked

Shen. "We can have our midday meal when we get back."

"I'll go with you," said Li. "They may invite us to a meal with wine."

"You know the proverb," said Shunü to her husband, "the world is full of fair-weather friends, who look down on you when you're down on your luck. Though Secretary Feng owes your family money, now that your father is dead and you are in difficulties he may not feel like paying you back promptly. Most likely he will refuse to see you. Better have a meal and go on."

"It's not far from here to the East Gate," countered Shen. "We can't lose anything by calling on him."

Li Wan, who was eager to lay his hands on that two hundred taels of silver, urged Shen on.

"Wait for me here," said Shen to his concubine. "If we are back soon, it will mean our trip was in vain; but if he keeps us to a meal, he is bound to pay me something. Then tomorrow we can hire a sedan-chair for you. You must have found it hard all these days on that donkey."

"Very well," said Shunü with a meaning glance at her husband. "Come back as soon as you can. Don't keep me waiting too long."

"How long do you think he'll be anyway?" asked Li Wan with a laugh. "Can't you let him out of your sight for a moment?"

As Shen Xiang was leaving, Shunü deliberately called Li back.

"If Secretary Feng invites you to a meal, please don't let him keep you too long," she said.

"Don't you worry," replied the runner.

By the time Li Wan walked down the steps of the inn, Shen Xiang had a good start of him. The runner was a careless fellow. He was quite familiar with this town, having often been here before, and even knew which was Secretary Feng's house. He was therefore not in the least anxious. After walking a few yards he looked round for a public latrine, then strolled slowly towards the East Gate.

When Shen Xiang saw that Li was not following him, he ran straight to Secretary Feng's house, where he was lucky enough to find Feng alone in the sitting room. They had been old friends in the capital, and Feng was delighted by this unexpected visit. But instead of greeting him Shen pulled at his sleeve.

"May I speak to you in private?" he begged.

Realizing that the situation was serious, Feng led him to the library, where Shen burst into tears.

"My dear nephew, what is the matter?" inquired Feng. "Don't waste time weeping if prompt action is needed."

"I expect you know how unjustly my father was done to death by that traitor," said Shen. "Now my two younger brothers who were with him have been murdered by Yang Shun and Lu Kai. I was the only one left at home, but they sent a warrant to our district and runners to take me to Bao'an. It looks as if our whole family is to be wiped out. The two runners escorting me mean mischief: I suspect they have orders to murder me when we reach the Taihang and Liang Mountains which are just ahead. So I have given them the slip, and come to throw myself on your mercy. If you can protect me, my father's spirit will be grateful to you in heaven. If you cannot, I shall dash my head against the stone steps and die here rather than at the hands of those traitors."

"Don't worry," said Secretary Feng. "I have a double wall behind my bedroom where you can hide and no one will find you. You had better stay there for a few days. I have a plan, if you will only wait."

"You are a second father to me!" cried Shen, bowing to express his thanks.

Then Feng took him by the hand and led him to the back of his bedroom, where he removed some planks from the floor to reveal an underground staircase. After fifty or sixty steps, they saw light and came upon three small rooms walled in so that no one could reach them. Every day Feng himself brought tea and food to Shen here; and because his household discipline was strict no one dared disclose the fugitive's presence.

Leopards can hide in mountain crags,
And crows in willow leaves;
Who need fear the government runners
In the house of a gallant friend?

Meanwhile Li Wan was proceeding in a leisurely fashion towards Secretary Feng's house at the East Gate.

"Is your master in?" he asked at the door.

"Yes," replied the old door-keeper. "He is."

"A gentleman in white called to see him. Did Secretary Feng admit him?"

"Yes. He has asked him to stay for lunch in the library."

Hearing this, Li settled down to wait with an easy mind; and at two in the afternoon a man in white came out   But when Li stepped forward hastily to accost him, he discovered this was not Shen but a stranger. By now the runner was both hungry and impatient, so he questioned the old door-keeper again.

"Why doesn't the gentleman your master is keeping for a meal come out?"

"He did come out just now."

"Doesn't your master have another guest in the library?"

"Not that I know of."

"Who was that gentleman in white who just left?"

"That is our master's brother-in-law, who often calls."

"Where is your master now?"

"He always has a nap after lunch. He must be sleeping now."

The fact that he was receiving the wrong answers to all his questions began to make Li worried.

"The truth is that I am here on business for His Excellency the Governor of Xuanfu and Datong," he said. "I have been escorting a state prisoner named Shen Xiang, a young gentleman from Shaoxing who said he was connected with your master and wanted to call on him. I followed him to your house, and he went in; but although I have waited all this time he has not come out yet. I suppose he is still in the library, though you don't know it. Please ask him to hurry up and come out, because we must be on our way."

"What are you talking about?" demanded the old man, feigning complete bewilderment. "I don't understand a word you say."

When Li suppressed his anxiety to explain the situation again in detail, the old man spat at him.

"You've been seeing ghosts!" he swore. "No Mr. Shen has been here! My master is in mourning, so he doesn't receive anybody outside the family. I am in charge of the gate and I announce everyone who goes in. How can you spin a yarn like that to me? I suppose you are one of those thieves who sneak around in broad daylight pretending to be government runners. Get out now, and don't pester me any more."

At this Li became really worried, and flew into a rage.

"Shen Xiang is an important state criminal!" he bellowed. "This is no joking matter. Please ask your master to come out, so that I can speak to him."

"Secretary Feng is sleeping now, and I dare not disturb him for nothing. You northern barbarians are fools!"

With that the door-keeper walked slowly off.

"The old idiot!" swore Li. "Why should he lose his temper just because I asked him to send in my message? Shen Xiang *must* be inside. I have the warrant on me, and this is not private business. I may as well go straight in."

He marched boldly into the hall and banged on the screen.

"It's time to go, Mr. Shen!" he shouted.

When there was no answer, he went on shouting until a servant-boy came out.

"Where is the door-keeper?" demanded the boy, staring at the runner from behind the screen. "Who let this fellow in to make so much noise?"

Before Li could call to him to stop, the boy walked out towards the west.

"Maybe the library is there," thought Li. "I'll have a look."

He turned west from the hall and headed down a long, deserted corridor till he came to a number of rooms which were obviously the women's quarters; then he dared go no further, but returned to the hall. At this point he heard shouting outside, and upon going to the gate found that Zhang Qian had come to look for him and was swearing at the door-keeper. The moment Zhang caught sight of Li, he started abusing him.

"A fine fellow you are!" he cried. "All you care about is food and wine, not how to do your job properly. You came into town at ten o'clock, and now it is nearly five in the afternoon; yet you are still hanging about here instead of making the criminal get a move on. What are you waiting for?"

"Curse it!" retorted Li. "What food have I had? I can't find him!"

"But you came with him into town."

"I stopped for a second at a latrine on the way. Then that damned southerner went ahead, and I couldn't catch up with him. I followed him all the way here, and the gateman to'd me a gentleman in white had been kept for lunch in the library; so I took it for granted it must be him. But though I've waited all this time, he still hasn't come out, and the gateman won't announce me. Not a drop of water has passed my lips, brother. Please wait here a few minutes while I fill my belly."

"How could you be such a fool?" exploded Zhang. "How dare you let a criminal like that out of your sight? Even if he did go to the library, you ought to have followed him in. Now who knows whether he is inside or not? Yet here you are talking as if nothing had happened. Well, you're responsible for this; it's nothing to do with me."

He started walking off, but Li hurried after him and caught hold of him.

"The fellow must be inside." insisted Li. "I'm sure he can't get away. We should both try to get him out, and you've had your meal — what's the hurry?"

"His concubine is still in the inn," replied Zhang. "Though I've asked the landlord to keep an eye on her, I don't feel happy about leaving her. She's the rope through the ox's nose: as long as she's there, we may be sure he'll come back."

"Right," agreed Li.

When Zhang had left, Li waited with an empty stomach till evening without seeing any sign of Shen. By sunset he was ravenous. Noticing a pastry shop next door, he went to pawn his coat for a few coins to buy dumplings. But although he was away for a few minutes only, he heard the sound of a gate being barred, and when he ran back he found Secretary Feng's house locked.

"Never have I been treated like this in all my years as a runner!" swore Li. "How high does he think a secretary's rank is, to put on such airs? Shen Xiang is the limit too. His concubine and baggage are in the inn, so even if he wants to spend the night here he ought to send us word. Well, it can't be helped; I'd better pass the night as best I can under the eaves. At daybreak I shall get hold of a more intelligent servant to talk to."

It was then the tenth month, and not too cold; but a wind sprang up in the middle of the night and rain fell. Soon Li's clothes were wet, and he shivered miserably. At dawn the rain stopped and Zhang Qian turned up again, sent by Shu-nü. He had with him the official despatch and summons, and they agreed that as soon as the gate opened they should push their way in. This they did. The old gateman could not stop them, and they created a great uproar in the hall. Presently the whole household had gathered round and begun shouting too, making the noise even worse; and when passers-by heard the din they clustered outside the gate to watch. Finally Secretary Feng walked out to see what the clamour was about. The servants heard him cough as he approached.

"The master is here!" they cried, hastily ranging themselves on both sides of the room.

"What is all this noise?" demanded Feng, entering the hall. The two runners stepped forward to pay their respects.

"Sir," they said, "we are here on a mission for the Governor of Xuanfu and Datong. We arrested the state criminal Shen Xiang at Shaoxing, and were escorting him through your district when he said he was related to you and wanted to call on you. Not daring to refuse him, we let him come. But that was yesterday morning, and he has still not come out. This is holding up our journey, yet your servants would not announce us. We hope, sir, you will kindly urge him to leave now."

Then Zhang Qian took from his wallet the warrant and the official despatch.

"Is this Shen Xiang the son of Shen Lian?" asked Feng, after reading these documents.

"Yes, sir," replied Li.

Feng put his hands over his ears and thrust out his tongue in dismay.

"What criminal negligence!" he exclaimed. "Shen Xiang is not only a state criminal, but the enemy of the prime minister. Who would dare shelter such a man? When did he come to my house, pray? You are raving! If this rumour reaches the authorities and they inform the Yan family, what will become of me? I would like to know how large a bribe you irresponsible scoundrels took to let such an important criminal go. And now you are trying to shift the blame to me! Throw them out, men, and bar the gate; otherwise we shall find ourselves involved. It will be no joke if the Yan family hears of this."

Still swearing, he went back to his room, while the servants pushed and shoved the two runners out and closed the gate behind them, still cursing them from inside. Zhang and Li stuck out their tongues and gaped at each other in consternation. "Yesterday you urged me to let him come to town," accused Zhang. "Now it's up to you to find him."

"Stop grumbling and let's go back to question his concubine," said Li. "She ought to know where he is. Then we can come back to get him."

"All right," said Zhang. "They are certainly devoted to each other. Yesterday when he didn't show up she went on crying for hours and insisted on waiting up for him. She must know where he is."

As they were talking, they hurried back to the inn. And the moment Shunü heard their voices from her room she ran to the door.

"Where is my husband?" she demanded.

"Ask him!" Zhang pointed at Li.

Li told her all that had happened the previous day.

"This morning I hurried to town without my breakfast but got nothing for my pains," said Zhang. "It doesn't look as if your husband can be with Secretary Feng, but in that case he must have gone somewhere else. He must have told you his plans, ma'am. If you tell us, we can go to look for him."

Before he had finished speaking, tears sprang to Shunü's eyes and she seized the two runners.

"Give me back my husband!" she cried.

"Your husband asked us to allow him to call on a relative, and we were good enough to let him go," they protested. "Now he's disappeared, and left us in this fix, yet you act as if we had hidden him somewhere. This is ridiculous!"

They bared their chests and sat down sulkily together.

Shunü ran to the door to bar their escape, then stamped her feet and screamed that injustice had been done. The old innkeeper hurried over to see what the matter was.

"Let me tell you what's happened, uncle," said Shunü. "My husband had no son at thirty, so he took me as his concubine, and I have been with him for two years. Because I have been with child for more than three months, he could not send me away; and I have followed him all this way, not letting him out of my sight once. Yesterday, because we were short of travelling money, he wanted to call on a friend; and that runner, Li, went with him. When he didn't come back last night, I began to have my suspicions; and now that these two have come back without him, I know they must have murdered him. Please help me, sir, and make them give me back my husband!"

"You mustn't jump to conclusions, ma'am," said the innkeeper. "These officers are not your husband's enemies. Why should they kill him?"

At that Shunu wept more bitterly than ever.

"I can tell you why," she sobbed. "My husband is hated by Prime Minister Yan, and these two men must have been sent by the Yan family or decided to ask for a reward from them. Just think, sir! Why should my husband suddenly go off without a word after bringing me all this way? And even if he wanted to, would Li Wan let him go? No, to curry favour with the prime minister these wicked men have made away with my husband. And what can a poor, lonely woman do? Please seize these murderers for me, uncle! Then I shall lodge a complaint at the yamen."

As she wept and stormed, Zhang and Li had no answer to make. Then the old innkeeper thought there must be something in what she said, and pitied her.

"Even if this is true, ma'am," he said, "your husband may not be dead. Why don't you wait another day?"

"It's all very well to tell me to wait another day, but who will be responsible for these two murderers? They may seize the chance to run away."

"If we had really murdered your husband and wanted to run away," declared Zhang, "why should we have come back here?"

"You counted on the fact that I am a helpless woman," retorted Shunù. "I suppose you thought you would kidnap me. Tell the truth now: where is my husband's body? You will have to confess when we go to court."

Hearing how convincingly she spoke, the innkeeper dared

say no more. Meanwhile forty or fifty people had gathered round, and when they learned the concubine's sad story they were furious with the two runners.

"If you want to lodge a complaint, ma'am, we'll take you to the military commissioner," they offered.

Shunü bowed deeply to them, weeping.

"Thank you for your kindness," she said. "Have pity on a lonely woman in distress and help me! Take these two murderers with you, and don't let them escape!"

"Never fear," they replied. "You can depend on us"

When the runners attempted to explain matters, they were silenced.

"There is no need for explanations," said the crowd. "Truth will always out. If you are innocent, why should you mind going with her to the yamen?"

Shunü shed tears as she went, and the crowd dragged Zhang Qian and Li Wan with them to the military commissioner's office. It was still too early, however, for that day's morning session.

Then Shunu, who had put on a white mourning apron, darted inside the palisade to where there was a big drum near the gate with a drum stick hanging from its frame. She seized the stick and beat the drum as loudly as she could. Shocked and startled, the yamen attendants and gate-keeper rushed forward and bound her.

"How dare you, woman!" they shouted.

Shunü fell sobbing to the ground, where she cried that she had been cruelly wronged. Then a shout was raised inside, the gate opened, and the military commissioner took his seat in court and asked who had beaten the drum. His lieutenant brought in Shunu, who wept as she related the misfortunes that had befallen her family and described in detail how Shen Lian and his sons had been killed, leaving only her husband, who had been murdered the previous day by the runners. She gave circumstantial evidence, and when the commissioner questioned Zhang and Li she pulled all their arguments to pieces. Moreover, she spoke so convincingly that they could not refute her.

"The prime minister is powerful and often plots the death of innocent men," reflected the commissioner. "What she says may be true."

He bid his lieutenant take Shunü and the two runners to the local Prefect He.

As soon as the prefect received this case, he sent for the innkeeper and cross-examined the four of them. The woman insisted that the two runners had murdered her husband, Li declared that he had been delayed by going to the latrine and lost his man, and Zhang and the innkeeper stated the facts as they knew them. The prefect did not know which of them was telling the truth. Shunü was so sad that it seemed her story must be true, yet Zhang and Li would not admit to murdering Shen Xiang. Finally Prefect He decided to detain the four of them while he went by sedan-chair to find out what Secretary Feng thought of the case. When Secretary Feng heard that the prefect had come, he hastily invited him into his sitting room, where they drank tea. But as soon as Shen Xiang's name was mentioned, Feng clapped his hands over his ears.

"That man is the prime minister's enemy," he declared. "Though I knew him in the capital, we were never close friends. Please don't mention Shen Xiang to me. If the Yans hear of this, they may make trouble for me."

Then he stood up.

"Since you have public duties to attend to, sir," he said, "I dare not detain you any longer."

After such a rebuff, the prefect had to leave.

"Judging by Feng's fear of the prime minister, he can hardly be sheltering Shen Xiang," he thought on the way back. "Perhaps the man was murdered by those runners after all. Or he may have called on Feng and been refused admittance, then gone to somebody else he knew."

Upon his return to the yamen, he summoned the four people in the case again.

"What other friends did your husband have in this district apart from Secretary Feng?" he asked Shunü.

"None, Your Honour."

"When did your husband leave? And when did they tell you he had disappeared?"

"My husband left the inn yesterday before lunch with Li Wan. At about four in the afternoon Zhang Qian went into town saying he was going to fetch them, and didn't come back till after dark. 'Brother Li is staying with your husband in Secretary Feng's house,' he told me. 'I shall go early tomorrow morning to call for them.' Today Zhang was out all morning, but he and Li came back without my husband. They must have murdered him! If my husband wasn't at Secretary Feng's house yesterday, Li should surely have looked for him and Zhang should have been worried too. Why should they reassure me? It's obvious what must have happened. They arranged on the road for Li to kill him that night, and this morning Zhang went back to town to help bury the corpse; then they returned to tell me my husband was missing. Avenge an unhappy woman, Your Honour!"

"I believe you are right," said the prefect.

And when Zhang and Li protested, he silenced them.

"Fine runners you are!" he exclaimed. "If you didn't plot his death, you allowed yourselves to be bribed into letting him escape. What more have you to say?"

He ordered his men to give them thirty strokes with the heavy bastinado; yet even when bleeding and torn they would not confess. Shunü was weeping bitterly, and pity for her made the prefect have the runners put to torture; but naturally they would not admit to a murder they had not committed, and though they were tortured twice they maintained a stubborn silence. When the prefect ordered them to be tortured again, however, they knew they could not stand any more.

"Shen Xiang cannot be dead, Your Honour," they pleaded.

If you will send officers with us, we promise to find him within a certain time and restore him to his wife."

Because the prefect was not certain of their guilt, he agreed. Shunu was sent to stay in a nunnery, while Zhang and Li were chained and despatched with four militiamen to find Shen, being ordered to report at the yamen every five days. The innkeeper was released, and a full report of the case was sent to the military commissioner.

Zhang and Li were loaded with chains and watched in turns by the four militiamen, who took their few taels of travelling money for food and drink, and sold their sword for liquor too. In a large district like this, through which travellers were constantly passing, they had not the slightest hope of finding the missing man. The search was simply a means of escaping torture.

Shunü, who was staying in the nunnery, went every five days to weep and wail in the yamen and threaten to commit suicide. And since the prefect could not solve the case, he demanded that the runners find Shen by a certain date. He called Zhang and Li in dozens of times and gave them so many strokes with the bastinado when they failed to find their prisoner that they could hardly move. At last Zhang Qian fell ill and died. And Li Wan, left alone, went to the nunnery to plead with the concubine.

"I am desperate," he told her, "so I will tell you the truth. Before we left Xuanfu, Secretary Jin Shao told us that Governor Yang had ordered us to kill your husband on the way, then get a certificate from the local authorities to close the matter. But although we agreed, naturally we would never have done such a cruel thing. As Heaven is my witness, however your husband escaped we had nothing to do with his disappearance; and if that is not the truth may my whole family perish! Now every five days the prefect summons me to demand the prisoner, and Brother Zhang has already been beaten to death. How unfair it will be if I die too! For your husband is *not* dead, and you are bound to meet again. So please have pity on me, ma'am, and stop weeping at the yamen. Give me a little more time in which to find him. You will be doing a good deed if you save my wretched life."

"I find it hard to believe that you have not murdered my husband," replied Shunü. "But since you say so, I'll stop going to the yamen and let you take your time looking for him. Mind you search hard, though, and leave no stone unturned."

Li Wan assented and left.

The prefect had set a time limit for the recapture of Shen Xiang and summoned the runners constantly because Shen was an important criminal wanted by Governor Yang, and because his concubine kept coming to beg that justice be done. At last, however, Li Wan's luck turned, and something happened to save his life. Governor Yang and Censor Lu had been taking counsel day and night how best to flatter the Yan family, in the hope that they might soon be ennobled; but now Secretary Wu Shilai in the Ministry of War heard of Yang Shun's slaughter of innocent people to gain credit, and presented a memorial denouncing him indignantly and accusing Lu Kai of abetting him in his evil courses. The emperor, who was then offering sacrifices to invoke the blessing of Heaven, was furious to hear of this massacre for it meant that the harmonious influences must have been impaired. He ordered the imperial police to arrest the culprits and bring them to the capital for punishment. Since the emperor was angry, Yan Song could not save his protégés entirely; but by putting in a good word for them he contrived that they should merely be deprived of their ranks instead of executed. Thus Yang Shun and Lu Kai, who had killed innocent citizens to curry favour with the mighty, simply covered themselves with shame.

When the Prefect of Jining heard that Yang Shun had been dismissed from office, he was willing to let Shen Xiang's case drop; the more so since Shunü had stopped coming to beg him to take action, and one of the runners was dead while the other kept entreating him to be merciful. So the prefect freed Li Wan from his chains and gave him a writ ordering him to make a careful search for the missing man, which was tantamount to releasing him. Li Wan felt as relieved as a criminal who receives an amnesty. After kowtowing again and again, he left the yamen and made off as fast as he could. Since he had no money left, he begged his way home.

Meanwhile Shen Xiang had been staying in Secretary Feng's secret chamber for many months, learning all that was happening outside from his host, and rejoicing to think that Shunü was still in the nunnery near by. After a year, when Zhang Qian had died, Li Wan had fled, and the case was dropped, Feng vacated three inner chambers for Shen Xiang so that he could study in the house, but would not allow him out nor let outsiders know of his presence. And because he was harbouring an outlaw in his house, Feng did not take up office again after completing his three years of mourning.

Time sped like an arrow, and soon eight years had passed. Yan Song's wife died, but instead of accompanying his mother's coffin to their home in the country Yan Shifan persuaded the prime minister to obtain permission for him to remain in the capital "to wait on his father." In fact, however, he spent the whole period of mourning drinking and enjoying himself with his concubines; and because the emperor was himself a dutiful son, when he heard of this he was displeased. There was a priest at that time named Lan Daoxin, who was able to commune with spirits, and the emperor summoned him to ascertain whether his ministers were good or bad.

"I summon only real deities from the upper regions who speak the truth and cannot flatter," said the priest. "If the oracle happens to offend Your Majesty, I hope you will pardon me."

"I desire to hear the truth from Heaven," replied the emperor. "This in no way concerns you, and I shall certainly not be angry with you."

Then the priest traced a charm and read an incantation, whereupon the sand on his tray began to move and the following lines appeared on it:

On a high hill grows foreign grass;
Both father and son are ministers of state;
The sun and moon have lost their brightness,
And heaven and earth are upside-down.

"Can you explain this to me?" asked the emperor.

"I am an ignorant man," replied the priest. "I cannot understand it."

"*I* understand it," said the emperor. "A high hill stands for the character Song, and foreign grass for Fan. This is therefore a reference to Yan Song and Yan Shifan. I have long suspected that they were usurping authority and injuring the state, and now that Heaven has confirmed this I shall know how to deal with them. See that you do not say a word of this to others."

The priest kowtowed.

"I shall not speak of it to anyone," he promised. Then, taking his reward, he left.

After that the emperor began to treat Yan Song coldly, and a censor named Zou Yinglong took this opportunity to present a memorial to the throne impeaching the prime minister and his son. He pointed out that Yan Shifan had taken advantage of his father's position to sell official posts and ranks and commit other crimes, and urged that he should be executed. He also recommended that since Yan Song had encouraged his profligate son and gathered a clique to injure good people, he should be dismissed from his post in order to reform the government. The emperor was delighted to receive this memorial. He promoted Zou to the rank of an advisor to the Board of Transmission and sent Yan Shifan to be tried by the chief justice, who banished him to the frontier. Yan Song was ordered to retire to the country too. Soon after this the Inspecting Censor of Jiangxi, Ling Run, reported that Yan Shifan had refused to do military service but was acting as a local despot, seizing people's property, sheltering outlaws, making secret overtures to the Japanese pirates and plotting high treason. The emperor decreed that the case should be investigated, and when the chief justice reported that the charges were true Yan Shifan was promptly executed and all his property confiscated. As for Yan Song, he ended his days in an old men's home, while all those who had suffered at his hands had their property and posts restored.

When Feng heard this good news, he lost no time in telling Shen Xiang that now he could go out, and Shen hurried to the nunnery to look for Shunü. After embracing each other they wept. At the time of leaving Shaoxing, Shunù was nearly three months gone with child, and she had given birth to a son in the nunnery who was now ten years old. Shen was happy to find she had taught the boy herself, so that he could already read the Five Classics.

Feng decided to go to the capital to apply for an official post, and he advised Shen to accompany him to clear his father's name, leaving his concubine for the time being with the Feng family. Shen took his advice, and they travelled to Beijing. When Feng called on Advisor Zou, told him of the injustice done to Shen Lian and his sons, and showed him a report written by Shen Xiang, Zou promised to take the matter up. The next day Shen Xiang sent in his report; and soon an imperial decree was issued stating that since Shen Lian had been killed on account of his loyalty to the state, his official status should be restored and he should be posthumously promoted one rank to commend his virtue. His wife and son should return home, and their confiscated property should be returned in full by the local authorities. Shen Xiang, who had long been a government stipendiary, was now appointed a magistrate.

Then Shen Xiang addressed the following memorial to the throne:

"When my father, Shen Lian, was at Bao'an and saw Governor Yang Shun slaughter innocent people for the sake of personal aggrandizement, he wrote verses to express his indignation. Then the censor Lu Kai, acting on secret instructions from Yan Shifan, inspected the area and conspired with Yang to execute my father and kill my two brothers. I myself barely escaped with my life. Thus the unjustly slain received no burial, and our family was nearly wiped out. No other family can have suffered as much as ours! Now Yan Shifan has been punished; but as long as Yang Shun and Lu Kai remain alive, those wrongly slain at the frontier have not been avenged, and the three murdered members of my family must be wailing in the nether regions. I fear this is not in accordance with the requirements of law and justice."

The emperor sanctioned Shen's request, and Yang and Lu were taken to the capital, condemned to death, and sent to gaol to await execution. Then Shen Xiang went to take his leave of Feng before going to Yunzhou to escort his mother and youngest brother back to the capital to live near his friend. After that he intended to go to Bao'an to find his father's remains and take them home for burial.

"I have received news of your mother from Yunzhou," said Feng. "She is well, and your youngest brother is already studying in the district school. Let me send someone to fetch them, while you go in search of your father's remains that is your most important task. You can join your mother when that is done."

Shen agreed and travelled with all speed to Bao'an, where he searched for two days without finding a single clue. On the third day he was sitting down to rest by the roadside when an old man came out of a nearby house and invited him in to have some tea. Shen saw a scroll hanging on the wall on which were mounted two memoranda of Zhuge Liang bearing a date, but no signature. He gazed at this intently, as if unable to tear his eyes away.

"Why are you so interested in that scroll?" asked the old man.

"May I ask who wrote it?" inquired Shen.

"It was written by my deceased friend, Shen Lian."

"Why do you keep it?"

"My name is Jia Shi. When Mr. Shen was sent to stay here
he lodged in my house, and we became sworn brothers. When
tragedy overtook him I was afraid of being involved, and fled
to Henan; but I took these two pieces of writing with me and
mounted them on one scroll. Whenever I look at it, I feel as
if I were seeing my old friend again. Only after Governor
Yang was dismissed dared I return here. Shen Lian's wife and
his youngest son, Shen Qiu, have moved to Yunzhou, where I
frequently go to see them; and I have just sent a man to tell
them that the Yans have fallen and Mrs. Shen's wrongs can
now be avenged. I expect young Mr. Shen will come before
long to fetch his father's coffin; so I have hung this scroll in
the hall, in order that he may recognize his father's writing."

Shen Xiang hastily kowtowed, addressing Jia Shi as his uncle
and benefactor.

"Who are you?" asked Jia, having helped him to rise.

"I am Shen Xiang, and this is my father's writing."

"I heard that Yang Shun sent runners to your district to
seize you, so that he could destroy your whole family," said
Jia. "I thought you had been murdered by him. How did you
escape?"

As Shen told him all that had happened in Jining, Jia exclaimed in pleasure and surprise, then told his servants to prepare a meal for his guest.

"You must know where my father was buried," said Shen
Xiang. "Will you show me the place so that I can pay my
respects?"

"After your father was murdered in gaol, I stole his body
and gave it burial," replied Jia. "But I have never dared
speak of this before. Now you can take his remains to your
home, and my efforts will not have been wasted."

They were on the point of leaving when a young gentleman
rode up.

"What a coincidence!" cried Jia, pointing to the newcomer.
"Here is your younger brother."

And indeed it was Shen Qiu who alighted to greet them.

"This is your eldest brother, Shen Xiang," Jia told him.

The brothers felt as if they were meeting in a dream, and embracing each other they wept. Then with Jia leading the way, the three of them went together to Shen Lian's grave — a mound covered with wild brambles and grass. The old man bade them kowtow, and they fell crying to the ground. But soon Jia urged them to rise.

"We must discuss important business now," he said. "Don't give way to grief."

At that the brothers dried their tears.

"When your two brothers were unjustly killed," Jia told them, "there was a kind gaoler with a sense of justice named Mao, who pitied them and buried them west of the city. Though Mao is dead now, I know the place. You had better take their remains with your father's coffin, so that the sons' spirits can dwell with their father's. What do you think?"

"We could ask nothing better, uncle," they replied.

That same day they went with Jia to the west of the city and were overcome with grief at the sight of the place. The next day they prepared coffins and chose an auspicious date on which to open the graves and remove the three corpses, which, thanks to the loyalty and integrity of the dead men, had not decomposed in the least. After shedding more tears, the brothers ordered a carriage to take the three coffins away, then said farewell to Jia Shi.

"I would like to have this scroll to hang in our ancestral temple," said Shen Xiang. "I hope you will agree, uncle."

Jia thereupon gave them the scroll, and when they had thanked him with tears in their eyes they left. Shen Qiu took the coffins to Zhangjiawan, whence they would be conveyed by boat, while Shen Xiang went back alone to Beijing to see his mother. Then, after making his report to the authorities, he thanked Feng for his assistance and left for home.

All the officials in the capital were full of praise for Shen Lian's loyalty and justice, and admired the brothers for travelling so far with the coffins; therefore they sent them gifts,

money and travelling credentials. Shen Xiang, however, accepted only one credential. When he reached Zhangjiawan he
chartered a large junk, which a hundred men towed rapidly
along. In a few days they reached Jining, where Shen Xiang
had the junk moored while he went alone into the city to let
the Feng family know that all was well; then he escorted Shunü
and her ten-year-old son to the boat. They paid their respects
first to Shen Lian's coffin, then to Shen Xiang's mother; and
when the old lady saw how big her grandson was, she was
overjoyed. She had believed the whole family destroyed; but
now she had her sons and grandson with her, while all their
former enemies had died in misery. This shows that the wicked
invariably come to a bad end, whereas the good prosper at last.

When they reached Shaoxing in Zhejiang Province, old Mr.
Meng and his daughter, Shen Xiang's wife, welcomed them
six or seven miles outside the city. Thus the whole family was
reunited, joy mingling with their sadness. As the boat moored
at the harbour, the local officials came to pay their respects
to the dead; all the former property of the Shen family was
restored; and after the two brothers had interred the coffins
in their ancestral graveyard, they observed three years of
mourning so dutifully that their praise was on everyone's lips.
The local governor also had a temple built for Shen Lian,
where sacrifices were held in spring and autumn; and the
scroll with his handwriting has been kept there to this day.

After the three years of mourning Shen Xiang went back
to the capital and was appointed a magistrate. Since he proved
a good official, he was soon promoted to a prefectship.
Shunü's son passed the examinations early in his career, and
became a palace graduate during the same year as his uncle,
Shen Qiu; and all their descendants were scholars. Because
Feng had saved Shen Xiang's life, the whole capital praised
his gallantry, and he was appointed Minister of Civil Affairs.
One day he dreamed that Shen Lian called on him and said:
"Because I am loyal and just, Heaven has made me the
guardian spirit of Beijing. You are to be the guardian spirit

of Nanjing.   Tomorrow at noon we must go to our respective posts."

Feng woke up puzzled.   But the next day at noon he suddenly saw carriages coming to welcome him, and passed peacefully away.   Thus the two friends became deities.

Loyal and just during life, they are now immortal
As gods who will be known through eternity.
All evil-doers will certainly go to Hell,
For thus is made manifest the justice of Heaven.

The Tattered Felt Hat

Now if Fate is against it, 'tis folly to wed;
But if Fate has ordained it, you've nothing to dread;
Though the billows roll high and the thunderclouds form,
Still your conjugal vessel will weather the storm!

During the Zheng De period (1506-1521), there lived in the main street of Kunshan in Suzhou Prefecture a man named Song Dun, who came of a long line of officials and whose wife belonged to the Lu family. They engaged in no trade but lived on the rental from Song's ancestral estate, and though they were over forty had neither son nor daughter.

One day Song said to his wife, "You know the proverb: Bring up sons for your old age and store up grain against famine. You and I are over forty, yet we have no children. Time flies like an arrow and soon our hair will be white, but who will see to our funeral?" Saying this, he shed tears.

"Your forebears were good men who did no evil and you are their only descendant," said his wife. "Heaven will never let your line die out. After all, children can be born to elderly couples. If the time is not ripe, even if children are born to you they will die young; and you will just have a great deal of work for nothing, and a great deal of needless grief."

Song nodded his agreement. He was wiping away his tears when they heard a cough from the hall and someone called out, "Is Yufeng at home?"

It was the custom in Suzhou, regardless of social status, for friends to call each other by their second name; and Song Dun's second name was Yufeng.

Song cocked his head to listen, and when the visitor called

197

out a second time he recognized the voice of his friend Liu Shunquan. Liu had inherited a great junk in which he carried goods for various merchants to different provinces; and because he had prospered in this traffic he kept all his property on the boat. The junk itself was worth several hundred taels of silver, being made entirely of fragrant *nanmu* wood. In the south, with its network of rivers and canals, many families follow the waterman's trade.

Liu Shunquan was Song Dun's best friend. Thus upon hearing his voice Song joined him immediately. Instead of bowing ceremoniously, each shook his clasped hands in greeting. Then they sat down and tea was served as usual.

"How is it that you had time to call today?" asked Song.

"I have come to borrow something from you," replied Liu.

Song smiled.

"What can you lack on your splendid boat that you want to borrow from my poor house?" he asked.

"I wouldn't trouble you for anything else, but you have enough and to spare of this. That is why I am presuming on your kindness."

"Certainly, I won't grudge you anything I have."

Now Song Dun and his wife, being childless, had been burning incense and offering prayers for a son in many temples, and had made wrappers and bags of yellow cloth to carry the paper cash used in sacrifice. After each such pilgrimage they would hang these very reverently in their Buddhist shrine at home. Liu Shunquan was forty-six, five years older than his friend, but he had no son either. Recently he had heard that a salt merchant from Huizhou had built a temple to the goddess of child-birth outside the West Gate of Suzhou in order to pray for offspring, and that this temple was always thronged with pilgrims. Since Liu had to go to Fengqiao just outside Suzhou on business, he decided to offer incense at this temple; but having no cloth bags to hold the sacrificial paper he had come here to borrow some. When he explained this, however, Song remained silent.

"Don't you want to lend them?" asked Liu. "If I spoil one, I shall give you two new ones in its place."

"It's not that at all," replied Song. "I was thinking that if the goddess there is so powerful, I would like to accompany you. When is your boat leaving?"

"Straightaway."

"My wife and I have two sets of bags and wrappers. We can take one each."

"Very good."

When Song went in to tell his wife that he meant to go to Suzhou to offer incense, she was pleased too. Then from the wall of their Buddhist shrine he took down the two sets of bags and wrappers, one for himself and the other for his friend.

"I'll go on ahead and wait for you aboard," said Liu. "Come as soon as you can. The junk is under Sima Bridge at the West Gate. If you don't mind our rough and ready ways, you can share our simple meals. Don't trouble to bring rice." ·

Having agreed to this and hastily packed some incense, candles, sacrificial paper and other offerings, Song put on a new white silk gown and went straight to the West Gate to board the junk. With a fair wind they covered over twenty miles in less than half a day, and moored at Fengqiao as dusk was falling. An old poet wrote of this place:

> As the moon sets, crows caw under a frosty sky;
> Near the maples and fishermen's fires my sleep is troubled;
> And the toll of midnight bells from Hanshan Temple
> Reaches the traveller's boat.

The next morning they rose before dawn, washed, had a simple meal, rinsed their mouths and hands, and put the paper cash in the yellow wrappers and the other paper offerings and invocations in the yellow bags. Then, these bags round their necks, they went ashore and walked slowly to the temple. It was barely dawn, and though the temple gate was open the gate to the shrine was still closed; so they wandered through the covered walks admiring the buildings until the temple gate creaked and an acolyte appeared, who invited them in. No other pilgrims had arrived yet, and the candlesticks were still empty; but the acolyte lit their candles at the temple lamp and took their invocations to intercede for them with the goddess. After Liu and Song had offered incense and worshipped, each gave a few dozen coins to the acolyte, burned the paper cash and left. Liu invited Song back to his boat, but Song declined. Then Liu returned his wrapper and bag to Song, and after thanking each other they separated, Liu returning to Fengqiao to meet some merchants.

Since it was still early, Song decided to go to the East Gate to get a boat home, and was just starting off when he heard groaning near by. Upon investigating, he found a low matting shed propped against the temple wall; and in this shed an old monk lay dying, too weak to answer any questions. Song was gazing at the monk with concern when a man accosted him.

"Why are you staring at him, sir?" asked the stranger. "Do you want to do a good deed?"

"What good deed can I do?"

"This monk comes from Shaanxi. He is seventy-eight this year and says he has never eaten meat all his life — he did nothing but chant the Buddhist sutras. Three years ago he started collecting alms here to build a temple; but when he could find no patron he built this shed and settled down here to go on chanting his sutras. There is a vegetarian eating-house near by, where he used to go for a meal each morning; but he never ate anything afternoon. Some people who were sorry for him gave him money and rice with which he paid the eating-house, never keeping a cent for himself. Since recently he fell ill, he has eaten nothing for a fortnight. Two days ago he could still open his mouth to speak, and when we asked him why he was clinging to life in spite of so much suffering he told us that his time was not up and he must wait another two days. Today he can no longer speak, and may die at any moment. If you feel sorry for him, sir, why don't you buy him a simple coffin and cremate him? That would be a good deed. When

he said his time had not yet come, he may have meant that
he was waiting for you."

"I came here today to pray for a son," thought Song. "If
I do a good deed before I go back, Heaven will surely hear
my prayer."

So he asked: "Is there an undertaker here?"

"Yes. There's Mr. Chen's shop just round the corner."

"Could I trouble you to take me there?"

The other led Song to the undertaker's shop, where they
found Mr. Chen supervising his men as they sawed wood.

"I have brought you a customer, Mr. Chen," said the
stranger.

"If you want to choose wood for a coffin, sir," said the undertaker, "we have the genuine, two-ply, superfine Maoyuan
wood inside. If you want one ready-made, just take your pick
of those we have here."

"I want a ready-made one," Song told him.

"This is the finest quality," said Chen, pointing to one.
"This costs three taels."

Before Song could begin to bargain with him, the stranger
put in: "This gentleman wants to do a good deed by buying
a coffin for the old monk in that shed. This will reflect credit
on you too, Mr. Chen, so don't charge him too much."

"If that's the case," replied the undertaker, "how dare I
make a profit? You can have it for cost price — one tael and
sixty cents — but not a cent less."

"That is fair enough," said Song.

Then he thought: "The silver I brought with me is worth
little over half a tael, and I have less than one hundred coppers left after offering incense. That means even if I give him
all I have, it's less than half the price. . . . I know what to
do! Liu Shunquan's boat is not far away."

"I agree to that price," he told the undertaker. "But I must
call on a friend to borrow the money. I'll be back presently."

Mr. Chen made no objection.

"As you like, sir," he said.

The other man, however, was annoyed.

"You offered to do a good deed, but now you are backing out," he declared. "If you have no money, why did you come here?"

While he was still speaking, a number of people pass-ed down the street saying what a pity it was that the monk whom they had heard chanting sutras a fortnight ago was now dead.

"Do you hear that, sir?" demanded the stranger. "The old monk is dead. He is watching intently in the nether regions to see whether you will bury him or not."

Song did not reply immediately.

"I have agreed to take this coffin," he was thinking, "and if I don't find Liu at Fengqiao I can't just sit there waiting for him. A tradesman doesn't care who buys his goods; so if some other customer comes along and offers a little more, Mr. Chen will sell this coffin to him. Then I shall be breaking my promise to the monk."

Accordingly, he took out his silver and asked for the balance to weigh it. To his surprise, he found that because it was an ingot it weighed more than it looked; in fact it was worth over seventy cents. Having handed this to the undertaker, he took off his new white silk gown.

"This gown cost more than one tael," he said. "But if you think it worth less, let me leave it with you as a deposit which I shall redeem later. If you are willing to take it, however, please count it in."

"I will make bold to take it, sir," said the undertaker, "if you will excuse my presumption." So he accepted the silver and the gown.

Then Song took from his head a silver pin worth about twenty cents of silver and gave it to the man who had brought him here.

"I'll trouble you to exchange this silver pin for some coppers to pay for the miscellaneous funeral expenses," he said.

"What a good heart the gentleman has!" cried all who were

watching in the shop. "Since he has paid for the major expenses, we local people ought to pay for the minor ones." And they went off to collect money.

When Song went back to the old monk's hut and found him indeed dead, he wept as bitterly as if he was one of his kinsmen. Although unable to account for the sharpness of his grief, he could not bear to gaze at the dead man, but turned away with tears in his eyes. By the time he reached the East Gate the regular passenger boat had gone, so he hired a sampan to take him home. His return so late at night without his gown but with a sad look on his face made his wife think he must have been fighting. She hastily asked what had happened.

"It's a long story," replied Song, shaking his head.

After going into the Buddhist shrine to hang up the two sets of bags and wrappers and kowtow before the image, he went back to his room, sat down and asked for some tea. Then he told his wife the whole story of the monk.

"You did the right thing," she said. "I don't blame you."

His wife's goodness turned Song's grief to joy.

At the fifth watch that night, while they were both sleeping, Song dreamed that the old monk had come to his house to thank him.

"You were fated to have no son," said the monk, "and your span of life was destined to end today. But because you showed such charity, Heaven has decreed that you shall live for another six or seven years; and because you are my benefactor I shall become a son in your house to repay you for your kindness in giving me a coffin."

Song's wife also dreamed that a golden arhat entered her room. She cried out in her sleep, waking her husband, and they told each other their dreams. Uncertain whether to believe them or not, they were lost in wonder.

Plant peas, and you will harvest peas;
Plant gourds, and gourds you reap alone;

Let each man strive to do good deeds,
For each will reap what he has sown!

Then Song's wife conceived and in due course gave birth
to a son whom they called Jin, which means golden, because
she had dreamed of a golden arhat. The parents' happiness
can be imagined. By this time Liu Shunquan had a daughter
called Yichun, and when the children were a few years old
and someone suggested that they should be engaged to each
other, Liu was quite agreeable. Song Dun, however, wanted
his son to marry the daughter of some renowned old family,
not of a waterman. Though he did not raise any objections,
at heart he was unwilling.

When Song Jin was six his father fell ill and died. As the
proverb says: The fortunes of a house depend entirely on its
master, ten women are not as good as one man. After Song
Dun died and his wife took charge of the household there
were several famines, and the district authorities took advantage
of the fact that she was a widow to raise her taxes. Unable
to deal with the situation, she had to sell all her property by
degrees and rent rooms in which to live. To begin with she
put on an appearance of poverty; but later, because there was
no one bringing money in, she reached the end of her resources;
and in less than ten years, having become really poor, she died
of sickness.

After burying his mother Song Jin had nothing left but his
bare hands, and driven out by his landlord had nowhere to
go. Luckily he had learned to write and calculate as a child;
and it happened that a local provincial scholar named Fan,
who had just been appointed the magistrate of Jiangshan in the
province of Zhejiang, wanted an accountant. Someone recommended Song Jin, and when Fan sent for him and saw
how young and handsome he looked, he was favourably impressed. Having tested the lad and found that he could write
both standard characters and a free running hand and had
mastered both multiplication and division, Fan made him stay

in his library, gave him a new suit of clothes and dined with
him at his own table. It seemed nothing was too good for the
young man. Then, choosing an auspicious day, Magistrate
Fan set off in the official junk with Song Jin for his new post.

Now though Song Jin was poor he came from an old family,
therefore now that he was Magistrate Fan's accountant he would
not lower himself to behave like a lackey or allow the servants
to take liberties with him. Fan's stewards, who had hoped to
take advantage of his youth, did not like the airs he gave
himself; and when their party reached Hangzhou and had to
continue their journey by land they approached the magistrate.

"This boy Song Jin is here to write and keep accounts for
you, sir," they said. "He ought to know his place. But he has
no manners at all, and you have been far too good to him. It
doesn't matter letting him sit and eat with you on board ship;
but once we are travelling by land you ought to keep him at
a proper distance, sir. We humbly suggested that the most
satisfactory thing would be to make him write a covenant declaring himself your bondsman; for then he will not dare take
liberties later in the yamen."

Like wax in their hands, the magistrate let himself be persuaded. But when he called Song Jin to his cabin and bid him
draft such a covenant, Song Jin naturally refused. After pressing him for some time the magistrate grew angry, and ordered his men to strip the lad and drive him away. Then they
laid rough hands on Song Jin, tore off all his clothes except
for a shirt and drove him ashore, where he stood for several
minutes speechless with anger. Sedan-chairs and horses were
waiting on the bank for Magistrate Fan, but Song Jin had to
turn away with tears in his eyes. With no money or valuables
on him, he begged for food in the streets by day and sheltered
in old temples by night. Poor as he was, because he came from
an old family he still had some pride. He would not clamour
for alms like those beggars who fawn and cringe without any
sense of shame. If he got something to eat, well and good;
if not, he would go hungry. In this way, eating one meal and

missing the next, he soon became pale and thin and lost all his former good looks.

When lovely flowers are washed by rain,
  Their crimson hue is lost;
And fragrant herbs will fade away,
  Their verdure nipped by frost.

It was then late autumn, the wind was chilly, and it suddenly began to pour with rain. Thinly clad and half starved, Song Jin shivered hungrily in the War God's Temple at Beixinguan, not daring to put so much as his head outside from seven in the morning till noon, when at last the rain stopped and he tightened his belt and ventured out. He had not taken many steps when he met a man whom he recognized at once as his father's best friend, Liu Shunquan. Too ashamed to face him, Song Jin walked on with lowered head and downcast eyes. But Liu, who had recognized him too, laid hold of him from behind.

"Aren't you Song Jin?" he asked. "How did you get into this state?"

Song Jin shed tears and clasped his hands before him as he bowed.

"I am so shabbily dressed that I dared not greet you, uncle," he said. "But since you ask me. . . ." He proceeded to explain how the magistrate had abused him.

"Poor boy!" said Liu. "If you would like to work on my boat, I shall see that you have enough to eat and wear."

Song Jin fell on his knees.

"If you will have me, uncle," he declared, "I shall look on you as my second father!"

Liu then led Song Jin to the river, and went aboard first to tell his wife what he had done.

"This suits both sides," said Mrs. Liu. "I have no objection at all."

Thereupon Liu beckoned to the lad from the stern, bidding him come aboard; and having taken off the old cloth gown he was wearing he gave it to Song Jin, then led him aft to see his wife and Yichun, who was standing there too.

"Bring some rice for him to eat," said Liu, when Song had walked back to the stern.

"There is rice," replied Mrs. Liu, "but it is cold."

"We have hot tea on the stove," put in Yichun.

She filled an earthenware pitcher with boiling tea, while Mrs. Liu took some pickled vegetables and cold rice from the cupboard and offered them to Song.

"We can't live as comfortably aboard as at home, Master Song," said Mrs. Liu. "You must just take us as you find us."

As Song Jin started on the rice and pickles, it began to drizzle again.

"There's an old felt hat in the back cabin," said Liu to his daughter. "Fetch that for Master Song to wear."

Finding one side of the hat torn, Yichun deftly took a needle and thread from her hair and sewed it up, then tossed it on the cabin roof.

"Here!" she called. "Take this!"

Song Jin put on the old felt hat, and when he had washed down the cold rice with tea Liu told him to clear up and swab the deck. Then Liu went ashore to see some merchants, not coming back till night. The next morning when he got up, he saw Song Jin sitting in the stern doing nothing.

"The boy has only just come here," thought Liu. "We mustn't let him get into lazy ways."

So he shouted: "Hey, there! After eating our food and wearing our clothes, you shouldn't sit idle. If you have nothing better to do, you can plait some ropes. They always come in useful."

"Certainly," replied Song quickly. "I'm at your service."

Then Liu gave him a bundle of hemp out of which to make rope.

A man who's by another fed
Will hardly dare to raise his head.

After that Song Jin was careful to keep hard at work from dawn till dusk. Since he was a good clerk and accountant he made up the bills for all the goods they carried, and never slipped in his reckoning; hence the owners of other boats often asked him to take his abacus over and help them make up their accounts, while their clients liked and respected him too as a smart young fellow.

When Liu Shunquan and his wife saw how reliable and useful Song Jin was, they began to treat him better, giving him good food and good clothes and passing him off as their nephew. And since Song was happy and contented, he grew plumper and healthier till all the watermen envied him his good looks.

Soon more than two years had passed.

"I am growing old," thought Liu one day, "and I have only this one daughter. I must find a good husband for her. Someone like young Song would suit us down to the ground, but I wonder what my wife would say to that?"

That evening he drank a good many cups with his wife, then suddenly pointed at his daughter who was beside them.

"Yichun is growing up," he remarked to his wife, "but we haven't married her off yet. What shall we do about it?"

"It's important to find a son-in-law who will support us in our old age," said Mrs. Liu. "Why aren't you doing anything?"

"I've been giving the matter a good deal of thought, but it's hard to find a really suitable man. A clever handsome lad like young Song is one in a thousand, but where can we find another like him?"

"Well, why not marry her to Master Song?"

Liu pretended to be taken aback.

"What?" he cried. "A man without a family to fall back on, who works for me and has not a cent of his own? How can we marry our daughter to him?"

"Master Song comes from an official family and is the son of an old friend of ours," retorted Mrs. Liu. "When his father was alive there was talk of Song Jin marrying our daughter —

have you forgotten that? Though he's had bad luck, he's a handsome young man who can write and make up accounts. Such a son-in-law will be no disgrace to us, and he will look after us when we grow old."

"Are you sure you won't change your mind, my dear?"

"Why should I?"

"Very well then!"

The fact is that Liu, who was afraid of his wife, had long wanted Song Jin for his son-in-law but feared that Mrs. Liu might not agree. Now that she approved he was delighted, and calling Song Jin in he proposed the match in his wife's presence. At first the young man declared himself unworthy; but when he saw that Liu was in earnest and would not ask him for a cent he agreed. Then Liu went to a geomancer to find an auspicious day for the wedding, and having told his wife the date they set sail for Kunshan. There he gave Song Jin a cap and silk gown, and dressed him in new clothes from head to foot so that he looked more handsome than ever, while Mrs. Liu prepared clothes and trinkets for her daughter. When the happy day arrived the kinsmen of both families were invited to a great feast, and Song Jin became Liu's son-in-law. The following day all the relations came to offer congratulations and the feasting continued for three days. After the marriage, it goes without saying, the young couple loved each other dearly. And Liu Shunquan's business prospered too.

Another year and two months passed quickly, and Yichun gave birth to a daughter whom the young parents loved dearly, taking it in turns to carry her. But the baby contracted smallpox just after her first birthday, and physic proved unavailing, for in twelve days she died. In his bitter grief at the loss of this child, Song Jin fell a prey to consumption. Cool in the morning, he was feverish every evening. His appetite failed and he wasted away till he was nothing but skin and bones and could barely drag himself along. At first Liu and his wife called in physicians and questioned fortune-tellers, in the hope that the young man would recover; but his illness went from bad to worse, until after a year he looked more like a ghost than a man and was too weak to write or use his abacus. Then the old couple considered him a thorn in their flesh and longed for his death, but he did not die.

"We were counting on him to support us in our old age," they would complain to each other bitterly. "Yet now look at the state he's in — the walking corpse! He's a dying snake who has coiled himself round our necks and won't be shaken off, and he's ruined our dear daughter's life as well. What can we do? We must think of a way to get rid of this wretch, so that Yichun can find a good husband."

After discussing the matter at length they hit upon a plan, which they kept secret from their daughter. On the pretext that they must collect goods from the north bank of the river, Liu piloted the junk to a desolate spot near Wuxi where nothing could be seen for miles around but lonely hills and the deserted river, void of any sign of life. The wind was slightly against them that day, and Liu deliberately steered out of his course to ground the junk on the sandy shore. He then told Song Jin to get into the river to push the boat off, and cursed him when he proved slow.

"You consumptive devil!" he cried. "If you aren't strong enough to shove off the boat, at least you can save us a little money by cutting some firewood ashore."

Feeling rather ashamed, Song took a chopper and struggled ashore. As soon as he was out of sight his father-in-law pushed the boat off, headed it in the opposite direction, and set off downstream under full sail.

Song reached a wood where he found plenty of timber, but too weak to fell it he picked up some fallen branches and brambles instead and bound them with dry vines into two bundles. Not having the strength to carry them over his shoulder, he decided his best plan was to tie both bundles together with another long vine and drag them after him as a cowherd drags his buffalo. He had trudged some distance when he realized that he had forgotten the chopper and had to go back for it and fasten it to his load, which he then pulled slowly back to the shore. But upon reaching the place where they had moored he found no junk — only the misty river and sandy islets stretching to the horizon. He headed upstream searching as he went, but not a trace of the boat could he find, and as the sun set in the west he knew that he had been abandoned. Having nowhere to go he sobbed bitterly in despair, until, choking, he fell senseless to the ground. When he came to himself he saw an old monk by the shore, but did not know where he came from.

"Where are your companions?" asked the old monk, leaning on his staff. "This is no place in which to linger."

Hastily rising to his feet, Song Jin greeted the old man and told him his name.

"I have been tricked and abandoned by my father-in-law," he said. "Now I am alone with nowhere to turn. I beg you to help me, father, and save my life!"

"My humble monastery is not far from here," replied the monk. "If you will spend the night with me, we can think of some plan tomorrow."

Filled with gratitude, Song Jin followed the monk for a few hundred yards to a thatched building, where the old man struck fire from his flint and cooked some gruel.

"What enmity was there between you and your father-in-law?" he asked.

Song told him how he had married into the waterman's family and fallen ill.

"Do you then hate your father-in-law?" inquired the monk.

"When I was a beggar," replied Song, "he was kind enough to take me into his family. It is my unhappy fate to have fallen ill and been abandoned — how can I blame other people for that?"

"You speak like a good man," said the old monk. "Your illness was caused by grief, so it cannot be cured by any physic but only by purifying your heart and resting. Have you embraced the Buddhist faith? Do you ever chant sutras?"

When Song replied that he had not, the old monk took a book from his sleeve and gave it to him.

"This is the *Vajrapani Dharani* handed down by Buddha," he said. "I will teach you this, and if you read it once a day you will rid yourself of vain desires, improve your health and derive incalculable benefit."

Now since Song Jin had been a monk in his previous existence who spent all his time chanting this sutra, he had only to hear it once today to be able to recite it. He sat down with the old monk to practise yoga and chant the sutra with closed eyes, and as dawn approached fell asleep. When he awoke he found himself seated on a wild, grassy slope with no monk or temple in sight, although the *Vajrapani Dharani* lay in his lap and he could recite it. Marvelling at this, Song rinsed his mouth with water from a pool and chanted the sutra. Immediately his cares seemed to melt away, strength returned to his limbs, and understanding that Providence had sent a saint to earth to save him he bowed to heaven in thanks. He was still homeless, however, like seaweed drifting on the ocean; and he wandered along gnawed by hunger until, catching sight of a building on the wooded hill in front, he determined to ply his old trade once more and beg for food there. Thus it came about that his bad fortune turned to good, and hardships gave place to prosperity.

> *Each time you reach your pathway's end,*
> *You'll find another course;*
> *Each time you reach a fountain-head,*
> *You'll find another source.*

Upon reaching the hill in front, Song Jin found no sign of human life, but there were swords and lances planted between the trees. Puzzled though he was, he pressed forward boldly to the mouldering temple of a local deity, where he discovered eight large chests securely locked and covered with pine branches and straw.

"This must be loot some bandits have hidden," he thought.

"They have planted these swords and lances here to scare people away. I don't know where they stole these things, but I see no reason why I shouldn't take them."

Sticking pine branches in the ground to mark his path, he made his way out of the wood to the river bank. And luck was certainly with him now, for there he found a big junk which had been buffeted in a storm and put in to the shore to have its damaged rudder repaired.

"I come from Shaanxi and my name is Qian," Song Jin told the boatmen, acting as if frightened half out of his wits. "I came south with my uncle to do business; but while passing here we were robbed and my uncle was killed. Because I pretended to be his servant and had been ill for a long time, they spared my life and ordered one of their gang to keep an eye on me in the temple and watch the loot while they went to rob someone else. Luckily a poisonous snake killed the man who was guarding me last night, so I could escape. Will you take me off with you?"

The men in the junk looked sceptical.

"There are eight big chests belonging to my family in the temple, and it isn't far from here," Song assured them. "Won't some of you come ashore and help me carry them to the boat? I promise to give you one chest of goods; but we must make haste. If the robbers come back it will be too late, and we shall be in danger."

Now the men on the boat would travel far in their search for wealth; so as soon as they heard there were eight chests of goods they all volunteered to go. At once sixteen men were picked, who followed Song to the temple with eight poles and quantities of rope. Sure enough, they found eight great chests there, all of them very heavy; but with two men to one chest they were able to take them all. When Song Jin had hidden the lances and swords in the thick undergrowth, they carried the eight chests to the boat. By now the rudder had been repaired too.

"Where do you want to go?" they asked Song.

"I want to go to Nanjing to look for some relatives," he replied.

"We are bound for Guazhou," they said. "We can take you on your way."

They cast off and travelled more than a dozen miles before stopping for the night. Then, believing this Shaanxi merchant — as they took Song to be — to have plenty of money, they bought wine and meat to congratulate him on his escape. The following day a strong westerly wind sprang up, they hoisted sail and in a few days reached Guazhou, only two or three miles from Nanjing. Here Song Jin chartered another small boat, on which he loaded the seven heaviest chests, leaving one chest for the boatmen who had aided him, as he had promised. But how they opened the chest and divided the spoil is another story.

Having put up at an inn by Longjiang toll-gate, Song Jin called in a blacksmith to open the chests and discovered that they were packed with gold, jade and other jewels; for this was the accumulated loot of years, not just a single haul from one family. When Song had sold the contents of one chest for several thousand taels, in order to avoid arousing the innkeeper's suspicion he moved into the city, where he dressed in the finest silk, lived on the fat of the land, and bought slaves to serve him. By selling all but the best jewels in the six remaining cases, he raised tens of thousands of silver taels with which he bought a great mansion inside Yifeng Gate, remodelled the rooms, pavilions and gardens, and furnished the whole most sumptuously. He also opened a pawnshop outside his house, and bought several farms and dozens of bondservants, including ten experienced stewards and four beautiful pages to wait on him. Soon all Nanjing knew of this Mr. Qian, who never stirred from his door but in a carriage or on horseback and whose house was filled with gold and silver.

As the ancients say: A man's way of life affects his health and appearance. Now that Song Jin was rich, he became healthy. He filled out and his cheeks grew ruddy, till he was a different being altogether from the old, haggard Song with his beggarly looks.

When autumn comes, the moon shines yet more bright;
When fortune smiles, a heavy heart grows light.

Let us return now to Liu Shunquan. After tricking his son-in-law into going ashore, Liu headed his boat downstream and set sail before a favourable wind, so that in next to no time they covered thirty miles. While the old couple were secretly rejoicing, Yichun knew nothing of what had happened. Imagining her husband was still on board, she prepared a cordial for him and called to him to come and drink it. When there was no answer to her calls, she assumed he must be sleeping in the stern, and started forward to look for him. Then her mother seized the bowl of physic and hurled it into the river.

"That consumptive devil is gone!" she shouted. "Stop thinking about him!"

"Where is he?" demanded Yichun fearfully.

"Your father saw that he was not going to get better, and was afraid he might infect the rest of us; so he sent him ashore for firewood, then sailed away."

Calling in horror upon heaven and earth, Yichun seized hold of her mother.

"Give me back my husband!" she screamed.

When Liu Shunquan heard sobbing and shouting from the cabin, he came to reason with her.

"Child," he said, "listen to me! If a girl marries the wrong man, she will suffer for it all her life. This consumptive was bound to die sooner or later anyway — he was not the husband destined for you. It's better to make a clean break now, so as not to waste your youth. I shall find you another husband to support you. Stop thinking about Song Jin."

"What have you done?" cried Yichun. "This was a cruel, wicked, vile trick! It was you who proposed this match to Song Jin, and as husband and wife we should live and die together. How can you undo our marriage? Even if he was bound to die, we should have let him die in peace. How could you abandon him in that lonely place? If he dies because of me, I shall kill myself. If you have any feeling for me, quickly take the boat back upstream to find him. Otherwise, every-one will condemn you."

"When the consumptive found the boat gone, he must have made for some village to beg for food," said Liu. "We should never find him. Besides, coming downstream with a fair wind we are miles away. We had better let it go at that. I advise you to give him up."

When Yichun saw that her father would not turn back, she sobbed wildly and ran to the bulwarks to throw herself over-board. Luckily her mother was quick enough to stop her; but Yichun swore that she would take her own life and went on crying as if her heart would break. Her parents, who had never suspected that their daughter would prove so stubborn, were forced to watch her all night; and the next morning they had to agree to go back upstream. But with the wind and current against them they covered only half the distance that day, and that night Yichun wept and wailed again and gave them no peace. By four o'clock in the afternoon of the third day they reached the place where they had stopped before, and Yichun went ashore herself to look for her husband. Finding two bundles of fuel and a chopper which she recognized as theirs, she knew her husband had been back here; but since Song Jin himself was gone the sight of these things made her sadder than ever. Refusing to give up, however, she insisted on making a thorough search, and her father had to accompany her. They walked a long way but saw only dark woods and rugged hills, with no trace of mortal man; and finally Liu per-suaded her to go back to the boat, where she spent another night weeping. On the fourth day, before daybreak, she in-sisted that her father should search with her again; but there was no sign of Song Jin in that desolate country, and Yichun cried all the way back to the junk.

"Where could my husband beg for food in this wild, lonely

place?" she wondered. "After his long illness he could not walk far. He left the chopper by the sandy cliff — he must have drowned himself there!"

Weeping bitterly, she made another attempt to throw herself into the river; but again her father stopped her.

"You can guard my body but not my heart," sobbed Yichun to her parents. "Since I am determined to die, you had better let me die early to rejoin my husband."

The old couple were upset to see the agony their daughter was in.

"Child," they said, "we have done you a wrong. We acted too hastily. But the damage is done now, and it's no use regretting it. Take pity on us, because you're the only child we have; and if you die we shan't survive you long. So forgive us, daughter, and don't take this so much to heart. We shall write a bill and have it posted up in all the villages and towns along the river; so that if he is still alive he will see it and come back. If after three months there is no news, you hold a funeral and sacrifice to him, and we won't grudge any expense."

Then Yichun dried her eyes.

"If you will do that," she said, "I shall die content."

Liu Shunquan immediately wrote a notice asking for news of his son-in-law, and had this posted up in the towns along the river where everyone could see it. But three months passed without any news.

"My husband must really be dead," said Yichun.

She speedily prepared mourning and put it on, then set up a shrine, sacrificed to Song Jin and engaged nine monks to chant masses for three days and three nights. She made an offering of her trinkets too, in order to obtain a blessing on her husband. Their fondness for their daughter made Liu Shunquan and his wife afraid to oppose her; so she mourned for several days, wailing at dawn and again at dusk until all the neighbouring boatmen were moved. When Liu's old clients knew of this not one but felt sorry for Song and pitied his

young wife. And not till after six whole months did Yichun
cease weeping.

"Our daughter has stopped crying at last," said Liu to his
wife then. "Now that she is getting over it, we should urge
her to marry again. For what help can a young widow be to
her old parents in an emergency?"

"You are right," agreed his wife. "But I'm afraid she will
refuse. It will take time to talk her round."

A month later, on the twenty-fourth of the twelfth month.
Liu brought his junk back to Kunshan for New Year. And
that evening, after drinking with a relative, he felt embolden-
ed to reason with his daughter.

"It will soon be New Year," he said. "Why don't you take
off that mourning?"

"A widow should mourn all her life," retorted Yichun.
"How can I take it off?"

"What?" Her father glared at her. "Mourn all your life?
You'll wear mourning or not as I think fit."

When Mrs. Liu heard her husband speak so roughly, she
intervened.

"Let Yichun wear mourning till the end of the year," she
said. "She can take it off after she's sacrificed on New Year's
Eve."

Realizing that her parents meant to put pressure on her,
Yichun started crying again.

"You plotted to kill my husband," she sobbed, "and how
can I lose my chastity and betray Song Jin? I would rather
die in my widow's weeds than live without them."

Liu would have flared up, but his wife scolded him and
pushed him to his cabin to sleep. Yichun cried again all that
night, and on New Year's Eve after sacrificing to her husband
she started weeping once more, till her mother persuaded her
to stop. Then they sat down to their New Year's Eve dinner;
but the old couple were put out to see that their daughter
would touch neither meat nor wine.

"Child," they said, "even if you remain in mourning, what

does it matter if you take a little meat? Young people have to keep up their strength."

"To someone who is waiting for death even these vegetable dishes are too much," replied Yichun. "What meat do I need?"

"If you won't have any meat," said Mrs. Liu, "at least drink a cup of wine to cheer yourself up."

"Not a drop of wine can reach him under the ground," sighed Yichun. "Thinking of him, how can I drink?"

Then she burst into tears again and went fasting to bed. And her parents, seeing that she was not to be persuaded, gave up all attempts to make her remarry.

The following verse was made in praise of Yichun's chastity:

> *Chaste wives and widows of the past*
> *Have not this boatman's lass surpassed;*
> *She'd sooner die than prove untrue,*
> *And more than this no wife can do!*

We shall now go back to Song Jin, who, after a year and eight months in Nanjing, had his affairs in excellent order. Bidding his stewards look after his estates and taking with him three thousand taels of silver, four servants and two handsome pages, he chartered a boat to Kunshan to find his father-in-law. When the neighbours told him that Liu Shun-quan had left for Yizhen three days previously, Song Jin bought cloth with his silver, went to Yizhen, and placed his goods with a well-known agent. The following day when he walked down to the harbour to look for Liu's boat he caught sight in the distance of his wife in deep mourning at the prow, and realizing that she had remained true to him instead of marrying again he was deeply moved. Returning to his lodging, he sought out his landlord.

"There is a beautiful boatwoman in mourning on the river, Mr. Wang," said Song. "I have found out that the boat she is in belongs to Liu Shunquan of Kunshan, whose daughter she is. I lost my wife nearly two years ago, and I would like to take this woman as my second wife."

He took ten taels of silver from his sleeve and gave them to Wang.

"Please buy yourself a drink with this trifle and consent to be my go-between," he begged him. "If you succeed, I shall reward you well. As for the marriage gift to the girl's family, I'm willing to spend up to a thousand taels."

Happy to receive so much silver, Wang went to the wharf and invited Liu Shunquan to a tavern, where he ordered a good meal and asked Liu to take the seat of honour.

"I am a common boatman," said Liu in surprise. "Why do you treat me like this? You must have a reason."

"Drink three cups of wine and then I'll tell you," replied Wang.

"I won't sit down until you have explained," declared Liu, his suspicions aroused.

"In my lodging house," Wang told him, "there is a Mr. Qian from Shaanxi, who possesses thousands of taels of silver. His wife died nearly two years ago, and because he admires your daughter's beauty he would like to marry her; in fact he offers you a marriage gift of a thousand taels and has asked me to act as go-between. I hope you won't refuse."

"Of course we would be only too glad if our child could marry a rich man," replied Liu. "But my daughter is determined to remain a widow. If we so much as hint that she should marry again, she threatens to commit suicide. I'm afraid I must decline your kind offer."

He was starting to leave when Wang pulled him back.

"This feast was Mr. Qian's idea," he said. "I'm only acting as host for him. Since the table is laid, you mustn't go away. It doesn't matter if we fail to make a match of it."

When Liu had sat down and they were drinking, Wang raised the subject again.

"Mr. Qian is very much in earnest over this request," he said. "I hope you will consider it carefully when you go back to your boat."

Liu, however, was so frightened by his daughter's repeated

threats to jump into the river that he did nothing but shake his head, not daring to assent.

When the meal was over they parted, and Wang went back to tell Song Jin what the old boatman had said. Then Song realized that his wife was completely faithful to him.

"Never mind if you were not successful," he said to Wang. "I want to hire his boat to take goods upstream. Do you think he will agree to that?"

"All these boats are for hire," replied Wang. "Of course he will agree."

Indeed, as soon as Wang told Liu that Mr. Qian wished to hire his boat, Liu consented readily. Then Song ordered his servants to move his luggage aboard, leaving the cloth on shore till the next day. When Song Jin came to the junk, dressed in a brocade gown and sable cap and attended by two handsome boys in green velvet coats holding censers and wands, Liu and his wife did not recognize him but took him for a nobleman from Shaanxi. Husband and wife know each other better than anyone else, however; and when Yichun peeped round from the stern of the boat, although she could not swear that it was her husband, she was amazed at the likeness. Then she heard the gentleman call out in her direction as soon as he came aboard:

"I am hungry and would like something to eat. If your rice is cold, give me some hot tea with it."

This set her wondering.

Then the gentleman said to his servant:

"After eating my food and wearing my clothes, you shouldn't stay idle. If you have nothing better to do, you can plait some ropes. They always come in useful."

Since this was exactly what Liu had said to Song Jin when first he came to their boat, it set Yichun wondering even more.

Later, when her father served tea to his passenger, the gentleman said:

"You have a tattered felt hat in your back cabin. Will you lend it to me?"

Too slow-witted to think this strange, Liu went to ask his daughter for the hat. But as Yichun handed it to her father she chanted:

> "Though the felt hat is tattered,
> I mended it myself.
> I think of the wearer of the hat —
> How changed from his former self!"

When the gentleman heard this chanting from the stern, he understood. And after taking the hat from Liu he chanted back:

> "The common fellow has been transformed
> So that his own folk don't know him;
> Though he returns in rich brocade,
> He never forgets the old felt hat."

That night Yichun said to her mother: "I believe this Mr. Qian in our front cabin is none other than Song Jin. How could he know otherwise that we have a tattered felt hat? He looks like my husband, too, and nobody else could have said the things he did. Will you ask him?"

"You silly girl!" laughed her father. "That consumptive devil of yours has probably rotted away long ago. Or if he didn't die, he must be a beggar somewhere. How could he become so rich?"

"When we asked you to take off mourning and marry again, you threatened to drown yourself," said her mother. "But now that you see this rich gentleman, you claim he is your husband. Suppose he says he isn't — won't you lose face?"

Yichun blushed with shame and dared say no more, but Liu called his wife aside.

"Don't snub the girl," he said. "Marriages are made in heaven. The other day Mr. Wang invited me to the tavern and told me this Mr. Qian from Shaanxi is willing to g.ve us a thousand taels if he can marry our girl; but because she's so stubborn, I didn't promise him   Today she actually seems to be interested

in this man; so why not seize the chance to marry her to him?
Then we can live in comfort for the rest of our lives."

"You are right," said his wife. "This Mr. Qian may have
had some such idea in mind when he hired our boat. Tomorrow
you can go and ask him."

"I will," agreed her husband.

The next morning after the gentleman had risen and washed,
he stood at the prow of the junk toying with the felt hat.

"Why do you keep looking at that hat, sir?" asked Liu.

"I like the stitching on it," was the reply. "This must be
the work of a very skilful needlewoman."

"Our daughter sewed it," replied Liu. "It's nothing to speak
of. The other day Mr. Wang brought me a message from you,
sir. I wonder if you were in earnest?"

"What message?" asked the other deliberately.

"He said," replied Liu, "that you lost your wife nearly two
years ago and had never married again, sir, but wanted to make
my daughter your wife."

"Would you be willing?" asked the gentleman.

"This is more than I could hope for," replied Liu. "Of course
I am willing. The only trouble is that my daughter is so loyal
to her last husband that she has determined never to remarry.
So I dare not promise anything."

"How did your son-in-law die?"

"Unfortunately he fell ill with consumption. Then one day
when he went ashore to collect firewood I made the mistake
of thinking he was aboard, and cast off. We posted up notices
asking for news of him for three months, but never found him.
He must have drowned himself in the river."

"No," said the gentleman. "Your son-in-law did not drown
himself. After meeting a holy man who cured him of his illness,
he came into a great fortune. If you want to meet your son-in-
law, please ask your daughter to come here."

Yichun, who had been eavesdropping, sobbed when she heard
this.

"Heartless man!" she cried. "I have mourned for you for

three years, and suffered ten thousand hardships because of you. Why will you still not tell the truth?"

At that Song Jin shed tears too.

"Dear wife!" he called. "Let me see you!"

Then they clasped each other and wept.

"This doesn't seem to be any Mr. Qian, wife," said Liu. "We had better apologize to him."

So the two old people entered the cabin and bowed again and again.

"Father! Mother!" exclaimed Song Jin. "There is no need to be so polite! But please don't abandon me next time I fall ill."

The old couple did not know where to look for shame.

Then Yichun took off her mourning and threw the shrine to her dead husband into the river. Song ordered his servants to pay their respects to their mistress, while Liu and his wife killed a chicken and heated wine to entertain their son-in-law. This was a feast of welcome and a reunion too. When the table was laid, Liu described how his daughter had abstained from meat and wine; and Song, shedding tears, poured wine for his wife and begged her to take some meat. Then he turned to the two old people.

"You abandoned me hoping to kill me," he said. "So there is no love between us and no reason why I should recognize you. It is only for your daughter's sake that I am drinking your wine today."

"If my father had not left you on that shore," protested Yichun, "how could you have become prosperous? Besides, my parents were good to you before that. You should remember their kindness to you, not their cruelty."

"Very well," agreed Song. "I shall do as you say. I have a home and rich landed property now in Nanjing; so you old folk can retire and come there with us to live happily together."

For this Liu and his wife thanked him again and again.

The following day, when Wang the innkeeper heard what had happened, he came to the boat to offer his congratulations, and

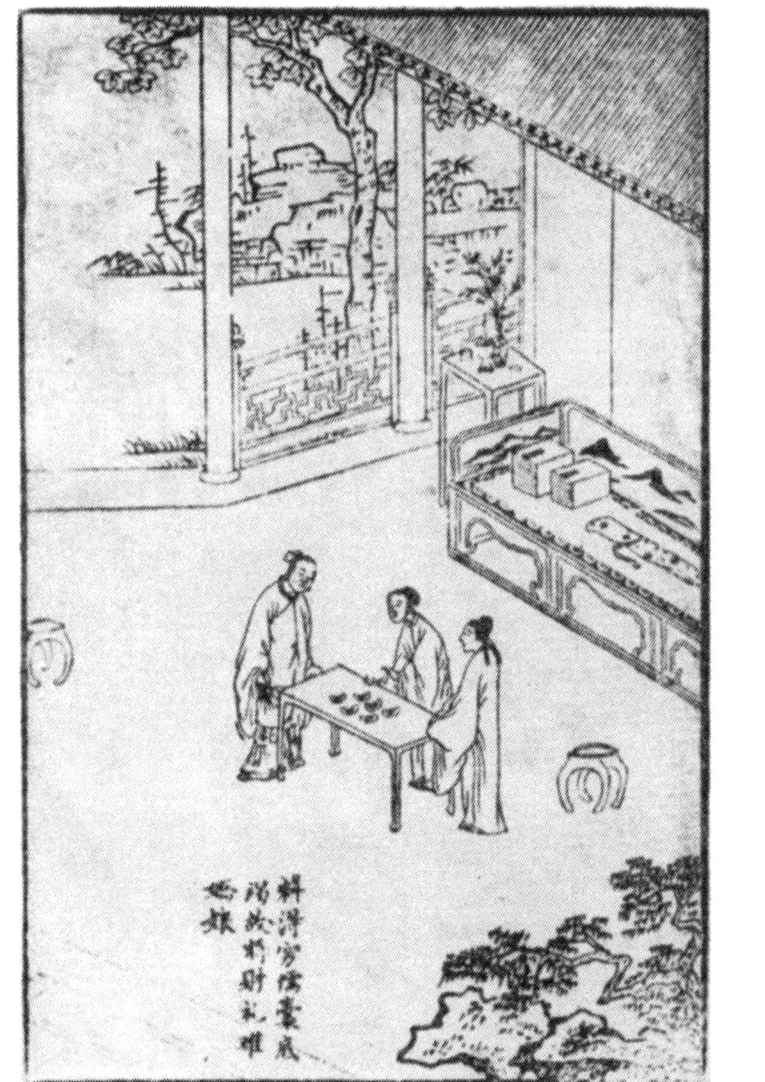

料得芳盟費凝眸
場破約財以謀
也難

杜十娘怒沉百宝箱

they feasted for another day. Song then left three of his servants
with Wang to sell the cloth, while he travelled back by boat
to Nanjing to spend three days in his fine house before going
to Kunshan with his wife to bow before his father's grave. He
also made rich presents to all his kinsmen.

By this time Magistrate Fan was no longer in office but had
come home. When he heard that Song Jin had returned a rich
man, to avoid meeting him on the street and being slighted he
hid himself in the country for over a month, not daring to ven-
ture into town.

After Song Jin had attended to all his business in Kunshan
he went back to Nanjing, where the whole family lived happily,
enjoying their wealth and splendour. When Yichun noticed
that her husband went every morning to the Buddhist shrine to
pray to Buddha and chant sutras, she asked the reason, and Song
Jin told her how the old monk had taught him the *Vajrapani
Dharani* sutra and cured his disease. Thereupon Yichun embraced the faith too and asked her husband to teach her the
sutra, which they chanted together till old age. They both lived
to be over ninety, dying peacefully at last in their beds; and
their descendants remained one of the richest families in Nanjing, many of them passing the official examinations.

The Courtesan's Jewel Box

Our story starts with the invasion of Korea by the Japanese general Hideyoshi in the twentieth year of Wan Li period (1592). When the King of Korea appealed for help, the Son of Heaven sent troops across the sea to save him; and the Board of Treasury proposed that since the grain and silver allocated to the troops were insufficient for the expedition a special tax should be raised by the sale of places in the Imperial Colleges. To this the emperor agreed.

Now this system had many advantages for those with money. In addition to having better facilities for studying and passing the examinations, the students of these colleges were assured of small official posts. Accordingly, the sons of official or wealthy families who did not want to sit for the county examination took advantage of this scheme to purchase a place in one of the Imperial Colleges. So the number of students in both the colleges in Nanjing and Beijing rose to over one thousand each.

One of these students was called Li Jia. A native of Shaoxing in Zhejiang Province, he was the oldest of three sons of a provincial treasurer. Although a licentiate, he had failed to pass the prefectural examination, he had purchased a place in the Imperial College at Beijing under the new system; and during his residence in the capital he went with a fellow-provincial and fellow-student, Liu Yuchun, to the singsong girls' quarter. Here he met a celebrated courtesan called Du Wei, who, because she was the tenth girl in the quarter, was also known as Decima.

She was sweetness and loveliness incarnate;
Her fine eyebrows were arched like distant hills;
Her eyes were as clear as autumn water;
Her face was as fresh as dew-washed lotus;

Her lips were as crimson as ripe cherries.
Ah, the pity of it! that this lovely maid
Should be cast by the roadside in the dust.

Since Decima became a courtesan she had met countless young
men of rich and noble families who had not hesitated to spend
all they possessed for love of her; so the other singsong girls
used to say:

When Decima is at the feast,
The poorest drinker drains a thousand cups;
When in our quarter Decima appears,
All other powdered faces look like ghosts.

Though Li was a gay young fellow, he had never seen such
a beautiful girl. At his first meeting with Decima he was absolutely charmed by her and fell head over heels in love. And
since he was not only handsome and amiable but open-handed
and untiring in his pursuit of her, the attraction soon proved
mutual. Realizing that her mistress was grasping and heartless,
Decima had long wanted to leave her; and now that she saw
how kind and devoted Li was, she wished to throw in her lot
with him. Although the young man was too afraid of his father
to marry her, they fell more and more deeply in love, passing
whole days and nights together in pleasure and remaining as
inseparable as if they were already husband and wife. They
vowed solemnly never to love anyone else.

Their love was deeper than the sea,
And more sublime their faith than mountain peaks.

After Li became Decima's lover, other wealthy men who had
heard of her fame tried in vain to gain access to her. At first
Li spent money lavishly on her, and the procuress, all smiles
and blandishments, waited on him hand and foot. But when
more than a year had sped past, Li's money was nearly exhausted. He could no longer be as generous as he would have
liked, and the old woman began to treat him coldly. The provincial treasurer heard that his son was frequenting the courtesans'

quarter, and sent letter after letter ordering him to come home; but the young man was so enamoured of Decima's beauty that he kept postponing his return. And later, when he heard how angry his father was with him, he dared not go back.

The proverb says that friendship based on money will end once the money is spent. Decima, however, loved Li so truly that the poorer he grew the more passionately attached to him she became. Her mistress told her repeatedly to send Li about his business and, seeing that the girl refused to do so, she began to insult him in the hope that he would leave in anger. But her insults had no effect on Li, who was naturally of a mild disposition, so she could do nothing but reproach Decima every day.

"In our profession we depend on our clients for food and clothing," she said. "As we speed one guest from the front door, another should be coming in by the back. The more clients we have, the more money and silk we shall heap up. But now that this dratted Li Jia has been hanging around for more than a year, it's no use talking about new clients — even the old ones have stopped coming. We seem to have got hold of a Zhong Kui[1] who keeps out devils, because not a soul will come near us. There'll soon be no smoke in our chimney. What's to become of us?"

Decima, however, would not quietly submit to this. "Mr. Li did not come here empty-handed," she retorted. "Look at all the money he has spent here!"

"That was before: it's *now* I'm talking about. You tell him to give me a little money today for fuel and rice for the two of you. In other houses the girls are a money-tree which needs only to be shaken to shower down riches: it's just my bad luck that I've got a girl who keeps the money away. Every day I have to worry how to make ends meet, because you insist on supporting this pauper. Where do you think our food and clothes are coming from? Go and tell that beggar of yours that, if he's

---

[1] According to Chinese mythology, Zhong Kui was a chaser of ghosts.

any good at all, he must give me some silver; then you can go off with him and I'll buy another girl. Wouldn't that suit us both?"

"Do you really mean it?" demanded Decima.

"Have I ever told a lie?" replied the old woman, who, knowing that Li had not a cent left and had pawned his clothes, thought it would be impossible for him to raise any money. "Of course I mean it."

"How much do you want from him?"

"If it were anyone else, I would ask for a thousand taels; but I'll ask a poor devil like him for only three hundred. With that I could buy another girl to take your place. But there's one condition: he must pay me within three days, then I shall hand you over straight away. If he hasn't paid after three days, I'll give him a good beating with my cane, the wretch, and drive him out, gentleman or no gentleman! Nobody will be able to blame me either."

"Although he is away from home and has run out of money," said Decima, "he should be able to raise three hundred taels. But three days is too little. Can't you make it ten?"

"The young fool has nothing but his bare hands," thought the procuress. "Even if I give him a hundred days, he won't be able to get the money. And when he fails to produce it, however thick-skinned he is he won't have the nerve to turn up again. Then I can get my establishment under proper control once more, and Decima will have nothing to say."

"Well, to humour you," she said, "I'll make it ten days. But if he doesn't have the money by then, don't blame me."

"If he can't find the money by then, I don't suppose he will have the face to come back," said Decima. "I am only afraid that if he does bring the three hundred taels, you may go back on your word."

"I am an old woman of fifty-one," protested the procuress. "I am worshipping Buddha and fasting ten days every month. How could I lie to you? If you don't trust me, I'll put my palm

on yours to make a pledge.   May I become a dog or swine in
my next life if I go back on my word!"

Who with a mere pint pot can gauge the sea?
The bawd, for all her scheming, was a fool
To think, because the scholar's purse was light,
She could so easily frustrate their love.

That night in bed Decima discussed her future with Li.

"It's not that I don't want to marry you," said the young
man.   "But it would cost at least a thousand taels to buy your
freedom, and where can I get that now that all my money is
spent?"

"I have already spoken to my mistress," replied Decima. "She
wants only three hundred taels, but it must be paid within ten
days.   Although you have come to the end of your allowance,
you must have relatives and friends in the capital from whom
you can borrow.   If you raise this sum, I shall be yours; and
we shan't have to suffer the old woman's temper any more."

"My friends and relatives here have been cold-shouldering me
because I have been spending too much time with you," said Li.
"Tomorrow I'll tell them that I am packing up to leave and
coming to say goodbye, then ask for money for my travelling
expenses.   I may be able to collect three hundred taels."   So he
got up, dressed and prepared to take his leave.

"Be as quick as you can!" urged Decima as he was going out.
"I'll be waiting for good news."   And Li promised to do his
best.

On leaving the house, Li called on a number of relatives and
friends, pretending that he had come to say goodbye.   They were
pleased to hear that he was going home, but when he mentioned
that he was short of money for his journey they said nothing.
As the proverb says: To speak of a loan is to put an end to
friendship. They all, with good reason, considered Li as a young
rake whose infatuation with a courtesan had kept him away
from home for more than a year, and they knew that his father
was furious with him.

"Who knows whether he is telling the truth?" they thought. "Suppose we lend him money for the journey and he spends it on girls again, when his father hears of it he will attribute the worst motives to us. Since we shall be blamed in any case, why not refuse altogether?"

"I am so sorry!" said each in turn. "I happen to be short at the moment, so I can't help you." Li received exactly the same answer from each of them, not one of his acquaintances proving generous enough to lend him even ten or twenty taels.

He called at house after house for three days without succeeding in borrowing a single cent; but he dared not tell Decima this and put her off with evasive answers. The fourth day, however, found him in such despair that he was ashamed to go back to her; but after living so long with Decima he had no other dwelling place and, having nowhere else to spend the night, he went to his fellow-provincial, Liu, and begged a bed of him. When Liu asked why he looked so worried, Li told him the whole story of how Decima wanted to marry him. Liu, however, shook his head.

"I don't believe it," he said. "Decima is the most famous courtesan in that quarter and her price must be at least ten pecks of pearls or a thousand taels of silver. Her mistress would never let her go for three hundred taels. The old woman must be annoyed because you have no money left but are monopolizing her girl without paying her; so she has thought of this trick to get rid of you. Since she has known you for a long time, she has to keep up appearances and can't drive you away outright; and, knowing that you are short of cash, she has asked for three hundred taels in order to appear generous, giving you ten days in which to raise that sum   They believe that if you can't get the money in time, you won't have the face to go back; while if you do, they will jeer at you and insult you so that you can't stay anyway. This is the kind of trick such people always play. Think it over for yourself and don't let them take you in. In my humble opinion, the sooner you sever relations with them the better."

When Li heard this he was filled with misgivings and remained silent for a long time.

"You mustn't make a wrong decision," went on Liu. "If you really want to go home and need money for the journey, your friends may be able to raise a few taels. But I doubt if you could get three hundred taels in ten months, let alone ten days, for people nowadays are simply not interested in their friends' troubles. Those women knew that you could never borrow such a sum: that's why they named this figure."

"I suppose you are right, my friend," said Li.

But, still unwilling to give up the girl, he continued to call on acquaintances to ask for a loan, no longer going back to Decima at night. He stayed with Liu for three days, until six of the ten days had passed, by which time Decima had become so anxious that she sent her little servant-boy out to look for him. The boy found Li on the main street.

"Mr. Li!" he called. "Our mistress is expecting you!"

Li, however, felt too ashamed to go back and said: "I am busy today. I will come tomorrow."

But the boy had his instructions from Decima and, taking hold of Li's coat, he would not let him go. "I was told to find you," he said. "You must come with me."

So Li, who was of course longing for his mistress, accompanied the boy to the courtesans' quarter. But when he saw Decima he was silent.

"What progress have you made?" asked Decima.

Li shed tears and said nothing.

"Are men's hearts so hard," she said, "that you cannot raise three hundred taels?"

With tears in his eyes, Li answered: "It is easier to catch a tiger in the mountain than to find a friend in need. I have been hurrying from house to house for six days, but I have not been able to borrow a cent; and it is because I was ashamed to come to you empty-handed that I have stayed away for the last few days. Today you sent for me, and I come feeling overwhelmed with shame. It is not that I haven't done my best, but people are heartless."

"Don't let the old woman hear you," said Decima. "Stay here tonight, and we'll talk it over." Then she prepared a meal and they enjoyed the food and wine together.

In the middle of the night Decima asked: "Couldn't you get any money at all? What will become of me then?"

But Li had no answer for her and could only shed tears.

Soon it was dawn and Decima said: "In my mattress I have hidden one hundred and fifty taels of silver which I have saved up, and I want you to take that. Now that I have given you half the sum, it should be easier for you to find the other half. But there are only four days left: don't lose any time." Then getting out of bed she gave the mattress to Li, who was overcome with joy.

Ordering the servant-boy to carry the mattress for him, Li went straight to Liu's lodging, where he told his friend all that had happened that night. And when they unpicked the mattress they found in the cotton padding many silver pieces which, when weighed, totalled one hundred and fifty taels. Liu was very much impressed.

"The girl must really be in love with you," he said. "Since she is so much in earnest, you mustn't let her down. I will do what I can for you."

"If you help me now," replied Li, "I shall never forget it."

Then Liu kept Li in his house, while he went round himself to all his acquaintances. In two days he borrowed one hundred and fifty taels which he gave to Li, saying: "I have done this not so much for your sake as because I am touched by the girl's devotion to you."

It was a happy Li, beaming with smiles, who came to Decima with the three hundred taels on the ninth day — one day earlier than the appointed time.

"The other day you could not borrow a cent," said Decima. "How is it that today you have got one hundred and fifty taels?" And when Li told her about his fellow-student Liu, she pressed her hands to her forehead in token of gratitude. "We must thank Mr. Liu for making our wish come true!" she cried.

They passed the night in great joy together, and the next morning Decima rose early and said to Li: "Once you have paid the money, I shall be able to leave with you. You had better decide how we are going to travel. Yesterday I borrowed twenty taels from my friends which you can take for the journey."

Li had, in fact, been wondering where he was going to get the money for their journey, but had not liked to mention this difficulty. Now he was delighted to receive this twenty taels.

As they were talking, the mistress of the house knocked at the door.

"This is the tenth day, Decima!" she called.

When Li heard this, he opened the door to invite her in. "Thank you, aunty," he said. "I was just going to ask you over." And he placed the three hundred taels on the table.

The procuress had never thought that Li would produce the money. Her face fell and she was about to retract, when Decima said:

"I have worked here for eight years, and I must have earned several thousand taels for you in that time. This is the happy day on which I am to start a new life — you agreed to that yourself. The three hundred taels are here, not a cent less, and they have been paid on time. If you break your word, Mr. Li will take the money away and I shall immediately commit suicide. Then you will lose both the money and me, and you will be sorry."

The old woman had nothing to say to this. After long thought she finally had to fetch her balance to weigh the silver.

"Well, well," she said at last. "I suppose I can't keep you. But if you must go, go at once. And don't think you're going to take any clothes and trinkets with you." She pushed them out of the room, and called for a lock with which she padlocked the door.

It was already autumn. Decima, just risen from her bed and

not yet dressed, was still wearing old clothes. She curtseyed
to her mistress and Li bowed too. Then as husband and wife
they left the old woman's house together.

Like a carp escaping from a golden hook,
They scurried off, not to return again.

"Wait while I call a sedan-chair for you," said Li to Decima.
"We can go to Mr. Liu's lodging before deciding on anything."
But Decima demurred.

"My friends have always been very good to me," she said,
"and I ought to say goodbye to them. Besides, they were kind
enough to lend us the money for our travelling expenses the
other day: we ought to thank them for that." So she took Li
to say goodbye to the other courtesans.

Two of these girls, Yuelang and Susu, lived near by and were
Decima's closest friends. She called first on Yuelang, who,
surprised to see her dressed in old clothes and with no ornaments in her hair, asked what had happened. Decima told her
and introduced Li to her. Then, pointing to Yuelang, Decima
told Li:

"This is the friend who lent us the money the other day. You
should thank her." And Li bowed again and again.

Presently Yuelang helped Decima to wash and comb her hair,
sending at the same time for Susu. And after Decima had made
her toilet, her two friends brought out all their emerald trinkets,
gold bracelets, jade hairpins and ear-rings, as well as a brocade
tunic and skirt, a phoenix girdle and a pair of embroidered slippers, until soon they had arrayed Decima in finery from head
to foot. Then they feasted together, and Yuelang lent the lovers
her bedroom for the night.

The following day they gave another big feast to which all
the courtesans were invited; and not one of Decima's friends
stayed away. After toasting the happy couple, they played wind
and stringed instruments, and sang and danced, each doing her
best to give the company pleasure. And this feast lasted till
midnight, when Decima thanked each of her friends in turn.

"You were the chief among us," said the courtesans. "But now that you are leaving with your husband, we may never meet again. When you have decided on which day to set out, we shall come to see you off."

"When the date is settled, I shall let you all know," said Yuelang. "But Decima will be travelling a long way with her husband, and their resources are rather limited. We must be responsible for seeing that she doesn't have to go short on the way." The other courtesans agreed to this, then left, while Li and Decima spent the night again in Yuelang's room.

When dawn came Decima asked Li: "Where are we going from here? Have you any plan?"

"My father is already angry with me," replied Li, "and if he hears that I have married a singsong girl, not only will he make me suffer for it, but you will feel all the weight of his anger too. This has been worrying me for some time, but I have not yet thought of a way out."

"A father cannot help loving his son," said Decima, "so he won't be angry with you for ever. But perhaps, since going straight home would offend him, we had better go to some beauty spot like Suzhou or Hangzhou for the time being. You can then go home alone and ask some relatives or friends to persuade your father to forgive you. Once you have made your peace with him you can come to fetch me, and all will be well."

"That is a good idea," agreed Li.

The next morning they said goodbye to Yuelang and went to Liu's lodging to pack their baggage. When Decima saw Liu she kowtowed to him to thank him for his assistance, and promised to repay him in future.

Liu hastily bowed in return. "You must be a remarkable woman," he said, "to remain loyal to your lover even after he became poor. I merely blew upon the fire in the direction of the wind. Such a trifling service is not worth mentioning."

The three of them feasted all day, and the following morning chose an auspicious day for the journey and hired sedan-chairs and beasts. Decima also sent her boy with a letter to Yuelang

to thank her and bid her farewell. When they were leaving,
several sedan-chairs arrived bearing Yuelang, Susu and the other
courtesans who had come to see them off.

"You are starting on a long journey with your husband and
you are short of money," said Yuelang. "So we have prepared
a little gift to express our love. Please accept it. If you run
short on your journey, you may find it useful." She told a
servant to bring over a gilt box of the type used for carrying
stationery; but since this was securely locked, its contents could
not be seen. Decima neither declined the gift nor opened it,
but thanked them all. By now the chairs and beasts were
ready, and the chair-bearers and grooms asked them to start.
Liu offered the travellers three cups of wine in parting, and
he and the courtesans saw them to Chongwen Gate where, wiping
away tears, they all bid their friends farewell.

Uncertain whether they would meet again,
They bade farewell, with tears on either side.

In due course Li and Decima reached Luhe River where they
were to take a junk. They were lucky enough to find an official
despatch boat returning to Guazhou and, having settled the
amount of their fare, they booked places on this junk. Once
aboard, however, Li discovered that he had not a cent left.
Although Decima had given him twenty taels, it was all gone!
The fact was that Li had stayed in the courtesans' quarter until
he had nothing but old clothes to wear; so as soon as he had
money he naturally went to redeem a few of his gowns at the
pawnshop and to have new bedding made. What was left
of the silver was enough only for the sedan-chairs and beasts.

"Don't worry," said Decima, when she saw his anxiety. "The
present that my friends gave us may prove useful." Thereupon
she took a key and unlocked the box. Li, standing beside her,
was too ashamed to look into the case as Decima took out a
silk bag and placed it on the table.

"See what's in that," she said.

Li picked up the bag, which was quite heavy; and when he

opened it he found it contained exactly fifty taels of silver. Decima meantime had locked the box again without saying what else it contained.

"How generous of the girls to give us this!" she exclaimed. "Now we have enough not only for the road but to help towards our expenses when we visit the beauty spots in Suzhou or Hangzhou."

Surprised and delighted, Li rejoined: "If not for your help, I should have died far from home without a burial place. I shall never forget how good you have been to me." After that, whenever they talked of the past Li would burst into tears of gratitude, but Decima would always comfort him tenderly.

After an uneventful journey of several days, they reached Guazhou Harbour where the junk moored. Li booked another passenger boat, had their luggage put aboard and arranged to set sail the next morning at dawn. It was midwinter and the full moon was as clear and bright as water.

"Since we left the capital," said Li to Decima as they sat together in the bow of the junk, "we have been shut up in the cabin with other passengers so that we couldn't talk freely. But today we have the whole boat to ourselves and can do as we please. Now that we are leaving North China and coming to the Changjiang Valley, don't you think we should drink a little wine to celebrate and to cheer ourselves up?"

"Yes," said Decima. "I haven't had a chance to chat or laugh for a long time. I feel just as you do."

Li got out the wine utensils and placed them on the deck, then spread a rug on which they sat down together to drink to each other, until they were both under the spell of the wine.

"You had the loveliest voice in all your quarter," said Li, raising his cup to Decima. "The first time that I saw you and heard you sing so divinely, I lost my heart to you. But we have been upset for so long that I haven't heard your heavenly voice for many days. Now the bright moon is shining on the clear waves; it is midnight and there is no one about — won't you sing for me?"

Decima was in a happy mood, so, clearing her throat and tapping her fan on the deck to keep time, she sang. Her song was about a scholar who offered wine to a girl, and was taken from the opera *Moon Pavilion* by Shi Junmei of the Yuan Dynasty. It was set to the air known as "The Little Red Peach Blossom."

As her voice reached the sky, the clouds halted to listen;
As her voice reached the waves, the fish frolicked for joy.

Now on another junk near by there was a young man called Sun Fu, who was a native of Xinan in Huizhou. He had an estate worth millions of cash, for his family had dealt in salt in Yangzhou for generations; and now, at twenty years of age, he too had entered the Imperial College in Nanjing. This Sun was a dissolute young man who frequented the courtesans' quarters in search of amusement or to buy a smile from the singsong girls: indeed, he was one of the foremost in the pursuit of pleasure.

Sun's boat was moored at Guazhou Harbour too on this particular evening, and he was drinking alone to drown his boredom when he heard a woman singing so clearly and exquisitely that not even the song of a phoenix could compare with her voice. He stood up in the bow and listened for some time until he realized that the singing came from the next boat; but just as he was going to make inquiries, the song ended. The servant whom he sent to put discreet questions to the boatman found out that the adjacent junk had been hired by a certain Mr. Li, but was unable to learn anything about the singer.

"She must be a professional, not a respectable girl," thought Sun. "How can I contrive to see her?" Preoccupation with this problem kept him awake all night.

At the fifth watch a high wind sprang up, and by dawn the sky was filled with dark clouds. Soon a snowstorm was raging.

Trees on the hills are hidden by the clouds,
All human tracks are blotted out below:

And on the frozen river in the snow
An old man fishes from his little boat.

Since this snowstorm made it impossible to cross the river, all boats had to remain in the harbour. Sun ordered his boatman to steer closer to Li's junk; and then, having put on his sable cap and fox fur coat, he opened the window on the pretext that he was watching the snow. Thus he succeeded in catching sight of Decima, for when she had finished dressing she raised the curtain of the cabin window with one slender white hand in order to empty her basin into the river. Her more than earthly beauty made Sun's head swim, and he fastened his eyes to the spot where she had appeared, hoping to gain another glimpse of her; but he was disappointed. After some reflection, he leaned against his cabin window and chanted aloud the lines by Gao Xueshi on the plum blossom:

Like a hermit resting on some snow-clad hill;
Like a lovely girl in some glade beneath the moon.

When Li heard someone chanting poetry in the next boat, he leaned out to look just as Sun had hoped he would. For Sun's plan was to attract Li's attention by this means in order to draw him into conversation. Now, hastily raising his hands in greeting, Sun asked:

"What is your honourable name, sir?"

After Li introduced himself he naturally asked to know Sun's name. And, when Sun had introduced himself, they chatted about the Imperial College until very soon they were on friendly terms.

"It must be Heaven's will," said Sun, "that this snowstorm should have held up our boats in order that we should meet. I am in luck. Travelling by junk is thoroughly boring, and I would like to go ashore with you to a wineshop where I can profit by your conversation while we drink. I hope you won't refuse."

"Only meeting you by chance," replied Li, "how can I impose on you like this?"

THE COURTESAN'S JEWEL BOX

"Oh, come," protested Sun. "Within the four seas all men are brothers."

Then he ordered his boatman to put down the gang-plank, and told his boy to hold an umbrella for Mr. Li as he came across. He bowed to Li at the bow and followed him politely ashore.

A few paces brought them to a wineshop. They went upstairs, chose a clean table by the window and sat down. When the waiter had brought wine and food, Sun asked Li to drink; and as they drank they enjoyed the sight of the snow. After they had exchanged the usual platitudes about scholarship, Sun gradually steered the conversation around to courtesans; and now that they had found a common interest — since both young men had much experience in this field — they began to talk frankly and to exchange confidences.

Presently Sun sent his servant away, and asked in a low voice: "Who was the girl who sang on your junk last night?"

Li, only too ready to boast of his conquest, announced truthfully: "That was Du Wei, the well-known courtesan of Beijing."

"If she is a courtesan, how did you manage to get hold of her?"

Then Li told him the whole story: how they had fallen in love, how Decima had wanted to marry him, and how he had borrowed money to redeem her.

"It must, no doubt, be very pleasant," said Sun, "to be taking home a beauty. But will your honourable family approve?"

"I have no anxiety on the score of my first wife," replied Li. "The only difficulty is that my father is rather strict, and I may have trouble with him."

This gave Sun the opening he had been waiting for.

"Since your respected father may disapprove, where do you intend to lodge your beauty?" he asked. "Have you discussed it with her?"

"Yes, we have discussed it," replied Li with a frown.

"And does she have a good plan?" demanded Sun eagerly.

"She wants to stay for a time in Suzhou or Hangzhou," answered Li. "And when we have visited the beauty spots there, I will return home first to ask friends or relatives to talk my father round; then, when he is no longer angry, I shall fetch her back. What do you think of this plan?"

Sun looked thoughtful for a while, pretending to be very much concerned.

"We have only just met," he said at length, "and you may take offence if a casual acquaintance advises you on such an intimate matter."

"I need your advice," protested Li. "Please don't hesitate to speak frankly."

"Well then," said Sun. "Since your father is a high provincial official, he must be very jealous of your family reputation. He has already expressed displeasure because you visited low haunts: do you think he will allow you to take a singsong girl as your wife? As for your relatives and friends, they will all take their cue from your respected father. It will be useless to ask their help: they are bound to refuse. And even if some of them are foolish enough to plead your cause to your father, once they realize that the old gentleman is against this marriage they will change their tune. So you will be causing discord in your family, and you will have no satisfactory answer to take to your mistress. Even if you enjoy the scenery in Suzhou and Hangzhou for a time, you cannot live like that indefinitely. Once your funds run low you will find yourself in a dilemma."

Only too conscious that all he possessed was fifty taels, the greater part of which was already spent, when Sun spoke of possible financial difficulties Li nodded and admitted that such, indeed, was the case.

"Now I sincerely want to give you some advice," went on Sun. "But you may not like to hear it."

"I am very much obliged to you," said Li. "Please speak frankly."

"I had better not," declared Sun. "Casual acquaintances shouldn't come between lovers."

"Never mind about that," protested Li.

"As the ancients said, women are fickle," argued Sun. "And singsong girls in particular are likely to prove untrue. Since your mistress is a well-known courtesan, she must have friends everywhere. There may be some former lover of hers in the south, and she may be making use of you for the journey here so that she can join another man."

"Oh, no, I don't think so," said Li.

"You may be right," replied Sun. "But those young southerners are notorious philanderers; and if you leave your mistress by herself, she may succumb to one of them. On the other hand, if you take her home you will make your father angrier than ever. In fact, there seems to be no way out for you.

"Now the relationship between father and son is sacred and inviolable. If you offend your father and abandon your home for the sake of a courtesan, you will be universally condemned as a dissolute wastrel. Your wife will not consider you worthy to be her husband, your younger brother will cease to respect you as his elder, and your friends will have no more to do with you. You will find yourself a complete outcast. So I advise you to think this thing out carefully today."

This speech left Li at a complete loss. Hitching his seat nearer to Sun, he demanded earnestly: "What do you think I should do?"

"I have a scheme which would be very much to your advantage," replied Sun. "But I fear you may be too fond of your concubine to consider it, and I will have wasted my breath."

"If you have a good plan to restore me to the bosom of my family, I shall be tremendously grateful to you. Don't hesitate to speak."

"You have been away from home for more than a year, so that your father is angry and your wife displeased with you. If I were you, I would be unable to eat or sleep for remorse. But your worthy father is angry with you only because you have let yourself become infatuated with a courtesan and are spending money like water. You are showing yourself unfit to inherit

his property, for if you go on in this way you are bound to
bankrupt your family; so if you return home now empty-handed,
the old gentleman will vent his anger on you.   But if you are
willing to part with your concubine and to make the best of a
bad bargain, I don't mind offering you a thousand taels for her.
With this sum, you can tell your father that you have been
teaching in the capital instead of squandering money, and he
will certainly believe you.   Then peace will reign at home and
you will have no more trouble: at a single stroke you will have
turned calamity into good fortune.   Please consider my offer
carefully.   It's not that I covet your courtesan's beauty: I just
want to do what I can to help you out."

Li had always been a weak character who stood in great awe
of his father; so Sun's argument convinced him completely and,
rising from his seat, he bowed to express his thanks.

"Your excellent advice has opened my eyes," he said.   "But
since my concubine has come all these hundreds of miles with
me, I can't sever relations with her too abruptly.   I'll talk it
over with her, and let you know as soon as I gain her consent."

"Break it to her gently," said Sun.   "Since she is so fond of
you, she can't want to estrange you from your father.   I am
sure she will help to restore you to your family."   They went
on drinking till dusk, when the wind dropped and the snow
ceased.   Then Sun told his servant to pay the bill, and walked
hand in hand with Li back to the boat.

You should tell a stranger only one third of the truth;
To bare your heart to him is far from wise.

Now Decima had prepared wine and sweetmeats on the junk
for Li, but he did not come back all day.   At dusk she lighted
the lamp to wait for him, and when he came aboard she rose
to welcome him; but she noticed that he seemed flustered and
upset.   As she poured a cup of warm wine for him, he shook
his head in refusal and went without a word to his bed.   Decima
was disturbed.   Having put away the cups and plates and helped Li to undress, she asked:

"What has happened today to make you so sad?"

Li's only answer was a sigh. She repeated her question three or four times until he was asleep, and by then she was so uneasy that she sat on the edge of the bed unable to close her eyes. In the middle of the night the young man woke up and heaved another great sigh.

"What is preying so heavily on your mind?" asked Decima. "Why can't you tell me?"

Li sat up, drawing the quilt around him, and tried several times to speak; but he broke off short each time and tears poured down his cheeks.

Then taking Li in her arms Decima comforted him with kind words, saying: "We have been lovers for nearly two years and won through a thousand hardships and difficulties; and you have not looked depressed once during all this long journey. Why are you so upset now when we are about to cross the Yangzi and settle down to live happily ever after? There must be a reason. As husband and wife we shall live and die together, so we should discuss our troubles together too. Please don't keep it from me."

After she had begged him several times to speak, with tears in his eyes Li said: "When I was stranded far from home you were good to me and attached yourself to me in spite of every hardship, so that I am inexpressibly grateful to you. But I have been thinking things over. My father is a high provincial official who is a stickler for convention and a very stern man. If I anger him so that he drives us out of the family, we shall be forced to wander homeless, and what will become of us then? That would mean a complete break with my father, and we could not be sure of a happy married life either. Today my friend Sun from Xinan discussed this with me while we were drinking, and now I feel quite broken-hearted."

"What do you mean to do?" asked Decima, greatly alarmed.

"A man in trouble cannot see his way clearly," said Li. "But Mr. Sun has thought out an excellent plan for me. I am only afraid you may not agree to it."

"Who is this Mr. Sun? If his plan is good, why shouldn't I agree to it?"

"His name is Sun Fu. He is a salt merchant from Xinan and a gallant young scholar. He heard you singing last night, so he asked about you; and when I told him our story and mentioned that we would not be able to go home, he offered a thousand taels for your hand. If I had a thousand taels, it would be easy for me to face my parents; and you would have a home too. But I can't bear to part with you: that's why I am sad." When he had said this, his tears fell like rain.

Taking her arms from his shoulders, Decima gave a strange laugh.

"He must be a fine gentleman to have thought out this plan," she said. "You will recover your thousand taels, and I shall no longer be an encumbrance to you if I can go to another man. What could be more reasonable and high-principled? This plan suits us both. Where is the silver?"

"Since I hadn't got your consent, my love," said Li, who had stopped crying, "the money is still with him. It hasn't yet changed hands."

"Mind you clinch with him first thing tomorrow," urged Decima. "You mustn't miss this opportunity. But a thousand taels is a lot of money; be sure it is properly weighed and handed over before I cross to the other boat. Don't let that salt merchant cheat you."

It was now the fourth watch, and since dawn was approaching Decima got up and lighted the lamp to dress herself.

"Today I am dressing to usher out an old client and welcome in a new," she said. "This is an important occasion."

She applied her rouge, powder and scented oil with great care, then arrayed herself in her most splendid jewels and most magnificent embroidered gown. Her perfume scented the air and she was a dazzling sight.

By the time she had finished dressing it was already dawn and Sun had sent a servant to their junk for a reply. When Decima stole a glance at Li and saw that he looked pleased, she urged him to give a reply at once and possess himself of the silver as soon as possible. Then Li went to Sun's boat to announce that Decima was willing.

"There is no difficulty about the money," said Sun. "But I must have the lady's jewel case as a pledge."

When Li told Decima this, she pointed to her gilt box.

"Let them take that," she said.

Then Sun, in great exultation, promptly sent the thousand taels of silver to Li's boat. When Decima had looked through the packages and satisfied herself that the silver was of the finest and the amount was correct, she put one hand on the side of the boat and beckoned to Sun with the other, so that he was transported with joy.

"May I have that box back for a minute?" she asked, parting her red lips to reveal pearly teeth. "It contains Mr. Li's travel permit which I must return to him."

Satisfied that Decima could not escape him now, Sun ordered his servant to carry back her gilt box and set it down on the deck. Decima took her key and unlocked it, disclosing a series of drawers inside; and when she told Li to pull out the first drawer, he found it filled with trinkets, pearls, jade and precious stones, to the value of several hundred taels of silver. These jewels, to the consternation of Li, Sun and the others on the two boats, Decima suddenly tossed into the river.

Then she told Li to pull out a second drawer containing jade flutes and golden pipes, and a third drawer filled with curious old jade and gold ornaments worth several thousand taels. All these, too, Decima threw into the water.

By this time the bank was thronged with spectators. "What a pity!" they exclaimed.

As they were marvelling at her behaviour, she drew out the last drawer in which there was a casket. She opened the casket and they saw that it was packed with handfuls of bright pearls and other precious stones such as emeralds and cat's-eyes, the like of which they had never seen before and the value of which they could not even guess at. The onlookers cried out loudly in admiration. When Decima made as if to toss all these jewels into the river too, a remorseful Li threw his arms around her and wept bitterly, while Sun came over to plead with her also. But Decima pushed Li away and turned angrily on Sun.

"Mr. Li and I suffered many hardships to come here!" she cried. "But you, to gratify your lust, lied cunningly to him in order to break up our marriage and destroy our love. I hate you! After my death, if I become a ghost, I shall accuse you before the gods. How dare you think of enjoying me yourself!"

Then Decima turned to Li.

"I led the unhappy life of a courtesan for many years," she said, "and during that time I saved up enough to support myself in my old age. But after I met you, we swore to love each other all our lives. When we left the capital I pretended that this box was a present from my friends, whereas actually it contained jewels worth over ten thousand taels of silver with which I intended to fit you out splendidly, so that when you returned to your parents they might feel well disposed towards me and accept me as one of the family. Then I could have remained happily with you ever after. But you did not trust me and were easily swayed by lies; and now you have abandoned me midway, caring nothing for my true love. I have opened this box in front of all these people to show you that a paltry thousand taels is nothing to me. I had jewels in my casket, but you, alas, had no eyes. Fate must be against me. I escaped from the bitter lot of a courtesan only to be cast aside by you. All of you here today can be my witnesses! I have not been unfaithful to him, but he has proved untrue to me!"

Then all who were present were moved to tears. They cursed and spat at Li, accusing him of ingratitude and disloyalty; while shame, unhappiness and remorse made the young man weep bitterly. He was turning to beg Decima's forgiveness when, clasping the casket in her arms, she leapt into the river. They shouted for help, but there was a thick mist over the river and the current was strong, so she could not be found. How sad that such a beautiful and famous courtesan should fall a victim to the hungry waves!

The watery deep engulfed that lovely form;
The river bore her from the world of men.

Gnashing their teeth in rage, the onlookers wanted to fall upon Li and Sun; and the two young men were so alarmed that they shouted to the boatmen to cast off, escaping in opposite directions. As he stared at the thousand taels of silver, Li longed for Decima; and he sat brooding all day in shame and sorrow until he lost his reason. He remained insane all his life.

As for Sun, he fell ill with fright and kept to his bed for over a month. But he was haunted day and night by Decima's ghost, who cursed him until he died a lingering death; and all men said this was a just retribution for the crime he committed on the river.

When Liu Yuchun completed his studies in the capital and packed up to return home, his boat also moored at Kuazhou; and while he was washing his face by the side of the junk, his brass basin fell into the river. He asked a fisherman to cast his net for it, but the man drew up a small casket; and when Liu opened this he found it full of priceless jewels, pearls and other treasures. Liu rewarded the fisherman well and put the casket at the head of his bed. That night he dreamed that he saw a girl coming over the waves of the river, whom he recognized as Decima. She came up to him and curtseyed, then told him how faithless Li had proved.

"You were kind enough to help me with one hundred and fifty taels," she said. "I meant to repay you after we reached our destination, and although I was unable to do so I have never forgotten your great kindness. So this morning I sent you this casket through the fisherman to express my thanks. We shall never meet again." Suddenly awaking, Liu realized that Decima was dead, and he sighed for her for several days.

Later generations, commenting on this, condemned Sun for his wickedness in plotting to obtain a beautiful girl for a thousand taels of silver. Li they considered beneath contempt because, like a fool, he failed to understand Decima's worth. As for Decima, she was a pearl among women; the pity was that instead of finding a husband worthy of her, she wasted her affection on Li. This was like casting bright pearls or rare jade before a blind man, and resulted in her great love changing to hate and all her tenderness vanishing with the flowing stream.

> *Those who have never loved had best be silent;*
> *It is no easy thing to know love's worth;*
> *And none but he who treasures constancy*
> *Deserves the name of lover on this earth.*

The Oil Vendor and the Courtesan

All young men like to boast of their adventures,
For there's no plain sailing in the sea of love;
Money without good looks will win no hearts,
Yet neither will looks without money prove enough;
And money and looks combined will still fall short
Without the wish to please and courtesy.
But a handsome youth who is considerate too
Will beat all rivals in the lists of love.

This verse, written in the metre of "Moonlight on the Western River," gives us the art of pleasing women in a nutshell.

"The singsong girl likes good looks and the bawd likes money," says the proverb. So a handsome and wealthy young man should find both women agreeable and be able to reign supreme in the courtesans' quarter, coming off victorious in all amorous encounters.

Something more is needed, however, and that is consideration, which can no more be dispensed with than the uppers of a shoe or the lining of a jacket. A girl's charm can be increased tenfold and her shortcomings discounted by a considerate lover; and what woman can resist a soft-spoken man who showers her with delicate attentions and studies her likes and dislikes? This is what we mean by consideration.

In the tournaments of love the considerate lover will win the day, for consideration will serve him instead of good looks and riches. Take the case of Zheng Yuanhe,[1] who lost his money and looks and became a beggar. When Li Yaxian met him in

---

[1] The story of Zheng Yuanhe and Li Yaxian was popular in the Tang Dynasty.

251

the snow she took pity on him, wrapped him in her embroidered gown, fed him on dainties and made him her husband, not for the sake of his money or his looks, but because Zheng was such an attentive young man that she could not bear to part with him. Consider how, when she was ill and wanted to drink horse-entrails soup, Zheng killed his best horse for her. One such incident is enough to win a girl's heart. When finally Zheng came first in the imperial examinations and she as his wife received a title, the beggar with his clapper became a counsellor at court, who left his wretched hovel to dwell in marble halls with silken coverlets; and their romance has been handed down through the ages.

When fortune frowns, gold sheds no light;
When fortune smiles, then iron looks bright.

The accession to the throne of the first emperor of Song was followed by seven reigns during which the people enjoyed peace and security. But after Emperor Hui Zong appointed evil ministers and gave all his time to pleasure, building parks and gardens instead of attending to affairs of state, there was great unrest among his subjects; and the Golden Tartars seized this opportunity to invade the country, so that the fair and flower-like empire was all but destroyed. The emperor and his son were taken as captives to the north, and only when Prince Kang[1] crossed the Yangzi on a clay horse and established himself as Emperor Gao Zong in the south was peace restored. But during these decades the people suffered indescribable hardships.

Now in Anle Village outside Kaifeng, capital of the northern empire, lived a man called Xin Shan whose wife's maiden name was Ruan. They kept a grocery shop and made a comfortable living by selling grain, as well as flour, beans, tea, wine, oil, salt and other commodities. Xin Shan was over forty, but he had no sons and one daughter only — Yaoqin — a pretty and intelligent child. Sent to the village school at the age of seven,

---

[1] A member of the imperial house of the Northern Song Empire who founded the Southern Song Dynasty.

she soon became a great reader. At ten, she could compose poems. And at twelve she was an accomplished lyrist, chess-player, calligrapher and painter; while the skill with which she plied her needle astounded all who saw her. All these arts came to her naturally.

Since Xin Shan had no son, he looked forward to being sup-ported by a son-in-law in his old age. But in view of his daughter's brilliance it was no easy matter to find a suitable husband for her; so he refused all the overtures of marriage that were made. Just at this time the Golden Tartars invaded China and besieged Kaifeng; and, although reinforcements could have been summoned to the rescue of the capital, the prime minister, set on surrender, forbade them to advance. Then the enemy's power increased, the capital was taken by storm, the emperor and his son were captured, and the people outside the city — frightened out of their wits — left their homes and fled with their old folk and children for their lives.

Xin Shan made off like the other refugees with his wife and twelve-year-old daughter, carrying their baggage on their backs. Fearfully as stray dogs, swiftly as fish escaping from the net, through cold and hunger they pushed desperately on. They were not overtaken by the Tartars; but they met some defeated government troops.

"The Tartars are coming!" cried these soldiers when they saw refugees with bundles on their backs. And they started fires to terrify the people.

Dusk fell as the panic-stricken fugitives scattered in all direc-tions, each concerned only for himself; and the troops seized this opportunity to loot, killing those who refused to part with their goods. Thus confusion was added to confusion and sorrow piled on sorrow.

Pushed and jostled by the troops, Yaoqin fell down; and by the time she struggled to her feet her parents had disappeared. Not daring to call out, she passed the night by some deserted graves at the roadside; but the next morning when she came out of hiding there was nothing to be seen save wind-swept dust and corpses strewing the road. All the refugees with whom they had travelled the previous day had disappeared. Yaoqin cried bitterly for her parents, but did not know how to find them. She could only press on southwards, sobbing as she went. Hungry and wretched, she had walked less than a mile when she saw a mud hut and decided to ask there for a drink of water. When she reached the hovel, however, she found it dilapidated and deserted, its inmates having long since fled. Then she sat down by the mud wall and cried as if her heart would break.

At this juncture, as luck would have it, who should come by but one of Xin's neighbours! This was Pu Qiao, a loafer and wastrel. The government troops had separated him from the rest of his party too, so he was travelling alone; and when he heard sobbing he hurried over to see what was the matter.

Yaoqin had known this man since she was a child, and in her loneliness and distress any neighbour looked like a friend. Drying her eyes, she rose to greet him.

"Have you seen my parents, uncle?" she asked.

"Yesterday those soldiers stole my baggage, and I have very little money left," thought Pu. "Here is a heaven-sent means of support! She's worth her weight in gold."

"Your parents are very upset to have lost you," he lied. "They have gone on ahead; but they told me, 'If you find our daughter, be sure to bring her back to us.' And they promised to reward me well."

Though Yaoqin was an intelligent child, distress had made her over-credulous, and quite trustingly she attached herself to Pu.

People who should never mix
Grow quite friendly in a fix!

"Your parents are travelling day and night," he told the girl, when he had fed her with some of his provisions. "If we can't overtake them on the road, we shall have to cross the river to Jiankang to find them. While we are travelling' I shall treat you as my daughter and you had better call me your father;

otherwise people may think I have been kidnapping little girls who have lost their way, and that wouldn't look good, would it?"

To this Yaoqin agreed; thus whether travelling on foot or by boat they passed for father and daughter. Upon reaching Jiankang they learned that the Fourth Prince of the Tartars was about to lead troops across the river; so, fearing that Jiankang would not be safe and knowing that Prince Kang had ascended the throne at Hangzhou, now renamed Linan, they took a junk to Runzhou then travelled by way of Suzhou, Changzhou, Jiading and Huzhou to the southern capital, where they put up at an inn.

Now in the course of this thousand-mile journey from Kaifeng to Linan, Pu had spent all his silver — he was even reduced to handing over his coat to settle the score at the last inn. All he had left was Yaoqin, and, eager to sell this living merchandise, as soon as he heard that a bawd at the West Lake named Mrs. Wang was buying girls, he brought her to the inn to inspect his goods and offer a price. In view of Yaoqin's good looks, Mrs. Wang agreed to pay fifty ounces of silver for her; and immediately Pu received the money he escorted the girl to the bawd's house.

"This is my own daughter, and it breaks my heart to have to part with her," the cunning man told Mrs. Wang. "If you treat her gently, she will do as you want; but you must be patient with her."

To the girl he said: "Mrs. Wang is a relative of mine. I am leaving you with her for the time being while I go to look for your parents; then I shall come to fetch you."

So Yaoqin went to Mrs. Wang quite happily.

How sad that such a clever miss
Should fall into a trap like this!

Mrs. Wang made Yaoqin new clothes and lodged her in an inner chamber, giving her good food and tea every day and speaking to her so kindly that she soon felt quite at home. But

when several days had passed with no news from Pu Qiao, Yaoqin started longing for her parents again, and with tears in her
eyes asked Mrs. Wang:

"Why doesn't Uncle Pu come back?"

"What Uncle Pu?"

"The Mr. Pu who brought me here."

"He told me he was your father."

"His name is Pu, but mine is Xin."

Then she related how after losing her parents in their flight
from the capital she had met Pu, who had reassured her and
brought her to Linan.

"Well, I never!" exclaimed Mrs. Wang. "So you're an orphan,
a crab without claws! I may as well tell you the truth: that
fellow Pu has sold you to me for fifty ounces of silver. We
are in the courtesan business here, and I already have three or
four girls — none of them very much to look at. Because I've
taken a fancy to you I mean to treat you as my own child; and
once you grow up I guarantee you will live on the fat of the
land."

When Yaoqin realized that Pu had deceived her, she burst
out crying and for a long time was inconsolable.

After that Mrs. Wang gave her a new name, Wang Mei, and
everybody in the house called her by this name. Taught music,
dancing and singing, she excelled in all these arts; and by the
time she was fourteen she was so lovely that all the young gallants of Linan brought her rich presents, marvelling at her beauty.
There were others who admired genius in a woman, and when
it was known that she was a skilled calligrapher and writer,
every day men thronged the door asking for her calligraphy or
poems. So she grew famous, and became known as The Flower
Queen. And some young men on the West Lake composed the
following verses about her:

> *What other maid can compare with The Flower Queen?*
> *She is poetess, painter, skilled calligrapher,*
> *And unequalled too in dancing, singing and music.*

We often compare the West Lake to the beauty Xi Shi;
But no beauty of old can compare with this wonderful girl.
Happy the man who is lucky enough to possess her!
Who would not be willing to die for such delight?

Since Yaoqin was so famous, by the time she was fourteen men came to negotiate for the first night with her; but she refused them all.   As for Mrs. Wang, she valued the girl as if she were made of gold, so when she saw that The Flower Queen was unwilling, she dared not cross her.

Another year passed.   Mrs. Wang asked Yaoqin to receive clients, but the girl was adamant.

"I will agree to it only after I have seen my parents and gained their consent," she declared.

While secretly indignant, Mrs. Wang did not want to offend the girl, so she let the matter drop.   One day, however, a rich man named Jin offered three hundred taels of silver for the first night with The Flower Queen, and this great sum of money induced Mrs. Wang to think of a plan, to which Jin agreed.   On the evening of the Moon Festival, The Flower Queen was invited to the West Lake to watch the tide from a boat.   Then three or four of the bawd's accomplices played drinking games with the girl until she was drunk, after which they carried her back to Mrs. Wang's house and laid her on the bed; and when she woke at dawn the next day she realized that she had been tricked into losing her maidenhead.   Lamenting her unhappy fate she rose and dressed, then threw herself down on a bamboo couch near the bed with her face to the wall and wept silently.   When Mr. Jin came up to her, she scratched his face till the blood came.   And since this was more than he had bargained for, he took his leave as soon as it was light.   By the time Mrs. Wang emerged from her room to beg him to stay, he was gone.

Now it is customary for men who enjoy the first night with a courtesan to receive congratulations from the girl's mistress the next morning, and for all the other bawds to compliment him too.   There is usually feasting for several days, while the young man often stays in the house for one or two months, or at least twenty days or a fortnight. So Mr. Jin's departure so early the next morning was quite unheard of. Uttering exclamations of dismay, Mrs. Wang threw on her clothes and hurried upstairs, where she found Yaoqin lying on the couch bathed in tears. Because she wanted to induce the girl to accept more clients, Mrs. Wang apologized profusely; but The Flower Queen said not a word, and finally the bawd had to leave her alone.

Yaoqin cried for a whole day, took neither bite nor sup, and declared that she was too ill to go downstairs or see callers. Mrs. Wang had no patience with such behaviour and wanted to punish her, but feared this would only make the high-spirited girl more stubborn. Yet if she gave way to her, instead of making money Yaoqin would receive no 'one, in which case she would be useless even if she stayed there for a hundred years. After racking her brains fruitlessly for several days, Mrs. Wang bethought her of a sworn sister of hers, Mrs. Liu, who was a frequent visitor at her house.

"Mrs. Liu has the gift of the gab, and she's on good terms with Yaoqin," thought the bawd. "I'll ask her to speak to the girl. If she can make her see reason, so much the better!"

She sent a maid to invite Mrs. Liu over; and when her friend had arrived and sat down in the front room, Mrs. Wang explained her problem.

"I can make even angels and goddesses lovesick," declared Mrs. Liu. "Just leave this to me."

"If you can do this," said Mrs. Wang, "I'll gladly kowtow to you. Have some more tea before you go to see her, so that talking won't make you thirsty."

"My mouth is like the sea," boasted the other. "I can talk all day without feeling dry."

After a few cups of tea Mrs. Liu went to the inner quarters, where she found Yaoqin's door locked. She knocked lightly and called: "Niece!"

Recognizing Mrs. Liu's voice, Yaoqin opened the door and they greeted each other. Then Mrs. Liu sat down beside the

girl at the table on which she noticed a piece of silk with a
woman's face drawn but not yet coloured on it.

"What a wonderful sketch!" she cried.   "How clever you are!
Lucky Mrs. Wang, to get such an intelligent girl as you — so
good-looking and so accomplished!   One could offer thousands
of ounces of gold and search the whole capital without finding
another like you."

"Don't tease!" protested Yaoqin.   "What good wind has
blown you here today?"

"I've been wanting to call for a long time," replied Mrs. Liu,
"but there's too much to do at home. I made time today, though,
to come over and congratulate you, because I hear you are a
woman now."

Yaoqin blushed scarlet and lowered her head without a word.
Knowing that she felt ashamed, Mrs. Liu moved her chair nearer
and took the girl's hand.

"You're not a soft-shelled egg, child," she said.   "Why be
so squeamish?   If you remain so bashful, how are you to make
big money?"

"What do I need money for?"

"Even if you don't want money, child, your mistress expects
a return on all she's spent on bringing you up.   Those who live
by a mountain depend on the mountain for a living, and those
who live by water depend on the water.   Not one of Mrs.
Wang's other girls is a patch on you.   You're the best melon
in her garden, and she treats you better than the rest.   An intelligent girl like you should understand that.   Yet I hear since
you had your first customer you've been refusing to see anybody
else.   What do you mean by such behaviour?   Who would feed
silkworms mulberry leaves if they refused to spin silk?   Since
your mistress shows you special consideration, you should do
something for her too, instead of giving the other girls reason
to find fault."

"Let them find fault.   What do I care?"

"Well, of course, talk is a small matter.   But don't you know
our ways?"

"What do you mean?"

"You girls are food, clothes and money to people in our profession. When we are lucky enough to get a good-looker, it's like a rich family acquiring a good piece of land. If the girl is still young, we hope she will grow up quickly; because once she's had her first man she's like a crop ready to be harvested — we can expect the money to start rolling in! As one man leaves by the back, another comes in by the front. Mr. Zhang sends rice, Mr. Li fuel; and clients just flock to our doors. That's what we call a successful house."

"You make me blush," said Yaoqin. "I'm not going to do anything like that."

Putting her hand to her mouth, Mrs. Liu crowed with laughter.

"You're not, eh?" she cried. "You won't have any say in the matter, miss! Mrs. Wang is head of this house, and if you don't obey her she can beat you within an inch of your life. Then you'll have to do as she wants. Your mistress has never treated you harshly because you're intelligent and pretty and used to kindness and she wanted to save your face and leave you some self-respect. But just now she was telling me that you don't appreciate your own luck: you don't know that eiderdowns are light and millstones heavy. So now she's angry and has asked me to speak to you. If you persist in being stubborn she may lose her temper, and then you'll be cursed and beaten. You can't escape. But don't make a bad start; because once you begin wrangling you may go on all day and every day, until you can't stand it any more and have to receive men. By then, though, you'll have lost your privileged position and the other girls will laugh at you. Take my advice: since you're in her power, you'd better do as your mistress says; then you'll find life very pleasant."

"I belong to a good family," said Yaoqin. "I was tricked into coming to this brothel. If you'll help me to find a proper husband, aunty, you'll be doing a better deed than building a nine-storied pagoda. But I'd rather die than prostitute myself."

"To get married is only right and proper, child," replied Mrs.

Liu. "Of course I won't gainsay that.   But there are different kinds of marriage."

"What do you mean by different kinds of marriage?"

"There's true marriage, sham marriage, sad marriage and happy marriage; there are marriages that are timely and marriages of necessity; marriages that end well and marriages that end badly.   Now, child, be patient while I explain this to you.

"What do we mean by true marriage?   Well, the ideal match is between a brilliant scholar and a beautiful girl; but such marriages are rare.   When two such people meet and fall in love, they can't bear to be separated for a moment and long to marry each other.   They are like two moths clinging together till death. This is true marriage.

"What is sham marriage?   It's when a young man loves a girl who doesn't want to marry him, but tricks him into spending a lot of money on her.   When the wedding day is fixed, she backs out.   But though the fool knows that she doesn't love him, he insists on marrying her and offers her mistress a bribe she can't resist, so that the girl's wishes are over-ridden.   Carried against her will to his house, she deliberately breaks the family rules, makes scenes or even carries on with other men, until her husband finds it impossible to keep her.   In six months or a year he lets her go back to the brothel.   Such a marriage is just a way of making money; that's why we call it sham.

"What is a sad marriage?   It's when a man loves a girl who doesn't care for him, and uses his position to force the mistress of the house — who is afraid of trouble — to consent to the match.   With tears in her eyes, the girl is compelled to go with him.   But once in his house she feels as if she were at the bottom of the ocean, for his family rules are so strict that she dare not lift her head; and she leads a miserable life, half as concubine half as servant.   This is a sad marriage.

"What is happy marriage then?   It's when a girl can choose her husband and has come across someone rich and gentle, whose wife is kind too but has no children.   He takes the girl in the hope that she will bear him a son; and if she does, she is treated as one of the mistresses of the family. So she has a comfortable life and good prospects. That is a happy marriage.

"What is meant by a marriage which is timely? It's when a courtesan who is still famous and sought after has had her fill of love and pleasure and chooses a really satisfactory husband. By stopping at the height of her success, she can make sure that no one will despise her. Such a marriage is timely.

"What is a marriage of necessity? It's when a girl has no desire to get married, but is forced to by the authorities, black-mailed into it, or disposed of in payment of a debt. In such cases she has no choice but to marry, whether the man is good or not; and all she can hope for is peace and quiet and a roof over her head. This is a marriage of necessity.

"What do I mean by a marriage that ends well? It's when a courtesan who is no longer young and has been through a great deal meets an honest fellow, and they are attracted to each other. Then she may hoist sail and go to live with him till old age. This is marriage that ends well.

"What do I mean by a marriage that ends badly? It's when a couple fall passionately in love, only to cool before long. Or when a man's parents are difficult or his wife jealous, so that after several quarrels he sends the girl back and demands a refund of his money. Or when the man becomes too poor to keep her, so that if she can't bear hardships she must leave him and take up her old trade again. These are marriages which turn out badly."

"What must I do now if I want to marry?" asked Yaoqin.

"Listen to me, child, and I'll tell you."

"I shall be indebted to you for ever for your advice."

"Marriage is a serious step," began Mrs. Liu. "Besides, you have already slept with a man, so that even if you marry tonight you won't be a virgin. It was a mistake to come here at all, but that was your fate; and now that your mistress has been to so much trouble to bring you up, she certainly isn't going to let you go until you have helped her for a few years and earned her a few thousand taels of silver. Besides, before marrying

you must find a good man. You wouldn't want an ugly, stink-
ing fellow, would you? But if you don't receive clients, how
are you to find a man you like? If you refuse to admit anyone,
your mistress will be forced to find some rich man to buy you
as his concubine. That is another kind of marriage. But your
husband may be old or ugly, or some illiterate country bully,
in which case you will lead a wretched life. It would be better
for you to be thrown into the river, for then at least there would
be a splash and people would pity you. So I advise you to do
as your mistress says and receive clients. Since you are so beautiful and accomplished, ordinary fellows won't dare approach you,
but only the sons of rich and aristocratic families who won't
disgrace you. While you enjoy love and pleasure in your youth
you will be helping your mistress in her business, and putting
something aside so that you don't have to ask help from anyone
in future. Then, in five or ten years, when you come across
someone you like, I shall act as your go-between and see that
you marry in style; and by that time Mrs. Wang will be willing
to let you go. Isn't this best for both parties?"

When Yaoqin smiled and said nothing, Mrs. Liu realized that
she was convinced.

"It's sound advice I've been giving you," she concluded.
"You'll live to thank me for it." Then she rose to go.

Mrs. Wang outside the door had heard every word; and when
the girl saw Mrs. Liu out and came face to face with her own
mistress, she retreated blushing into her room. The two bawds
returned to the front of the house and sat down.

"She's a very stubborn girl," said Mrs. Liu. "But thanks
to my persuasion the iron is melting. If you lose no time in
finding another client for her, she should be agreeable; and then
I shall come again to congratulate you."

Mrs. Wang thanked her friend profusely, and treated her to
a meal and wine before letting her go. Later the young men
of the West Lake made this song to describe Mrs. Liu's powers
of persuasion:

Oh, Mrs. Liu has a tongue so fast
She beats all orators of the past;
For she can argue black to white
Or wake a drunkard up at night;
She can make a fool of someone clever,
Or a girl say Yes! who once said Never!

After her talk with Mrs. Liu, Yaoqin accepted customers willingly; and soon so many were flocking to her she had not a moment to herself. She became so famous that Mrs. Wang charged ten taels of silver for a night with her; but even at that price men fought for her. Mrs. Wang was overjoyed to be making so much money, and Yaoqin was looking hard for a man she could love; but not one could she discover. As the proverb says: "It is easier to find a priceless jewel than a true lover."

Our story brings us now to an old man named Zhu who kept an oil shop outside Qingpo Gate in Hangzhou. Three years before this he had adopted a young refugee from Kaifeng called Qin Chong. This lad's mother had died when he was a child; and when he was thirteen his father, Qin Liang, had abandoned him to become a monk at Tian Zhu Monastery. A childless widower, Old Zhu treated Qin Chong as his own son, changing his name to Zhu Chong and keeping him in the shop to learn the trade. And at first all went well. But then Old Zhu developed kidney trouble, which meant that instead of working he had to sit or lie down all the time; so he engaged an assistant named Xin Quan to help with the business.

Four years passed in a flash, until Chong was a handsome young man of seventeen; but though of age, he had not married. A maid of over twenty in the household, called Orchid, had her eye on him and tried several times to hook him; but he was an honest lad. Besides, she was such an ugly slut that he was not interested. So one side was willing but the other was not.

When Orchid saw that she had made no impression on the young man, she started angling for the assistant, Xin Quan. A bachelor of nearly forty, he rose to the bait at once and often lay with the maid in secret.   Later, however, they felt Chong was in their way, and plotted together to have him driven out.

One day, the picture of injured innocence, Orchid complained to Old Zhu: "Master Chong has tried several times to seduce me.   He's a bad young fellow."

Old Zhu had trifled with the maid himself, so he could not avoid a twinge of jealousy.

Then Xin Quan stole some silver from the shop.

"Master Chong has been gambling outside," he told the old man.   "He has taken money several times from the till."

At first Old Zhu did not believe them.   But because he was growing senile they succeeded in convincing him.   Then he called Chong and rated him soundly.

Chong was smart enough to realize that he had Xin Quan and Orchid to thank for this.   But any attempt to clear himself would only stir up trouble and, if Old Zhu did not believe him, would make matters worse.   He took another line.

"There is not enough business to keep both Mr. Xin and me busy," he said to Old Zhu.   "Let him look after the shop while I go out as an oil vendor.   The money I make every day should double our turnover."

The old man would have agreed but for Xin Quan.

"It's not that he wants to be an oil vendor," said Xin, "but after stealing from you all these years he has quite a tidy sum tucked away.   And because he bears you a grudge for not finding him a wife, he doesn't want to work here.   He would like to set up on his own, so that he can marry and start a family."

"I've treated him as my own child, but he has no sense of gratitude," sighed Old Zhu.   "May Heaven curse him!   Very well.   Since he is not my own son and we don't seem able to get on together, I had better let him go."

He gave Chong three taels of silver and told him to go away, letting him take his clothes and bedding, however, which shows that after all the old man had a kind heart.   When Chong saw that his foster-father would not keep him any longer, he bowed four times and left, sobbing bitterly.

Now when Chong's father left for Tian Zhu Monastery, he had not told his son where he was going; so as soon as the lad quit Old Zhu's house he rented a small room by Zhongan Bridge, put down his luggage there, bought a padlock and locked the door, then trudged through the highways and byways in search of his father. But after searching several days to no purpose, he had to give up. During his four years in Old Zhu's house, the lad had been so loyal to his foster-father that he had not put by a cent for himself; hence all he possessed was the three taels given him when he left, and this was not enough to start any business. After cudgelling his brains, he decided that since oil was the only trade with which he was familiar, and the oil shops knew him, that would be the safest trade for him. So he bought a pole and casks, and spent what was left of his money on oil.

The merchant who sold oil to Zhu knew Chong for an honest fellow, and pitied him because another man's slander had cost the lad his job as shop assistant and reduced him to selling oil in the streets. To help him, this merchant chose the purest oil for him and gave him better weight than anyone else; and with these advantages Chong was able to give his customers better measure too. So he sold more oil than other vendors, and made a profit every day. But he lived frugally, saving his money or using it only to buy necessities. The one thing that worried him was the thought of his father.

"My foster-father changed my name to Zhu," he reflected. "How can people know that my real name is Qin? If my father looks for me, he won't be able to find me."

So he decided to use his original surname once more.

If an upper-class gentleman with a fine future wants to change his name, he can send a petition to the government or notify the Ministry of Ceremony or the Imperial College, for then an announcement will be put on the census list so that everybody knows of it. But how was a mere oil vendor to make his change of name known? Chong found a way. In large characters he wrote "Qin" on one of his oil containers and "Kaifeng" on the other, so that all could tell his surname and place of origin. And eventually everybody in the market came to know him by his true name, calling him Oil Vendor Qin.

It was then early spring, when the weather was neither too hot nor too cold. Hearing that there was to be a nine-day mass in Zhao Qing Monastery and calculating that a great deal of oil would be needed, thither Chong carried his casks. And the monks, who knew his name and had heard that his oil was better and cheaper than anyone else's, gave him all their custom. So for nine days in succession Chong carried his wares to the monastery.

No profit comes of venal ways;
It's honesty that always pays!

It was fine on the ninth day when Chong carried his empty casks out of the monastery, and there were many sightseers about. Walking along the lake-side, the young man feasted his eyes on the peach blossom, willows and painted barges with flutes and drums which were plying to and fro on the lake. And presently he set down his casks and pole in a clearing to the right of the monastery, and sat on a rock to rest. Near by, overlooking the lake, was a house with a fence and a gilded gate behind which grew some dwarf bamboos enclosed by a vermilion balustrade; while the front court, which was all that could be seen of the interior, was neat and clean. From this house now emerged several men in caps, accompanied by a girl. When they reached the gate the men bowed and walked off, and the girl went in again.

Chong's eyes had been riveted upon this girl, for never in his life had he seen so dainty a beauty. He sat there like one in a dream, unable to move. The simple lad had no experience of courtesans, and he was just wondering whose house this could be when a middle-aged woman and her maid came out.

"I was just going to send out for some oil!" exclaimed the woman at the sight of his casks. "And here is an oil vendor. Let's buy from him."

Then the maid walked over.

"Are you selling oil?" she asked.

"I've none left, ma'am," replied Chong. "But I can bring you some tomorrow."

The maid could read, so when she saw the characters on the casks, she told her mistress: "This oil vendor's name is Qin."

The woman had heard of this honest Oil Vendor Qin.

"We need oil every day," she told him. "If you will bring it here, we shall buy from you."

"Thank you, ma'am," replied Chong. "I'll come without fail."

Then the woman and her maid went in.

"I wonder what relation that woman is to the girl?" mused Chong. "I don't care if I make no profit each time I come, so long as I can have a good look at that girl."

He was picking up his pole to go, when a sedan-chair with a blue silk canopy and two pages running behind it stopped at the gilded door. The chair was set down, and the two pages went into the house.

"Strange," thought Chong. "Whom are they fetching?"

Presently two maids came out, carrying a bundle in a crimson rug and an inlaid bamboo box. When they had given these to the chair-bearers to put under the seat, the wonderful girl came out. At her heels were the two pages, óne with a lyre in a case, the other with some scrolls and a jasper flute hanging from his wrist. The girl mounted the chair and the bearers carried it once again along the way they had come, while the maid and pages followed behind. After this second and closer look, Chong wondered even more who the girl could be as he walked slowly off, his pole over his shoulder.

A few paces brought him to a tavern by the lake. He seldom drank, but today the sight of the girl had filled him with a pleasant melancholy; so putting down his pole he walked into the tavern, chose a table for one and sat down.

"Will there be other guests, sir?" asked the waiter. "Or are you drinking alone?"

"I am on my own," replied Chong. "Bring the best wine

you have and some fresh nuts.   I don't want any meat dishes."

As the waiter was pouring wine for him, Chong asked: "Whose is that house over there with the gilded gate?"

"That is Lord Qi's house," was the reply.   "A Mrs. Wang is living there now."

"Who is the girl who just went by in that sedan-chair?"

"That is the famous courtesan Yaoqin whom people call The Flower Queen.   She comes from Kaifeng, but was stranded here.   She is good at music, singing, dancing, chess, lyre-playing, calligraphy and painting; and she receives only grandees.   A night with her costs at least ten taels of silver; so ordinary fellows don't get a look in.   She used to live outside Yongjing Gate, but the place was too small; and six months ago Lord Ji, who is a friend of hers, lent them this house and garden."

When Chong heard that The Flower Queen came from the north too, he was reminded of his old home and felt even more drawn to her.   After drinking a few cups, he paid the score, took up his pole and left.

"What a pity that a beautiful girl like that should become a courtesan!" he thought.   "If she hadn't, though." he reflected with a smile, "I would never have seen her.   Life is short" — his imagination was running away with him — "and if I could hold such a beautiful girl in my arms for one night, I would die content.   But even if I peddle oil all day, I make only a few cents.   She's not for the likes of me.   I'm worse than the toad in the cesspool who longed to eat a swan.   All her friends are young noblemen.   Even if I saved enough silver, she would turn me away because I'm only an oil vendor."

But then he thought: "I've heard that the mistresses of such houses will do anything for money.   They would admit even a beggar if he could pay, so why not a respectable tradesman? Yes, if I had the silver, I'm sure they'd accept me! . . .   The question is — how to get it?"

So he muttered to himself all the way back, giving free rein to his fancy.

Was there ever such a madman?   A small tradesman whose

whole capital was barely three taels of silver — how could he dream of spending ten taels for one night with a famous courtesan? But where there's a will there's a way. After long consideration he came to a decision.

"Starting from tomorrow, when I've got back my outlay I'll put what's pure profit aside," he vowed. "If I make one cent's profit a day, in a year I shall have three taels and sixty cents; and in three years I shall have enough. If I make two cents a day, I shall need only a year and a half. If I make more, I shall have the sum in about a year."

Occupied with these thoughts he reached home, unlocked his door and went in. But after the daydreams in which he had indulged on the road, the sight of his bed filled him with melancholy; and he lay himself down without any supper to toss sleepless through the night, thinking of the beautiful girl.

Beauty kindled his desire,
Set his restless heart on fire.

At dawn Chong rose to fill his casks and breakfast, then locked his door and carried his oil to Mrs. Wang's house. Once at her gate, however, he dared not go in, simply putting his head inside to look round. Mrs. Wang, who had just risen but not yet combed her hair, was telling her maid what provisions to buy. And, recognizing her voice, Chong called her name.

When the bawd saw who it was, she laughed.

"Good man!" she cried, "you have kept your word."

Then calling him in, she bought a jarful of oil — about five catties. She offered a fair price, and when Chong did not dispute it she was very pleased with him.

"This jar will not last more than two days," she said. "If you come every other day, I won't buy from anyone else."

Chong assented, shouldered his load and left, regretting that he had not seen the girl. He was happy, though, to have made a regular customer of Mrs. Wang, for that meant that although he had not seen The Flower Queen this time, he might see her

the next time or the time after.   Still, to go all that way just
for one customer was not good business.

"Zhao Qing Monastery is near here," he thought.   "And
though they aren't celebrating any special mass, they must need
oil just the same.   I had better take my casks there.   If I get
several customers, I can sell all my oil in one trip."

The monks were very pleased to see him.   They all bought
from him, and Chong arranged to bring them oil every other
day.   As that day was an even number, he decided to come
out this way on the days which had even numbers, and to sell
his oil in the city on the odd days.   After this, whenever Chong
left the city he made straight for Mrs. Wang's house, ostensibly
to sell oil but actually to see The Flower Queen.   Sometimes
he saw her and sometimes he did not.   When he missed her
it made him sad; yet seeing her made him sad too, for then
he longed for her all the more.

After he had been there several times, everybody in Mrs.
Wang's household knew Qin the Oil Vendor.   Soon more than
a year had passed, and every day Chong put aside some pure
silver — sometimes three cents, sometimes two, never less than
one — and when he had a certain amount he made it up into a
packet.   Bit by bit he accumulated a large parcel of silver, how
much exactly he did not know.

One day — it was an odd day and raining so heavily that
Chong could not do business — pleased at the sight of his big
bundle of silver, he decided to have it weighed and see how
much it came to.   Taking an umbrella, he walked to the silversmith's across the road and asked if he could borrow their scales.

"How much silver can an oil vendor have?" thought the
silversmith, eyeing him contemptuously.   "The small balance
for less than five taels will be more than enough for him!"

But when Chong undid his bundle and showed his silver —
which being in pieces looked even more than it was — the silversmith, who was a mean, obsequious fellow, regarded him
quite differently.

"It's true that you can't judge by appearances!" he thought.

Hastily setting up the balance, he produced all his weights, large as well as small. And Chong found that he had exactly sixteen taels, not a cent more, not a cent less: in other words, a whole catty!

"If I set aside three taels as capital," thought Chong, "I shall still have more than enough for a night in the courtesans' house. But if I gave them all this loose silver, they will laugh at me. I'll have it cast into ingots while I'm here. That will look better."

He weighed out ten taels for a large ingot, and one tael and eighty cents for a small one, then paid the silversmith with a piece from the four taels and twenty cents that were left. After this, he laid out a few dozen cents on new shoes, socks and a new cap, went home to wash and starch his gown, and last of all bought some Persian incense to scent his clothes. On the next fine day he dressed himself up.

> *No lordling rich and great was he,*
> *But a youth as handsome as could be!*

He put the silver in his sleeve, locked his room and went straight to Mrs. Wang's house, feeling as if he were walking on air. But once at her gate his courage failed him.

"I usually come with my pedlar's kit to sell oil. How can I explain that I'm here today as a customer?" he wondered.

As he stood there hesitating, the gate creaked and Mrs. Wang came out.

"Aren't you doing business today, Master Qin?" she asked. "Where are you off to, dressed up so smartly?"

Chong had to pluck up courage to step forward and bow, and Mrs. Wang returned his greeting.

"I have come specially to see you, ma'am," he murmured.

The bawd was experienced enough to read his mind.

"Here is Qin Chong all dressed up and paying me a visit," she thought. "He must have taken a fancy to one of my girls; I suppose he wants to spend a night or an hour with her. Well, he's no millionaire, but whatever's in the basket can be used as food. We can make enough out of him to buy garlic."

So, beaming she asked: "Are you giving us your patronage, Master Qin?"

"I want to make a bold request. But I don't know how to begin."

"Don't be afraid. Come in and sit down, then we can talk."

Though Chong had often been to the house to sell oil, this was the first time he had been offered a seat. But since he was here today as a client, Mrs. Wang took him to the reception room, made him sit in the place of honour, and called for tea. When the maid came in with tea, she was so surprised to see Qin the Oil Vendor here as a guest that she lowered her head to giggle.

"What are you sniggering at?" demanded Mrs. Wang. "Where are your manners?"

Then, with a straight face, the maid carried out the used cups.

"Now, Master Qin," prompted Mrs. Wang. "What was it you wanted to say?"

"I just wanted to invite one of your young ladies to have a drink with me."

"Nothing but a drink? Surely you want to make love to her too!" declared the bawd. "You are an honest fellow — what put such romantic ideas into your head?"

"I have been dreaming of this for a long time."

"Well, you know all my girls. Which one do you fancy?"

"I want to spend one night with The Flower Queen."

"Don't talk nonsense!" Mrs. Wang was annoyed, for she could not believe he was serious. "Are you trying to make fun of me?"

"I mean what I say," protested Chong. "I wouldn't lie to you."

"Even a chamber pot has ears: haven't you heard what her price is? All your oil couldn't buy half a night with her! You had better pick one of the others."

"Whew! True sales talks!" Chong showed his tongue incredulously. "May I know how many thousand taels you ask for a night with The Flower Queen?"

When Mrs. Wang saw that he was joking, her face cleared.

"Not so much!" she said with a laugh. "Only ten taels, plus miscellaneous expenses."

"That's nothing, then," replied Chong, and produced from his sleeve the large ingot of bright silver. "Here is a good ten taels for you. And here" — handing her the smaller ingot — "is about two taels with which I'll trouble you to prepare a meal. If you will help me, I shall be indebted to you for ever and shan't forget to show my gratitude."

Mrs. Wang was unable to resist the large ingot. Fearing, however, that the oil vendor was acting on a sudden impulse which he might regret later, she felt she should sound him out.

"It's not easy for a tradesman to save up ten taels of silver," she said. "You had better think again."

"My mind is made up," replied Chong. "Don't worry, ma'am."

"Even so," said Mrs. Wang, as she put the silver in her sleeve, "there are other difficulties."

"What difficulties can there be since you are mistress of the house?"

"The young gentlemen who come to see The Flower Queen are from rich and aristocratic families. They are all scholars too; there's not an ordinary citizen among them. If she recognizes you as Master Qin the Oil Vendor, she will never receive you!"

"Please think of some way to get round her, ma'am," he begged. "If you help me I shall never forget your kindness."

When Mrs. Wang saw how determined he was, she frowned thoughtfully.

"I have it!" she cried at last with a smile. "With any luck you may succeed; but if you fail don't blame me. The Flower Queen hasn't come back yet from a feast she went to yesterday in Academician Li's house. Today Lord Huang has invited her to go boating. Tomorrow Mr. Zhang the poet and some others are asking her to a poetry meeting; and the day after was book-ed by Minister Han's son some time ago. So you'd better come the day after that. And you'll make a better impression if you don't come here this week to sell oil. Another thing: you don't look like an upper-class customer in that cloth gown. Wear silk or satin next time you come, so that the maids won't rec-ognize you. Then it'll be easier for me to spin some kind of yarn about you."

"I shall remember all you've told me," promised Chong as he took his leave.

For three days he stopped selling oil, and strolled about the streets in a second-hand silk gown he had bought at a pawnshop, to practise carrying himself like a scholar and a gentleman.

Before he meets his courtesan, poor fool,
He learns the ways of the Confucian school!

On the fourth day Chong went so early to Mrs. Wang's house that he found the gate still closed. He decided to take a stroll; but, not daring to pass the monastery for fear the monks laugh at his fine clothes, he walked in another direction. Upon his return he found the gate open; but there was a carriage outside and a number of footmen were sitting in the courtyard. Though Chong was a simple lad, he had all his wits about him; so instead of going in he beckoned quietly to the coachman.

"Whose carriage is this?" he asked.

"Minister Han's," was the reply. "We've come to fetch our young master."

When Chong realized that the minister's son had not yet left, he went to an inn for a meal. By the time he returned the carriage had gone, and as he entered the gate he met the bawd herself.

"I'm very sorry," she told him. "But The Flower Queen is not free today. Just now Master Han begged her to go with him to East Village to enjoy the early plum blossom; and he is such an old customer that I couldn't refuse him. He wants to take her to Ling Yin Monastery tomorrow, too, for a chess tournament.   Lord Qi has also asked for her several times; and since he is our landlord we can't very well refuse him either. He often stays three or four days when he comes, so I can't tell when he will leave.   If you really want a night with her, you must wait a little longer.   Otherwise I can refund you the money you gave me the other day."

"The only thing I'm afraid of is losing your help, ma'am," replied Chong.   "I don't mind waiting ten thousand years if I can have her in the end."

"That's all right, then," said the bawd.   "And there's another thing, Master Qin," she added as he was leaving.   "Come at about four in the afternoon next time instead of in the morning. Then I can tell you whether she is booked or not.   In fact, the later you come the better.   Don't take offence if this is all I can do for you."

"Indeed not," he protested.

Chong did no business that day, but went out the next morning with his pedlar's kit to sell oil inside the city, giving Qiantang Gate a wide berth.   And every evening, after his work was done, he dressed himself neatly and went to Mrs. Wang's house.   But The Flower Queen was never free, and he waited for more than a month in vain.

On the fifteenth of the twelfth month it snowed heavily, and when the snow stopped the wind whistled over the snowdrifts till they turned to ice.   It was bitterly cold, but the ground was dry.   After plying his trade for the greater part of the day, Chong dressed himself as usual and went to see what news there was for him.   Mrs. Wang greeted him with a beaming face.

"Today you have a ninety-nine per cent chance!" she said.

"What is it that is still uncertain?" he asked.

"The fact that she is not back yet."

"Will she be coming back?"

"Today Marshal Yu invited her to his home to enjoy the snow, and then they feasted on a boat in the lake.   The marshal is seventy, so of course he won't be making love to her, and he said he would send her back this evening.   Why don't you go to her room and have a cup of wine to warm you up while you wait for her?"

"Please lead the way, ma'am!"

Mrs. Wang led him through several winding passages and halls to a clean and airy building and two small chambers as wings. On the left was a room for the maids with little in it but a bed, table and chairs. On the right was The Flower Queen's bedroom, which was locked. In the sitting room in the middle hung a painting by a famous artist, while ambergris was burning in an old bronze censer on the table. The writing tables on two sides of the room were laden with curios, and the walls were hung with poems; but, ashamed that he was no scholar, Chong did little more than glance at them.

"If her sitting room is so elegant, her bedroom must be simply magnificent!" he thought. "And tonight I shall enjoy it to the full! Ten taels a night is really not too much."

Mrs. Wang offered him a seat and acted as hostess while maids brought in a lamp and laid a square table with six bowls of nuts and cakes and one hamper of delicacies. Even before tasting the wine you could smell its bouquet!

"Today all my girls are engaged, so there is no one but me to keep you company," said the bawd as she offered him wine. "Please drink a few cups and make yourself at home."

But Chong was not a good drinker, and he had too much on his mind to finish even one cup.

"I expect you are hungry," said Mrs. Wang. "Have some food before you go on with your wine."

A maid brought in two bowls of rice which she placed before him, with a bowl of soup. Mrs. Wang was a good drinker, and she did not touch the rice but kept the young man company with wine. After finishing one bowl, he laid down his chopsticks.

"The night is long," said Mrs. Wang. "Have some more."

So he ate another half bowl.

Presently a maid came in with a lantern.

"Your bath is ready, sir." she said

Although Chong had bathed before coming out, he dared not refuse, but went to the bathroom to wash, soap and scent himself again, then came back to the table. Mrs. Wang had ordered the food to be removed, keeping only the wine and a small stove to warm it. It was now after dusk and the bells in Zhao Qing Monastery had stopped tolling; but there was still no sign of The Flower Queen.

What can be more trying than waiting? As the girl failed to appear, Chong began to lose heart; but the bawd kept up a flow of banter and pressed him to drink until two or three hours had passed. Then they heard a commotion outside. The Flower Queen was back! When the maid announced her return, Mrs. Wang hurried out to meet her, and Chong stood up. Then Yaoqin was helped in, very drunk, by her maid. She halted at the threshold to gaze with drunken eyes at the bright candles, cups and dishes in the room.

"Who is drinking here?" she asked.

"Child," said Mrs. Wang, "this is that Master Qin I've told you about, who has admired you for so long and sent presents over. Because you were never free we have kept him waiting for over a month. But this evening luckily you have no engagements, so I asked him here to meet you."

"I've never heard of any Master Qin," retorted Yaoqin, turning away. "I won't see him."

Mrs. Wang put out both hands to stop her.

"He's a good man!" she declared. "I'm not fooling you."

So Yaoqin had to turn back. But as soon as she stepped into the room and saw Chong she recognized him, though she was too drunk to remember his name.

"I know this man, mother," she said. "He's not a respectable gentleman. If I admit him, I shall be laughed at."

"Child!" protested Mrs. Wang. "This is Master Qin who owns a shop inside Yongjing Gate. You must have seen him when we lived in that part of the city; that's why you know his face. Don't go mixing him up with other people! He begged so hard that I let him come, and I can't go back on my word.

So please put up with him for one night for my sake.   I know
I shouldn't have done this, and I'll make it up to you tomorrow."
   She pushed Yaoqin into the room, so that the girl had to greet
Chong, who pretended not to have heard a word.   Yaoqin
curtseyed to the young man and sat down beside him; but the
more she looked at him the more annoyed and suspicious she
felt.   At length she broke her silence to call for wine, which
she poured into a large cup.   Instead of offering this to the
guest as Mrs. Wang expected, she drank it straight off herself.
   "Child, you've already had too much!" protested the bawd.
"Don't drink any more."
   But Yaoqin would not listen.
   "I'm not drunk!" she retorted, then drained ten cups in succession.
   If she had been drunk before, she was now much more so.
She ordered a maid to unlock her room and light the lamp so
that she could lie down.   Then without letting down her hair
or removing her clothes, she kicked off her embroidered slippers
and threw herself on the bed to sleep. |
   "She's a spoilt, self-willed girl," said Mrs. Wang, much em-
barrassed.   "Something must have happened today to upset her;
but it's nothing to do with you.   I hope you will excuse her."
   "That's quite all right," Qin assured her.
   After drinking a few more cups he begged to be excused, and
Mrs. Wang saw him to Yaoqin's bedroom, whispering: "Don't
be too rough — she's drunk."
   To Yaoqin she called: "Get up, child, and undress so that
you can sleep properly."
   But Yaoqin was already sound asleep.   So the bawd had to
leave them.
   A maid cleared the table, then suggested: "Why don't you
go to bed now, Master Qin?"
   "I'd like a pot of hot tea, if there is any," he said.
   The maid brewed a pot of strong tea and brought it in, then
closed the door and went to her room.   Turning to look at The
Flower Queen, Chong saw that she was fast asleep on her silk

quilt, with her face to the wall. Although afraid she might catch cold after drinking, he did not like to disturb her; but, noticing another red silk quilt on the bedstead, he spread that gently over her. Next he trimmed the lamp, took off his shoes and lay down beside her, the tea pot in the crook of his left arm, his right arm over her waist. And not for a moment dared he close his eyes.

In the middle of the night Yaoqin awoke, overcome with nausea, and sat up shuddering. Putting down his tea pot Chong hastily sat up too, and supported her while she was very sick; holding the sleeve of his gown before her to avoid dirtying the bedding. Presently, her eyes still closed, she asked for tea to rinse her mouth. At that, the young man gently removed his gown and tossed it on the floor; then, happy to find the tea still hot, poured her a cup of the strong, fragrant brew. After two cups she felt much better and lay down again, quite exhausted, to sleep with her face to the wall. And Chong, having rolled up his soiled gown and put it in a corner, lay down once more beside her.

Yaoqin did not wake till the morning, when she turned over to discover someone lying beside her.

"Who are you?" she asked.

"My name is Qin," he said.

"Last night I was very drunk, wasn't I?"

She had only a hazy recollection of what had passed.

"Not very," he. lied.

"Was I sick?"

"No."

"Well, that's not too bad."

But after a little reflection she said: "No, I remember being sick and drinking some tea. Surely I couldn't have dreamed it?"

"Well," admitted Chong, "as a matter of fact you're right. I saw that you had had too much to drink, so I kept the tea pot warm for you. After being sick you asked for tea, and I poured you two cups."

"Was I sick on the bed?" demanded Yaoqin in dismay. "How disgusting!"

"I was afraid your bedding might be soiled, so I held out my sleeve."

"Where is your gown now?"

"Over there."

"What a shame to spoil your clothes!"

"My clothes are lucky to have been of service.'

"What a nice, considerate man!" thought Yaoqin, who was beginning to like him.

By this time the day was bright, and the girl got up. Suddenly she recognized the oil vendor.

"Tell me truly, now," she said, "who are you and what brought you here last night?"

"I can't lie to The Flower Queen," was the reply. "I am Qin Chong, who used to sell oil at your door."

He described how he had first seen her escorting a guest to the gate and getting into the sedan-chair; how much he had admired her and how he had saved up the money for a night with her.

"Because I was able to sleep beside you last night I count myself the happiest of men," he concluded. "I am quite content."

Yaoqin was very moved.

"Last night I was too drunk to entertain you, so you spent all that money for nothing," she said. "Don't you feel bad about it?"

"You are my goddess," replied Chong. "I'm afraid I didn't look after you well enough, and I am very lucky not to have made you angry. What more dare I hope for?"

"You are in business," she answered. "When you make money, why don't you keep it for your family? You shouldn't come to a place like this."

"I have no wife or children," was the rejoinder. "I am all alone."

"Will you ever come back?" she asked after a moment's silence.

"Last night the dream of my life came true, when I was able to be near you. How dare I hope for more?"

"What a wonderful man!" thought Yaoqin. "So sincere and honest! So kind and considerate too! He's one in a thousand. What a pity that he's a tradesman. If he were a gentleman, I would like to marry him."

Just then her maid brought in a basin of water and two bowls of ginger soup. Chong washed, but since he had not taken off his cap the previous night he did not have to do his hair. After drinking a little soup he stood up to take his leave.

"Don't go yet," said Yaoqin. "I want to talk to you."

"I admire you so much I would like to stay here a little longer," he replied. "But a man must know his place. I took a great liberty in coming here last night. If people hear of it, your reputation may suffer. So I had better leave early."

Yaoqin nodded. Then, dismissing her maid, she hastily opened her jewel box and took out twenty taels of silver.

"I behaved too badly last night," she said. "Take this for your business; but don't tell anyone I gave it to you."

Chong, of course, would not accept the money.

"I make money so easily," insisted the girl. "And this is just to thank you for your kindness last night. You mustn't refuse it. If ever you are short of cash, you must let me help you. You had better leave that soiled gown here, and I'll tell my maid to wash it for you."

"Please don't trouble," he replied. "I shall wash it myself. How can I take money from you?"

"Don't say that!" she protested. And thrusting the silver into his sleeve she gave him a little push. Seeing that he could not refuse, Chong accepted the money with a deep bow, then rolled up his soiled gown and went out past Mrs. Wang's room.

"Master Qin is leaving, madam!" called a maid when she saw him.

"Why are you leaving so early, Master Qin?" cried Mrs. Wang from her room.

"I have some business," he answered as he left. "I shall come to thank you another day."

Now though Yaoqin was not really interested in the oil vendor, she was touched by his devotion. Still suffering from the effects of wine, she rested that day instead of receiving guests, and her thoughts ran not on her other admirers but on Chong. In the words of this verse:

> You're a decent tradesman, sweetheart,
> Not a gentleman refined;
> Yet you've shown yourself so gentle,
> I can't fancy you unkind.
> Though I struggle to forget you,
> I can't drive you from my mind!

Let us go back now to Old Zhu. When Xin Quan and Orchid saw that the old man was bed-ridden, they began to carry on together quite openly. And after several disputes with him they decided to quit. They slipped away one night taking all the money in the shop with them.

The next morning when Old Zhu discovered his loss, he asked his neighbours' help; but although they posted up a notice and an investigation was made for several days, it came to nothing. By now, of course, the old man saw matters in their true light and repented of listening to Xin Quan and driving Chong away. Learning that the youth was living near Zhongan Bridge as an oil vendor, he decided to invite him back as a support for his old age. And fearing that Chong might bear him a grudge, he asked the neighbours to plead with the young man to return. Chong then packed up his things and went back to Old Zhu's house, where both of them wept at their meeting.

Old Zhu entrusted all his property to his foster-son, and by using his own twenty taels of silver Chong was able to get the shop in good shape again. Once more he sold oil over the counter and called himself Zhu Chong.

When, in less than a month, Old Zhu's illness took a turn for the worse, physic proved useless and he died, Chong beat his breast and wept as bitterly as for his own father. And the funeral, sacrifice, and interment of the coffin in the Zhu family graveyard outside Qingpo Gate were just as they should be, winning Chong great praise from his neighbours. When all this was over, he resumed business. His shop was an old firm which had done good business until Xin Quan's niggardly dealings drove customers away; but now that Chong was in charge all the old customers came back; so business was better than ever.

Since Chong was all on his own, he urgently needed an honest assistant, and one day a middleman introduced to him a man over fifty. This was none other than Yaoqin's father, Xin Shan. Lonely and helpless, he and his wife had wandered from place to place for several years, living from hand to mouth. Now, hearing that the southern capital had grown prosperous and most of the refugees from the north had settled there, they had come to Linan to search for their lost daughter. They could get no news of her, however, and soon all their money was spent and the innkeeper pressed them every day for payment. When they heard that an assistant was needed for an oil shop whose young manager, Zhu, also came from the northern capital, Xin Shan asked the middleman to recommend him. He knew the business, having once owned a grocery himself. And Chong was very sympathetic when he heard his fellow-townsman's story.

"Since you have nowhere to go, why don't you and your wife stay with me?" he suggested. "After all, we are virtually old neighbours. You can continue making inquiries about your daughter from here."

He gave Xin Shan two strings of cash to pay his bill at the inn. Then Xin brought his wife to meet Chong, who cleared out a room for the old couple and was pleased to find them a real help in the shop.

Swift as an arrow another year passed. It was high time for Chong to marry, and because he was well off and honest into the bargain, many families offered him their daughters for nothing. But after meeting an enchantress like The Flower Queen, Chong could take no interest in ordinary girls and determined to wed none but a beauty. So day after day slipped by, but brought him no nearer to marrying.

One who has seen the ocean thinks nothing of mere rivers;
One who has stood on a mountain top is not impressed by
*   clouds!*

Meanwhile, in Mrs. Wang's house, Yaoqin enjoyed such fame and pleasure that she had all the silks and satins and delicate fare she could desire. Yet whenever anything went wrong, when her admirers became jealous and quarrelled, or when she woke in the middle of the night drunk or unwell and found no one to care for her, then she would remember Master Qin's sterling qualities and wonder if they would ever meet again.

A year later, however, something happened to change her whole life.

There lived in Linan a young man named Wu, the eighth son of Wu Yue, Governor of Fuzhou. Thanks to his father's position Master Wu had plenty of money; and he liked to gamble, drink and amuse himself with singsong girls. He knew The Flower Queen by reputation; but although he sent several times to engage her for a night, she had heard such ill reports of him that she invariably excused herself. He called more than once with some other wastrels at Mrs. Wang's house; but still Yaoqin would not receive him.

Soon the Spring Festival arrived, when folk visit their family graves or go sightseeing. After several days of outings, Yaoqin was tired. Moreover, she had promised poems and paintings to a number of friends; so, ordering her maids to inform all callers that she was out, she closed her door, lit some fine incense, and set her desk in order. She had just taken up her brush when she heard shouting outside — it was Master Wu who had come with a dozen ruffians to demand that she accompany him to the lake. Refused once more by Mrs. Wang, he started smashing furniture in the hall, then charged straight for The Flower Queen's door, only to find it locked.

One way for a courtesan to avoid guests is to have someone lock her door from outside and say that she is out. But whereas simple customers can be fooled in this way, an old hand like Wu was not deceived by such a trick. He ordered his servants to smash the lock and kick open the door; Yaoqin was unable to hide herself; and Wu, shouting curses, bade two of his men drag her out. Mrs. Wang wanted to intervene and apologize; but the ugly turn things were taking made her slip away, and her whole household promptly went into hiding. Then with no consideration for Yaoqin's tiny bound feet, Wu's bullies hustled her out of the gate and through the streets, while their master swaggered behind. Only when they reached the West Lake and pushed her on the boat did they let go of her.

Clothed in silks and prized like a jewel, The Flower Queen had been pampered and cosseted ever since she came to Mrs. Wang at the age of twelve. Never before had she been so roughly and rudely treated. Once aboard, she turned towards the stern, hid her face in her hands and started sobbing. But instead of relenting, Wu nearly burst with rage. Fierce as the God of War, he jerked his chair round to face the shore, sat down with his bullies ranged beside him, and ordered the boatmen to cast off.

"You bitch!" he cursed. "You don't know how to appreciate an honour! If you don't stop crying, you whore, I'll have you whipped!"

Not to be frightened by this, Yaoqin went on sobbing. When the boat reached a pavilion in the middle of the lake, Wu went ashore, ordering the food to be served in the pavilion. But when he told his men to fetch The Flower Queen to amuse him, she clung fast to the railing of the boat, crying bitterly, and would not let go. So all Wu's pleasure was spoilt. After drinking a few cups of wine alone, he went back to the boat to drag the girl from the railing; but she stamped and screamed until the furious bully ordered his servants to remove her hairpins and trinkets. Then, with dishevelled hair, Yaoqin ran to the end of the boat to throw herself ino the water. But the men stopped her.

"Are you trying to frighten me?" demanded Wu. "Even if you kill yourself, it will only cost me a few taels of silver. Of course, I don't want you to do away with yourself here; so if you stop that noise, I'll let you go."

When Yaoqin heard this, she stopped crying; and Wu ordered the boat to moor at a quiet spot outside Qingpo Gate. There he had the girl's embroidered slippers torn off.

"Walk home if you can, you bitch!" he jeered, ordering his ruffians to set her ashore. "Nobody's going to see you back."

Then the boat cast off again and steered for the middle of the lake.

How could Yaoqin walk on her tiny, bare feet? Though she had talent and beauty, she reflected, she was a despised courtesan and not one of her rich and aristocratic admirers would be willing to help her now.

"How can I face the world again, even if I do get back?" she thought. "It would be better to die. But what a futile death! For all my reputation, any peasant woman is luckier than I. It's all thanks to Mrs. Liu, with her sugared tongue, that I'm in this fix today. Has there ever been a woman as unhappy as I?"

She felt more and more wretched, and finally broke down and cried as if her heart would break.

Now it happened that Chong had gone that day to sacrifice at Old Zhu's grave outside Qingpo Gate. Having sent the sacrificial vessels back by boat, he was walking home alone when he heard a girl crying. And drawing nearer he recognized the beauty at once, in spite of her dishevelled state.

"What has happened, Flower Queen?" he demanded, aghast.

When Yaoqin heard a familiar voice, she stopped crying and looked up to see that understanding, considerate Master Qin. Here was a friend in need! She poured out her whole unhappy story, and Chong, touched to the quick, shed tears of sympathy.

From his sleeve he took a white silk handkerchief over five feet in length, which he tore in half and gave to the girl to bind round her feet. He then wiped the tears from her face and fastened up her hair, comforting her as he did so. As soon as her sobs ceased he called a sedan-chair, asked her to be seated, and escorted her himself on foot to Mrs. Wang's house.

Now the panic-stricken bawd, not knowing what had become of the girl, was sending out everywhere to make inquiries, when who should arrive but Master Qin with The Flower Queen! Mrs. Wang was as pleased as if someone had returned her a gem of the first water. Besides, the young man had long since stopped peddling oil at her door and she knew that he had taken over the Zhu Family Shop and was doing well. Now that he was a substantial citizen, her attitude to him had naturally changed. And when she saw the state Yaoqin was in, learned what a terrible experience she had been through and that it was Master Qin who had rescued her, the old woman could not thank him enough. She insisted that he stay to a meal.

Late in the afternoon, when Chong had drunk a few cups, he rose to go. But The Flower Queen would not hear of his leaving.

"I have often thought of you, and longed to see you again," she said. "I'm not going to let you leave like this."

Mrs. Wang also urged him to stay.

Never had Chong been so happy. That evening Yaoqin played, sang and danced for him, using all her art to please him, until the young man felt he was in paradise and could scarcely contain himself for joy. And as night fell they went arm in arm to her bed-chamber, where Chong's bliss can be imagined.

"I want to speak to you from my heart," said Yaoqin later that night. "You mustn't refuse what I ask!"

"I'd gladly go through boiling water or fire to serve you," declared Chong. "How can I refuse you anything?"

"I want to marry you."

Chong laughed.

"Even if you married ten thousand times, you would never

choose a poor fellow like me," he replied. "Don't joke about such a thing. I am too far beneath you."

"I am perfectly serious," insisted Yaoqin. "When I was fourteen and they made me drunk to start me on this life, I wanted to marry but knew of no one suitable. I couldn't tell who would make a good husband, and was afraid of making a mistake I would regret all my life. Later, though I met many men, they were all rich young gallants who gave their time to wine and women because they cared only for pleasure. None of them had any real feeling for me. I've met no other man so trusty and true as you, sir. Besides, I understand you are not yet married; and if you don't despise me because of my profession, I would like to serve you all my life. If you refuse, I shall hang myself here with three feet of white silk to prove my sincerity. That will be better than dying miserably as I might have done yesterday at the hands of those boors, jeered at by everyone."

Having said this, she started sobbing.

"Don't distress yourself so," Chong entreated her. "It's beyond my wildest dreams that you should love me. How dare I refuse you? But how can a poor man like myself pay the thousand of taels needed to redeem you? Much as I long to, it's not in my power."

"That need not hinder us," she replied. "As a matter of fact, I have saved up money and valuables for my marriage and left them with friends. I needn't trouble you for a cent."

"Even if you redeem yourself, you are used to living in a large house and enjoying the best of everything. How will you manage in my house?"

"With you I shall be happy wearing cotton and eating the plainest food."

"And what if your mistress objects?"

"I can get round her."

So they chatted till dawn.

Yaoqin now collected the boxes which she had deposited with the sons of Academician Huang, Minister Han, Marshal

Qi and others, and asked Chong to take them home. This done, she took a sedan-chair to Mrs. Liu's house and told her that she wished to marry.

"Yes, that was my advice to you, wasn't it?" said Mrs. Liu. "You are still young, of course; but who is the man?"

"Never mind who he is, aunty. But I am acting on your advice, and this is going to be a true, happy marriage which ends well, not one of your sham, unhappy marriages which end badly. And if you will take my side, my mistress is bound to agree. I have nothing worthy to offer you; but as a sign of my gratitude here are ten taels of gold to make trinkets. Do help me by talking my mistress round! If you succeed, I shall give you another present for acting as my go-between."

When Mrs. Liu saw the gold, she smiled till her eyes seemed two slits.

"You are like a daughter to me, and you are doing the right thing!" she cried. "How can I accept a present from you? I shall just keep this gold for the time being to look after it for you. You can depend on me. But your mistress considers you a money-tree which needs only be shaken to shower down gold. She won't want to let you go, and will probably ask at least a thousand taels for you. Is he willing to pay that much? I'd better have a talk with him first."

"Never mind about that, aunty. Let's assume that I'm redeeming myself."

"Does your mistress know you are here?"

"No."

"Well, you stay here for lunch while I go to have a talk with Mrs. Wang. I'll let you know when I come back if she's agreeable or not."

Mrs. Liu took a sedan-chair to Mrs. Wang's house and was invited in. When she asked about the trouble with Master Wu, Mrs. Wang told her the whole story.

"In our profession it is safer and more profitable to keep more ordinary girls," said Mrs. Liu. "They aren't particular about whom they receive, and they admit clients every day.

That Flower Queen of yours has become so famous that she's like a piece of dried fish on the ground -- every ant wants a bite! Though she's a great attraction, she must cause you a lot of worry. And though you charge ten taels a night for her, she brings you more fame than money; because whenever those young lords come they bring friends who stay all night and make an immense amount of work. There are all their servants, whom you have to treat well, too. If you don't do exactly what they want, they start using foul language and smashing things up; and you can't complain to their masters either. Then there are the scholars and poets and chess-players, who demand several days of her time every month. And the sons of the best families keep fighting for her. If she accepts Zhang, she offends Li. When one man is pleased, another is sure to grumble. Take this trouble with Master Wu for example. What a fright it must have given you! Because if anything were to go wrong, you would lose your capital. You can't bring a lawsuit against an official family: you have to put up with whatever they do. Luck was with you this time, and the stormclouds have blown over, but if anything unfortunate were to happen, you could do nothing but wring your hands. I hear, too, the Wu means mischief, and is likely to make more trouble for you. And Yaoqin is a quick-tempered girl, who won't flatter people. She's bound to come to grief."

"That's what worries me too," replied Mrs. Wang. "This young Wu comes of a rich, powerful family — he's not just anyone — yet she wouldn't hear of admitting him. That's how all this trouble started. She was easier to manage when she was younger; but now that she's so well-known and all those rich gentlemen make so much of her, she's grown spoilt and insists on having her own way. She receives only the customers she likes; and if she's unwilling, nine bulls can't budge her."

"The least bit of fame goes to these girls' heads," agreed Mrs. Liu.

"I want your advice," said Mrs. Wang. "If a man could be

found willing to pay, wouldn't it be better to sell her? That would simplify matters and save me a lot of worry."

"You're quite right. If you sell her, you'll make enough to buy five or six others. In fact, if you drive a good bargain, you may even get ten girls for the money. It's well worth your while."

"I've been thinking it over. Those high officials never pay much: they expect to get everything cheap. But she's so particular that when someone's found who'll pay the right price, she may go into one of her tantrums and refuse. So if you come across a good customer, my dear, do act as go-between and help us. And if the girl refuses, I hope you'll make her see reason. She won't listen to me; but she trusts you, and you can get round her."

Mrs. Liu went into a peal of laughter.

"I am here now as a go-between!" she cried. "How much do you want for her?"

"Well, sister, you know how things are. In our profession we buy cheap but sell dear. Besides, look how famous she has been for the last few years. Is there anyone in the capital who hasn't heard of The Flower Queen? So how can I let her go for a beggarly three or four hundred taels? No, I want at least a thousand."

"Let me go and tell him," said Mrs. Liu. "If he's willing to pay so much, I'll come back. If not, I won't." Then, getting up to leave, she asked: "Where is the girl today?"

Mrs. Wang sighed.

"Since Wu insulted her that day," she said, "she's been afraid that he may come back to make more trouble; so she takes the sedan-chair every day to different houses to complain. The day before yesterday it was Marshal Qi; yesterday it was Academician Huang. Heaven knows where she is today."

"If you make up your mind and are firm with her, she will have to agree," said Mrs. Liu. "If she doesn't, I shall talk her round. But don't make any difficulties, now, if the man is willing!"

"I've given my word," replied Mrs. Wang. "I shan't go back on it."

Then she saw her friend to the door, and Mrs. Liu after a hasty leave-taking mounted her chair and was carried away.

Once home Mrs. Liu told Yaoqin: "Well, I've won your mistress over. She's given her consent. The moment you produce the silver, it can be settled."

"The silver is ready," replied Yaoqin. "Will you promise to come to our house tomorrow, aunty, please, to get this settled? We must strike while the iron's hot."

"Since it's all arranged, I'll certainly come," promised Mrs. Liu. Yaoqin then said goodbye and went home, but did not breathe a word of this to anyone.

At noon the next day, Mrs. Liu arrived.

"How about it?" asked Mrs. Wang.

"It's ninety per cent certain. But I haven't spoken to the girl yet."

Mrs. Liu went to Yaoqin's room and, when they had greeted each other and chatted for a little, asked: "Did your man turn up? Where is the money?"

"In those leather cases."

Yaoqin pointed to the head of her bed, then opened five or six cases and took out thirteen or fourteen packets containing fifty silver taels each. With the gold, gems and jade which she produced as well, she had not less than a thousand taels' worth.

Mrs. Liu's eyes sparkled at this sight, and her mouth watered.

"How smart the girl is for her age!" she thought. "How did she manage to save up so much? The girls in my house receive guests too, yet none of them has come anywhere near this. Whenever they have a little money in their pockets they spend it on nuts and sweets instead of saving it; so if their foot binding is worn out, I have to buy new for them. Mrs. Wang was really in luck to get a girl like this, who could bring in so much money *and* save so much to redeem herself. It's all here ready!"

Yaoqin guessed what was in Mrs. Liu's mind, and quickly fetched four rolls of Luzhou silk, two bejewelled hairclips, and two phoenix hairpins of jade.

"Here are a few presents for you, aunty," she said, putting them on the table. "I must thank you for acting as my go-between."

Then, beaming with joy, Mrs. Liu went back to Mrs. Wang.

"She wants to redeem herself for the amount you fixed, not a cent less," she said. "This is better than if some man were to buy her, because it means there are no middlemen asking for wine and tea, who have to be paid one or two per cent of the price."

Mrs. Wang was rather vexed, however, to learn that the girl had so much money in her cases. The fact is, these bawds are pleased only when all the extras their girls make come to them. If they suspect that a girl is keeping a private hoard, they will wait till she is out, then unlock her door and ransack her room. Because Yaoqin was well-known and her friends were all important men, and because she was making a great deal of money for her mistress and had a hot temper, Mrs. Wang had tried not to offend her. So she had never entered Yaoqin's room, not realizing that the girl had put by so much.

Mrs. Liu understood why Mrs. Wang's face had clouded.

"Now, sister, stick to your word!" she said. "These are her own savings, not money that should have come to you. She could have spent it all. Or if she were a bad girl she could have given it all to some lover, and you'd have been none the wiser. It's a good thing that she put it by. Besides, if she hadn't saved a cent, you couldn't have let her leave your house naked, could you? You'd have had to fit her out decently before marrying her off. But now that she has produced all these things, I'm sure she won't ask you for so much as a thread. You can keep the whole of this sum to line your purse. And though she is getting married, she is still your daughter. If she does well, she is bound to send you presents during festivals; and, since she has no parents, you will be her husband's mother-in-law. There'll be plenty of good things coming to you."

Consoled by this reasoning, Mrs. Wang gave her consent. Then Mrs. Liu brought out the silver, weighed it packet by packet, and gave it to Mrs. Wang. This done, she went through the gold, jewels and jade to reckon the value of each piece.

"I am deliberately marking them down," she told Mrs. Wang, "so that when you sell them you can make a few dozen taels extra."

Though a bawd, Mrs. Wang was fairly honest, and she agreed to all her friend's estimates. And when Mrs. Liu saw that she was won over, she told her pander to draw up a marriage agreement for Yaoqin.

"I had better say goodbye to my mistress and leave with you, aunty," said the girl. "Will you let me stay with you for a couple of days, until we have chosen an auspicious date for the wedding?"

After receiving so many presents from Yaoqin, Mrs. Liu did not want Mrs. Wang to change her mind and keep the girl after all. Anxious to see the matter settled, she agreed.

Yaoqin promptly packed her toilet case, jewel boxes, chests, bedding and other belongings, without taking a single object belonging to Mrs. Wang. Leaving her room with Mrs. Liu, she said goodbye to the other girls and to her mistress, who shed a few conventional tears. Then Yaoqin had her baggage carried to the sedan-chair and went off happily with Mrs. Liu, who cleared a good, quiet room for her and her chests. And all the girls in Mrs. Liu's house came to congratulate her.

That evening when Chong sent Xin Shan to Mrs. Liu to ask for news, he learned that the business was settled. Then, with Mrs. Liu as go-between, an auspicious day was chosen, the wedding was celebrated with flutes and drums, and great was the young couple's happiness on their wedding night.

The following day, when Xin Shan and his wife were introduced to the bride, they were amazed to recognize their child; and when they had exchanged their stories they embraced with tears of joy. Then Chong asked his father and mother-in-law to be seated so that he and Yaoqin could pay their respects. All their friends marvelled, and a feast was held to celebrate this double happiness.

Three days after the wedding Yaoqin asked her husband to send rich presents to the friends who had stored her cases, and to tell them that she was now married, thus showing that she had a sense of gratitude. She also sent additional gifts to Mrs. Wang and Mrs. Liu, to the delight of both.

After the honeymoon, Yaoqin opened her chests to disclose gold, silver and hundreds of lengths of silk and embroidery from Suzhou and Chengdu, worth more than three thousand taels. She gave the keys of her chests to her husband, who gradually bought houses and land and expanded his business, leaving the management of the oil shop to his father-in-law. In less than a year the family was wealthy enough to live in style with plenty of servants.

One day, to express his gratitude to the gods, Chong vowed to present all the temples and monasteries in the city with sufficient candles and oil for three months. He also undertook to burn incense, offer prayers, observe fasts and purify himself. Starting with Zhao Qing Monastery, he went by turn to Ling Yin, Fa Xiang, Jin Ze and Tian Zhu monasteries.

Now Tian Zhu Monastery, which is devoted to the worship of Guanyin, consists actually of three monasteries: Upper Tian Zhu, Middle Tian Zhu and Lower Tian Zhu, all of which are important centres of worship but can be reached only by mountain paths, not by boat. Bidding his servants carry up one load of candles and three of oil, Chong set off up the mountain by sedan-chair.

He went first to Upper Tian Zhu Monastery, and was welcomed by the monks in the hall where his father lit candles and tended incense. Now that he was prosperous and well fed, Chong had grown stout and changed so much that Old Qin did not recognize him. On one oil cask, however, the old man saw the word "Qin," and on the other "Kaifeng": and that set him thinking. What a strange coincidence, indeed, that these two oil casks should be brought to this monastery! After Chong had offered incense, Old Qin brought in a tea tray and the chief monk offered their patron tea. Then Old Qin spoke up.

"May I ask, sir, why you have these words on your casks?"

"Why do you ask?" inquired Chong, interested to hear a northern accent. "Are you from Kaifeng too?"

The old man replied that he was.

"What is your name?" asked Chong. "Why did you join this order? And how long have you been here?"

Then Old Qin told him his name and place of origin.

"When I reached here after escaping from the soldiery, I had no means of support," he said. "So I let my thirteen-year-old son be adopted by a Mr. Zhu. Eight years have passed since then, but being old and infirm I have never left the mountain to ask news of him."

Chong threw his arms round the old man and wept.

"I am your son!" he cried. "I used to sell oil for Mr. Zhu. It was because I wanted to find you, father, that I wrote these words on the oil cask. Who would have thought that we should meet here! This was surely ordained by Heaven!"

The monks, too, exclaimed in wonder.

After spending that day at the monastery with his father talking of the past, Chong changed the name on his written invocations to the gods of the two remaining monasteries from Zhu Chong back to Qin Chong. Having offered incense in Middle Tian Zhu and Lower Tian Zhu, he returned to ask his father to accompany him home, so that he could be well looked after. But Old Qin had lived so long as a monk that he was used to observing fasts and unwilling to leave.

"We have been separated for eight years," protested Chong, "and all that time I have been unable to look after you. Besides, I have just married, and my wife ought to pay her respects to her father-in-law."

Then Old Qin had to agree.

Chong had his father carried in the sedan-chair while he walked on foot. Once home, he brought out new clothes for the old man and asked him to be seated in the hall while he and Yaoqin paid their respects. Her parents were introduced too.

That day a great feast was spread; but Old Qin would not touch the meat or wine. And the following day all their neighbours brought presents to congratulate the family on their fourfold happiness: Chong's marriage, the reunion of Yaoqin's family, the reunion of Chong with his father, and the restoration of the Qin family name. So they feasted for several days.

Then Old Qin chose to return to his monastery; and Chong, not daring to thwart his father's wishes, spent two hundred taels to build a lodge there for him. Every month Chong sent him provisions and money, and every ten days he went to see the old man, while Yaoqin visited her father-in-law four times a year. He lived to be over eighty, dying peacefully one day during his yoga exercises. In accordance with his wishes, he was buried on the mountain near the monastery.

As for Chong and Yaoqin, they lived happily together till old age, and had two sons both of whom became famous scholars.

And even to the present day, when singsong girls want to praise a man for showing consideration, they call him "a Master Qin" or "an oil vendor."

The Old Gardener

Through wind and pelting rain all night,
My wooden door was bolted tight;
Today the dark red flow'rs are gone,
The willow's green is left alone;
And, come to sweep the moss away,
I stay my broom here in dismay;
For, starring all the steps near by,
The crimson, wind-blown petals lie.

This verse was written by a flower-lover.

During the Tang Dynasty there lived east of Luoyang a gentleman named Cui Xuanwei, a devotee of Taoism and a bachelor who passed his life like a hermit. In the spacious grounds of his house, planted with flowers, bamboos and trees, he built a hut where he lived by himself; and his servants, whose quarters were outside this garden, could not enter without a good reason. For more than thirty years Cui never left his garden; and in springtime when the trees were in bloom he loved to stroll there day and night.

One fresh moonlit evening, unwilling to leave his flowers and go to bed, he was sauntering alone among the blossoms when he saw the dark figure of a girl slipping through the shadows.

"Who can she be, and what is she doing at this time of night in my garden?" he marvelled. "I will watch where she goes."

The girl went neither east nor west but came straight up to Cui and dropped a low curtsey.

Bowing in return, Cui asked: "From whose house do you come, young lady? And what brings you here so late at night?"

Parting her red lips in a dazzling smile, the girl answered: "I live near by. I am going with some friends to the east gate to see my aunt, and we would like to rest for a while in your courtyard. May we?"

Odd as he found her sudden appearance, Cui gave his cordial consent. And the girl, after thanking him, went back the way she had come, to return presently leading a group of maidens through the flowers and willows. As each in turn greeted Cui, he saw in the moonlight that they were exquisitely dainty and ravishingly beautiful. Some were magnificently attired, while others were simply dressed; even the maids attending them were quite bewitching. He could not imagine whence they had come. After they had exchanged greetings, Cui invited them to his room and they sat down.

"May I ask your names?" he said. "And what relatives are you calling on, that you come to my humble house?"

"My name is Yang," a girl in green told him. "This is Miss Li and this Miss Tao," she went on, pointing to two other girls, one in white and the other in red. And so she introduced them all, the last being a young girl in scarlet named Shi Acuo.[1]

"Though we have different surnames, we are all cousins," said Miss Yang. "Several days ago, our eighteenth aunt whose name is Feng[2] said that she intended to call on us, but she has not come; and we thought since the moon is so bright tonight, we might pay her a visit. Another reason for our coming was that we wanted to take this opportunity to thank you for all your kindness."

Before Cui could answer, one of the girls announced: "Here is Aunt Feng."

Surprised and pleased they trooped out to meet her, while Cui stood to one side to watch.

"We were on our way to see you, Aunt," declared the girls when they had greeted the newcomer. "But our host asked us

---

[1] Yang means willow, Li plum, Tao peach, Shi and Acuo are two names for the pomegranate.

[2] Feng means wind.

to sit down for a few minutes, and now you've come! This shows how we have been thinking of each other!" They all curtseyed to her.

"I have often wanted to come to see you," replied their aunt, "but some business has always prevented me. Today I took advantage of a free moment."

"It is such a lovely night," said the girls, "won't you sit down, Aunt, and let us drink to your health?" They ordered the maids to fetch wine.

"Is it all right to sit here?" asked their aunt.

"We have a good host and the place is quiet," replied Miss Yang.

"Where is our host?"

When Cui stepped forward to greet Aunt Feng he noticed that her manner was rather breezy and fresh. He felt slightly chilled in her presence. Inviting her to his hut where the maids had set the table and chairs in order, he asked her to take the seat of honour. The girls sat in order of seniority, and Cui himself took the place of the host.

In no time the maids had brought wine and food and heaped the table with rare fruits and delicacies. The wine was strong and sweet as honey: nothing in that feast resembled earthly fare. By now the moon was so brilliant that the room was as bright as by day, and a heady fragrance filled the air. Guests and host drank to each other and, after a great deal of wine had been drunk, the girl in red filled a big goblet for her aunt.

"I would like to sing to you," she said.

> *"My cheeks are lightly rouged,*
> *My crimson robe is stained with crystal dew;*
> *My beauty fades so fast,*
> *But, cruel wind, I speak no ill of you!"*

Tender and clear, this song made all who heard it sad.

Then the girl in white presented another goblet to Aunt Feng.

"I have a song too," she said.

"My jade-clear skin was whiter than the snow
Beneath the moonlight of a bygone spring;
I dare not blame the breeze for my distress,
But mourn my beauty slowly vanishing!"

This song, even sadder than the first, upset Aunt Feng, who had drunk a few cups too many and was ready to flare up at a trifle

"In these lovely surroundings and at a good feast like this, why sing such depressing songs?" she demanded. "If they are levelled against me, I would ask you to remember your manners! Both the singers must drain a big cup of wine by way of punishment and sing another song."

She filled a cup and prepared to pass it over; but because she was tipsy she did not hold the cup firmly. Her sleeve caught on her chopsticks and all the wine was spilt. With anybody else it would not have mattered, but the wine went over Acuo — and Acuo was a pretty young girl who loved fine clothes and was wearing an embroidered scarlet gown. A single drop would have left a mark on this scarlet silk, so how much more a whole cup! The wine had gone to Acuo's head too, and when she saw her dress ruined she flushed with anger.

"*They* may have a favour to beg," she declared. "But *I'm* not afraid of you!" And she swept out.

"How dare she defy me, the drunken chit!" retorted Aunt Feng angrily, and prepared to flounce off too.

"Acuo is so young," pleaded the other girls, as they followed their aunt down the steps. "The wine has made her forget her manners, but please don't take offence. We shall bring her tomorrow to apologize to you."

In vain, however, did they urge Aunt Feng to stay. She blustered off eastwards. The girls then said goodbye to Cui and scattered among the flowers. Eager to see where they were going, he hurried after them; but he slipped on the mossy ground and fell, and by the time he scrambled to his feet the girls had disappeared.

"It couldn't have been a dream," he mused, "because I didn't go to sleep. And they can't have been ghosts, because they were dressed properly and spoke clearly. But if they were human, how could they vanish so suddenly?" In his bewilderment he speculated wildly.

In his room, the table and chairs were back in their usual places. Not a cup or dish remained from the feast, yet the air was filled with fragrance. While he marvelled at this, Cui realized that it could portend no evil, so he was not afraid. The next evening he was strolling again among his flowers, and came once more upon the girls, who were urging Acuo to go to apologize to her aunt.

"Why ask that old witch?" demanded Acuo, who was still angry. "Why not ask the gentleman here?"

Delighted with the idea, they said to Cui: "We all live in your garden, sir. Every year we are troubled by bad winds which will not leave us in peace, and in the past we always asked Aunt Feng to protect us. But since Acuo offended her yesterday, she may not be willing to help us any more. If _you_ will protect us, we shall repay your kindness as best we can."

"What power have I to protect you?" asked Cui.

"All we ask," replied Acuo, "is that every New Year's Day you should set a crimson banner painted with the sun, the moon and the stars on the east side of the garden. Then we shall be safe. New Year's Day is past now; but if you will set up a banner on the twenty-first of this month at dawn when the east wind begins to blow, we shall have no trouble that day."

"That is easy," said Cui. "I will certainly do that for you."

"Thank you so much!" they cried together. "We shall never forget your kindness." Then, with a waft of fragrance they were gone so swiftly that Cui could not follow them!

The next day, interested in knowing what would happen, Cui prepared the crimson banner. When he got up at dawn on the twenty-first there was, sure enough, a slight east wind; so he hastily set up the banner on the east side of the garden.

Almost immediately a sand-storm swept down upon the city, and many trees south of Luoyang were blown down; only the plants in Cui's garden came through unscathed! Then Cui realized that the girls were flower spirits, Acuo in her scarlet frock being the pomegranate, while Aunt Feng was the spirit of the wind. The next evening these flower fairies brought him several pecks of peach and plum blossom to express their gratitude.

"Thank you, sir," they said, "for saving us. Our only way to repay your kindness is to bring you these flowers. If you eat the petals you will live to a great age and regain your youth; and if you will continue to protect us in this way we shall enjoy long life too."

After taking their advice Cui did indeed appear younger and younger, until he looked like a man in his thirties. And later he became an immortal.

> *The Luoyang gardener who loved his flow'rs*
> *Set up a crimson banner every year;*
> *By eating petals he avoided death,*
> *And blossoms proved his homely elixir!*

Pray do not imagine, gentle readers, that this tale about the wind and flower spirits is pure fantasy. In the four seas and nine continents are many marvels which men's eyes have never seen, men's ears have never heard, and scholars have never recorded in histories or classical lore.

It may be argued, though, that since Confucius avoided mentioning the supernatural, we would do well to shun these subjects too. And yet it is a fact that people who love flowers enjoy good fortune, while those who harm flowers shorten their own lives. Since the hand of Providence is manifest here, tales about flowers cannot be dismissed as foolish talk. If you do not believe me, gentle readers, let me tell you another story about a gardener who met a fairy in his old age. Flower-lovers will show even greater respect to flowers after hearing this story, while if there are any among you who do not love flowers,

I hope by means of this tale to make flower-lovers of you too. Although not all can become immortals, everyone can find enjoyment in a garden.

You ask when and where the events in this story took place? The answer is: during the reign of Emperor Ren Zong (1023-1063), in Changle Village, outside the East Gate of Suzhou. In this village, which lay only half a mile from the city, lived an old man named Qiu Xian. Coming of a line of farmers he owned a small plot of land and a thatched cottage. His wife had died and he had no children.

Since boyhood Qiu had loved growing flowers or cultivating fruit trees. He had, in fact, neglected farming to concentrate on gardening, and whenever he came upon some rare plant he was happier than if he had picked up a jewel. Even when out on urgent business, if he happened to see some flowering trees in a house he would slip in with a conciliatory smile, regardless of whether he was welcome or not. If he found only common plants or trees which were then blossoming in his own garden, he would leave quickly enough; but if he discovered some rare plant which he did not possess, or some plant which, even though he possessed it, had ceased to bloom in his garden, then he would set aside his business and remain there all day unable to tear himself away. So he came to be called The Flower Maniac.

If Qiu met a flower-vendor with a good plant, he would insist on buying whether he had money with him or not — if he had no money he would pawn the clothes off his back. Some flower-vendors, knowing him, always raised their price when dealing with him, for he could never resist buying. Wastrels too, who had lost all their money, knowing his passion for flowers would break branches off rare plants they had discovered and stick them in mud as if they had roots, to deceive him. And he would always buy. The strange thing was, however, that when Qiu planted such shoots they always grew. And so, day by day and month by month he built up a fine garden.

Around this garden Qiu had raised a bamboo fence on which

he trained rambling roses, briar roses, banksia, dog roses, hibiscus, cherry and broom; while at the foot of the fence he grew hollyhocks, balsam, cock's comb, mallow and poppies, as well as winter sweet, lilies, spring and autumn lychnis, cyclamen, anemones, rhododendron, wild ginger, white butterfly, elecampane, convolvulus and other flowers. They looked like a bright silk screen when in bloom. And a few paces from the fence he set other rare plants, so that before one flower had faded another was in blossom.

Inside the old gardener's double wicket gate, which faced south, was a path fringed by bamboos and shade-giving cypresses. This led to a three-roomed cottage which, although it had only a thatched roof, was high and spacious with large windows. In the hall hung a small painting by an unknown artist, and the plain wooden couch, table and chairs there were spotlessly clean; there was not a speck of dust on the floor either. Behind the hall were two fine rooms, one of which was the old man's bedroom. He had every kind of flower under the sun and they all grew well, so that each season there seemed like spring.

> Proud plum, so arrogant and stark,
> Shy, fragrant orchids dear,
> Cool, elegant camellia blooms,
> And greengage dark are here.
> Chrysanthemum that braves the frost,
> Sweet apricot in rain,
> Narcissus like translucent jade,
> Prim peony's disdain.
> Magnolia glimmers by the steps
> With pomegranate rare;
> And golden lotus by the pool
> Is cool and fresh and fair.
> Hibiscus dazzles by the stream
> Near perfumed cassia spray;
> The pear tree shimmers in the night,
> At dawn the peach is gay.

The winter plum is sweet to smell,
And bright as silk the rose,
And spring seems ever present while
Each season comes and goes.

That garden held more flowers and aromatic herbs than you could count!

Qiu's wicker gate faced the great Chaotian Lake which joined Wusong River in the east, Zhenze Lake in the west, and Pangshan Lake in the south; so the view was delightful in all seasons, in bright or rainy weather alike. Here Qiu built an embankment which he planted with peach and willow trees, whose red blossoms and green leaves in spring rivalled the beauty of the famous West Lake in Hangzhou. He planted hibiscus along the bank and lotus of different colours in the water; and when these were in flower the whole lake seemed covered by a silk canopy and the air was filled with fragrance. Water chestnut gatherers sang as they paddled their small craft, and sailing boats raced each other when there was a wind, while under the willows fishermen who had moored their boats spread their nets to dry. Some fished, others mended their nets, lay drinking on the prow, or challenged each other to swimming contests. Their laughter could be heard all day.

On painted barges came pleasure-seekers, attended by musicians, to see the lotus, and when they turned home at dark, thousands of lanterns mingled with the light of glow-worms and the reflection of stars in the water till you could hardly distinguish one from the other. In late autumn, when cold winds blew and turned the maple leaves red or yellow, the withered willows and hibiscus on the bank contrasted with the white duckweed and red smartweed at the water's edge; and the mournful cries of the wild geese among the rushes pierced the sky. In the depth of winter, when snow clouds massed and snowflakes fell, all was white. The pageant of the four seasons defied description.

Across the huge expanse of Lotus Lake,
While boys pluck lotus merry fishers sing;
A host of flow'rs enfolds a small thatched hut,
Whose master mid the blooms is slumbering.

But enough of this.

The old gardener's first care every day was to sweep away the fallen leaves from under his flowers, then water each plant in turn. And at night he would water them once more. Great was his joy whenever a tree was about to blossom. He would heat wine or brew a pot of tea, then bow low and pour a libation while he uttered three prayers for the tree's longevity. This done he would sit under the tree to sip his drink slowly, and once under the influence of wine he would sing. When he was tired, he would lie under the tree with a rock as his pillow, remaining there from the time when the buds began to open until the tree was in full blossom. If the sun was strong, he would sprinkle the flowers with water from a whisk. If the moon was bright, he would stay up all night. If a storm sprang up, in his straw hat and fibre cape he would make a tour of inspection; and wherever he found a branch battered by the wind he would prop it up with bamboo. In bad weather he would get up several times at night to inspect his charges.

When blossoms faded the old man would sigh or even shed tears, but unwilling to part with the fallen petals he always swept them up gently with his whisk and put them in a dish so that he could enjoy them until they were withered, when he would place them in a clean vase. As soon as the vase was full, with a look of inexpressible sadness he would offer libations again of tea or wine, then carry the vase to bury it in the embankment. This he called "Burying the Flowers." If any petals were spattered with mud during a shower, he would carefully wash them clean and scatter them in the lake. This he called "Bathing the Flowers."

The old gardener could not bear to see branches or flowers plucked. He reasoned: "A plant blossoms only once a year, and for a few days only during one of the four seasons. It puts up with three seasons of neglect for the sake of these few glorious days when it dances in the breeze and smiles at all around like a true favourite of fortune. But then all too often it is cut off in its prime. These few days are hard to come by, but to destroy a plant is easy. If flowers could speak, wouldn't they complain? Flowers first bud, then bloom and quickly fade; thus their blossoming time is very short. Then think of all the butterflies, bees, birds and insects which attack a plant, and of the hot sun, bitter wind and pelting rain. Men ought to protect flowers from all this — how can they have the heart to pluck them instead?

"Think of the time it takes a seedling to put out roots, branches and tender twigs before it can blossom for men's delight. Isn't the tree lovely enough? Why must people pluck the flowers? For plucked flowers and broken sprays can no more be restored to the branch than dead men can be restored to life or severed limbs rejoined to the body. If plants could speak, wouldn't they speak with tears?

"Some folk cut beautiful sprays for their vases just to divert guests for a moment while they feast, or pick rare flowers for their concubines to wear in their hair for a day. It never occurs to them that guests can be entertained in the garden itself and women can use artificial flowers for their hair. One twig broken means one twig less on the bough, and one branch cut this year means one branch less next year. But why not lengthen the life of a plant so that we can enjoy it year after year? There are unopened buds, too, which are plucked with the flowers and doomed to wither on the broken bough. Isn't that the same as when children die? Some people don't love flowers, but pluck them just for a whim, giving them to anyone who asks for them or tossing them carelessly away by the roadside. Isn't this the same as when men are unjustly done to death and have no one to avenge them? If flowers could speak, wouldn't they voice their hatred?"

With this philosophy, Qiu never broke a twig nor hurt a bud

in his life. When he admired flowers in other gardens he would willingly linger there all day; but if the master of the house offered to pluck a spray or a blossom for him, he would utter a horrified refusal. If he saw men picking flowers he would beg them to stop, and if they paid no attention he would gladly go down on his knees to them to save a flower's life. Although people called him The Flower Maniac, they were often moved by his sincerity to desist, and then he would bow low to express his thanks.

Some boys who picked flowers in order to sell them were paid by Qiu to stop doing this. But if a flower was plucked in his absence, he would be most distressed when he discovered it, and seal the broken stem with mud. This he called "Doctoring the Flowers."

For the reasons already given, Qiu tried to keep people out of his garden. If relatives or friends wanted to come in and he could not very well refuse them, he would make this clear before admitting them. He also warned them that he did not like human breath to contaminate the flowers and that they must not go too close to the plants. And if some oaf picked a flower or bud behind his back, the old man would flush with anger and never admit him again, not even if the fellow cursed or struck him. So later on, when people learned what he was like, they dared not touch so much as a leaf of his.

Now wherever there are shrubberies or plantations birds will come to nest, especially if they find fruit or berries. If the birds would content themselves with feasting on the fruit, little harm would be done, but they invariably injure the buds too; so the old gardener scattered grain on the ground for the birds and prayed to them to be merciful. And the birds were sufficiently intelligent after eating their fill to fly low, warbling among the flowers, without injuring a single bud or swallowing a single seed. Hence Qiu's garden bore more fruit — larger and sweeter too — than any other. When the fruit ripened, he would gaze heavenward and sacrifice to the flower god before presuming to taste it, and offer some to all his neighbours before selling the rest. Yet every year he made enough money from his fruit to live on.

Since the old man found happiness among his flowers, he tended his garden for more than fifty years — from boyhood to old age — without wearying of it. In fact, he became healthier as the years went by, taking pleasure in his rough clothes and simple fare. When he had money to spare he would help the poor and destitute in his village; so all the villagers respected him and addressed him as Master Qiu, though he always called himself The Old Gardener.

From dawn till dusk he dug and trenched and hoed,
Till with a thousand blooms his garden glowed;
And such a loving vigil did he keep,
He could not bear to leave his plants to sleep.

We come now to the second part of our story. There was in Suzhou a cruel, crafty, mean young fellow named Zhang Wei who, coming from an official family, took advantage of his position to lord it over his neighbours and ruin innocent people. And woe betide anyone who offended him, for Zhang would not rest content until he had ruined the unfortunate man's family. His attendants were as savage as tigers or wolves, and some young vagabonds were always with him to help him in his evil deeds. They stirred up trouble wherever they went, and those injured by them were past counting. The time came, however, when Zhang crossed a man more powerful than himself who had him beaten within an inch of his life; and, when sued, this enemy pulled strings at court so that Zhang lost his case. Then, accompanied by four or five servants and his usual group of young ruffians, he went to the country to live down his humiliation; and his country house happened to be in Changle Village, not far from the old gardener's cottage.

One day, strolling half drunk in the village after his morning meal, Zhang passed the old gardener's gate and was struck by the fresh and pretty flowers on the fence and the cool groves of trees around.

"This seems a pleasant place," he remarked. "Whose is it?"

"This is the garden of old Qiu, The Flower Maniac," replied his servant.

"Ah, yes," said Zhang. "I did hear there was some old fool here called Qiu who grows very good flowers. So this is where he lives. Suppose we go in to have a look?"

"The old man is rather eccentric," answered his servant. "He won't let people look at his flowers."

"He may refuse others," retorted Zhang. "But he can't treat me like that. Go and knock. Don't keep me waiting."

At this time the peonies were in full bloom and the old gardener, who had just finished watering them, was enjoying himself beside the flowers with a pot of wine and two dishes of sweetmeats. He had not finished his third cup when he heard knocking and put down his drink to open the gate. When he discovered five or six men standing there smelling strongly of liquor, he feared that they must be wanting to see the flowers. "What brings you here, gentlemen?" he asked, standing in the gateway.

"Don't you know me, old man?" demanded Zhang. "I am the celebrated Lord Zhang. That estate over there belongs to me. Hearing that you have many good flowers in your garden, we have come specially to have a look."

"Why, sir," replied Qiu, "I haven't any rare trees, only common varieties like peach and plum which have finished blossoming. There isn't much else."

"You old scoundrel!" roared Zhang with an angry glare. "How can it hurt you if we just have a look? How dare you say you haven't any? Are you afraid we'll eat your flowers?"

"It's the truth I'm telling," insisted Qiu. "There really isn't much."

Zhang paid no attention to him, however, but stepped forward and pushed the old man aside so roughly that he went staggering. Then they all rushed in. When Qiu saw how fierce they were, there was nothing he could do but close his gate and follow them in. He cleared away his wine and sweetmeats, and then stood watching the intruders.

They saw that the garden was well stocked with plants, and the peonies were blooming in all their splendour. These were not just common varieties like "Jade Pavilion in Spring," but included the five famous species: "Yellow Pavilion," "Green Butterfly," "The Melon," "Dark Beast," and "Red Lion." The peony is the king of flowers, and the peonies of Luoyang are the best in the world, one plant of "Yao Yellow" or "Wei Purple" from that city costing five thousand cash.

Do you ask why Luoyang has the best peonies? It is because Wu Zetian, the wanton Tang empress who had two favourite ministers named Zhang, thought she would like, one winter's day, to stroll in the palace grounds, and issued the following edict:

"Tomorrow I shall walk about my park;
Send word at once to let the Spring God know.
Bid all the flowers blossom in the night,
Before the morning wind has time to blow."

Since the empress was a sovereign ordained by Heaven, the plants dared not disobey her. They all began to bud and blossom that night; and on the following day, when she went to her pleasure grounds, she saw red and purple flowers blooming in all their fragrance. The peony alone, too proud to flatter the empress and her favourites, had not put forth so much as one leaf. Then Empress Wu in anger had the peony banished to Luoyang, since when the peonies of Luoyang have become the best in the world. The following verse, set to the air "Jade Pavilion in Spring," praises the peony:

This flower, graceful in the breeze,
Takes pride of place in May;
But fears its beauty in the rain
May soon be washed away.
The pretty girl has sighed all day
And now, before her glass,

Blushes to think that peonies
Her loveliness surpass.

The peonies, planted opposite the old gardener's cottage, were surrounded by rocks from the lake; and around them he had erected a wooden frame with a cloth awning to keep off the sun. The plants ranged from six to over ten feet in height and the magnificent blooms, large as platters and of variegated colours, presented a dazzling sight. Zhang's party exclaimed in admiration and he himself stepped on to a rock the better to inhale the fragrance. But Qiu was very particular about this.

"Stand back, sir," he said. "Don't go up there."

Annoyed as he was with the old gardener for not admitting him more promptly, Zhang had been waiting to find fault.

"You live so near my house, don't you know who I am?" he cried. "With this gardenful of fine flowers, you coolly told me you had none. And now, instead of being thankful that I didn't take offence, here you are telling me what I can do! Does it spoil a flower to sniff at it? Just to show you who is master, I'll smell some more." Pulling the blossoms to him one by one, he started burying his nose in them.

Old Qiu was furious, but dared not say anything. He thought that Zhang would be leaving almost at once; but the scoundrel intentionally assumed the air of a connoisseur and said:

"Flowers like this call for a celebration. Let's have some wine and enjoy ourselves." He ordered his men to fetch wine quickly.

When the old gardener saw that Zhang meant to stay and drink there, he was even more alarmed.

"My cottage is too small," he said, stepping forward. "There is no place to sit. You had better just look at the flowers, sir, then drink your wine in your own house."

"We can sit here," retorted Zhang, pointing at the ground.

"The ground is dirty," protested Qiu. "How can you sit there?"

"Never mind," was Zhang's rejoinder. "I'll have a carpet spread over it."

Food and wine were brought in, a carpet was spread on the
ground and they sat in a circle to play the finger-game and
drink. Long and merrily they caroused, while Qiu sat on one
side fuming.

Then the loveliness of the flowers made Zhang conceive a
wicked plan. He determined to make this garden his! Looking
tipsily at Qiu, he said: "I never thought an old fool like you
could grow flowers. That is to your credit. Here, drink a cup
of wine with me."

The old gardener was in no mood to answer politely. "I
never drink," he growled. "But don't let me stop *you.*"

"Will you sell this garden?" demanded Zhang.

Qiu realized that this meant real trouble.

"This garden is my life," he answered fearfully. "How can
I sell it?"

"Nonsense!" cried Zhang. "Just sell it to me. If you have
nowhere to go, you can come to my house. I won't ask anything else of you but to grow flowers for me. What do you say?"

"You are in luck, old one!" chorused Zhang's followers. "His
lordship is being very good to you. Hurry up and thank him!"

As they began to put pressure on him, the old gardener,
numb with rage, turned his head away.

"What a surly old fool!" cried Zhang. "Why don't you
answer?"

"I've told you I'm not selling. Why do you keep asking?"

"Curse you! If you still refuse to sell, I'll send you to the
yamen with my card."

Old Qiu, who was furious, wanted to answer back. Then
he thought: "Zhang is a powerful man, and he is drunk. Why
should I take him seriously? I had better give him a soft
answer."

So swallowing his anger he replied: "You must give me a
day in which to consider, sir. How can this be decided so
quickly?"

"That's right," said the others. "You decide tomorrow."

By this time they were very drunk. Zhang and his roughs

got up to go while the servants packed up the remains of the feast. Afraid that they might pluck the flowers, Qiu stood before the peonies to protect them; and when Zhang stepped forward to climb on the rocks, Qiu pulled at his sleeve and said:

"Though a flower is a trifle, a lot of work has to be put in every year to raise these few blossoms; so it is a pity to hurt them. And if you pluck them, they will wither in a couple of days. Why commit such a crime?"

"Crime? You are raving!" shouted Zhang. "Tomorrow the whole garden will be mine, so even if I pick all the flowers, it is none of your business!"

He tried to push the old gardener aside, but Qiu seized hold of him and would not let him go.

"Even if you kill me," he insisted, "I shan't let you pluck the flowers!"

"Curse you, you old fool!" cried the others. "What does it matter if his lordship takes a flower? Why make such an ado about nothing? Do you think you can frighten us out of picking?"

Then they began to pluck blossoms at random. Crying out in despair, the old man let go of Zhang and made a desperate attempt to stop the others; but when he barred the way on one side he could not protect the other, and soon many of his peonies had been plucked.

"You bandits!" cursed Qiu, whose heart was bleeding. "Swaggering in to play the tyrant here! I'll make you suffer for this!"

He charged so hard against Zhang, who was drunk, that the bully lost his balance and fell over backwards.

"Help!" cried the others. "His lordship is hurt!" And throwing down their flowers they rushed up to beat the gardener.

One of them was sober enough, however, to realize that since Qiu was an old man they might easily kill him, so he stopped the others and helped Zhang up. But angry and ashamed because of his fall, Zhang proceeded to tear up all the plants so

that not a bud was left, strewing the ground with flowers which
he trampled underfoot. Unhappy flowers!

Torn down and crushed by wicked hands,
The tender plants lay dead,
As if a storm had scattered all
The petals soft and red.

The old gardener rolled on the ground in his rage, calling
on heaven and earth. Neighbours who heard the uproar rushed
in and, shocked to see the garden being laid waste, they urged
the cruel men to stop and asked what had happened. Some of
the neighbours who were Zhang's tenants apologized to him
on Qiu's behalf and bowed him obsequiously to the gate.

"Tell that old scoundrel," ordered Zhang, "if he hands over
the garden quietly, I'll let him off! If he refuses again, let him
beware!" Then he stalked furiously off.

Because Zhang was drunk the neighbours did not take his
threats seriously, but came back and made Qiu, who was still
weeping bitterly, sit up on the steps. Then after trying to comfort him, they left, closing the gate behind them. Some of them,
who felt Qiu had been wrong in the past not to let people in
to see his flowers, said:

"The old fellow is a bit queer in the head: that's why this
happened. It should be a lesson for him."

But others with a sense of justice protested: "How can you
say such a thing? You know the proverb: Spend a year on
growing a flower, enjoy it for ten days only. People who simply
enjoy the sight of the blossoms don't know what trouble the
gardener has had. Heaven knows to what pains he has been
to raise these wonderful blossoms. How can you blame him
for being fond of them?"

Meantime old Qiu, still grieving for his mangled plants, set
to work to pick them up. But the sight of them, trampled,
scattered and mud-stained as they were, made his tears fall
anew.

"My poor flowers!" he groaned. "I loved you too much to

injure one petal or leaf on any plant. Who could have thought
that you would come to this?"

As he was weeping, he heard someone call: "Why are you
crying so bitterly, Master Qiu?"

The old man turned to see a beautiful girl of about sixteen,
simply but tastefully dressed. He had no idea who she could
be and dried his tears to ask:

"Where are you from, young lady? What brings you here?"

"I live near by," said the girl. "I came because I heard your
peonies were in bloom. I did not expect to find them withered."

At the mention of peonies, Qiu broke down again.

"What is the matter?" asked the girl. "Why are you crying
like that?"

Then the old gardener told her how Zhang had destroyed
his flowers.

"So that is the reason," said the girl with a laugh. "Would
you like the flowers to return to their boughs?"

"Don't make fun of me, young lady. How can fallen blossoms return to the boughs?"

"In our family we know how to restore blossoms to the bough.
Our method always succeeds."

"Can you really do that?" Qiu's sorrow began to turn to joy.

"Of course," said the girl.

"If you will perform this miracle," said Qiu with a bow,
"I have no other way of thanking you, but whenever my flowers
blossom I shall invite you here to enjoy them."

"Stop bowing to me," replied the girl, "and fetch a bowl of
water."

As Qiu hurried in for the water he was thinking: "How
can she work such a miracle? Could she be making fun of me
because she saw me weeping?" But then he reflected: "No.
I have never seen this young lady before, so there is no reason
why she should make fun of me. It must be true."

Returning to the garden after hastily filling a bowl with
water, he discovered that the girl had disappeared. The flowers
were back on their stems, however, not a single petal remaining

on the ground. But whereas one plant bore one colour only before, red and purple were now mixed and pale and dark intermingled, with the result that the peonies looked more magnificent than ever.

> *Saint Han, we know, could colour flowers afresh,*
> *The fairy maid restored them to the bough;*
> *Since miracles are worked by honest faith,*
> *Do not despise The Flower Maniac now!*

Surprised and delighted, Qiu exclaimed: "I never thought the young lady could really do this wonderful thing." Thinking she was still among the flowers, he put down the water and stepped forward to thank her; but although he searched the whole garden she was nowhere to be found.

"Where can the young lady have gone?" he wondered. "She must be at the gate. I am going to beg her to teach me this art." He ran to the gate but found it closed, and when he opened it and looked out he saw two old men sitting there. These were his neighbours Yu and Shan, who were watching fishermen hang out their nets in the sun. They stood up to greet the old gardener.

"We hear Zhang Wei was here making trouble," they said. "But we were in our fields and so could not come to ask what was the matter."

"Yes," said Qiu. "I had a great deal of trouble with those scoundrels. Luckily a young lady came who knew a good way to save the flowers; but she left before I could thank her. Did you see which way she went?"

"If flowers are spoilt, how can you save them?" asked the two old men in surprise. "How long ago did this girl come out?"

"Just now," replied Qiu.

"We have been sitting here for some time," said his neighbours, "but no one came out. There can't have been any girl."

Then Qiu realized the truth. "In that case, she must have been a fairy!" he cried.

"Tell us how the flowers were saved," requested the old men. And when the old gardener described what had happened, they declared: "What an amazing thing! Let us go in and look."

They went in, and Qiu barred the gate behind them.

"This must be the work of a fairy!" exclaimed Yu and Shan after seeing the peonies. "No mortal could do such a thing!"

Then, while Qiu burnt his choicest incense and bowed to Heaven to express his thanks, the two old men said: "Your single-minded love for flowers must have moved the fairy to come down to earth. Tomorrow you should let Zhang's ruffians see this, to make them feel thoroughly ashamed."

"No, no," replied the old gardener. "Such men are like mad dogs. The best thing is to avoid them. Why should I ask them back?" And the two neighbours agreed that there was reason in this.

Since Qiu was very happy, he warmed up the wine he had been drinking and invited Yu and Shan to enjoy the flowers till it was dark. After they left they spread the news, so that by the next day all the villagers knew it and wanted to see the peonies but were afraid the old gardener might not let them. Qiu was, however, an intelligent man. The apparition of the goddess had filled him with a desire to leave the world and search for truth. He did not try to sleep that night but sat by his flowers, deep in thought, until it dawned on him that he had been to blame for the trouble with Zhang.

"I brought it on myself by selfishness," he decided. "If I were like the gods, who are kind to all, it would never have happened."

So the next morning he opened wide his garden gate to all who wished to come in. The few villagers who ventured in first found him sitting facing the flowers.

"You can come and see the plants whenever you like," Qiu told them, "so long as you don't pluck them."

And when this news spread, all the men and women in the village flocked to his garden.

The next morning Zhang Wei told his followers: "Yesterday that old ruffian knocked me down. Do you think I can let it go at that? Come on now to demand his garden. If he refuses, we'll get some more men to smash up the place completely."

"His garden is next to your house," said Zhang's friends. "You need not be afraid that he will refuse. But it was a mistake to spoil the flowers yesterday. We should have kept a few to enjoy ourselves later."

"Never mind that," said Zhang. "They will grow again next year. Let's go quickly before he has time to get up to any tricks."

They had not gone far when they heard that a fairy had appeared in Qiu's garden to restore all the broken flowers to the boughs, and that all his peonies had different colours now. But Zhang did not believe this.

"What good deeds has that old thief done to deserve a visit from a fairy?" he demanded. "And this fairy turned up just after we spoilt his flowers — as if she were his housekeeper! Depend upon it, the old man has made up this story and spread it because he is afraid we will go back. He wants to make out that he is protected by divine power, so that we will leave him alone."

Zhang's followers agreed with him. But when they reached the garden they found the double gates wide open and men and women streaming through, all of whom told the same story.

"It looks as if it really happened," said Zhang's men.

"Never mind!" retorted the bully. "I don't care if the fairy is sitting there — I'm going to ask for the garden!"

As they walked along the winding path to the thatched cottage, they saw that the news was true. And the flowers, strange to say, looked more splendid than ever now that so many people had come to see them, and seemed, indeed, to be smiling.

Though Zhang was very much taken aback, he did not abandon his scheme to obtain the garden; but after looking around for a short time he conceived another wicked plan.

"Let us leave now." he said to his men.

When they had gone out of the gate, his men asked: "Why didn't you demand the garden?"

"I have a good plan," said Zhang. "There is no need to argue with him: the garden will be mine tomorrow."

"What is your plan?"

"Wang Ze who practised black magic in Beizhou has recently revolted," replied Zhang, "so the Ministry of War has ordered all prefectures and districts to prohibit sorcery and arrest all magicians. Our district has offered three thousand strings of cash as a reward for information about sorcerers. Well, tomorrow I shall send Zhang Ba to the yamen to accuse Qiu of sorcery, on the grounds that he has restored these flowers to their stems. The old man will admit his guilt under torture and be thrown into gaol; then the garden will be publicly auctioned, but who will dare to buy it? It is sure to fall to me, and I shall pocket the three thousand strings reward as well."

"This is a fine plan," said his men. "We must lose no time in carrying it out."

They went straight into the city to write the charge, and the next morning Zhang Ba was sent to the prefectural yamen to inform against the old gardener. Zhang Ba was Zhang Wei's ablest lackey and he knew the yamen officials well.

Since the city prefect was anxious to discover magicians, when he heard that the whole village had seen this miracle he naturally believed the charge and sent officers and constables with Zhang Ba to arrest Qiu. Zhang Wei, who had paid all the necessary bribes, told Zhang Ba and the constables to go ahead while he and his men followed. The constables marched straight into the garden, but the old gardener thought they had come to see his flowers and paid no attention. Then they rushed forward with a shout and bound him.

"What have I done?" asked Qiu in terror. "Why have you arrested me?"

Cursing him as a magician and a rebel, they dragged him away without a word of explanation. And when the neighbours gathered round in consternation to ask what had happened, the constables said:

"Why do you ask? He is guilty of a great crime. How do we know you haven't had a part in it?"

At this the villagers were afraid and slipped away lest they become involved. Only Yu, Shan and a few other good friends followed the old gardener at a distance.

After Qiu's arrest, Zhang came with his men to lock up the garden. First they had a good look round to see if there were any people left inside, then they locked the gate and went back to the yamen. The constables had already ordered Qiu to kneel on the platform, and the old gardener noticed that there was another man kneeling beside him but did not recognize the informer. The runners, all of whom had been bribed by Zhang, had prepared the instruments of torture.

"Where do you come from?" shouted the prefect. "How dare you practise magic here to deceive the people? What followers have you? Tell the truth now!"

This was like a cannon shot in the dark — the old gardener did not know who had attacked him.

"My family has lived for generations in Changle Village," he said. "I am not a magician from other parts. I know nothing about magic."

"The other day by means of black magic," declared the prefect, "you caused fallen blossoms to go back to the boughs. Can you deny that?"

Then Qiu realized that his accuser must be Zhang Wei. He told the prefect how the bully had demanded his garden and trampled the flowers, and how a fairy maid had appeared. The prefect, however, was too prejudiced to believe him.

"Many men practise religion all their lives in the hope of achieving godhead," he scoffed, "yet even then they cannot meet a fairy. Why should a fairy appear to you just because you weep? If a fairy did reveal herself to you she would leave her name so that people should know her, instead of disappear-

ing without a word. Whom do you think you are fooling? No
doubt about it, you are a magician! Put him to torture!"

With a shout of assent the runners rushed forward like tigers
or wolves, threw Qiu to the ground, caught hold of his ankles
and were just about to torture him when the prefect was seized
by such dizziness that he nearly fell off his seat. Too faint to
preside over the court, he ordered that Qiu be pilloried and
imprisoned until the next day when the trial should continue.

As the gaolers led Qiu away weeping, he saw Zhang Wei.

"Lord Zhang," he said, "I have done you no wrong. Why
should you do this cruel thing to destroy me?"

But Zhang turned away without a word and went off with
his lackey Zhang Ba and the other young vagabonds.

By now old Yu and Shan had arrived and learned the charge.

"This is gross injustice!" they said. "But never mind. Tomorrow we shall get all the villagers to bail you out."

"I hope so," responded Qiu tearfully.

"Curse you, you criminal!" shouted the gaolers. "Stop
snivelling and get a move on!"

With tears in his eyes Qiu went to the gaol, where his neighbours sent wine and food for him. The gaolers did not give it
to him, however, but consumed the gifts themselves. And at
night they chained the old man to his pallet so that he became
a living corpse, unable to move an inch.

"I wonder what fairy it was that saved my flowers but gave
that bully a chance to slander me," he sighed. "Ah, fairy! if
you will pity me and rescue me, I will give up my home and
practise religion."

As he was musing, the fairy who had visited him the previous
day appeared again.

"Mercy, fairy!" cried Qiu desperately. "Save me!"

The fairy smiled.

"Do you want me to end your agony?" she asked. And
stepping forward she pointed a finger at him, whereupon his
chains were loosed and fell to the ground. The old gardener
knelt down and kowtowed.

"May I know your name, fairy?" he requested.

"I am The Keeper of Flowers and I serve the Heavenly Empress in the Western Paradise," she replied. "Because you loved your flowers so well, I made them whole again, little thinking this would give that bully a chance to slander you. Fate must have decreed that you should suffer this trial; but tomorrow you will be set free. As for Zhang Wei, the flower spirits informed the Heavenly Emperor how the wretch injured flowers and plotted to kill you, and he has died. The hangers-on who abetted him in his evil courses have been visited by calamities too. If you devote yourself in future to religion, in a few years I shall come to carry you to Heaven."

The old gardener kowtowed again.

"Please tell me, goddess, how to practise religion," he begged.

"There are many ways," replied the fairy. "It depends upon a man's nature. Since you started by loving flowers, you will achieve godhead through flowers. If you feed yourself on blossoms, you will finally be able to fly."

After she had informed him how to draw nourishment from flowers, Qiu kowtowed again to thank her; but when he stood up she had vanished. Raising his head he saw that she was standing on top of the prison wall, whence she beckoned to him saying:

"Come up and leave with me."

But when the old man had climbed half way up he felt exhausted; and as he reached the top he heard the crash of gongs below and men shouting: "The magician has escaped!"

Terror made him lose his grip and fall headlong, to wake in a cold sweat on his pallet. Remembering clearly, however, what had passed in the dream, the conviction that all would be well gave him comfort.

A man who's free from selfish imperfection
May rest assured of heavenly protection.

Zhang Wei, meantime, who had seen that the prefect was convinced of Qiu's guilt, was exulting.

"The gardener is a cunning old rogue," he said, "but now let him spend a night on a prison pallet, leaving his garden for us to enjoy."

"The other day when the garden was still his we didn't have too good a time," said his men. "Now that it is yours, we can enjoy it to our hearts' content."

"That is right," said Zhang.

So they went out of the city together and ordered the servants to prepare wine and food. They marched to Qiu's garden, opened the gate and went in; and although the neighbours felt indignant, they were too afraid of Zhang to protest. But when Zhang and his men reached the thatched cottage, they found all the peonies scattered on the ground again — not a single flower remained on its stem!

They marvelled at this, and Zhang said: "It does look as if the old scoundrel is really a magician. Otherwise how could these peonies change back again so quickly? Could there really have been a fairy?"

"He knew that your lordship wanted to enjoy the flowers," suggested one young fellow, "so he has played this trick to make us feel foolish."

"Well," said Zhang, "since he has played this trick, we can enjoy the fallen blossoms."

With that they spread the carpet and sat on the ground as before. They drank heartily, and two extra bottles of wine were given to Zhang Ba as his reward. They caroused till the sun was sinking in the west and they were half drunk, when a great wind sprang up.

> *Flung to the winds the courtyard grass!*
> *Muddied and spoilt the pond!*
> *Borne in the air the roar of beasts,*
> *Tempest-torn pines beyond!*

Caught up by this swirling wind, all the flowers on the ground were transformed in a twinkling into girls about a foot high. But before the men had finished crying out in amazement, the girls shook in the wind till they attained the size of human beings. They formed a bevy of beauties in magnificent clothes, and the men were dazzled by their loveliness. A girl in red began to speak.

"We have stayed here for many years," she declared, "and been well looked after by Master Qiu. We never thought to see the day when ruffians would pollute us with their foul breath and savage us with their cruel hands, nor that they would bring a false charge against Master Qiu and plot to seize this place. Now we have our enemies before us! Let us fall on them to requite the kindness of our friend and to avenge the cruel insult to ourselves!"

"You are right," replied the rest. "We must lose no time, otherwise they may run away."

Then, raising their arms, they swept forward; and their long sleeves, fluttering like pennons in the wind, sent cold shivers down the men's spines.

"Ghosts! Ghosts!" cried the men. And throwing down their cups they fled in confusion with no thought for each other. They stumbled over rocks, grazed their faces against the branches of trees, slipped, fell, and staggered to their feet only to fall again. When this confusion had lasted for some time they counted their number, and found that Zhang Wei and his lackey Zhang Ba had disappeared. By now the wind had dropped, and with lowered heads they ran home like rabbits through the gloaming, thankful to escape with their lives. After the servants had recovered from their alarm, they asked some bold young tenants to go back with torches to search for the missing men. Returning to the garden they heard groans issuing from under a great plum tree, and when they raised their torches to look they discovered Zhang Ba, lying with a broken crown against the trunk of the tree, unable to rise. Two of the tenants helped him home while the rest searched the garden; but they found everything quiet and still. The peonies under their awning were blooming as before — not a blossom was broken — but cups and plates littered the cottage, where wine had been

spilt everywhere.   Gaping in surprise, they gathered together
the utensils and started searching again.   The garden was by
no means large, yet they went round it three or four times without finding any trace of Zhang Wei.

"Could he have been blown away by the wind or eaten by
the fairies?" they wondered.   "What can have become of him?"

After hanging around for some time, since there was nothing
they could do, they decided to go home for the night and make
a fresh search the next day.   As they reached the gate, however,
they met another group of men with lanterns coming in.   These
were old Yu, Shan and a few other neighbours who had come
to see whether it was really true that Zhang Wei and his men
had met ghosts, that he had disappeared and that a search party
was looking for him.   When the tenants declared that this was
indeed the case, the old men were amazed.

"Don't go yet," they said.   "We'll help you to look once
more."

They made another careful search, only to be disappointed
again; and the tenants were making for the gate, sighing, when
Yu and Shan said: "If you won't be coming back tonight, may
we lock the gate?   It is our duty to keep watch here."

By this time, having lost their leader, Zhang's men were like
a snake without a head   All their swagger gone, they answered·
"Of course!   Of course!"

Just as they were leaving, however, a tenant called out from
the east corner of the fence: "I've found the master!"   And
they all rushed over

The worker pointed up.

"Isn't that the master's gauze cap with soft flaps hanging on
the ash bough?" he asked.

"If the cap is here, its owner must be near by!" cried the
others.

But they had not groped more than a few paces along the
fence when one of them exclaimed in horror.

From the cesspool at the east corner a man was projecting
upside-down, and by the shoes and socks and lower garments

they could tell that it was Zhang. In spite of the filth the tenants dragged his body out, while Yu and Shan, secretly thanking the gods, left with the other neighbours. Some of Zhang's men carried his corpse to the lake to wash, and others went home to inform his family, who wept and wailed as they prepared clothes for the funeral. That same night the fracture in Zhang Ba's skull proved fatal, and he died just before dawn. Thus retribution came to two evil-doers.

> *Two knaves have bid the world farewell,*
> *Two wicked ghosts have gone to hell!*

The next day the prefect felt well enough to preside over the court; and he was about to try the old gardener again when a constable reported how the informer, Zhang Ba, and his master, Zhang Wei, had both died the previous night. The prefect could not believe in this new miracle until more than a hundred of the local peasants and elders arrived with a joint petition which stated that Qiu was no magician but a flower-lover who did good deeds, and that Zhang Wei had been punished by Heaven for accusing the old gardener falsely. They explained and accounted for the whole affair.

The prefect's dizziness the previous day had made him suspect that injustice might have been done, and now he saw the truth. After ordering the immediate release of Qiu, who had fortunately not yet been tortured, he gave him a notice bearing the official seal to hang outside his garden gate, in order to prevent people from injuring his plants. The villagers expressed their gratitude to the prefect and left the court, and when Qiu had thanked all his neighbours, he went home with them. Yu and Shan unlocked the garden gate and went in with their friend; and when the old gardener saw his peonies blooming as before, he was very moved. Then there was merry-making for several days, for the neighbours gave feasts to celebrate Qiu's return, and he prepared feasts to thank all who had helped him.

After that the old gardener accustomed himself to feeding on flowers until he was able to do without cooked food: he also gave all the money from his fruit sales as alms. So in a few years' time, his hair, which had been white, turned black again and his cheeks became as ruddy as those of a young man.

On the fifteenth day of the eighth month one year, Qiu was practising yoga under his blossoms beneath a bright sun and cloudless sky when a holy breeze sprang up and coloured clouds rose like vapour As clear music sounded in the air and rare incense was wafted from above, blue phoenixes and white storks alighted in his courtyard and The Keeper of Flowers appeared in the sky, surrounded by pennons, canopies and fairy maids making music. When the old gardener saw her, he prostrated himself on the ground.

"Qiu Xian, your time has come!" said the goddess. "I have requested the Heavenly Emperor to appoint you Protector of All the Flowers on Earth, and you are to go to Heaven now with your house. Your task will be to bless those who love and cherish flowers and to punish those who neglect and destroy them."

When Qiu had thanked her by kowtowing towards the sky, he ascended the clouds with the fairies, while his thatched cottage and garden rose slowly from the ground and floated southwards. Old Yu, Shan and all the villagers who witnessed this knelt down and saw the old gardener raise his hand in farewell to them from the clouds, where he remained in sight for a long time. After this the village was renamed Fairy Village or Flower Village.

> *It was the gardener's love for flow'rs*
> *That moved the goddess to appear;*
> *His garden soared with him to Heav'n,*
> *No need for any elixir!*

Marriage by Proxy

*I bring wine with me here every day on my fisherman's
boat;*
*From the depth of the flowering reeds my soft melodies
float;*
*Wind is hushed on the lake, and no shadows of clouds
sail by,*
*While as bright as green glass are the water and radiant
sky.*

This verse was written by Yang Bei of the Song Dynasty
during a visit to Lake Taihu, which lies ten miles southwest
of Suzhou. Do you ask how large the lake is? It measures
nearly seventy miles from east to west and forty miles from
north to south, has a circumference of one hundred and sixty
miles and an area of sixty thousand acres. The largest of its
seventy-two islands are the two called East Dongting and
West Dongting, which rise sheer out of the water; while the
other islets, near and far, seem sometimes to be floating on
the lake and sometimes to have disappeared beneath the
waves.

East Dongting and West Dongting are in the middle of
the lake, completely surrounded by water, so that you must
take a boat and brave the wind and waves to reach them. The
people here are clever traders, who sell their wares in all
parts of the country; thus the merchants have a saying: "The
men of Taihu could drive a hard bargain even in Heaven."

Our story is about a rich man named Gao Zan, who lived
on West Dongting. As a young man he dealt in grain in the
south, and finally he became wealthy enough to open two

331

pawnshops and hire four assistants to run them for him while he lived in comfort at home. His wife, a daughter of the Jin family, bore him a son whom they named Gao Biao, and a daughter, Qiufang, who was two years older than her brother. Gao Zan engaged an experienced old tutor to teach his two children; and since Qiufang was an · intelligent child, after studying from the age of seven to twelve she had read all the classics and could write excellent essays and poems. At thirteen she left the classroom to devote herself to such womanly accomplishments as needlework and embroidery in her own chamber; and by the time she was sixteen she was remarkably beautiful.

Since his daughter was so lovely and talented, Gao Zan resolved not to marry her to any ordinary fellow, but only to a gentleman and a scholar, who must be both brilliant and handsome. He was not concerned about the amount of the wedding gifts, and was willing to give his daughter a handsome dowry so long as a suitable match could be found for her. Many of the local gentry sent to ask for her hand; but when Mr. Gao discovered that the suitors possessed only average abilities and indifferent looks, he turned them all down.

Since Gao Zan was a rich man, go-betweens spread the news of his daughter's beauty and intelligence far and wide, reporting that her father was even willing to lose money over the marriage provided he could procure a handsome and accomplished son-in-law. The result was that every young man with the least pretension to talent or good looks tried his luck and asked a go-between to present his case as favourably as possible; but most of them proved to be quite mediocre. And after being deceived time and again by matchmakers, Gao Zan finally lost patience.

"In future let us have no more empty talk," he declared. "If you find anyone outstanding, bring him to see me; then I can soon tell whether he suits me or not and we shall save all this trouble."

After this, the go-betweens thought twice before approaching Mr. Gao.

Let us turn now to a young scholar named Qian Qing who lived in Wujiang in the Suzhou Prefecture. This youth had studied the classics, possessed a wide knowledge of things ancient and modern, and was as handsome as you could wish. He came of a poor family of scholars and had been unfortunate enough to lose both his parents while yet a child; so he was all alone in the world, and by the time he was old enough to marry could not afford to take a wife. Instead, he lived with his old servant, Qian Xing, who did a little peddling which was barely sufficient to keep them both alive. Indeed, they often went hungry. Luckily, however, the year that Qian Qing passed the district examination, a rich cousin of his who lived outside the North Gate of Wujiang invited him to his house to continue his studies.

This cousin, Yan Jun, was the same age as Qian Qing, both of them being eighteen that year. But since Yan was the senior by three months, Qian addressed him as his elder brother. Yan's father had died, and he had only his old mother left. He, too, was unmarried.

"Why, story-teller," you may object, "Qian Qing did not marry because he was poor. But how did it happen that Yan Jun, who was so well off, was still a bachelor at eighteen?"

Well, there was a reason for this, reader. Yan Jun had such a high opinion of what was due to himself that he had sworn to marry none but a beauty, and had not yet succeeded in finding a wife. He happened to be extraordinarily ugly himself, yet he always dressed in brilliant reds and greens, and chuckled to think what a fine figure he cut. He was, moreover, such an ignoramus that he could hardly write a complete sentence; yet he insisted on introducing classical tags and historical allusions into his conversation to air his knowledge. Although Qian Qing realized that he had nothing in common with such a man, since the latter was making it possible for him to continue his studies he deferred to his cousin's wishes in every way; and Yan became so attached to Qian that he consulted him about everything and they were on the best of terms.

To proceed with our story, however. One day at the beginning of the tenth month, a distant relative named You Zhen, who was a shrewd trader and had borrowed capital from Yan to start a fruit shop, came back from the Dongting islands with several loads of oranges and presented some to Yan as the first of the season. While on the islands You had heard the story of Gao Zan's search for a son-in-law, and he happened to mention this quite casually to Yan, who immediately pricked up his ears.

"I have always wanted to make a good match, but never succeeded," thought Yan. "Now here is this eligible girl. With my looks and attainments, to say nothing of my wealth, if I send a matchmaker over to present my case well, I should be sure of success."

After a sleepless night he got up at dawn to wash and dress hurriedly, then called on You Zhen, who was just taking down his shutters.

"What brings you here so early, sir?" asked You.

"I want to ask you a favour," replied Yan. "I came early to make sure not to miss you."

"What is it you would like me to do?" inquired You. "Come in and sit down while you give me your instructions."

Yan Jun went in, and after they had greeted each other ceremoniously they took their seats in the places of guest and host.

"I have come to ask you to act as my go-between," said Yan.

"It is very good of you to put me in a position to earn a go-between's fee, sir. What family do you have in mind?"

"The Gao family on West Dongting Island which you mentioned yesterday. That would be an ideal match, and I hope you will consent to arrange it for me."

You Zhen chuckled.

"Forgive me if I speak frankly, sir," he said. "If it were

any other family I would gladly go; but you must find some other matchmaker to call on Mr. Gao."

"Why do you refuse?" asked Yan. "You brought this up in the first place; so what makes you ask me to find another go-between?"

"I am not exactly refusing," said You, "but old Gao is such an odd character that he will be difficult to talk round. That's why I'm hesitating."

"On other matters," countered Yan, "he may try to trick you, and prove a difficult customer; but all a go-between has to do is to bring a young couple together, and that is a good deed, provided his daughter is not set against marriage. Men and women have got to marry; and however odd this Gao is, he can't treat a go-between rudely. So what are you afraid of? It seems to me you're deliberately making difficulties because you don't want to help. I shall just have to find someone else, that's all. But don't expect to be invited to my wedding feast."

Saying this, he rose in a huff to go.

Now You Zhen, who had borrowed money from Yan, usually deferred to all the latter's wishes. When he saw that his patron was angry, he hastily changed his tune.

"Don't be offended," he said. "Please sit down, and let us discuss the matter again."

"If you're willing to go, say so," retorted Yan. "If not, what is there to discuss?"

But while grumbling like this he sat down once more.

"I am not deliberately making difficulties, but that old Gao is a real eccentric," explained You. "Other families lay down conditions for the bride, but he imposes them on the bridegroom. He won't give his daughter to any man until he's seen the fellow and is satisfied with him. In view of all these difficulties, I'm afraid you may go to a lot of trouble for nothing. That's why I don't dare undertake such a tricky business."

"But judging by what you say, it's the simplest thing in the world," replied Yan. "If he wants to see me, let him. I'm not deformed. I've nothing to be afraid of."

You Zhen could not help laughing.

"Don't take offence, now," he said. "But the fact is that although you are not ugly, Mr. Gao has turned down plenty of handsomer men than you. If you don't let him see you, you have some slight chance of success. But if he sees you, there is not one chance in ten thousand."

"The proverb says that go-betweens must know how to lie," countered Yan. "You can assure him that I am a most handsome man. For all you know, this match may be predestined, in which case you will win his consent at once without his demanding an interview."

"But what if he does insist on one?"

"We can settle that later if necessary. Do go and speak for me."

"Very well, to please you, I will."

"Be sure to do your best," urged Yan as he stood up to go. "If you bring this off, I'll give you twenty taels of silver and return you your note of hand, besides paying the usual go-between's fee."

"Of course I'll do what I can," replied You.

As soon as he reached home, Yan Jun sent a servant with fifteen cents in silver to You, to cover his expenses on the boat the next day. And that night again he could not sleep a wink.

"If he doesn't do his best, but comes back with more excuses, this trip will have been in vain," he thought. "I had better send a smart servant with him to hear what he says. Yes, that's a good idea!"

As soon as it was light he called his servant boy, Xiao Yi, and told him to accompany You Zhen to the Dongting islands. But even after Xiao Yi had left, Yan could not set his mind at rest; so he hastily washed and combed his hair, then went to a nearby temple to consult the oracle there. He burned incense and bowed before the shrine, then shook the container holding divination sticks until one fell out. When he picked

it up, he found that it was Number Seventy-three; and on the
wall under this number he read:

Their pledge once plighted in the fragrant bower,
  No message did she send;
In vain he hopes to join his love once more,
  In failure all will end!

Although Yan Jun was no scholar, the meaning of these lines
was clear enough.

"Curse it!" he swore, as shaking his sleeves in disgust he
strode out of the temple.

Upon reaching home, he sat down to consider the situation.

"Why should this end in failure?" he wondered. "Can he
really object to my looks? Men are not like women in this
respect — it's enough if a man is presentable — why should
Mr. Gao want a second Pan An?"[1]

He picked up a mirror and studied himself in it for some
time; but soon the sight was more than even he could bear.
Slamming the mirror down on the table, he sighed heavily and
remained sitting there in utter dejection for a long time.

Let us return, however, to You Zhen and Xiao Yi, who had
hired a fast boat with three rowers. There was no wind that
day and the lake was still; the oars creaked as the boatmen
pulled on them, and by two in the afternoon they had reached
the landing stage before Mr. Gao's house on West Dongting.
Xiao Yi presented the visiting card, and when Mr. Gao invited
them in and inquired into their business, You replied that he
had come as a go-between to ask for Miss Gao's hand in
marriage.

"Whom do you represent?" asked Gao.

"A relative who lives in my district. He is well-to-do, his
property being on a par with your own, sir. Although only just
eighteen, he is a fine scholar."

"What does he look like? I have made it clear that I won't
accept anyone before seeing him."

---

[1] An ancient scholar celebrated for his good looks.

Knowing that Xiao Yi was behind his chair, You Zhen had to tell a barefaced lie.

"There can be no question about his looks," he said. "He's a splendid-looking fellow in every way! He's a fine scholar too. When he took the preliminary test at fourteen, the examiner placed him first on the list. Because he has been mourning for his father for the last few years, he has not entered a school, nor can he take the county examination; but all the old scholars who have seen his compositions say he is good enough to take the provincial and palace examinations. I am not a professional matchmaker; but because I often buy fruit in your honourable district, I happened to hear that you wished to select a suitable husband for your beautiful and accomplished daughter. It struck me immediately that my relative would make an excellent match for her; so I have made bold to call on you."

Gao Zan was delighted.

"If your relative is both handsome and talented, how can I refuse him?" he said. "But I shall not be satisfied till I have seen him. If you will bring him to my humble house, there should be no further difficulty."

"I am not exaggerating, sir, as you will see for yourself later," said You. "But my relative is a young gentleman who seldom leaves his study, and he may not be willing to come. If I prevail on him and we succeed in arranging a match, all will be well. But if we should fail, he will be ashamed to go home and is sure to bear me a grudge."

"If he is as good as you say," replied Gao, "we are bound to make a match of it. But since I never leave anything to chance, I must see him. If he doesn't want to call on me, I can call on you; and you can introduce him to me casually in your house. How about that?"

You Zhen dreaded to think what would happen if Mr. Gao went to Wujiang and found out how ugly Yan Jun was.

"If you have set your heart on seeing him, sir," he said

hastily, "I will bring him here to pay his respects. How can we trouble you to go so far?"

Having said this, he prepared to take his leave; but Mr. Gao would not let him go, and hastily ordered a meal to be served. They drank together till nearly nine, when Gao Zan urged You to stay for the night.

"I have bedding on board my boat," replied You, "and we must start early tomorrow morning; so I will say goodbye to you now. When I bring my young kinsman to pay his respects, I shall impose on your hospitality again."

Then Mr. Gao saw him to the junk and gave him a packet of silver for his boat-fare; and You, after thanking him, went aboard. The next morning he and Xiao Yi travelled under full sail before a favourable wind, reaching Wujiang in less than half a day.

Yan Jun was standing at his gate waiting for them, and hurried to meet them.

"Here you are at last!" he exclaimed. "How did you get on?"

You Zhen described in detail all that had passed between him and Mr. Gao.

"He insists on seeing you, sir," he concluded. "What's to be done?"

When Yan's jaw dropped and he said nothing, You suggested that they talk it over later, then went home.

Yan Jun went back into his house and called for Xiao Yi to cross-examine him, for he was not sure that You had told him the truth. Xiao Yi, however, confirmed the go-between's story. Presently, after cudgelling his brains, Yan hit on a way out of this difficulty, and went to call on You again.

"Since hearing what you had to say, I have thought of a plan," he said.

"What is your plan?"

"My cousin, Qian Qing, who is studying in my house, is a little better-looking and cleverer than I am. I'll ask him to go with you tomorrow and pass himself off as me. If we can fool

Mr. Gao for the time being, he won't be able to back out once we have exchanged betrothal gifts."

"If he sees Mr. Qian," said You, "he will have no earthly reason to refuse. I'm only afraid Mr. Qian may not be willing."

"He is my cousin," retorted Yan, "and we are on the best of terms. Why shouldn't he take my place for a while if I ask him? I'm sure he won't refuse."

He went home and took his dinner that evening with Qian in the study, providing specially good food and wine for the occasion.

"I impose on your kindness every day," said Qian in surprise. "Why should you provide such a feast today?"

"First have a few cups of wine," said Yan. "Then I want to ask you a small favour, which you must promise not to refuse."

"There's nothing I won't do for you if I can," replied Qian. "But in what way can I be of service to you?"

"The fact is, cousin," answered Yan, "that You Zhen who keeps the fruit shop across the road is trying to arrange a match for me with the daughter of the Gao family on West Dongting Island. He gave Mr. Gao such a flattering description of my talents and good looks that the old man insists on my visiting him before exchanging presents. You talked it over with me yesterday. The point is this. If I go, I may not live up to You's description; and then not only will You lose face, but the match may fall through. So I want you to take my place and go with You Zhen to see Mr. Gao. If you help to deceive him and make the wedding possible, I shall be ever so grateful and reward you handsomely."

Qian Qing thought this over.

"I would gladly do anything else for you," he said. "But I'm afraid this can't be done. Mr. Gao might be taken in for a time; but when he finds out the truth, you and I will both be in an awkward position."

"All I want is to trick him for a time," replied Yan. "I'm not afraid of his finding out after the exchange of presents.

Since he doesn't know who you are, he can only blame the go-between; and what harm will that do you? Besides, he lives miles away on West Dongting, and it will take him some time to find out the truth. Don't worry, but just go ahead. There's nothing to be afraid of."

Qian did not reply immediately, for he was thinking hard. To fall in with his cousin's wishes would hardly be honourable; yet to refuse would mean offending the man who was supporting him. He was in a dilemma.

"My dear cousin," said Yan seeing him hesitate, "you know the proverb: The sky can't fall because there will always be someone to prop it up. I shall take the whole responsibility, don't worry."

"Well," said Qian, "I look far too shabby to pass myself off as you."

"I know how to fix that," replied Yan.

No more was said on the subject that night.

The next morning Yan rose early and went to the study to order a servant-boy to fetch a leather case of bright silk and satin clothes in the latest style, which had been scented with ambergris so that they gave off a pungent odour. Yan gave his cousin a complete new outfit, including new socks and silk slippers; and when he found that his caps would not fit Qian, he bought him a new one. He also gave him two taels of silver.

"Please take this trifle for the time being," he said. "I shall show my gratitude more substantially later. The clothes are yours to keep too. All I ask is that you don't mention the matter to anyone. I've arranged with You Zhen for you to leave tomorrow morning."

"Just as you please," replied Qian. "I'll borrow these clothes for the time being, and return them when I come back. But I can't accept this silver."

"The men of old shared horses, carriages and fur coats with their friends," said Yan. "Even if I didn't need your help, I would have thought nothing of giving you these few poor clothes. They are just a small expression of my gratitude; and if you refuse I shall feel very uncomfortable."

"Since you are so kind, I will accept the clothes. But I can't take the silver."

"If you persist in refusing, I shall think you are unwilling to help."

Then Qian accepted the silver.

That same day Yan had another meeting with You Zhen. You was most reluctant to undertake this trip; but not liking to offend Yan, he finally consented. Then Yan hired a boat and prepared provisions, bedding and so forth for the journey. He also ordered three servant-boys to act as attendants, one of them being Xiao Yi, who had accompanied You on his previous trip. All three were smartly dressed in silk, and Yan bade them be sure to address Qian as their master — not by his own name — when they reached the island. These preparations took most of the night, and they rose early the next morning to help Qian with his toilet. Everything he put on was new, and a delicious perfume was wafted from his splendid clothes when he moved. He looked more elegant than ever!

You Zhen was invited to a meal in Yan's home with him and his cousin; then they were escorted to the boat by Xiao Yi and the two other servants. Once again they had a favourable wind, and travelling under full sail reached West Dongting Island at dusk and spent the night on the boat.

The next morning after breakfast, when they judged Mr. Gao should be up, Qian wrote a formal visiting card couched in most respectful terms in Yan Jun's name, and Xiao Yi took this card to Mr. Gao's house to announce that Mr. You had brought his young master to pay his respects. Mr. Gao's servants, who recognized Xiao Yi, hastened to pass on his message; whereupon Mr. Gao ordered the guests to be admitted at once. Then, followed by You, the false Yan Jun entered the reception room; and when Mr. Gao saw how dignified, handsome and beautifully groomed the young gentleman was, he was most favourably impressed.

They exchanged greetings and Mr. Gao asked Qian to take the seat of honour; but the latter declined on the grounds of his youth, and finally they sat down facing each other, Gao Zan inwardly applauding the young man's modesty.

Once seated, You Zhen broke the silence to express his gratitude for Mr. Gao's hospitality on the occasion of his previous visit.

"Not at all!" rejoined Mr. Gao. "So this young gentleman is your relative, Mr. Yan! The other day I omitted to ask his honourable second name."[1]

"I am really too young to be entitled to a second name yet," replied Qian politely.

"His second name is Boya (Elder Refinement)," put in You.

"Aptly chosen! Aptly chosen!" declared Gao warmly.

"You flatter me, sir," returned Qian.

Then Mr. Gao made inquiries about Yan's family, and Qian answered each question in the most gentlemanly manner.

"Well, he seems quite brilliant outwardly," thought Mr. Gao. "But what about his learning, I wonder? I'll ask the tutor and my son to meet him, to see what sort of scholar he is."

Accordingly, when tea was served for the second time, he ordered his servant to go to the library and invite the tutor and the young master in to meet the guests. Very soon a scholarly-looking gentleman in his fifties came in, leading a lad who still wore his hair about his shoulders. All stood as greetings were exchanged.

"This is my son's tutor, Mr. Chen, from the prefectural college," said Mr. Gao. "And this is my son, Gao Biao."

The boy was remarkably handsome.

"If the son is like this, the daughter must be well worth looking at," reflected Qian. "Yan is a lucky fellow."

When the tea had been brought in a third time, Mr. Gao turned to the tutor.

-----

[1] A young scholar was often given a second name when he grew up, and this was the name generally used in polite address.

"Our worthy guest comes from Wujiang," he said. "Though young, he is a good scholar."

Mr. Chen took the hint at once.

"Wujiang is noted for its men of letters," he remarked to Qian, "and the men of that district show exceptional discernment. Who would you say are the three most famous men from your district and in what way did they distinguish themselves?"

Qian promptly named the three men, after which he and the tutor embarked on a discussion; and, realizing that Mr. Chen's scholarship was no more than average, the young man let himself go. He introduced classical quotations and allusions to events in ancient and modern history, until the tutor was quite overcome and could only exclaim:

"What talent! What remarkable genius!"

As for Mr. Gao, he was so delighted he could hardly sit still; and presently he despatched a servant with orders that a specially good meal be prepared. At once attendants arranged tables and spread them with every kind of delicacy, and Mr. Gao, bowing with the cup and chopsticks in his hands, offered Qian the seat of honour. But Qian declined, and sat down facing his host as before. Then, in a twinkling, the tables were spread with three soups, ten main dishes and a number of side plates.

Do you ask how this could be done so promptly? The fact was that Mrs. Gao doted on her daughter, and when she heard that the go-between had brought young Mr. Yan, she hid behind the screen to have a look at him. The moment she saw how handsome he was and how well he talked, she lost her heart to him and guessed that her husband would do the same. So she had a feast ready as soon as it was ordered, and it was served like lightning. The five men had rice after their wine, and more wine after their rice, feasting till the sun was sinking in the west, when Qian and You rose to take their leave. Gao Zan could not bear to part with them, and begged them to be his guests for several days; but Qian would not hear of this, and finally Mr. Gao had to let him go.

First Qian Qing took his leave of Mr. Chen, thanking him for his instruction; then he expressed his gratitude to his host.

"We shall be making an early start tomorrow, sir," he said, "so I shall not come back to say goodbye."

"Your visit has been so short that I have not been able to entertain you properly," replied Mr. Gao. "Forgive me if I have been remiss."

Gao's son also bid them farewell, and Mrs. Gao presented them with food and wine for the journey, as well as a packet of silver for their boat-hire.

"I am quite satisfied with young Mr. Yan's attainments and appearance," said Mr. Gao, taking You Zhen aside. "I shall be delighted if you will complete all arrangements for the wedding."

"I shall carry out your wishes," promised You.

Gao Zan saw them to their boat, where they parted, then he and his wife spent the whole night discussing their future son-in-law.

The next morning Qian and You set sail; but since the wind was against them they did not reach home till late that night. Yan Jun was sitting up alone by candlelight eagerly awaiting their news; and they went in to tell him all that had happened. Hearing that there were no difficulties in the way of his match, Yan was overjoyed, and he hastened to choose an auspicious day that same month for the exchange of betrothal presents. As an expression of gratitude he also returned You Zhen's note of hand for twenty taels of silver. Then he selected the second day of the twelfth month for the wedding; and since Mr. Gao had found a son-in-law after his own heart, and his daughter's dowry had long since been ready, he raised no objections.

Soon it was the end of the eleventh month, and the happy day was fast approaching. In those parts they did not observe the ancient custom of sending the bridegroom to fetch the bride; but the bride's mother usually escorted her to her husband's home. Gao Zan, however, having chosen such a wonderful son-in-law and boasted of him to all and sundry, now insisted that Yan should come to his house for a wedding feast to which he would invite all his friends and relatives. When You Zhen heard this he was appalled, and lost no time in telling Yan.

"Well," said Yan, "I shall have to go myself this time."

You stamped his foot.

"The other day when Mr. Qian went, the whole household was staring at him for hours!" he cried. "They could paint his portrait from memory. How am I to explain it if someone quite different shows up this time? The marriage will be broken off, and I shall be disgraced!"

At this, Yan began to abuse his go-between.

"I told you that this marriage was predestined," he grumbled. "If you had let me go the first time, we should not be in this fix today. This is all your fault for telling me how difficult old Gao was and persuading me to send my cousin instead. Now it appears Mr. Gao is only too easy to get on with — as soon as we proposed it he agreed to the match. This is because I was fated to marry his daughter: it has nothing to do with his seeing Qian Qing. Besides, now that he has accepted my gifts, his daughter belongs to me. Dare he deny that? What can he do if I go there myself this time? Can he stop the marriage?"

"Of course he can stop it!" You shook his head. "The girl is still in his house. If he refuses to put her in the sedan-chair, there is nothing you can do."

"I'll take a few extra men with me," said Yan. "If he's willing, so much the better. If not, we'll break our way in and carry her off; then let him take the case to court if he likes. I have the girl's horoscope as evidence; so if he calls the wedding off, he will be in the wrong!"

"You mustn't think of anything so rash," entreated You. "A powerful dragon is no match for a snake in its own lair. However many men you were to take, you couldn't compete with a local family who can call in more and more people to their aid. And if big trouble were to come of it and we were involved in a lawsuit. the old man would swear that the man who came to ask for his daughter's hand was not the same as the bridegroom. Then the magistrate would be bound to question the go-between, and under torture I should have to admit the truth. Even Mr. Qian's career might be ruined. That would be no joke!"

"In that case I'll just stay away," said Yan after a moment's thought. "I'll trouble you to go tomorrow to tell Mr. Gao that I have already called on him once, and in this part of the country we don't follow the custom of fetching the bride. They had better just send the girl over here as is usually done."

"That simply won't work," replied You. "Old Gao was so delighted with his future son-in-law that he has been boasting of his brilliance and good looks ever since; so all his relatives and neighbours are waiting for the bridegroom to fetch the bride in order to see him for themselves. Someone has got to go."

"What's to be done then?" demanded Yan.

"In my humble opinion the only thing to be done is to ask Mr. Qian to take your place again, and carry through the imposture to the end. Once we have brought your bride home, your family is powerful enough to prevent Mr. Gao from carrying her off. After you are married, of course, you must expect to be heartily abused by the old man; but that need not worry you."

"You are right," agreed Yan after some hesitation. "But this is *my* wedding, and now someone else is going to enjoy the ceremony in my place. What's more, it's going to be very difficult to persuade him to go."

"Well, you have no way out," said You. "And Mr. Qian will enjoy only the short ceremony of fetching the bride, while you will be happy for the whole of your life."

Thereupon, pleasure mingled with his exasperation, Yan Jun took his leave of You Zhen and went to the library to find Qian.

"My dear cousin," he said, "I have another favour to ask of you."

"What can I do for you this time?"

"The third of next month is my wedding day, and on the second I should go to fetch the bride. I'm afraid I must trouble you to take my place again."

"When I took your place last time," said Qian, "the occasion was relatively unimportant. But how can I take your place in a serious ceremony like fetching the bride? It's out of the question."

"Of course there is something in what you say, cousin," replied Yan. "But since you went the first time, her family knows you; and if I were to go now it would look most suspicious. Not only would they break off the marriage, but they might even bring a lawsuit against me in which you would be involved. You mustn't let your scruples ruin everything. Once you have brought my bride home, I shan't be afraid, no matter what he says. This is the only way out, cousin. You must do me this last good turn."

When Qian had given way to such earnest entreaties, Yan engaged the necessary musicians and attendants, promising them handsome rewards when they returned with the bride if they would keep his secret. And none of them dared refuse.

At dawn on the morning of the second, You Zhen came to Yan's house to help sort out the presents for the bride's family and the largesse to be distributed among Mr. Gao's servants. When all was ready, including a scholar's hat, round collar, silk belt and black boots for Qian, food and bedding were carried down to the boats. There were two large junks, one for the bride and another for the bridegroom and go-between, as well as four smaller junks for the attendants, and four fast boats to escort the junks and carry messages. To the sound of gongs and trumpets these ten boats set sail on the lake, and their progress was enlivened by the continuous discharge of firecrackers.

Late that afternoon the boats reached West Dongting and moored several hundred yards from Mr. Gao's house. While You Zhen went on ahead to announce their arrival, the presents were alloted to different bearers, the gaily decorated sedan-chair for the bride was made ready, and hundreds of torches and lanterns were lit. Then to the sound of flutes and drums Qian Qing, splendidly dressed, was carried by eight bearers in a chair with silk hangings to Mr. Gao's house. Since all the islanders far and near had heard of the wonderful talent and good looks of Mr. Gao's future son-in-law, they crowded round to watch as eagerly as if this had been a religious procession. And when they saw how finely Qian held himself in his chair, as beautiful as a jade statue, they exclaimed in admiration.

"This brilliant young scholar and his beautiful bride will make a fine couple!" cried some of the women who knew Gao's daughter. "Mr. Gao has certainly picked himself a good son-in-law."

Meanwhile a great feast had been spread in Gao Zan's house, which was packed with friends and relatives; and before evening fell red candles cast a ruddy light over the hall. The guests heard music sound as a messenger from the boats announced that the bridegroom's chair was already at the gate; and the groomsmen, with red silk over their shoulders and flowers in their hats, hurried to the courtyard to greet Qian and read him a poem of welcome. Then with much ceremony he was ushered into the hall, where he poured a libation of wine and bowed before the goose.[1] After this he was introduced to all Gao's relatives in turn, and they marvelled at his beauty. Presently tea was served, and the guests were offered fruit and sweetmeats before sitting down to dinner. Since this was a special occasion the bridegroom consented to sit in the seat of honour, with all the other guests around him. And as he feasted in the hall to the accompaniment of music, his attendants were entertained in another room.

As Qian sat there in the seat of honour listening to the flow of compliments on his appearance and on Mr. Gao's good

---

[1] In ancient times the bridegroom sacrificed a wild goose at his marriage, and a goose continued to figure in later wedding ceremonies

fortune in finding such a son-in-law, he smiled wryly to himself.

"They are staring at me as if I were a being from another world," he thought. "Presently I shall wake up from this delightful dream; but what will these people do when they discover the truth? . . . Today I am acting as a substitute for Yan; I wonder when I shall be a bridegroom myself? I'm afraid my wedding won't be nearly such a splendid affair."

These depressing reflections spoilt his enjoyment of the feast.

Mr. Gao and his son kept pressing the bridegroom politely to drink; but not wanting to keep his cousin waiting Qian rose presently to leave. Mr. Gao insisted on his staying a little longer and eating some more; but when his followers had finished feasting and it was late, Xiao Yi came up to Qian and urged him to go. The young man ordered Xiao Yi to distribute the largesse they had brought, then stood up to take his leave. It was after midnight, and the bride's dowry had already been sent down to the boat. Mr. Gao was just about to escort the young couple to their chairs when the boatmen came running up to the house.

"A storm has sprung up — we can't sail tonight!" they cried. "You must wait until the wind has dropped."

The fact was that at midnight a great gale had blown up.

That wind uprooted trees, swirled dust on high,
And lashed the lake till billows reached the sky!

The drumming and fluting had drowned the sound of the storm; but now that Mr. Gao ordered the musicians to stop playing they could hear the wind roar. Everyone was amazed, and You Zhen stamped in annoyance. Mr. Gao was very much put out too, but he had to invite all his guests to take their seats again, after which he sent a man outside to keep an eye on the weather.

By dawn the wind was higher than ever. It drove dark storm clouds before it, and soon snow was falling. Everybody gathered by the windows to watch the sky and discuss what was to be done.

"This wind may blow for some time," remarked one.

"A wind that springs up at midnight doesn't usually die down till the following midnight," said another.

"Even if the wind dropped, the snow would make travelling impossible," put in a third.

"I'm afraid the snow's coming down faster and faster."

"This is a bitterly cold wind. When it stops, the lake may freeze."

"The lake never freezes over completely; but a snowstorm can be really dangerous."

While the guests were commenting like this on the weather, Mr. Gao and You Zhen were growing more and more anxious. After a time breakfast was served; but by now a regular gale was blowing and the snow was coming down more thickly than ever. It was out of the question to cross the lake that day; yet if they let this auspicious day go by, there might not be another suitable day that month. Besides, for the bridegroom who had arrived so bravely with flutes and drums to go back without his bride would be a great pity.

Among the guests was an old man called Zhou Quan, one of Mr. Gao's neighbours, who often settled local disputes. When he saw that Gao Zan was at a loss, he made a suggestion.

"In my humble opinion," he said, "there is a simple solution to this."

"What do you advise?" asked Mr. Gao.

"It would be a pity to let this auspicious day go by without the wedding. So, since your future son-in-law is here, why not marry the young couple at once? This feast can serve as their wedding feast, and they can go home in peace and comfort when the wind drops. Wouldn't that be the best plan?"

"An excellent idea!" said all the guests.

Mr. Gao had already had this same proposal in mind, and he was most grateful to old Zhou for expressing it so opportunely. He immediately ordered his servants to prepare for the wedding.

To return to Qian Qing, however. Though he was here in his cousin's place, he had no real part in this wedding, so at first he was not worried by the storm. And although taken aback by Zhou Quan's proposal, he did not think for a moment that Mr. Gao would consent to it. When Mr. Gao agreed so readily, he was absolutely horrified. He looked round for You Zhen to protest on his behalf; but the go-between was a heavy drinker, and because it was cold and he was in low spirits he had drained one goblet after another until he was completely drunk. He was lying back, snoring, on his chair. So Qian was forced to speak up for himself.

"An important ceremony like marriage should not be carried out in such a casual manner," he said. "We had better choose another auspicious day, when I will come again to fetch the bride."

But Mr. Gao would not hear of this.

"We are already as good as one family," he objected. "And since your worthy father is dead, you can make decisions for yourself."

This said, he retired to the inner chambers; and although Qian assured Mr. Gao's kinsmen and neighbours that he had no wish to get married here, they all supported Mr. Gao. At his wit's end, Qian finally made an excuse to withdraw, in order to consult Xiao Yi. But although Xiao Yi agreed that such a wedding would be most irregular and declared Mr. Qian must refuse to go through with it, he had no alternative solution to offer.

"I have already refused time and again," Qian told him. "But Mr. Gao won't take no for an answer. And if I persist in my refusal, it will only arouse his suspicions. I want to do the best I can for your master in this important matter. I swear by heaven and earth I have no intention of betraying him!"

As they were talking, the guests came out in a body to look for the bridegroom.

"Marriage is a fine thing, and your father-in-law has already made up his mind," they said. "Don't hesitate any longer, sir!"

Then Qian, speechless with dismay, had to suffer himself to be ushered back into the hall. After lunch the wedding feast was spread. The groomsmen in their red silk sashes directed the ceremony, and the bride and bridegroom clad in wedding robes entered the hall, performed the customary rites and became man and wife.

> *They celebrate a marriage here today;*
> *The newly wedded couple should be gay;*
> *But while the bride is glad, the groom is sad,*
> *And her delight is matched by his dismay!*

When the wine was finished the guests left, and Mr. and Mrs. Gao escorted Qian to the bridal chamber. The bride's attendant took off the bride's headdress and urged the young husband to go to bed; but to her surprise he refused, and she had to put the bride to bed first, then withdrew. As the maids closed the door, they called out a final word of encouragement to Qian.

"Don't wait up for me!" mumbled the young man, whose heart was thumping like a doe's.

The maids, who had been hard at work all night and were practically dozing where they stood, went to sleep at once. Qian had meant to sit up by candlelight till dawn; but he had forgotten to ask for candles, and when the one in his room went out he did not like to call for another; so he just lay down disconsolately on the edge of the bed fully dressed, without having so much as looked at the bride. The next morning he rose as soon as it was light and went to her brother's study to wash and comb his hair. And the old couple, attributing this to youthful bashfulness, did not think it strange.

Although the snow had stopped now, the wind was blowing as hard as ever. Mr. Gao prepared a congratulatory feast, at which Qian made himself thoroughly drunk, so that it was very late before he went to his room, and the girl was already asleep.

Too tired to sit up all night, the young man again lay down fully dressed upon the edge of the bed, not daring to touch so much as the bride's coverlet.

The next morning the wind had dropped a little and he wanted to leave; but Mr. Gao insisted on his staying for one more day. Again he drank hard all day, and managed to whisper to You Zhen while they were at table how he had spent the last two nights fully dressed. But although You expressed approval, he secretly doubted the truth of this statement. Under the circumstances, however, there was nothing he could do.

Now Mr. Gao's daughter, Qiufang, had stolen several looks at her husband since the wedding, and was delighted to find him so handsome. But she could not understand why he had passed two night fully dressed, and wondered if he were offended because she had not waited up for him. On the third night she told her maids to stay up until her husband came in and ask him to retire first. The girls did as they were told, and when Qian came in unfastened his belt and took off his hat for him; but at this he took fright and leapt hastily on the bed to fling himself down fully clad on its innermost edge. Very upset, the bride lay down fully dressed too; but she did not like to mention the matter to her parents.

The fourth day dawned clear and fine, and Mr. Gao ordered a boat so that he and his wife could escort their daughter across the lake, Mrs. Gao and Qiufang sharing one junk, Mr. Gao, Qian Qing and You Zhen another. The vessels were hung with coloured streamers, and the gay fluting and drumming could be heard for miles around. Xiao Yi, however, who was very uneasy as to what his master would say to him on his return, boarded one of the smaller craft and went on ahead of the others.

And now it is time to return to Yan Jun, who had been waiting eagerly ever since despatching Qian to fetch his bride. When he heard a great storm spring up at midnight of the second day, he was most worried; for he feared the wind and snow would delay the travellers and the auspicious day might go by before his bride could be brought home. Little did he think they could not cross the lake! Decorated candles and a wedding feast were ready; but although he sat up all night there was no sign of his bride, and he became more anxious than ever.

"I hope they haven't set sail in this storm," he thought. "If they're on the lake now, they must be in great danger."

But then it occurred to him: "If they haven't set sail and my father-in-law knows the auspicious day has passed, he probably won't send her. We shall have to choose another auspicious day, and goodness knows how long that will mean waiting. This suspense is killing!"

Presently, however, he reflected: "If You Zhen has any sense, he will persuade Mr. Gao to send her over, and I needn't trouble whether the day is an auspicious one or not — I shall make her my wife as soon as possible."

Troubled by such disturbing thoughts, he could not sit still, but kept pacing to the gate to look out.

On the fourth day, when the wind dropped, he guessed that he would soon have news; and, sure enough, shortly after noon Xiao Yi arrived.

"The bride will soon be here," reported Xiao Yi. "She's only a few miles away."

"How did it happen her father was willing to let her leave after the auspicious day had passed?"

"Mr. Gao was so anxious not to let the auspicious day go by that he insisted on celebrating the marriage at once. Mr. Qian took your place, sir, as bridegroom for three days."

"Do you mean to say Mr. Qian has spent the last three nights in the bridal chamber?"

"Yes, sir. But he didn't touch your bride. He just lay there without moving."

"You dog!" swore Yan. "Do you expect me to believe a tale like that? What did I send you there for? Why didn't you make him refuse? How could you let him do a thing like that?"

"I did speak to him, sir. But Mr. Qian said: 'I just want

to do what's best for your master.   I swear by heaven and earth I have no intention of betraying him!' "

Rage welled up in Yan Jun's heart.   After giving Xiao Yi a blow which sent him reeling, he rushed furiously outside to settle scores with Qian.   As it happened, the boats had just come alongside the shore.   After taking the precaution of asking You Zhen to keep Mr. Gao company, Qian leapt ashore and, conscious that he had nothing to reproach himself for, made his way boldly and confidently to Yan's house.   When he saw Yan he smiled, and prepared to greet him and tell him all that had happened.   But Yan was too base himself to understand honour in another.   Glaring at Qian as if his cousin were his worst enemy, he charged at him without giving him a chance to speak.

"Curse you!"   He gnashed his teeth with rage.   "You have been having a fine time, haven't you?"

Still swearing, he grabbed Qian's hat and hair and began to kick and pummel him.

"Curse you!" he shouted.   "You double-crosser!   Enjoying yourself at my expense!"

Qian attempted to justify himself; but Yan was too busy beating him to pay any attention, and none of the servants dared intervene.   At last, in a panic, Qian shouted for help; and Gao's party, hearing the commotion, hurried ashore to see what had happened.   When they saw this vicious-looking character beating the bridegroom, they did not know what to make of it, but hastened forward to try to stop the fight — in vain.

Then Mr. Gao questioned Yan's servants, and they, realizing that further concealment was impossible, told him the truth. Immediately he flew into a rage, and fell to cursing the go-between.

"You scoundrel!   How dare you play such a trick!"

With that he rushed forward and began to belabour You Zhen.

When Mr. Gao's servants charged forward indignantly to give the ugly stranger a good beating, Yan's household rallied to their master's defence, and joined battle with Mr. Gao's forces.   Thus whereas at first Yan and Qian, Gao and You, had been struggling alone, now the two parties were skirmishing wildly. And more and more people gathered round to watch, till soon the street was blocked and traffic stopped.

Just at that moment, fortunately, the local magistrate happened to arrive in his sedan-chair at the North Gate after seeing off a superior officer. When he heard the din and saw that a fight was going on, he stopped and ordered his runners to arrest the rioters. Immediately the crowd scattered, leaving only Yan, who was still clutching Qian, and Gao Zan, who would not let go of You Zhen. Since they were all shouting at once, the magistrate could not make out what had happened; and he ordered them to be taken to his yamen so that he could examine them properly, without interruption. First he questioned Gao Zan, as the oldest of the four.

"I am a native of West Dongting Island, Your Honour," said Mr. Gao. "My name is Gao Zan. I chose a handsome and talented husband for my daughter, and on the third of this month he came to fetch his bride; but because the storm made it impossible for them to leave that day, I persuaded him to celebrate the wedding in my house. Imagine my surprise today, upon our arrival here, when this ugly ruffian set upon my son-in-law and started beating him cruelly. When I asked the reason, I was told that the hideous wretch had bribed the go-between to trick me into giving him my daughter by sending young Qian to my house to impersonate him! If you will question the go-between, Your Honour, you will understand their vile plot."

"What is the go-between's name?" demanded the magistrate. "Is he here?"

"His name is You Zhen," replied Mr. Gao. "There he is!"

Then the magistrate dismissed Gao Zan and called You Zhen forward.

"By your tricks and lies you are responsible for this fraud," said the magistrate sternly. "Tell the truth now, if you want to avoid a heavy sentence!"

You Zhen attempted to deny the charge, until the magistrate grew angry and ordered the ankle-press to be brought. Although a rogue, the go-between had never yet been tortured, and now he was frightened into telling the truth: how Yan Jun had sent him to propose the match, how Gao Zan had insisted that he must have a handsome and talented son-in-law, how Qian Qing had gone in Yan's stead, and how finally the wedding had taken place. All this he recounted in detail.

The magistrate nodded.

"That sounds like the truth," he said. "Although Yan Jun went to so much trouble, someone else finally carried off his prize. No wonder he was angry! But he should never have played such a trick in the first place."

Thereupon he called for Yan Jun, to question him.

After hearing You Zhen's truthful account of the matter and seeing that the magistrate was in a kindly mood, Yan decided not to withhold evidence. And his account tallied with that of the go-between.

Last of all, the magistrate called Qian Qing forward. And when he saw how badly bruised the handsome youth was, he felt sorry for him.

"You are a scholar and have passed the district examination," he said. "You should understand what is seemly. How was it that you consented to fetch a bride for someone else? How could you lend yourself to such deceit?"

"I did so against my will," replied Qian. "Yan Jun is my elder cousin, and because I am poor he has allowed me to live in his house and continue my studies there. He begged me so persistently to go that I was forced to agree. It seemed the only thing to be done at the time."

"Wait a minute!" said the magistrate. "If you did this to oblige a relative, why did you marry the girl?"

"The idea was that I should simply fetch his bride for him," said Qian. "But that storm blew for three days, making it impossible to cross the lake; and then Mr. Gao, not wanting to let the auspicious day go by, insisted that the wedding take place at once."

"Since you were only a substitute, you should have refused."

At this point, Yan Jun stepped forward to kowtow.

"Your Honour!" he cried. "The very fact that he consented to the wedding proves his double dealing!"

"Silence!" thundered the magistrate. "Attendants! Remove that man!"

The runners pushed Yan back to his place, and the magistrate continued to examine Qian.

"Can you maintain that you consented to the marriage from purely unselfish motives?" he demanded.

"Ask Mr. Gao," replied Qian. "He will tell you that I refused again and again. But when he insisted I was afraid that further refusal would arouse his suspicion and spoil my cousin's chances of success. That is why I went through with the ceremony. But though I spent three nights in the bridal chamber, I never once removed my clothes and left the bride strictly alone."

The magistrate burst out laughing.

"Young men are hot-blooded and unsteady," he declared. "Do you mean to tell us you spent three nights in the same bed without touching the bride? You can't fool us like that!"

"It is the truth, Your Honour," replied Qian. "If you don't believe me, tell Mr. Gao to go and ask his daughter. You will soon know whether I am lying or not."

"If the girl is fond of him, she won't tell the truth," thought the magistrate.

He hit on a better expedient, and bade an attendant send a good old nurse to the boat where Mr. Gao's daughter was, to make discreet inquiries, ordering her to return as soon as possible.

Presently the nurse came back and confirmed what Qian had said.

"Then she is my wife!" cried Yan. "I am still willing to take her!"

"Hold your tongue!" roared the magistrate. Then he called for Gao Zan again.

"To which of them do you want to marry your daughter?" he asked.

"From the first I took a fancy to young Mr. Qian," replied Gao. "And my daughter has gone through the wedding ceremony with him. Although the young man's behaviour was strictly honourable, they are husband and wife in name at least. For my daughter to marry Yan Jun now would not only go against my wishes, but against hers too."

"I agree with you entirely," said the magistrate.

But Qian would not consent to this.

"I acted as I thought best," he protested. "Now if you declare the girl my wife, my three nights of self-denial will have been wasted. Better find the young lady a new husband altogether. I don't want to do anything which may arouse suspicion and cause talk."

"If the girl marries someone else," replied the magistrate, "your two trips across the lake to deceive her father will have to be counted against you, and will jeopardize your career; whereas by taking her as your wife you can make amends for your misconduct. Besides, your good faith has been made clear and the girl's family is willing; so who can suspect your motives now? Don't be stubborn. My decision is already made."

Then he took up his brush and wrote:

"Gao Zan wishes to find a suitable husband for his daughter; this was only natural. Yan Jun persuaded someone to impersonate him — something quite unheard of. And when the handsome bridegroom was accepted, they did not know that he was a substitute.

"Qian Qing crossed the lake twice and spent three nights in the bridal chamber, but remained true to his cousin. The storm helped him, for Heaven willed this marriage. Thus a brilliant young scholar wed a beautiful bride. They make a well-matched couple.

"The schemer has only himself to blame for his failure to win a wife. Since the girl has been married to Qian, there is no need for a second ceremony.

"Yan Jun did wrong to lay such a plot and to beat his friend; but since his scheme has failed he will not be further punished. However, the money he has prepared for the wedding shall be given to Qian as a recompense for the beating.

"You Zhen, who was responsible for all this trouble, must be severely punished."

Having written this verdict, the magistrate bade his runners give You thirty strokes with the heavy bamboo, then drive him out without making him sign a confession; for he did not wish Qian Qing's impersonation to become generally known.

Then Mr. Gao and Qian bowed in thanks, and the whole party left the yamen. Yan Jun was the picture of shame; but he dared not express his rage, and hanging his head slunk furtively away. Not for several months, however, did he dare show himself on the streets again. As for You Zhen, he went home to nurse his wounds.

Mr. Gao invited Qian to his boat and thanked him warmly.

"If not for your brilliant and honourable conduct, which won the magistrate's respect," he said, "my daughter would almost certainly have been handed over to that ruffian. Today I must beg you to come back to stay with us for a few days, for I do not know what relatives you have left at home."

"Both my parents are dead," was the reply. "And I have no other close relatives."

"In that case," replied Mr. Gao, "I hope you will live with us and allow me to provide for you while you continue your studies. What do you say?"

"If you will do so, sir," answered Qian, "I shall be more grateful than I can say."

That evening they set sail from Wujiang, and reached West Dongting the next morning. When the islanders heard this story they marvelled, and not one but admired Qian's integrity.

Later Qian passed the highest examinations and became an official; and both he and his wife lived to a ripe old age.

Although the lovely maid was nearly trapped by ugly Yan,
His wicked plan worked out to the advantage of young Qian.
The moon shines cold and bright above the waters of the lake,
Where home across the water fly the loving duck and drake.

The Proud Scholar

There was a talented scholar in the Jia Qing period (1522-1566) named Lu Nan, a native of Junxian County in Daming Prefecture. Lu was a fine-looking man with an arrogant manner, who held himself aloof from the dusty world. Able to write essays at eight and poems at ten, he could dash off thousand-character compositions at a moment's notice; and since he loved drinking and gallant deeds but was careless in little things and scorned all mundane matters, he came to be known through the country as the greatest genius of that age. All his friends were well-known scholars and high officials; moreover, because his forbears had held important posts for several generations, Lu was extremely wealthy and lived like a prince. He owned a fine, stately mansion at the foot of the Fuqiu Mountain outside the county town; all his concubines were beautiful and sang divinely; while he amused himself by teaching music to his pages whom he had selected for their looks. As for his other servants and retainers, they were too many to count. The grounds behind Lu's house were several acres in extent; and here he had the most skilful workmen construct a pleasure park with a lake and artificial hills, which he called the Garden of Songs.

Now since all flowers like warmth, the best-known varieties come from the south, for the north is so cold that most flowers are killed by the frost here and few good plants can be grown, the rare exceptions being those cultivated by high officials and rich families. Since Junxian where Lu Nan lived was an out-of-the-way county, it was more difficult to buy flowers there than in Beijing, and none of the high officials' gardens were much to boast of. Not content, however, to be like everyone else, the scholar spared no expense to purchase rare plants and

curious rocks from distant provinces, until his garden became
the wonder of the district.   And, indeed, it was extraordinarily
beautiful.

Here are terraces and quiet courtyards,
And curious boulders, planted with rare blooms;
The lake pavilion leads to the bamboo copse,
A breezy summer-house stands beside the pines,
Among winding pools as green and clear as grass,
And mossy hummocks bright as emerald;
Here peacocks roost beside the peonies,
And cranes step gracefully between the flowers;
In deep green shade a little bridge is seen,
From crimson blossoms soars a lofty tree,
While mist makes all ethereal as a dream,
And hillsides washed by rain seem newly-dyed.
Magnolia barges float through water lilies,
A swing flies up and down through willow boughs;
Red balustrades are a foil for painted railings,
And bamboo matting for embroidered curtains.

No emperor could have been happier than Lu Nan as, by
day and by night, he enjoyed the flowers and birds in his pleasure garden.   When friends called, he would feast them till
they were drunk; when he met a man after his own heart, he
would insist on entertaining him for weeks and months; and
no one in distress was turned away empty-handed from his door.
Thus, as his fame spread, there was no end to the visitors who
called on him.   His hall was always filled with guests, and his
wine cup was never empty.

Since Lu was both brilliant and well-read, he imagined that
to pass the imperial examinations was as easy as picking up a
needle; but he had a run of bad luck.   Though his essays were
magnificent, they did not please the examiners; and after failing
several times and finding no one to recognize his genius, he
gave up all thought of an official career and stopped taking the
examinations, to spend all his time with poets, swordsmen,

Taoists or learned monks, with whom he discussed philosophy and swordsmanship, or gambled, drank and explored the beauties of the countryside. He now called himself The Hermit of Fuqiu, and wrote the following verse:

I soar aloft upon proud wings,
And stride to Heaven's gate,
Raising my gown as I tread the fragrant path.
A great wind sweeps the sea,
But I fasten my reins upon a bough of jade
And feed on jasper blossoms,
Delighting in the heavenly beauty here,
And singing the song of the phoenix.
Though the world of men is debased,
It cannot sully my plumage.

We come now to another character in our story, Wang Chen, the magistrate of Junxian County, who had a high opinion of himself because he had passed the palace examinations at an early age. A rapacious, suspicious-minded man, Wang loved wine and often sat up drinking all night; but since coming to this county he had met no one who was a match for him. When the magistrate heard that this brilliant scholar, Lu Nan, who was so highly regarded and well connected, not only possessed the best garden in the district but was also a good drinker, he longed to meet him, and invited him to the yamen. But Lu was not like most scholars, who try by every means to make the acquaintance of the local magistrate, begging friends to introduce them or styling themselves his students and sending him presents at festivals, for the sake of the advantages like to accrue to themselves. The most servile, if the magistrate invites them to his yamen, feel as honoured as by a gift from the emperor, and paste the invitation on the wall to impress their friends and relations. And while those with more backbone may not stoop quite so low as this, they certainly accept any invitation the magistrate may send them. Yet Lu Nan ignored five or six invitations from Magistrate Wang, on the pretext that he would never enter a yamen.

Do you ask why Lu should behave like this? It was because he was so brilliant himself that he looked down on everybody else, in his overweening pride considering rank and riches as no better than worn-out shoes. Had princes or ministers invited him to a banquet without calling in advance to pay their respects, he might well have refused; and he certainly would not have called on them first. A man like this, too haughty to be an emperor's subject and too arrogant to be a baron's friend, could not be expected to call on a mere magistrate.

Well, now an odd customer like Lu was up against a tiresome, difficult character like Magistrate Wang. Most men will give up inviting somebody after he has refused four or five times; but this magistrate did not know when to stop, and when he saw that Lu would not come to him he decided to call on Lu instead. To make sure that the scholar would not be out, he sent a messenger with his card to arrange a date. This messenger went straight to Lu's house, and handed the card to the door-keeper.

"His Honour has an important message for your master," he said. "Please announce me."

The gate-keeper dared not delay but took him straight into the garden to find Lu Nan. When the messenger saw winding emerald pools and green hills all around him, while bamboos and shady trees showed each other off to advantage and the birds in their branches chirped in harmony, he was charmed. Never had he seen anything to equal this. He felt he had wandered into paradise.

"No wonder my master wants to visit this garden," he thought. "I've never seen anything so lovely. How lucky I am to have had a chance to come here. This is a sight I shall never forget."

He feasted his eyes as he walked down winding paths, past terraces and pavilions, till he came to a place filled with plum trees whose blossom was like scented snow, its cool fragrance penetrating to his very bones. In the middle of the trees was an octagonal pavilion with red and green tiles and carved and painted beams. A horizontal wooden placard proclaimed in bold characters that this was The Pavilion of Gleaming Jade; and here three or four guests were drinking as they enjoyed the plum blossom, while beside them five or six beautiful girls played stringed and bamboo instruments or sang, marking time with clappers. The gate-keeper stood outside with the messenger until the singing was over, then delivered the magistrate's card while the messenger stepped forward.

"His Honour told me to give you his best regards, sir," he said to the scholar. "Since you won't visit him in town, he would like to call on you here; but he doesn't want to come while you are out and miss you; so he has sent me to find out on which day he can come to receive your instructions. His Honour has also heard of the beauty of your garden, and is eager to see it."

You cannot bring two people together by force; but when Lu Nan knew that the magistrate instead of taking offence at his repeated refusals intended to call on him, he was rather favourably impressed.

"Though this man is a mean, despicable fellow," thought Lu, "he is the magistrate; and respect for talent is after all a virtue in an official. If I refuse him again, I will lay himself open to a charge of narrow-mindedness and intolerance.... But a vulgar upstart like that can't possibly understand essays or have any real appreciation of poetry. He has no knowledge of the classics either, but was lucky enough to pass the palace examinations and is puffed up with his own importance. I doubt if he has read many books, and philosophy will be quite beyond him; so what interest can there be in his conversation? I had better not ask him here."

On the other hand, as the magistrate was so eager to come, Lu felt it would be impolite to refuse him; and as he was considering the matter a servant brought up more wine. That gave Lu an idea.

"If he can drink," said the scholar to himself, "that will make up to a certain extent for his vulgarity."

So he asked the messenger: "Can your master drink?"

"He certainly can, sir. Wine is his life."

"How much can he drink?"

"All I know is that he often sits up drinking all night, and won't stop until he has had enough. How much exactly he drinks I don't know."

"So the boor can drink," thought Lu, pleasantly surprised. "That's one up for him."

"Since the magistrate wants to see the plum blossom in bloom, let him come tomorrow," he said, ordering a servant to give one of his cards to the messenger. "I shall prepare wine and food and be waiting for him here."

Having received this reply, the messenger left with the gate-keeper and went back to the yamen, where he gave Lu Nan's card to the magistrate. But that same evening, while Magistrate Wang was looking forward to seeing Lu and his plum blossom the next day, he heard that the new judicial commissioner of the province was arriving unexpectedly, and had to set off at once to the prefectural city, making his excuses to Lu. The magistrate had to wait for the commissioner's arrival and pay his respects in due form; so by the time he returned to his county several days had passed and the plum blossom had fallen.

> *Blossoms as bright as jasper heap the steps,*
> *Petals like jade surround the painted rails.*

Disappointed to have missed the plum blossom, Magistrate Wang expected that Lu would invite him again; but the scholar had issued his last invitation rather unwillingly, and after it was declined he thought no more of the matter. Why should he invite the magistrate again?

Soon it was the middle of spring, and the magistrate sent another messenger to convey his wish to see Lu's garden at this season. A scene of utter loveliness met the messenger's eyes: blossoms bright as embroidery and grass soft as a carpet, where butterflies and bees flitted to and fro, while orioles sang and swallows twittered. Presently he reached a peach grove, where the blossoms were like myriads of rosy clouds or thousands of swathes of crimson silk. It was a magnificent sight!

Lu Nan and his friends were singing and drinking lustily among the peach trees, when the messenger presented Magistrate Wang's card.

"Go and tell the magistrate that he can come now, if he likes," said Lu expansively. "There is no need to arrange another date."

But his guests protested.

"We are having a good time here," they said, "but if he comes we shall have to stand on ceremony and stop enjoying ourselves. Ask him some other day."

"Right you are," said Lu. "Let him come tomorrow." He gave the messenger a card and sent him off.

But unluckily, just as the magistrate was about to leave the yamen the next day, his wife had a miscarriage and fell senseless to the ground. Frightened nearly out of his wits, her husband was in no mood for a feast, so he sent to decline Lu's invitation again. Mrs. Wang did not recover till the end of the third month, by which time the peonies blooming in the scholar's garden were the admiration of the whole district, for they were lovely flowers. Magistrate Wang had been so disturbed and depressed by his wife's illness that for nearly three weeks he had neglected his work but drowned his sorrows in drink. When he heard that Lu's peonies were out he longed to see them, but after breaking his appointment twice he did not like to make another. Instead, he sent a gift of three taels of silver to Lu, mentioning his wish to see the flowers. Lu named a day for the magistrate's visit but declined the gift, which, however, he was finally forced to accept.

The day chosen was fine, and Magistrate Wang was just about to set off after the morning session when his attendants announced that one of the secretaries of the Ministry of Civil Affairs was passing here on his way home to see his parents; and since this was an important official, how could Wang ignore him? He had to hurry out of the city to welcome this superior, present him with gifts and entertain him to a feast. He hoped that the man would move on in a couple of days, leaving him time to see the peonies; but it turned out that this secretary was fond of sightseeing, for he spent about a week there and asked the magistrate to accompany him to all the beauty spots in the neighbourhood. When Wang sent another messenger to Lu, he learned that the peonies had faded and the scholar had gone away a couple of days before to the mountains.

Soon spring gave place to summer, and in a snap of the fingers it was middle of the sixth month. Knowing that Lu Nan had come back for the summer, Magistrate Wang sent a request to see his lotus in bloom; and the gate-keeper who took in the magistrate's card returned presently to say that his master wished to speak to the messenger, and took him to a lotus lake nearly two acres in size, bordered by green willows and shady ash trees and bright with pink lotus and green lotus leaves. This lake was called Turquoise Lake, and in the middle of it was a pavilion called The Pavilion of Silken Clouds, which could be reached only by boat, for there was no bridge leading to it. It was here that Lu found coolness in summer.

When they had rowed to the island, made fast their boat and jumped ashore, the messenger saw a pavilion with red balustrades and green gauze windows. The scent of lotus was carried by the breeze; goldfish sported among the water weeds; swallows nested under the eaves of the pavilion; herons flew under the trees and wild ducks swam near the shore. In the pavilion were a wicker bed covered with matting, a stone couch, and a censer of rare incense beside a vase of lotus on a bamboo table. With his head and feet uncovered, Lu was lying on the stone couch with an old book propped up before him and a cup of wine in his hand. Beside him were bowls of peaches and lotus root, plums and melons, as well as several wine dishes. A servant-boy was holding a wine pot while another fanned the scholar, who was draining his cup after every few lines he read with quiet enjoyment.

"We are all born of parents," thought the messenger, standing at one side and not daring to approach. "What has he done to deserve such comfort? Even our magistrate, who has passed the palace examinations, has his worries. He's not half as happy as this."

Just then Lu looked up and saw him.

"Are you from the yamen?" he asked.

"Yes, sir."

"That magistrate of yours is a peculiar fellow. He makes so many appointments but never turns up; and now he wants to see my lotus — it's a bit of a bore, you know. How does a man like that come to be an official? I've no patience with him. If he wants to come, let him; but I'm tired of making appointments that he doesn't ever keep."

"His Honour greets you, sir," said the messenger. "He has always admired your genius and longed to receive your instructions as a thirsty man longs for a drink; but urgent business has prevented him each time from coming. I hope you will name another day, so that I will have an answer for him when I go back."

When Lu heard how plausibly the man talked, he let himself be persuaded.

"In that case, let him come the day after tomorrow," he said.

Having got this reply and asked for a card, the messenger rowed back with the gate-keeper to the bank shaded by willows, and returned to the yamen to report on his errand.

Two days later, accordingly, when Magistrate Wang had dealt with his official business, he set out at noon to call on Lu. But Magistrate Wang was already suffering from a touch of the sun, for this was the hottest part of the summer; so the noonday sun like a crimson ball of fire was too much for him. While on the road he felt heaven and earth spin round, and fell fainting from his sedan-chair. His attendants hastily helped him up and carried him back to the yamen, where he gradually revived;

but he had to order his men to make his excuses once more to
Lu and send for a physician; and it was more than a month
before he could attend to his official duties.

One day, when Lu was going through the presents sent to
him in his library, he came across Magistrate Wang's gift.

"There has been no friendship between us," thought the
scholar, "so how can I accept a gift from him without doing
something in return?   I must pay him back in one way or
another."

So in the middle of the eighth month he invited the magistrate
to watch the moon with him on the night of the Moon Festival.
Magistrate Wang, who had been hoping for this, was delighted
to receive the invitation and sent a messenger at once to convey
his greetings to Lu and say that he would certainly come.   But
since the magistrate was the head of this district, Lu was naturally not the only one to invite him to a feast. A whole week
before the festival some of the local gentry and Wang's colleagues started asking him to meals, and as he was fond of drinking he did not refuse any of them.   Then, on the evening before
the festival, he declined outside invitations and prepared a feast
at home to enjoy in the courtyard with his wife.   That night
the moon was brighter than usual, and husband and wife drank
to each other till they were tipsy before going to bed.   The
magistrate had not fully recovered from his recent illness and
for the last few days he had been drinking too much; so when
on top of that he caught cold by sitting outside so late, he fell
ill again.   Thus his engagement with Lu to enjoy the moon had
to be cancelled; and he was forced to spend a few days in bed.

Presently the time came for cassia to bloom, and one day,
when he had no business to attend to, Wang started longing
once more to see Lu's garden.   As luck would have it, a man
arrived just then from the south to borrow money, bringing with
him two great jars of Huishan wine; so the magistrate sent one
jar to Lu and the scholar was very pleased, for there were few
things he liked better than good wine.

"Whatever his administration or literary gifts are like, he is quite a connoisseur of wine," thought Lu.

So he invited Magistrate Wang to come two days later to see his cassia. As the proverb says: Man's every bite and sup are preordained. That a magistrate, the head of a district, should condescend to visit a local scholar was strange enough; yet something always happened to prevent their meeting. When Lu invited him to see the cassia, Magistrate Wang determined to spend the whole day in the scholar's garden to make up for all his past disappointments; but while he was still in bed that morning a runner announced that Judge Zhao of Shanxi was passing here on his way to the capital; and since the judge was the magistrate's former tutor, Wang had to get up at once, wash and dress hurriedly, and take a sedan-chair to the river to welcome him and invite him to a feast. Because they were tutor and pupil and knew each other well, the judge naturally stayed for several days; and by then the cassia flowers had fallen.

Its golden grains flew dancing in the wind,
Its fragrant petals scattered on the ground.

Now Lu was a gallant, straightforward man, who would not stoop before superiors but was kind to inferiors; so after the magistrate had made all these humble and respectful advances, Lu believed that Wang must value talent, and began to feel well-disposed towards him. It was now the end of the ninth month and the chrysanthemums in his garden were out. He had many varieties of chrysanthemums but the rarest were Stork's Wings, Cut Velvet, and The Beauty, which are highly prized for their petals of many colours and their large, beautiful flowers. Remembering that the magistrate had asked to see his garden several times but never been able to come, Lu decided to ask him over while the chrysanthemums were in bloom to repay his courtesy; so he wrote an invitation for the next day. When Lu's servant reached the yamen, the magistrate was in court; so he went in, knelt down and presented the invitation.

"My master pays his respects to Your Honour," he said. "The

chrysanthemums in our garden are out, and he would like you to come tomorrow to enjoy them."

The magistrate had been hoping to see these chrysanthemums, but after breaking his word so many times had felt too embarrassed to raise the subject. This invitation was just what he wanted.

"Give your master my greetings," he replied. "I shall come early tomorrow to receive his instructions."

The servant went back with this message to Lu.

"Magistrate Wang sends you his greetings," he reported. "He will come early tomorrow morning."

Now when Magistrate Wang said he would go early, this was only his manner of speaking; but the servant by a slip of the tongue reported him as having said "early in the morning." And this slip of the tongue resulted in Lu's offending the magistrate, losing the whole of his great fortune, and very nearly losing his life into the bargain.

"How ridiculous this magistrate is," thought the scholar. "Who ever heard of arriving for a feast early in the morning? The only possible explanation is that he has heard so much about my garden that he wants to spend the whole day here."

So he told the cooks: "The magistrate will be coming early tomorrow morning. Have the feast ready in good time."

The cooks bustled about their kitchen all night to get ready. And the next morning Lu summoned his gate-keeper.

"If any guests call today, tell them I am not at home," he said. "There is no need to announce them."

Then he sent a man with his card to invite the magistrate over. By breakfast time a banquet was ready in the garden of The Hall of Happy Feasts. There were two tables only, for no other guests had been invited, and the tables were splendidly appointed.

> One single feast in a rich man's house
> Would keep a poor man for half a year.

When Magistrate Wang took his seat in court that day, he

intended to make short work of the cases in order to keep his appointment. One of the lawsuits, however, concerned nine robbers who had been captured by the county constables with some of their loot. This case, according to the magistrate's henchmen, involved a large band of robbers on the river; and there was nobody to claim the loot, which was considerable.

The magistrate, whose greed was aroused, had the robbers tortured. And one of them, who was a cunning rogue, confessed as soon as he was put in the leg-screws where he had hidden silver and other valuables worth hundreds of thousands of cash. In his eagerness to lay hands on such a treasure, the magistrate forgot all about the feast. He had the torture stopped and sent his right-hand man and some able runners with the robber to collect the hidden treasure, while the rest of the thieves were sent back to gaol and the loot was taken to the treasury.

The magistrate adjourned to a back room to wait for news. He waited from eight in the morning till two in the afternoon, and the attendant on duty served wine and food twice before the runners came back.

"This is a strange business," they reported. "We dug everywhere, but couldn't find a trace of any treasure."

The magistrate went back to the court in a fury and called the prisoners out to torture them all again; but when it came to the turn of the robber who had taken the magistrate's men to find the treasure, he could stand no more pain. For this man had already been cruelly tortured, and when the runners discovered that he was lying and there was no treasure they had beaten and kicked him savagely. As soon as they put the screws on him again, he fell dead.

The magistrate was a little disconcerted to see that the prisoner had died under torture, and he ordered the gaolers to bring him round; but try as they might they could not revive him. Then Magistrate Wang had an idea.

"Take the prisoners back to gaol," he ordered. "I shall try them again tomorrow."

His men understood and carried the dead robber back with

the rest to gaol, none of them daring to breathe a word of his death. And the gaoler made out a certificate stating that the man had died of sickness in prison, so that the corpse might be removed the next day.

Thoroughly disgusted with the whole business, Magistrate Wang now remembered the feast to which Lu had invited him, and set off. But it was already four o'clock in the afternoon as his runners accompanied him to Lu's house.

Now after Lu Nan had waited from early morning till ten o'clock, he sent a man to find out what was delaying his guest; and when the messenger came back to report that the magistrate was still trying culprits, Lu was rather annoyed.

"If he arranged to come first thing in the morning, why is he still busy in the yamen?" he wondered.

He waited and waited, but there was still no sign of the magistrate; so Lu, now quite exasperated, sent another man with his card to the yamen.

"I should never have asked him," he thought. "But I suppose now I shall just have to put up with it."

Nothing is more trying than waiting; and time dragged as the messenger failed to return.

"Strange!" thought Lu.

He sent another man after the first, and presently they came back together.

"They are still torturing some prisoners," announced the first messenger. "The gateman said: 'His Honour is angry; you'd better not disturb him.' Since he would not let me in, I couldn't deliver your card and dared not come back before."

Lu was already in a bad temper, and when he heard that the magistrate was torturing robbers in order to find hidden loot he flew into a rage.

"This grasping, cruel fool has no good in him at all," he declared. "But now I know what he's like. Well, it's fortunate that he hasn't come."

Ordering his servants to remove the lower table, he sat down in the place of honour at the table in the middle.

"Bring me warmed wine in big cups!" he shouted. "Look sharp! I want to get rid of the bad taste this has left in my mouth."

"His Honour may soon arrive," said the servants.

"What if he does?" retorted Lu. "Is my wine for a greedy, cruel boor like him? Besides, he has broken his word six or seven times already; he won't be coming today either."

When the servants saw how angry he was they dared say no more, but filled his cup and brought in dishes, while pages played stringed and wind instruments. After a few cups Lu called to a servant-boy:

"Come and massage me! Waiting for that cad has tired me."

After ordering the garden gate to be closed, he took off his cap and outer garments, bared his feet and let down his hair. Then one servant massaged him while others sang to him. He also bade them change his wine cup for a large goblet, and after draining several goblets his spirits rose and he drank long and deep until he was quite tipsy. Then he had the dishes removed for his attendants to eat, keeping only some fruit to go with the wine. After draining a few goblets more, he was thoroughly drunk. He dropped his head on the table and began to snore, while his servants, not daring to awake him, ranged themselves respectfully on either side.

The gate-keeper, meanwhile, did not know that his master was drunk. The scholar had many visitors, who came and went as they pleased, for Lu never refused callers or cared when they left; so the gate always remained wide open; and though the gate-keeper had been told to close it today, he paid no attention to his instructions. Besides, he knew that if the magistrate did turn up he would have to admit him in any case. Presently, when the sun was setting behind the hills, he saw the magistrate approaching in the distance, and hurried in to announce him. But upon reaching The Hall of Happy Feasts he discovered to his dismay that his master was dead drunk.

"His Honour is here!" he exclaimed. "Why has our master drunk himself into this state?"

When the other attendants heard that the magistrate was there, they gazed at each other in consternation but did not know what to do.

"Though the feast is ready, there'll be no waking our master," they said. "What's to be done?"

"You had better wake him, so that he can entertain the magistrate even though he is drunk," said the gate-keeper. "How can we ignore a guest who has been specially invited?"

So the servants stepped forward and shouted at Lu at the top of their voices; but do you think they could wake him? And when they heard voices and footsteps and knew that the magistrate had entered the garden, they scattered in fright, leaving Lu there alone. But this incident made mortal enemies of the good host and his distinguished guest, bringing about the ruin of Lu's fortune and causing his rare flowers to vanish like a dream.

> *'Tis Fate decrees both wealth and poverty,*
> *All fortune or disaster is ordained.*

Upon reaching the scholar's gate, Magistrate Wang was surprised not to find Lu Nan there to welcome him; nor was there a single servant in attendance.

"Is there anybody here?" shouted the runners. "Go and announce that His Honour has arrived."

When no one answered, the magistrate assumed that the gate-keeper had gone in already to report his coming; so ordering his men to stop shouting he went in. On the inner gate was a horizontal white placard bearing the name of the garden in green characters. Passing through this gate he saw avenues of cypresses, and rounding a corner he came to an arch with the inscription: Far from the dusty crowd. Beyond this arch was a path lined by pine trees, and as he walked through the pine wood Magistrate Wang saw hills at a distance with pavilions wrapped in mist set among trees, flowers and bamboos. He was struck by the ingenious layout of these grounds and the beauty of the scenery.

"Here indeed is an exceptional man," he thought.

Puzzled as he was to hear no one coming and see no sign of Lu advancing to greet him, Magistrate Wang concluded that the scholar must have taken a different path to look for him and thus they had missed each other. After wandering east and west with his attendants through the garden in search of his host, he came to a ·large, three-roomed building among hundreds of chrysanthemums, which were bright with frost, and myriads of maples, whose leaves shone like red silk reflecting the evening clouds. There were golden clusters of oranges too, and hundreds of pink and crimson hibiscus flowers by the pool, the red flowers contrasting with the green water of the lake, over which waterbirds skimmed.

"Since he invited me to enjoy the chrysanthemums, he must be here," thought the magistrate.

So he alighted from his sedan-chair before the hall and went in. He found no feast there, however, but only a man with rumpled hair and bare feet, who had rested his head on the central table in the place of honour and was snoring. There was nobody else. The magistrate's retainers marched forward.

"His Honour is here!" they shouted. "Get up!"

Magistrate Wang looked closely at the sleeping man and observed that he was not dressed like a servant; and when he saw the cap and gown beside him, he ordered his men not to shout but to see who it was. Then a runner who had been here before to bring an invitation scrutinized the scholar carefully and recognized him.

"Your Honour," he reported, "it's Mr. Lu who is lying here drunk."

The magistrate flushed crimson with anger.

"The insolence of the fellow!" he cried. "Getting me here to insult me!"

He was tempted to order his men to destroy the garden, but fearing this might seem undignified he suppressed his anger, swept into his chair and bade his men return to the yamen. The

chair-bearers carried him back the way they had come, but not
a soul did they meet on the way.

It was then evening, and lanterns were lit to light the road.
All the runners shook their heads and showed their tongues in
amazement.

"He's only a college scholar," they said.   "How dare he treat
a magistrate with such contempt?   Who ever heard of such a
thing?"

These comments, which the magistrate overheard from his
chair, only added to his indignation.

"Lu Nan may be talented, but he is under my jurisdiction,"
he thought angrily.   "Though he refused several invitations from
me, I was willing to call on him and sent him silver and wine —
I could hardly have been more condescending.   Yet he still insults me like this!   Even if I were his equal instead of a magistrate, he ought not to have behaved so rudely."

Still fuming with anger, he reached the yamen and retired
to his private quarters.

Only after the magistrate had left did Lu's servants and pages
dare to come out of hiding.   They found their master still fast
asleep in the hall; and not till after eight o'clock that evening
did he wake.

"While you were asleep His Honour came," they told him.
"But finding you sleeping he left immediately."

"Did he say anything?"

"We were afraid we might not know how to answer him, sir,
so we kept out of his way."

"Serves him right," said Lu.

He summoned the gate-keeper and gave him thirty strokes.

"Why didn't you close the gate," he demanded, "instead of
letting that vulgar upstart in to soil my ground?"

Then he called for his chief gardener.   "Tomorrow morning
see that you get water to wash the path he has defiled," he
ordered.

Last of all he sent for the messenger who had come before
to bring him the silver and the jar of Huishan wine; and the

messenger, not daring to conceal this, took them back to the yamen.

When Magistrate Wang reached his rooms and his wife greeted him, she saw that he was nearly bursting with anger.

"What can have happened at a feast to annoy you so much?" she asked.

Her husband told her what had passed.

"Well, you've only yourself to blame," she said. "You're the magistrate here, and whatever you do there will be people to fawn on you. Why did you cheapen yourself so many times by calling on a common citizen? Even if he is a genius, what good will that do you? If you were insulted today, it's no more than you deserved."

This lecture from his wife enraged the magistrate even more, and for a long time he sat in his armchair too angry to say a word.

"What's the use of sulking?" demanded his wife. "Don't you know the saying: A magistrate has power to ruin families?"

At that the magistrate saw light and, setting aside his former respect for talent, made up his mind to destroy Lu Nan. He remained silent, reflecting how best to deal with the scholar. Nothing less than Lu's death would satisfy his hatred.

The next day, after the morning session, he called in a trusted clerk named Tan Zun for consultation. Tan was an able man, who had always abetted the magistrate in embezzling government funds, for he was a wily old official. Having told him Lu's offence, Magistrate Wang declared that he meant to take vengeance by convicting the scholar of some crime.

"To get even with Lu Nan," said Tan, "Your Honour will have to use caution. You must pin on him some serious crime, for which there can be no pardon before you can have him executed. Just an ordinary impeachment won't do, I'm afraid; in fact it may even get Your Honour into trouble."

"How is that?" asked Wang.

"Lu and I belong to the same district," replied Tan, "and I know that he has many high official connections and is very rich. Though he behaves wildly because he fancies himself a genius, he has never broken the law; so if you have him arrested, on however serious a charge, he will appeal to a higher court and you won't be able to condemn him to death. But then he will hate you and try to take revenge. He may make things difficult for Your Honour."

"While there is something in what you say," replied the magistrate, "a man who behaves as recklessly as Lu must have done wrong in one way or another. I want you to make a careful investigation, so that I can deal with him."

Tan agreed, and no sooner had he left when the silver and wine presented to Lu Nan were brought back. The return of these gifts touched Magistrate Wang on the raw again; but as he had no other way of venting his anger he cursed the messenger, had him given twenty strokes, and made him take the silver and wine.

> *If we all refrained from hurting others' feelings,*
> *There need be no one gnashing his teeth in rage.*

Acting on Magistrate Wang's orders, Tan Zun set to work to discover what crimes Lu had committed. But days and months sped past and by the end of the year he was in a quandary, because he had found nothing, yet the magistrate kept demanding results. One day he was sitting disconsolately at home wondering how they could possibly trap Lu Nan, when a woman burst in. He recognized her as his servant Niu Wen's sister-in-law, the wife of Niu Cheng. The woman, who was about thirty and not bad-looking, curtseyed to Tan.

"Excuse me, sir," she said, "but can you tell me where my brother-in-law is? I'm lucky to find you in."

"He is at the yamen. What do you want him for?"

"It's like this, sir. The year before last my husband borrowed two taels of silver from Lu Cai, who works for Mr. Lu the scholar; and these last two years we have paid him interest. This year my husband went to work as a hired hand for Mr. Lu, who always pays the wages for the first half of next year

at the end of this year. When my man got the money and was
given a good meal with wine, he was very pleased; but just as
he was going out of the gate he was stopped by Lu Cai, who
knew that the wages had been paid and demanded his two taels
back. My husband told him since it was the end of the year
he needed the money and couldn't pay; but Lu Cai said he
must have his silver, and so they started quarrelling. Then my
husband was fool enough to curse Lu Cai as a slave, and for
that he got beaten up by Lu's men. After being beaten he came
home in a rage; and what with growing angry after that big
meal and catching cold when he stripped to fight, that night
he ran up a fever. He has been ill for eight days and now he
can't even swallow water. The doctor says he fell ill with
indigestion and a chill, but that he can't be cured; and now that
he is dying I have come to ask his brother what to do."

When Tan heard this he was overjoyed.

"So that's how it is," he said. "Well, if your husband recovers,
so much the better; if not, let me know at once and I guarantee
to avenge you and get you enough money to live on in comfort
for the rest of your life."

"It is very kind of you, sir, to help us," she replied.

As they were talking, Niu Wen came back; and when his
sister-in-law had explained the situation to him they decided to
go back to her house together.

"If anything happens," Tan reminded them as they left, "be
sure to let me know at once."

To this Niu Wen agreed. In less than an hour he and his
sister-in-law had reached Niu Cheng's home, opened the door
and entered. The room was deathly quiet, and when they went
up to the bed they were startled to find Niu Cheng stark and
cold, for he had been dead for some time. His wife burst into
loud sobs, and the neighbours came to see what had happened.

"He was strong as a tiger!" they exclaimed. "How could
he die so suddenly? What a shame!"

"Stop crying now," said Niu Wen to his sister-in-law, "and
come with me to my master. We'll see what can be done."

So the woman locked her door and begged the neighbours to keep an eye on things while she went off with Niu Wen.

"They must have gone to lodge a charge," said the neighbours. "This is a serious affair involving a man's life; we had better report it too, in order to clear ourselves." So they set off for the yamen too.

Soon the news of Niu Cheng's death had spread far and wide, and someone reported it to Lu Nan. The scholar had been informed of the fight between Niu Cheng and Lu Cai several days before; and because he was angry to find a servant of his turning money-lender and squeezing the poor, he had Lu Cai given thirty strokes, took Niu's note of hand from him and dismissed him. He was waiting for Niu Cheng, to return him his note of hand; and when he heard of Niu's death, he sent men to seize Lu Cai and take him to court. But Lu Cai, who had heard of Niu's death too, had fled to avoid trouble. No one knew where he had gone.

When Niu Wen and his brother's wife burst into the yamen to announce Niu Cheng's death, Tan Zun was mightily pleased. After going in quietly to inform the magistrate, he came back to them, told them what to say, and took down their depositions accusing the scholar Lu Nan of beating Niu Cheng to death because Lu had wanted to seize Niu's wife but failed. Then Tan told Niu Wen and his sister-in-law to beat the drum at the yamen gate and demand revenge. Obeying him implicitly, they pounded the drum violently with a faggot and shouted "Murder!" And the yamen runners, who had received their instructions from Tan, did not stop them.

When Magistrate Wang heard the drum, he took his seat in court and ordered the plaintiffs to be brought in. He was reading their plea when Niu Cheng's neighbours arrived too; but he ignored the neighbours to concentrate on the accusation brought against Lu Nan. After asking a few questions for form's sake, without any further investigation he ordered his men to hale Lu Nan before him at once.

"His Honour is very angry with Lu," Tan told the runners.

"So when you go there, arrest all the men in his household, leaving only the women and children alone."

The runners knew of the magistrate's grudge against Lu; since the scholar had a large household they decided that a strong force was needed to break in, so they mustered about fifty men who were fierce as tigers. Winter days are short, and it was a cold evening with an overcast sky and a bitter north wind. To please the magistrate Tan treated the police to a meal. Then carrying a torch apiece, they ran to Lu's house, broke in with shouts and seized whatever they could lay hands on. The scholar's servants, who could not imagine what had happened, darted wildly in all directions; the children cried, and the whole household was thrown into confusion.

Mrs. Lu was sitting by the stove with her maids when she heard shouting and scuffling outside. Thinking a fire had broken out, she hastily told her maids to investigate; but before they had taken a single step a servant came to the door.

"Look out, ma'am!" he cried. "A mob of men with torches have forced their way in!"

Mrs. Lu assumed that bandits were upon them, and her teeth chattered with fright as she bade her maids close the door. Before she had finished speaking, however, there was a glare of torches and strange men had rushed into the room.

"Spare us, prince!" screamed the maids, unable to escape.

"You fools!" replied the men. "We are not brigands, but officers sent by the magistrate to arrest Lu Nan."

When Mrs. Lu heard this, she realized that her husband was in trouble for the disrespect he had shown the magistrate.

"If you are the police, where are your manners?" she asked. "Even if my husband is required to appear at the yamen, it must be for some common lawsuit; it can't be a case of high treason. Why didn't you come in the daytime, instead of bursting in at night like robbers with so many men carrying torches and arms? We shall report you in court tomorrow and see that you are properly punished."

"Just give us Lu Nan," retorted the officers. "You can report us if you like."

Having ransacked this room, picking out all the choicest objects that pleased them, they went on to the rest, frightening the concubines so that they hid under their beds. When the constables had searched the whole house without finding Lu Nan, they concluded that he must be in the garden and trooped out to look for him there. The scholar was drinking with a few guests in a winter pavilion, while actors sang and played to them. The messenger he had sent after Lu Cai was reporting his failure to find him, when two other servants rushed upstairs.

"Master!" they shouted. "There's trouble!"

"What trouble?" asked Lu, by now half drunk.

"We don't know exactly, but a mob has broken in, and they're looting and seizing everyone they meet. They have just fought their way into your room, sir."

This alarm sobered the guests completely.

"What can this mean?" they asked, getting up. "Let's go and see."

The scholar, however, looked quite unconcerned.

Then they saw flickering torches, and the police rushed upstairs, while the terrified actors scattered in all directions looking for somewhere to hide.

"Who dares behave so outrageously here?" demanded Lu furiously. "I'll have you arrested!"

"Our magistrate wants you," retorted one of the officers. "I'm afraid you can't arrest us."

"Get moving!" cried another, putting a rope round the scholar's neck.

"What have I done?" demanded Lu. "How dare you treat me like this? What if I refuse?"

"You refused to come when you were invited, but you can't refuse this time because you're under arrest — understand?"

Then one pulled the rope, while others pushed and tugged, and so they got the scholar downstairs. They arrested more than a dozen servants too, and wanted to arrest the guests as well; but some of the constables knew that the guests came from noble families and were well-known scholars, so they dared not touch them. Leaving the garden, they made their way noisily back to the yamen. The worried guests followed to see what would happen; while the servants who had hidden themselves came out of hiding and, on Mrs. Lu's instructions, took silver to beg some of the yamen officers for news.

Lanterns and torches made the court where Magistrate Wang was waiting as bright as by day; and all voices were hushed. The police led Lu Nan to the foot of the dais, and looking up he saw the magistrate seated there like the King of Hell, with murder in his face, while runners were ranged on either side like attendant devils. At this display of might, the scholar's servants trembled. Then the constables stepped forward and reported:

"We have brought Lu Nan, Your Honour."

They dragged their prisoners to the platform and made the servants kneel on one side, Niu Wen and his brother's wife on the other. Lu Nan alone remained standing defiantly in the middle. When the magistrate saw that the scholar would not kneel, he examined him closely and gave a short laugh.

"Here is a fine petty tyrant!" he exclaimed. "So unmannerly in a public court — no wonder he fears neither man nor devil outside! But I'll ask you to spend a few days in our gaol before I deal with you."

Lu Nan took a few steps forward and drew himself up to his full height.

"Send me to your gaol if you like," he declared, "but you must give me the reason. What crime have I committed that your men should come at night to arrest me and seize my property?"

"You have attempted to seduce another man's wife and beaten Niu Cheng to death. These are serious offences."

When the scholar heard this he smiled.

"I was wondering what all the excitement was about," he said. "So it's on account of Niu Cheng! I suppose you merely want

me to pay with my life; but why all this flurry and hurry? Niu
Cheng was one of my bondsmen, who died after a tiff with my
servant, Lu Cai. I was in no way responsible for his death.
But even if I had beaten him to death, the law does not re-
quire a master to pay with his life for the death of a bondsman.
If you want to accuse me of a crime I never committed, to satisfy
a private grudge, it's easy for you to pass false sentence; but
I'm afraid you will find it hard to silence public opinion."

"It was a free man you killed!" thundered the magistrate.
"The case is quite clear, yet you maintain that he was your slave.
You insult the judge and refuse to kneel in court. It is easy
to see from your insubordinate behaviour here how high-handed
you must be in daily life. Before I try you for murder, you
shall be properly punished for such insolence to your magistrate."

He ordered his men to beat the prisoner; and the runners
strode forward to seize Lu.

"You can kill a gentleman but not humiliate him," cried the
scholar. "I am a gentleman and I am not afraid to die. Hurry
up and pass judgement. Have me sliced to pieces or decapitated
if you like; but I will not stand the indignity of the bastinado!"

Ignoring his protests, however, the runners threw him to the
ground and gave him thirty strokes; then, when the magistrate
ordered them to stop, Lu was taken with his servants to the gaol.
Niu Cheng's corpse was to be given a proper coffin by the local
authorities and taken to the mortuary for an autopsy; and Niu
Wen, his sister-in-law and the other witnesses were released on
bail pending a further summons. As Lu was helped out of court
by two servants, bleeding and bruised from his beating, he lifted
his head and cried aloud in his rage.

At the yamen gate his friends came up to ask: "Why were
you bastinadoed?"

"For no fault of mine," replied Lu. "My servant Lu Cai
caused a man's death, and Magistrate Wang wants to satisfy a
private grudge by holding me responsible. He means to condemn me to death, that's all!"

"What injustice!" exclaimed his friends, aghast. "Well, we

have decided what to do: tomorrow we shall get all the local gentry to speak to the magistrate. He can't ignore public opinion, and will have to set you free."

"Don't worry about me," replied Lu. "Let him do his worst. I have one important request though: please tell my family when you go back to send plenty of wine to the gaol for me."

"You had better not drink so much now," they cautioned him. Lu simply laughed.

"A man should make merry while he can," he answered. "Poverty and riches, fame and humiliation, are external things which can make no real difference to a man. Why should I stop drinking just because he wants to destroy me?"

As they were talking, a gaoler gave the scholar a shove from behind.

"Get moving!" he said. "You can talk another time."

This gaoler, Cai Xian, was one of the magistrate's trusted men. Lu glared at him.

"Cùrse you!" he shouted. "Mind your own business while I am talking."

"I like that!" retorted Cai Xian indignantly. "You are a felon now. You had better stop playing the gentleman here; it will get you nowhere."

"Who's a felon?" roared Lu. "What can you do if I refuse to move?"

Before Cai Xian could reply, some more experienced attendants' pushed him aside and contrived to get the scholar into the gaol. Then his friends left, and his servants went home to report all that had happened to Mrs. Lu.

Now when Lu Nan left the court, Tan Zun followed close on his heels to listen to what was said; then went back to the yamen and reported the scholar's conversation with his friends to the magistrate. So the following morning, on the pretext of sickness, Magistrate Wang did not attend to business and his gateman did not accept the local gentry's petition. In the afternoon, however, the magistrate suddenly took his seat in court, summoned the plaintiffs, witnesses and coroners, and had

Lu and his servants brought out of gaol for an examination of Niu Cheng's corpse.

The coroners, knowing what was expected of them, described slight bruises as serious injuries; and the witnesses, who realized that the magistrate had a grudge against Lu, testified that the scholar had beaten Niu Cheng to death. Then Magistrate Wang tricked Lu into producing the deed proving Niu Cheng his bondsman, and tore it up alleging that it was a forgery. Tortured and condemned to death, the scholar was given twenty strokes, then clapped in a cangue and sent to the gaol for the condemned. His servants, after being given thirty strokes each and sentenced to three years' penal servitude, were allowed out on bail; the dead man's wife, Niu Wen and the witnesses were dismissed; a final decision on the coffin and the corpse was postponed pending orders from above; and a detailed report of the case was sent to the higher authorities, describing how Lu had insulted the court by refusing to kneel and setting forth his crimes. Though the local gentry sent in another petition on Lu Nan's behalf, the magistrate ignored it.

Lu, you must know, was used to a life of luxury. If he had so much as a boil, doctors would be summoned; so how could he bear a heavy beating? As soon as he reached the prison he fell senseless to the ground. Luckily the turnkeys, knowing he had money, looked after him well and provided him with plasters and powder, while his wife sent a physician to the gaol to attend him. So in less than a month he recovered. Then a continuous stream of friends and relatives began to visit him, and the gaolers, delighted with the bribes they received, allowed visitors to come and go as they pleased.

Among the gaolers, however, was Cai Xian, one of Magistrate Wang's flunkeys. He went straight to report the situation to his master, who immediately swooped down on the gaol and caught five or six men in Lu's cell. Since they were all well-known scholars, he dared not punish them but sent them away; but Lu was given another twenty strokes and all the turnkeys were severely penalized. These men, realizing that was Cai

Xian's work, gnashed their teeth with rage; but since he was a favourite with the magistrate they dared not touch him.

Lu Nan had been accustomed to fine mansions, silken garments and delicious fare, with flowers and trees to delight his eyes, sweet music to divert his ears, and beautiful concubines to share his bed at night. Now, however, after leading a life as carefree as an immortal's, he was suddenly a prisoner, confined to a low, tumbledown cell. He saw nothing but condemned criminals, who scowled and raged like a pack of devils or ghosts; and he heard nothing but the clank of chains and shackles, the bells tolling the nightly roll-call, the gongs sounding the watches, and the dismal prison ditties. Though Lu was a high-hearted man, he could not help feeling depressed and longing for wings to carry him away, or an axe to hack down the gate and set the captives free. Whenever he recalled his humiliation, he bristled with anger.

"Here am I," he thought, "who have always fancied myself a stout fellow, fallen into the hands of this scoundrel. How am I to get out of here? And even if I succeed in getting out, how can I face the world again? What is the point of living on? I had better find some way to take my own life."

But on second thoughts he decided against suicide.

"King Tang of the Shang Dynasty and King Wen of the Zhou Dynasty suffered imprisonment," he reflected, "while Sun Bin and Sima Qian endured the indignity of mutilation. Yet these ancient sages bore the humiliation and bided their time. Why should I kill myself? ... I have friends all over the country, many of them officials, who will not stand idly by to watch my distress. They may not have heard yet how grossly abused I have been. I had better write to them, asking them to appeal to a higher court to redress my wrongs."

Thereupon he wrote a great number of letters, which his servant despatched.

Some of Lu's friends lived in retirement, others held office; but each and all were horrified when they received his letters. A few went straight to Magistrate Wang to entreat him to pardon the scholar, while others begged the higher authorities to help. These higher authorities, who had heard of Lu Nan's genius and felt he should be released, sent the county reports back to the county magistrate, and hinted that the scholar's family should make a formal appeal to them, so that they could suggest removing him to a different court for retrial.

Taking comfort from such messages, Lu told his family to appeal to various courts; and finally it was decreed that his case should be investigated in the prefectural court. The prefectural judge already knew of the case, having received a great many letters on the subject — especially from Lu's district. As for Magistrate Wang, within a few days he received dozens of letters urging him to pardon Lu; and, while he was still wondering what to do, he found that the higher authorities were sending back the reports. A few days later, when the judicial court notified the county that Lu Nan should be taken away for retrial, the magistrate realized that his superiors intended to release Lu, and his heart sank.

"The clever devil!" he thought. "Sitting here in gaol, how has he managed to interest all the higher courts in his case? Once he slips through my fingers, he will never rest until he has taken vengeance. Prompt action is called for. A weed will grow again unless you pull up its roots."

That night he sent Tan Zun to the gaol to bid Cai Xian make out a certificate of sickness and have Lu taken that same night to a quiet spot and killed.

Now the assistant magistrate in this county, Dong Shen, was a senior licentiate who was an able administrator and a just and merciful judge. When Magistrate Wang wrongly condemned Lu Nan to death, Dong felt great indignation; but as a subordinate he could not protest. Each time he went to inspect the gaol, however, he chatted with Lu, and so they became friends. He happened to go to the gaol that night and when he found Lu missing but no one would tell him what had become of the scholar, Dong grew angry and threatened to beat the gaolers. Then they whispered to him:

"His Honour sent Tan Zun here to have Lu Nan killed, and he has been taken to the back."

"How could the magistrate of a district do such a thing!" exclaimed Dong, greatly shocked. "No, no. You scoundrels must have decided to take his life because he wouldn't pay you all you demanded. Take me there this instant."

Not daring to disobey, the turnkeys led him to an alley behind the gaol, where they came suddenly upon Tan and Cai. Dong ordered these men to be arrested, then stepped forward to where Lu was lying on the ground, his whole body black and blue, his hands and feet bound, and a sand bag on his face to stifle him.

When Dong had bid his men remove the sand bag and called Lu Nan by name, the scholar, who was not fated to die, gradually regained consciousness. But he was unable to speak until they had unfastened him, carried him inside and given him a hot drink. Then he told them how Tan Zun had ordered Cai Xian to beat him, and they had tried to murder him. After reassuring the scholar and telling the gaoler to help him to bed, the assistant magistrate took Tan and Cai to the hall. Though he knew that the magistrate was behind this, now that the plot was discovered Wang would certainly not admit his complicity; and if Dong wrung a confession from Tan Zun, who was his superior's right-hand man, the magistrate would lose face. That would never do. So he summoned Cai Xian alone and urged him to confess that he and Tan, failing to blackmail Lu, had attempted to murder him. Cai, however, insisted that he had been carrying out the magistrate's instructions, until finally Dong lost patience and ordered him to be tortured.

Now the turnkeys hated Cai Xian because he had won them a beating by informing against them to the magistrate; so they brought the tightest leg-screws, and as soon as they put them on him Cai started shrieking and cried out that he would confess. But when Dong bid them stop, the turnkeys, eager to take their revenge, pretended not to hear and tightened the screw even more until Cai shrieked and howled, calling on all his ancestors.

in his pain. Only after Dong had repeated his order several times did the gaolers stop. Then Cai was given paper and brush and had to write what he was told.

"Don't let these men go," Dong ordered the turnkeys when he had the confession in his hands. "I shall come back after I have seen the magistrate."

He returned to the yamen and sat up all night to prepare a report, which he handed to Magistrate Wang in person at the next morning session. The magistrate was already wondering why Tan Zun had not come back, and when he saw Dong's report he was flabbergasted; but though he hated his subordinate for thwarting him, there was nothing he could do about it. After reading the report, he shook his head solemnly several times.

"Can this be?" he demanded incredulously.

"I saw it with my own eyes," replied Dong. "If Your Honour does not believe me, you can summon the three men to question them. Tan Zun was not so bad, but Cai Xian's attitude was quite inexcusable: he even tried to smear you. Your Honour ought to punish him as a warning to others."

At this hint that his secret was known, the magistrate turned purple; and, fearing that if the truth came out his reputation would be ruined, he had to sentence Cai Xian to penal servitude. After this, however, he bore the assistant magistrate a grudge; and later, when he found his subordinate guilty of trifling with women, he reported him to his superiors and had him dismissed from office. But that is another story.

Since the magistrate's plot had failed, he sent reports to all his superior officers and to many influential men in the capital declaring that Lu Nan was a local despot who gloried in his wealth, courted the powerful, had beaten a citizen to death and shown insolence in court, and was offering bribes to extricate himself from gaol. By making the case out as extremely serious and giving it such publicity, he hoped to intimidate all those who might have helped the scholar. He also told Tan to have bills denouncing Lu printed in the name of Niu Cheng's wife and posted up everywhere, then reported this to the prefectural

government. The prefectural judge was a coward who feared
to take any responsibility; and when he saw the magistrate's
report and the bill, to avoid trouble he simply forwarded them
to his superiors. But once a case had been through the prefectural court, other officials do not like to challenge the verdict;
so though Lu Nan had hoped to be released, his sentence was
confirmed and he was sent back to the county gaol.

Lu hoped that when the magistrate left this post, his case
would be re-examined; but the authorities considered Magistrate
Wang as a bold, forceful man who had overthrown a notorious
local despot; so his fame reached the capital and he was promoted to the Imperial Board of Scrutiny. And once Wang was
a powerful official no one dared to question his verdict, however
many strings Lu pulled.

Once, it is true, a censor named Fan took pity on the scholar
and had him released; but when Wang heard of it he told a
colleague of his that Fan had accepted bribes and was attempt-
ing to free an important criminal, with the result that the censor
was dismissed from his post and Lu imprisoned once more in
the county gaol. So later, even though some officials knew that
injustice had been done, no one dared risk his own post to vin-
dicate Lu Nan.

Time passed quickly, until Lu had been a prisoner for more
than ten years, during which time two new magistrates had come
and gone. Niu Wen and his brother's wife were dead, but Wang
had been promoted to the post of chief censor and was so powerful that Lu gave up all hope of release. Little did he know
that his trials were coming to an end when a new magistrate
was appointed to that county named Lu Guangzu, a native of
Zhejiang Province. This magistrate was a wise and learned
man, with great talent and administrative ability; and just before he left the capital Wang puzzled him by urging him not to
be taken in by Lu Nan.

"Though Lu Nan was sentenced during the censor's term of
office, many years have passed since then," he thought. "Why

is he still interested in the case? And why should he warn me to be on my guard? There must be a reason."

When he reached his new post he questioned some of the local gentry, and they all pleaded for Lu, saying how unjustly he had been punished. Suspecting that since the scholar was rich he might have bribed these men, the new magistrate did not place too much faith in what they said; but when he made further inquiries he received the same answer.

"How could an official condemn a man to death because of a private grudge?" he marvelled.

He determined to report the truth to his superiors, to right the wrong.

But then he thought: "When I send in my report, I shall be ordered to investigate further before setting him free. I had better release him first and then make my report."

He took out the files of the case and studied them carefully, but could find no way to reverse the judgement.

After poring over the records several times he came to the conclusion: "To settle this case I must find the true culprit — Lu Cai."

Thereupon he offered his constables a reward of a hundred taels for the capture of Lu Cai by a certain date; and in less than a month the man was arrested. Knowing that escape was impossible, Lu Cai confessed without being put to torture, and Magistrate Lu issued the following decree:

"Since Niu Cheng, after drawing his wages from the Lu family, quarrelled with Lu Cai who demanded the payment of a debt, it is clear that Niu Cheng was a hired hand in the Lu household. And the law does not require a master to pay with his life for the death of a hired hand. Moreover, it was Lu Cai who lent money to Niu Cheng, demanded its repayment and fought with him; therefore it was wrong to let Lu Cai go free and condemn Lu Nan. As Lu Cai fled from justice and involved his master in great trouble, he deserves death and shall be executed. Lu Nan has been unjustly imprisoned for many years and shall now be released."

That same day Lu Nan was led out of gaol, freed from his cangue, and sent home. The whole yamen was amazed, even Lu himself marvelling at this unexpected turn of events. Then Magistrate Lu wrote a detailed account of how the trouble had started and the scholar had been wronged, and called on the provincial judge to deliver the report. When the judge heard that Lu had already been released, he suspected bribery.

"I understand Lu Nan's family is very wealthy," he said. "Don't you care what people may say?"

"I care only about enforcing the law," replied the magistrate, "not about gossip. All I ask is whether a man is innocent or guilty, not whether he is rich or poor."

Hearing how honourably he spoke, the judge asked no further questions but said:

"In ancient times, when Zhang Tang was tribune, there was not a single innocent man in prison. I admire you for following in his footsteps." Then the magistrate respectfully took his leave.

Upon Lu Nan's return home, his whole family was overjoyed and all his friends and relatives came to congratulate him. After a few days his servants brought word that the new magistrate had come back to the county yamen, and Lu decided to call to thank him. For this he dressed plainly in black garments and a private citizen's cap.

"You owe so much to him," said the scholar's wife, "you ought to take some gifts to show your gratitude."

"Judging by his actions, he is a gallant man," replied Lu, "not one of those mean, money-grabbing fellows. To send him gifts would be an insult."

"Why should it be an insult?"

"I have been wronged for more than ten years, during which time all the higher officials were afraid to take my part; but as soon as Magistrate Lu came here he found out the truth and boldly released me. Without great wisdom and great courage, he would never have done such a thing; and if I repay him now with gifts, it will mean that though he understands me I have failed to understand him. That would never do."

So he went to the yamen empty-handed.

As Lu Nan was a talented scholar, the magistrate treated him with respect and invited him to his inner hall. When Lu met his benefactor he bowed but did not kneel; and the magistrate, secretly impressed, bowed in return, then told his attendants to fetch a chair and place it at one side.

Can you imagine such a thing, readers? Lu Nan had been imprisoned for years as a felon, so the magistrate who released him from gaol was his greatest benefactor; and even if Lu had knocked his head on the ground till it bled, it would not have been too much, yet he only bowed. Any other official would have taken offence at such insolence; but this magistrate paid no attention and simply called for another chair, thus showing his magnanimity and great respect for talent.

Who would have thought that when Lu saw that he was to sit on one side, he was the one to feel offended?

"Your Honour may condemn me to death," he declared, "but not to sit on a lower seat."

The magistrate immediately rose and bowed again.

"I beg your pardon," he said, and asked Lu to take his chair. Then they discussed past and present affairs, and got on so well together that they regretted not having met earlier. Indeed, soon they were fast friends.

When Chief Censor Wang heard that the new magistrate had released Lu Nan, he was angry and sent a trusted man to present a memorandum to the court accusing both Magistrate Lu and the provincial judge. To clear himself, the provincial judge wrote a detailed account of how Wang, when a magistrate, had falsely accused Lu on account of a private grudge; so the emperor dismissed Wang from office, while the provincial judge and Magistrate Lu remained at their posts. Tan Zun had left the yamen and was making a living by engaging in unjust lawsuits; but when the magistrate knew this, he reported it and had Tan imprisoned and sentenced to exile at the frontier. Lu

Nan, conscious that he had narrowly escaped death, gave up all idea of seeking an official career to take pleasure in wine and poetry, and gradually squandered his entire fortune without a qualm.

Lu Guangzu was an incorruptible magistrate, who loved the people as if they were his children, sought out evil-doers and put an end to vicious practices; so that wicked men trembled before him, and there was no more banditry, the people of his county revered him as a sage, and his fame spread to the capital; but because he had no friends in high places he was merely promoted to the post of a secretary in the Ministry of Rites in Nanjing. When he was leaving the county, the people clung to his carriage and lay down before it to prevent his leaving; wailing was heard all along the road, and common citizens escorted him for several dozen miles. Lu Nan accompanied him for nearly two hundred miles, then still loath to part from him, bid farewell with tears.

Later Lu Guangzu was set in charge of the Ministry of Rites; and Lu Nan, who had by then dissipated his whole fortune, went south to live with his old friend. Minister Lu treated him as an honoured guest, supplied him with one thousand cash every day for wine, and let him visit the best mountain and river scenery. And the scholar wrote poems wherever he went, which were known throughout the capital.

One day, when Lu Nan visited the temple dedicated to Li Bai at Caishi Rock, he met a priest with bare feet who struck him as an exceptional man. Lu invited this stranger to drink with him, and the priest offered him some white liquid from his gourd which the scholar found had a strangely delicious flavour.

"Where does this wine come from?" he inquired.

"I brewed it myself," was the answer. "I have a lodge at the foot of the Five Elders' Peaks in the Lushan Mountains. If you will come with me, I shall see that you have enough to drink."

"If you have such good wine," replied Lu, "I shall be glad to accompany you."

He wrote a letter on the spot to Minister Lu to bid him fare-well, and left empty-handed as he was with the priest. When the minister saw the letter he was impressed.

"He drifted here and now he has drifted away," he said. "The whole universe is but a temporary lodging house, and human life ephemeral as a mayfly. This man was a true romantic!"

He sent men time and again to look for Lu Nan in the moun-tains, but they could not find him. Some ten years later, how-ever, when Minister Lu had retired and the government sent an official to inquire after his health, he despatched his second son to the capital to express his thanks to the court; and in the capital some of his servants met Lu Nan, who asked them to send his greetings to his old friend. The scholar is said to have become an immortal, and a later poet wrote of him:

This scholar lost his freedom through misfortune,
But with wine and poetry despised great nobles;
Though he drifted away at last, taking nothing with him;
His reputation will endure for ever.

The Tangerines and the Tortoise Shell

Each day I fill my cup with wine;
My little garden blossoms gay;
Each day I sing and dance for joy,
And cast all gloom and care away.
The past is but an empty dream,
Great men have died and turned to clay;
Then strive no more for rank or fame,
But take your pleasure while you may.

This poem, set to the air of "Moonlight on the Western River" and written by Zhu Xizhen of the Song Dynasty, states that since fame and fortune in human life are ordained by Heaven men should enjoy themselves while they can. Just think how many heroes in the *Histories of the Past Seventeen Dynasties* failed to win the wealth and rank they deserved. A scholar might be able to dash off a thousand-word despatch on horseback; but when he was out of office his writings were not thought fit to cover a pickle jar. A warrior might be able to split a willow at a hundred paces; but when he was out of office his arrows were not thought fit to boil a pan of rice. Yet fools and dolts who were born lucky passed the examinations with a mere smattering of knowledge, or were appointed to high military posts although they knew little of the art of war. Truly, all depends upon destiny.

Well does the proverb say: If you are fated to be poor, the gold you dig up will turn to copper; if you are fated to be rich, the paper you pick up will turn to cloth. Everything is determined by fate; for as Wu Yangao wrote:

401

Luck is a wight of many pranks,
Who heedeth no man's curse or thanks,
Now here, now there, now up, now down,
Dispensing ruin or renown.

And according to the famous philosopher Zhu Xi: "Who does not want a golden chamber?   Who does not want his granaries filled with grain?   But no amount of planning will procure you something which is not in your stars; nor can you determine your children's fortune."

And Su Dongpo said: "Why scramble after fame which is paltry as the kingdom on a snail's horn, or profit which can be balanced on the head of a fly?   It is not worth it.   Everything is predestined, which is to be weak and which strong."

In fact, what all these famous men were trying to say is best expressed by the old saw: Man proposes, Fate disposes.

"Why, story-teller," you may protest, "if what you say is true, a man need not study the arts of peace and war but can just wait idly for good fortune without following any trade; and a wastrel can live on what Heaven sends or on his family inheritance.   Wouldn't this stop men from striving to better themselves?"

No, readers, let me explain.   Only when a family is fated to go down in the world does a loafer appear in it; only when a house is destined to fall does it produce a wastrel.   This is the general rule.   But there are, of course, also unexpected reversals of fortune, when a poor man becomes wealthy overnight or a rich man is suddenly left penniless.   So we cannot be sure of anything at all.

Listen now to the story of Jin Weihou, a native of Kaifeng, the capital of the Northern Song Dynasty.   Jin was a merchant who rose early, slept late, and spent all his waking hours thinking how best to make money.   As soon as he was comfortably off he hit on a plan to keep what he had: he spent his loose silver only, saved each tael of fine silver he got, and when he had collected a hundred taels melted them into one great ingot.   This he tied with a red cord and put by his pillow, where he could play with it at night before sleeping.   After years of skimping and scraping, he had eight such ingots, no more and no less; but then money came and money went, and, unable to make up another hundred taels, he gave up saving.

Jin had four sons, who prepared a feast on his seventieth birthday to congratulate him.   The respect they showed him made the old man happy.

"Heaven has been kind to me," he said.   "I have worked hard all my life, and now we are quite well off.   Thanks to my economy, I have saved up eight great ingots of silver which lie beside my pillow, tied in pairs with red cord.   I mean to choose an auspicious day to give you two ingots each.   And I hope you will treasure them all your life."

His four sons were overjoyed.   After thanking their father they left the table in the highest of spirits.

The old man was slightly drunk as he lit his lamp and went to his room.   He looked tipsily at the eight great ingots which formed a glistening white row by his pillow, and after stroking them several times he lay down with a chuckle.   Just as he was dropping off to sleep, however, he heard footsteps by his bed and feared thieves had broken in.   He listened carefully, and seemed to hear men hesitating to advance but nudging each other to step forward.   The lamp before the bed was still burning dimly, and when he parted the bed curtains and looked out, he saw eight big fellows in white gowns and red belts, who stepped forward with a bow.

"We are brothers sent by Heaven to serve you," they told him.   "It was good of you, sir, to bring us up and look after us all these years without making use of our services.   Your time is nearly up now.   We were to have stayed with you till you left this world; but today we heard that you mean to send us to wait on your sons; and, since we are not destined to serve them, we have come to say goodbye.   We are going now to live with a certain Mr. Wang in a neighbouring village; but we shall

meet once more." Having told him their new master's name
and address, they turned and left.

Surprised and bewildered, the old man jumped out of bed.
Not stopping to put on his shoes, he chased barefoot after the
eight men, whom he could see making for the door. In his haste
however he tripped over the door sill and fell, then woke up
to find that it was all a dream.

Old Jin immediately got up, trimmed the lamp and looked
by the pillow. His eight great ingots had gone! He thought
over all that had been said in the dream, and every word of it
was true. Then he heaved a sigh and a lump came into his
throat.

"I can't believe that my hard-earned savings are going not
to my sons but to strangers," he muttered. "Still, they told me
quite clearly this Mr. Wang's name and where he lives. I shall
make inquiries."

There was no more sleep for him that night, and the next
morning as soon as he got up he told his sons what had happened. Two of them were taken aback, two were sceptical.

"Evidently the silver wasn't destined to be ours," thought the
first two. "That must be the reason for this strange happening."

"The old man has obviously repented of his generosity,"
thought the two who were sceptical. "On second thoughts he
couldn't bear to part with his silver; that's why he's spun us
this yarn."

When Jin saw that two of his sons did not believe him, he
was all the more eager to get at the truth. So he asked his way
to the village he had been told of in the dream, and there sure
enough lived a Mr. Wang. Knocking at the door and entering,
Jin saw that bright candles were lit in the hall and sacrifices had
been set out for the gods. When he asked the reason for this,
the servants went to find their master; and presently Mr. Wang
appeared, greeted the old man and invited him to be seated.
Then he asked Jin what had brought him here.

"Something is puzzling me," said Jin. "And I have come to

see if you can shed any light on it. But I notice that you are offering sacrifices today. May I ask the reason?"

"Recently my wife fell ill," replied Wang, "and I consulted a fortune-teller, who declared that she would get better if her bed were moved. Yesterday, still ailing, she thought she saw eight big fellows in white gowns and red belts. 'We used to be in the Jin family,' they told her. 'But we have done with them now and come to you.' Having said this they crawled under the bed; and my wife broke into a cold sweat, after which she felt better. When we moved the bed, there in the dust we found eight great silver ingots bound round the middle with red cord. We have no idea where these have come from; but since Heaven has been so kind to us we have bought offerings to sacrifice. Now you have come to question me, perhaps you know something about this?"

Stamping his feet, Jin answered: "It took me a lifetime to save up that silver. Last night I had a dream too, and when I woke the silver had vanished. But in the dream my ingots mentioned your name and address; that's how I found my way here. It is the will of Heaven; I can't complain. But if I could see them once more I should feel better."

"That is easy," said Mr. Wang.

He left the room, smiling, and returned with four serving boys each of whom was carrying a tray bearing two ingots fastened with red cord — the selfsame ingots Jin had treasured.

The old man's eyes nearly started from his head, but there was nothing he could do. Big tears rolled down his cheeks as he stroked the silver.

"Fate must be against me," he said, "if I am not allowed to keep these."

Though Wang ordered the boys to put the ingots away again, he felt rather sorry for the old man. So he got out three taels of loose silver, put them in a packet and offered it to Jin as a parting gift. Jin, however, was unwilling to take it.

"I have been too luckless to keep my own," protested the old man. "How can I take yours?"

He declined again and again, until Wang pushed the silver up his sleeve. Wanting to give it back, Jin fumbled for the packet but could not find it. He blushed with confusion. And finally, since Wang insisted that he accept it, he bowed and left. Upon reaching home he told his sons what had happened, and they sighed. He also mentioned Mr. Wang's kindness in giving him three taels as a parting gift; but when he searched in his sleeve he could not find the silver, and was forced to conclude that he must have dropped it on the way home.

In fact, while Jin was modestly refusing the silver Wang had thrust the packet through a hole in the lining of his sleeve; and by the time the old man felt for it to return it, it had already dropped out and rolled under the door sill. Later, when the floor was swept, Wang got it back. So it seems that each bite or sup we take is preordained. Jin, who was not destined to possess money, could not keep even three taels, let alone eight hundred. But Wang, who was destined to possess it, could not get rid of three taels. Thus, regardless of either man's intentions, a have became a have-not and a have-not became a have.

I shall tell you now of a man who, though he came to grief every time on firm land and had to live from hand to mouth, found an extraordinary treasure in a far-away place you would never dream of visiting and became fabulously rich. Such a strange thing can seldom have happened before. But, as the verse says:

> *If honour and riches are your lot,*
> *It makes no odds if you're wise or not;*
> *And if 'tis your fate to be rich beyond measure,*
> *Far out in the ocean you'll find a treasure.*

During the Cheng Hua period (1465-1487) of our dynasty, outside the West Gate of Suzhou there lived a man named Wen Shi, who was so clever that he could turn his hand to anything. He learned chess, calligraphy and painting, could dance and sing after a fashion and play most musical instruments tolerably well. While he was a child, a fortune-teller predicted that he

would become very wealthy; and, confident of his own gifts, instead of applying himself to any business he lived in idleness until he had run through most of his patrimony. When he realized that he had not much left, and saw that other men often succeeded in doubling or trebling their capital by trading, he decided to go into business too. But, whatever he tried, he lost money.

One day, hearing that fans sold well in Beijing, Wen found a partner and laid in a stock of fans. He bought some fans of the best quality, skilfully made and covered with gold paper, and sent these with gifts to well-known scholars, requesting them to write a few lines or paint a picture on the paper of these fans, for then they would fetch about a tael of silver apiece. He also bought slightly inferior fans which could be painted in the style of the masters and sold as the genuine article to unsuspecting purchasers, this counterfeiting, indeed, Wen could do himself. Last of all, he bought some of the cheapest white paper fans, bare of any calligraphy or painting, which cost only a few dozen cash; but even these Wen was certain he could sell at twice their original price. Then, choosing an auspicious day, he packed his fans in a box and set off for Beijing.

How could he guess that it would rain almost every day that summer in Beijing? It remained so cool that the sale of fans started late, and autumn set in early. Then at length the weather cleared, and some dandies started looking for Suzhou fans to tuck in their sleeves or flourish as they walked. When they came to buy, however, and Wen opened his box, he exclaimed in horror. For in Beijing things grow mouldy in the summer, and the unusual humidity this year had made the ink and glue on the fans stick tightly together. When he opened them by force, he tore the paper. All the fans which were worth money because of their calligraphy and painting were ruined; only the inferior white ones were unspoiled. But how much were they worth? By the time he had sold them at a loss to raise money for his journey home, all his capital had gone.

All Wen's ventures ended in a similar way. He not only

lost money himself, but usually ruined his partners into the bargain. So his friends nicknamed him Unlucky Wen.

In a few years his whole estate was gone, and he had not
even succeeded in getting a wife. He eked out a miserable
existence by occasional copying work and odd commissions. But
because he was a witty fellow, who knew plenty of jokes and
anecdotes, he made an entertaining companion and no party was
complete without him. So although he could never acquire
property, he never went hungry.

Having once lived in style, Wen did not mix very well with
the common run of spongers. Some friends who were sorry for
him recommended him as a private tutor, but respectable families
considered him too much of a dilettante. Thus he could please
no one: the rich and their hangers-on alike jeered at him for his
lucklessness. But so much for this.

One day Wen heard that over forty merchants in the neighbourhood — the usual Zhangs, Lis, Zhaos and Qians — were
about to set off on a trading trip overseas.

"I have no roots here," he thought, "and no means of livelihood. I might as well go with them to see the sights abroad;
then I shan't have lived in vain. They will surely not refuse
me; and I shall have a pleasant trip instead of worrying about
food and fuel at home."

As he was turning the matter over in his mind, up came Zhang
Chengyun, a merchant who specialized in overseas trade. Because he could recognize rare jewels, was generous and ready to
help the unfortunate, his companions called him Canny Zhang.
Wen now told this merchant what he was thinking.

"Nothing could be better," said Zhang. "We often find these
voyages dull; but if you come, with your jokes and stories the
days will pass quickly. I'm sure everybody in our party will
be glad to have you. But we are all taking goods and you have
nothing. It would be a pity to make the trip empty-handed.
I'll see if we can't raise enough for you to buy a little merchandise to take along."

"It is very kind of you to suggest it," replied Wen. "But I am afraid no one else will be as generous as you."

"Well, I can but try," said Zhang as he left.

Just then a blind fortune-teller passed by, sounding his gong; and Wen, finding a coin in his pocket, stopped the man and asked to know his fortune.

"Your luck is amazing," declared the blind man. "No ordinary wealth is coming to you, but a fortune!"

"I am only going on this trip for pleasure," thought Wen, "to pass the time. What business can I do abroad? Even if they do raise some money for me, it won't amount to much. So how can I possibly make a fortune? This fellow must be lying."

Just then Zhang came back, fuming.

"Mention money and friendship is finished!" he said. "Those merchants are a strange lot. When I told them you were coming, they were all pleased; but when I asked them to help, not one of them would. So two of my best friends and I have raised one tael of silver for you. It's not enough for any goods, but you can buy some fruit to eat on board. We shall look after your food."

Wen thanked him warmly as he accepted the silver.

"Hurry up and pack," said Zhang, starting off. "We're going to leave at once."

"I have nothing to pack," replied Wen. "I shall be with you immediately."

Weighing the silver in his hand, he looked at it with a smile. "What can I get with this?" he wondered.

But as he walked on he saw vendors with baskets lining the streets.

> Red as flames that blaze afar,
> Bright as newly risen star;
> Ere the frost how few you find:
> Juice yet tart, unwrinkled rind.
> Better far than Farmer Li's;
> Su has none as fine as these;

Good as fruit from warm Swatow,
Famed Fuzhou they rival now!

On the two Dongting islands in Lake Taihu the sun is as
warm and the soil as fertile as in Fujian or Guangdong, where
the world famous tangerines of Shantou and Fuzhou grow; and
the Dongting tangerines have the same colour and fragrance as
these. When first ripe they taste a little sour, but they soon
sweeten; and their price is only one-tenth that of the Fuzhou
fruit. These tangerines are called Dongting Reds.

"With one tael of silver I can buy over a hundred catties of
these tangerines," thought Wen. "They will quench my thirst
on the junk, and I can share them with my friends to show my
appreciation of their kindness."

So he bought the tangerines, had them packed in a bamboo
crate, and hired a man to carry them with his luggage to 'the
boat. The merchants clapped their hands and laughed when
they saw what he had brought.

"Here come Mr. Wen's precious wares!" they cried.

Though made to look a fool, Wen swallowed his resentment
and boarded the ship; but he dared not mention the tangerines
after this. Soon the junk set sail and reached the open sea,
where all that could be seen were rolling silvery waves tossing
up snowy foam, and floating reflections of the sun, the moon
and the stars.

They sailed before the wind for several days — how far exactly they could not tell. Then they sighted land and saw from
the junk a populous city with towering walls, which they knew
must be the capital of some country. Having moored in a harbour where they would be safe from storms, the seamen pegged
down the mooring rope, cast anchor and made everything fast.
Then most of the crew and passengers went ashore, and discovered that this was the land of Killah,[1] where some of them
had been before.

---

[1] According to Chinese and Arab accounts, Killah or Kalah was an important trading post in the Middle Ages; but whether it lay in southern
India or the Malay Archipelago we do not know.

In this country Chinese goods could fetch three times their original cost, and the same was true of goods carried from here to China. By taking merchandise from one to the other you might gain a profit eight or nine times your original outlay; so merchants risked their lives to make this trip. All Wen's friends had traded here before and knew where to find agents, lodgings and interpreters; so they went ashore to dispose of their wares, leaving Wen behind to keep an eye on the boat. Indeed, as he was a stranger to the place he had nowhere to go. While sitting there idly, he suddenly remembered his tangerines.

"I have never opened that crate," he thought. "The fruit may be spoiling. Now that the others are out of the way, I may as well have a look."

He asked a sailor to hoist the crate up from the hold. When he opened it, the fruit on top looked all right; but to make quite certain he took all the tangerines out and spread them on the deck. And this was the beginning of the change in his luck.

The tangerines gleamed like fire all along the deck, looking from a distance like thousands of points of fire or the sky on a starry night. And when the natives on the shore saw this, they drew near.

"What are these fine things?" they asked.

Wen did not answer. He had noticed a few white spots on one or two of his tangerines, which he now picked out, peeled and ate. Meantime more people had gathered on the shore.

"Oh, they're to eat, are they?" they exclaimed, laughing.

Then one more enterprising than the rest asked: "How much does one cost?"

Wen did not understand their language; but a sailor who did raised one finger in fun, and said: "One coin each!"

Then the man who had asked the price undid his gown, revealing a red cotton waist-band from which he took a silver coin.

"Let me try one," he said.

Wen weighed the coin in his hand, and reckoned that it was worth about a tael.

"How many does he expect for this?" he wondered. "There

doesn't seem to be a balance here. I'll give him one first to see."

He picked out a big tangerine which was a lovely red, and handed it over. The other man took it and fingered it curiously. "What a beauty!" he said.

As soon as he split it open he was struck by its fragrance, and all near him cried out in admiration because it smelt so sweet.

This foreigner did not know how to eat a tangerine, but he peeled the skin as he had seen Wen do. Instead of dividing it into quarters, though, he stuffed the whole thing into his mouth, let the sweet juice pour down his throat, then swallowed the fruit pips and all.

"Marvellous!" he exclaimed, laughing heartily, then produced another ten silver coins from his waist-band. "I'll buy another ten to present to the chief."

Delighted with this unexpected luck, Wen picked out ten more tangerines for him; and when the onlookers saw this they came forward to buy too. Some bought one tangerine, others two or three; but all paid with silver coins, and all went away delighted.

Now the people of this country used silver coins with different designs on them. Those with dragons and phoenixes on them were considered the most valuable, then those with human figures, animal figures, and trees, and lastly those with water-weeds. All were of pure silver, however, and weighed the same. The first man to buy the tangerines had used the coins designed with water-weed, happy to think that he was buying such excellent wares at so reasonable a price; for they were just as fond of driving a good bargain as the Chinese.

Before long, two-thirds of the tangerines were sold. Those of the crowd who had not brought money bitterly regretted their lack of foresight and hurried home to fetch some. And Wen, seeing that he had not much fruit left, decided to put the price up.

"I am keeping the rest for myself," he announced. "These are not for sale."

Then someone offered to pay double.

"Just my bad luck, coming so late," he grumbled, as he bought two tangerines for four coins.

When the others saw this they complained: "We still want to buy. Why do you let him raise the price?"

"Didn't you hear?" demanded the last customer. "He said he wouldn't sell."

As they were arguing together, who should arrive but the man who had bought the first ten tangerines. He galloped up on a grey horse, dismounted and pushed his way through the crowd.

"Don't sell them one by one!" he shouted. "Don't sell them one by one! I want to buy the lot. Our chief wants them to send to the khan."

When the others heard that, they stepped back to watch from a respectful distance. Wen had all his wits about him, and he realized at once that here was a good customer. Hastily taking out all the tangerines from his crate, he counted them and discovered there were little more than fifty left.

"Just now I said I meant to keep these for my own use," he declared. "I don't want to sell them. But if you'll add something to the price, I'll let you have a few more. I am already selling at two coins each."

Then the other picked up a big saddle bag from the horse's back and took out some coins bearing the tree design.

"How about one of these for each?"

"No," replied Wen. "I want the same as before."

The other smiled and took out another coin with the dragon and phoenix design.

"How about one of these?"

But again Wen replied: "No, I want the same as before."

The man laughed.

"One of these is worth a hundred of the others," he said. "I wouldn't have given you these in any case: I was only joking.

If you prefer the water-weed coins to these you must be a fool. But if you will sell all your fruit to me, I am quite willing to add another small coin to the price."

Wen counted his tangerines and found there were fifty-two left, and for these he received no less than one hundred and fifty-six of the water-weed coins. His customer wanted the bamboo crate too, and tossed him another silver piece for it; then fastened the crate to his horse, cracked his whip and rode joyfully off. At that the rest of the crowd scattered, seeing that there was nothing more for sale.

When they had gone, Wen went to the cabin and weighed one of the coins. It was nearly nine-tenths of a tael, and others which he weighed were the same. He had about a thousand coins in all, and having given two to the sailors as a tip he wrapped up the rest.

"That blind fortune-teller was right," he chuckled.

He waited cheerfully for the merchants' return to tell them this joke.

"Why, story-teller, you must be wrong!" I seem to hear some-one say. "If silver there was so cheap and they did business like that, why didn't those merchants who regularly carried silk and brocade overseas sell for silver coins? Then they could have made a hundred times as much profit!"

No, reader, you don't understand. The people of that country liked to barter goods for silk and brocade. And only by taking goods could our merchants make a profit; for if they sold their wares for money the people of Killah always used the coins stamped with dragons and phoenixes or human figures, so that even if the price was good the silver did not weigh much. Therefore such transactions were not profitable. When Wen sold his tangerines he was paid in their inferior coins; but since these weighed the same as the coins of higher value, he made money.

"No, story-teller, that doesn't make sense either," you may protest. "For in that case why didn't all the merchants just sell fruit for the water-weed coins, and make a bigger profit? Why should they lay out so much capital on other merchandise?"

That is not the way to look at it, reader.   Wen's success was a pure chance.   If he had taken fruit a second time and not been so lucky, in three or four days his tangerines might have gone bad.   Before his luck changed his fans were spoilt, although fans are much less perishable than fruit.   One cannot argue like that.   Enough, however, of this.

After the merchants had found their agents and purchasers and come back to the junk to dispose of their goods, Wen told them what had happened.

"What luck!" they exclaimed, surprised and delighted.   "So the one without capital has been the first to make a profit."

"Everybody calls him Unlucky Wen," said Zhang, clapping his hands.   "Now his luck has evidently turned."   Then he addressed himself to Wen.   "These coins will not buy you many goods here," he warned him.   "Your best course would be to purchase a few hundred taels' worth of Chinese goods from your friends to exchange for some rare local products which will sell at a great profit once we get home.   That would be better than keeping this silver without using it."

"I never have any luck," answered Wen.   "Each time I tried to do business I invariably lost all I had invested.   Now thanks to your kindness I have been able to come here and make a profit without capital.   I have never known such luck in my life!   How dare I tempt providence by trying to make more money?   If I were to fail again as usual, I couldn't hope for another scoop like this with my Dongting Reds."

"We can do with more silver," said the merchants.   "And we have plenty of goods with us.   Can't we do a deal which will be to the advantage of both sides?"

But Wen was adamant.

"A man who has been bitten by a snake shudders at the sight of a straw rope three years later," he said.   "The mere mention of goods makes me break into a cold sweat.   I'll just take this silver back with me."

The others clapped their hands together in astonishment.

"What a pity not to make several times the profit," they said, "when it's yours for the taking."

Then they went ashore again to barter their goods in the warehouses for native products.

During the next fifteen days Wen saw many fine sights and was well content, for he did not desire anything more. Then, the merchants' business at an end, they boarded their junk and after sacrificing to the gods and drinking to the success of their voyage set sail again.

Some days later, the weather changed.

> *Then dark clouds hid the noon-day sun and white waves*
>   *washed the sky;*
> *The fishes fled into the deeps, the dragons writhed high;*
> *Then like a draggled, storm-tossed crow behold the stagger-*
>   *ing boat,*
> *The very islands, so assailed, could barely keep afloat.*
> *The seamen, buffeted like chaff, before the tempest flew;*
> *The ocean boiled up heaven-high like some magician's brew.*
> *The storm god cackled loud and long to show his awful*
>   *might;*
> *Each hapless seaman shuddered, and his face grew deathly*
>   *white.*

When this gale sprang up, the seamen shortened sail and steered no definite course, but scudded before the wind until they sighted an island. They reefed sail and stood in for the land, but on drawing nearer saw that it was uninhabited.

> *Great trees grew high to touch the sky,*
>   *Rank grass was everywhere;*
> *The jungle showed no sign of life,*
>   *But tracks of fox and hare.*
> *Who ruled this desolate domain?*
>   *Was this some dragon's lair?*
> *Or who could tell if mortal man*
>   *Had ever ventured there?*

The sailors dropped their iron anchor at the stern of the boat, then landed with their mooring pegs to make the vessel fast.

"You can rest here," they told the merchants, "till the storm has blown over."

Wen with his silver had wished he could grow wings to fly home instead of sailing, so he felt doubly impatient now that they were waiting for the wind to drop.

"I'm going ashore to have a look at this island," he told the others.

"What is there to see on a desert island?" they demanded.

"Well, there's nothing to do on board, anyway," he retorted.

Still dizzy after their tossing in the storm, his friends could not stop yawning and would not go with him. But summoning up his resolution he leapt ashore. Then lo and behold —

> *An ancient shell transformed his fate,*
> *And made a poor man rich and great!*

If I had been there then, reader, and able to foretell the future, even if I were lame I would have tottered after him with a stick. It would have been worth it! But nobody else had such luck: all his friends were too lazy. Since no one would go with him, Wen tried to impress his friends by clambering straight up to the summit of the island, using creepers to haul himself up. The hill was not high, so it was not too strenuous a climb, though there was no path through the wild grass. When he reached the top and gazed at the vast ocean all around him, he felt as forlorn as a floating leaf, and shed sad tears.

"For all my cleverness, bad luck has dogged me the whole of my life," he thought. "All my property has melted away, so that I had to come empty-handed on this trip. And although by a stroke of good fortune I have made over a thousand silver coins, Heaven alone knows whether I am destined to enjoy them or not. I am on a desert island, not on firm ground, and my safety still depends on the dragon king of the ocean."

In the midst of these melancholy reflections his eye fell on a strange object projecting from the wild grass in the distance, and going nearer he discovered an empty tortoise shell as large as a bed.

"I never knew there were tortoises as big as this," he marvelled. "I swear no living soul has ever seen such a thing, and no one would believe me if I told them of it. I haven't bought a single thing since coming abroad; but if I take this home with me as a curiosity and people see it, they won't be able to say all Suzhou men are liars. Besides, if I were to saw the top from the bottom and put four legs on each half, they would make two beds."

Taking off his cloth leggings, he knotted them together and tied them to the shell to pull it along. When he neared the shore and his friends saw him dragging something after him, they hailed him with laughter.

"Is that another boat you've got there, Mr. Wen?" they demanded.

"This is my foreign merchandise, I'd have you know," replied Wen.

When they looked up and saw an object resembling a two-layered bed without legs, they were amazed.

"What an enormous tortoise shell!" they exclaimed. "But what have you lugged it here for?"

"It's such a curiosity," replied Wen, "I thought I'd take it along."

"You wouldn't buy anything good," they chuckled. "Now what do you intend to do with this?"

"I know what he can do with it," said one. "If anyone has a really serious problem to settle, he can use this shell for divination. The only trouble is there aren't herbs big enough to heat it with!"

"When the physicians need tortoise shell for their ointment, they can break this up," proposed someone else. "It's as big as several hundred small ones put together."

"Never mind whether it's useful or not," said Wen. "It's a rarity, and it hasn't cost me anything; so I'm going to take it back with me."

He called a sailor, and between them they hoisted the shell on board. If it had looked big out in the open, here on deck it seemed enormous; and had this not been a sea-faring vessel, there would have been no room for such a huge object. The merchants laughed loud and long.

"When we get home and are questioned about our cargo," said one, "we'll tell them Mr. Wen has been dealing in out-size tortoises."

"Don't you laugh!" retorted Wen. "I shall be able to turn it to account. It's bound to come in useful."

Paying no attention to their laughter, he cheerfully fetched water, washed the shell inside and out and wiped it dry, then put his purse and luggage inside and roped the two ends of the shell together so that it became a trunk.

"Look!" he said, beaming. "Here is a use for it right away."

"Well done! Well done!" They roared with laughter. "We always said Mr. Wen was a clever fellow!"

The next morning the wind dropped and they set sail again, and in a few days reached the coast of Fujian Province. No sooner had they moored when a group of agents and brokers whose business it was to watch out for overseas traders came aboard. They laid hold of the merchants, crying: "Deal with Mr. Zhang!" "Come to Mr. Li!" And only when the merchants set off to see their habitual dealer did these agents leave.

Wen and his friends went to a big shop belonging to a Persian dealer, where they sat down and waited. When the dealer heard that traders from abroad had arrived, he hastily gave his cooks money and ordered them to prepare a feast for several dozen men. Having given his instructions, he walked over to the shop.

This Persian's surname was Ma, and his personal name

Baoha.[1] He dealt only with sea-faring merchants, bartering Chinese goods for their rare merchandise, and his capital ran into hundreds of thousands of silver taels. All traders who sailed the seas knew him well; Wen alone of his party had never met the man before. This Persian had been in China for many years, and in dress and behaviour was not very different from the Chinese; but he kept his eyebrows shaved and his beard clipped, while his deep-set eyes and high nose gave him an odd look. He came out now to greet the merchants, and they sat down together. Then, after two rounds of tea, he stood up and invited them into a great hall where a splendid banquet was spread.

It was a time-honoured custom that when traders arrived from abroad their dealers should entertain them before talking business and disposing of their goods. Now, holding a cloisonné tray with a chrysanthemum design, their host bowed.

"May I see the invoice of your goods, gentlemen?" he asked. "Then we can decide how to sit."

Do you know the reason for this, reader? The fact is that this Persian valued money above everything else. When he saw an invoice for goods worth tens of thousands of taels, he would ask the owner of this precious merchandise to take the seat of honour and place the others according to the value of their wares, without any consideration for age or family status. So each merchant from the junk, knowing the amount and value of his friends' goods, took his wine cup and sat down, leaving Wen standing alone.

"I have never met this gentleman before," said the Persian. "I take it he is new to the trade and has not bought much merchandise."

"This is a good friend of ours, who accompanied us for the sake of the trip," they replied. "He has money but didn't in-

---

[1] Ma, the abbreviation for Mohammed, was the surname given to most foreigners from Islamic countries. Baoha might be a transliteration of some name like Abu Hassan or Abu Hamid

vest in any goods, so we shall have to ask him to take the lowest seat today."

Blushing for shame, Wen sat down, while the Persian took the place for the host, and the feast began. One merchant boasted how much cat's eye he had purchased, another how many emeralds. While they boasted and bragged, Wen had not a word to say, and he began to regret that he had not taken their advice and bought some goods; for now, though he had several hundred taels of silver in his wallet, he could take no part in their conversation.

"Still," he thought with a sigh, "I had no capital at all to start with. I've had more than my share of luck, so I should be content."

Occupied with these reflections, he had no heart to drink, but looked on while his friends played drinking games and feasted merrily. Their host was an experienced man. He saw that Wen looked unhappy, but could not draw attention to it and simply invited him to drink a cup or two of wine. Then the merchants rose from the table.

"We have had enough wine and it is late," they said. "We had better go back to the boat. We shall bring you our goods tomorrow."

Thereupon they took their leave; and their host, having seen that the table was cleared, went to bed.

Early the next morning the Persian went to the harbour to call on the merchants. And the first thing he set eyes on when he boarded the junk was the huge object cluttering its deck. He started with astonishment.

"To which of you does this precious thing belong?" he asked. "You didn't mention it yesterday at dinner. Is it not for sale?"

The merchants laughed and pointed at Wen.

"This treasure belongs to our friend here," they said.

"And he seems likely to have it on his hands for some time," added one.

The Persian glanced at Wen, and flushed red with consternation and anger.

"After all these years we have done business together how could you play such a trick on me?" he reproached the merchants. "Why did you make me offend a new client by giving him the lowest seat?"

Then, taking Wen by the arm, he said to the others: "Let us leave your goods for the time being. I must first go ashore to apologize to Mr. Wen."

The merchants were nonplussed. About a dozen of them who knew Wen well or were naturally inquisitive followed the Persian back to his shop to see what would happen. The dealer led Wen in, set the central chair straight in the place of honour and, ignoring all the others, urged Wen to be seated.

"I have been very remiss," he said, "very remiss. Please sit down."

Wen was consumed with curiosity.

"Can the old tortoise shell really be valuable?" he wondered. "Can I possibly be so lucky?"

The Persian left them, to return presently and invite them into the hall where they had feasted the previous day. Again they found several tables laid, but the chief table was even more sumptuous than the last time. The dealer toasted Wen.

"This gentleman ought to take the seat of honour," he told the rest. "For all the other goods on your boat are nothing compared with what he has. I have been very remiss, very remiss."

Amused and curious, not knowing what to make of this, the merchants sat down. And after three cups of wine the Persian came to the point.

"May I ask, sir," he inquired of Wen, "whether this treasure of yours is for sale?"

Wen was no fool. "If I'm offered a good price for it, why not?" he answered promptly.

On hearing these words the dealer was nearly overcome with joy. Beaming with smiles he rose from his seat.

"Name your own price," he said. "You will not find me niggardly."

Wen, of course, did not know how much the shell was worth, and was afraid of exposing his ignorance if he asked for too little, or of being laughed at if he asked for too much. He thought so hard that his cheeks flamed and his ears burned, but he could not name a price. Then Zhang winked at him and, putting his hand behind his chair where their host could not see it, raised three fingers and made a dash with his second finger.

"Ask that," he whispered, meaning three thousand taels.

But Wen shook his head and raised one finger.

"Even this seems too much," he replied softly.

"How much do you mean?" asked the Persian, who had observed this interchange.

"Judging by the sign he just made," said Zhang jokingly, "I assume Mr. Wen means ten thousand taels."

The Persian laughed heartily. "You must mean that he doesn't want to sell and is merely joking with me," he said. "How could such a precious object be worth so little?"

When the merchants heard this they were flabbergasted Rising from their seats they pulled Wen outside

"What luck!" they exclaimed. "It must be worth a fortune! But we have no idea what price to ask. You had better name an exorbitant figure and let him bargain it down."

Still Wen hesitated, ashamed to speak.

"Go on. Go on," his friends prompted him.

"You can speak frankly," said the Persian.

Then Wen asked for fifty thousand taels. The dealer, however, still shook his head.

"Too little! Too little!" he protested. "I can't allow that."

He took Zhang aside and talked to him privately.

"You have made many trips abroad, sir," he said, "and everybody calls you Canny Zhang. Is it possible you don't know what this shell is? You can't be in earnest about selling, but just want to make a fool of me."

"I will be frank with you," replied Zhang. "Wen is a good friend of mine, who accompanied us on this trip for his own pleasure, but didn't make any purchases. He came across this shell by accident when we put in to an island during a storm; and not having paid for it he has no idea of its price. If you will give him fifty thousand taels for it, he can live in luxury for the rest of his life and will be perfectly satisfied."

"In that case," said the Persian, "I want you to be guarantor. I will make it well worth your while. But you must promise not to go back on our bargain."

He bade his assistant bring brushes and ink, folded up a piece of strong paper specially designed for contracts, and handed a brush to Zhang.

"I will trouble you to take charge and to draw up an agreement so that we can settle this business," he said.

Zhang pointed to a fellow merchant.

"This gentleman, Chu Zhongyin, writes a good hand," he said, passing the paper and brush to him.

Chu ground the ink on the ink-stone, spread out the paper, and taking up his brush wrote as follows:

MEMORANDUM OF AGREEMENT WITH ZHANG CHENGYUN AND PARTY

The Suzhou merchant, Wen Shi, having brought, carried and transported from abroad one large tortoise shell, and Ma Baoha, the Persian, having agreed and covenanted to buy the said tortoise shell for fifty thousand taels of silver, both parties hereby agree that after the signing of this contract one party shall hand over the goods and the other party the money. And if either party attempt to retract, he shall forfeit one-tenth as much again as the sum herein before agreed upon.

This was written out in duplicate, then the date was put down and all present signed as witnesses. Zhang's name headed the list, and Chu as clerk signed last. After this the two documents were put together and the date and the word "contract" written over the junction of the two sheets, so that half of the characters appeared on each. This done, Wen and the Persian, as the two principals sealed the agreements, followed by all the rest.

"Our middlemen's fee should not be too low," said Zhang when it came to his turn. "Not if you want this business to go smoothly."

"You need not worry about that," replied the Persian with a smile.

When the signing was completed, the dealer fetched a casket of silver from an inner room. "Let me first pay the middlemen's fee," he said, "before I go on to what I have to say."

The merchants gathered round as he opened the casket to show the packets of silver inside. There were twenty packets, each containing fifty taels of silver, making a thousand taels in all. The Persian presented this casket with both hands to Zhang.

"You might distribute this while you are all here," he suggested.

The feast and contract had taken the merchants so much by surprise that they had been rather dubious about the genuineness of the transaction; but now that the Persian brought out this glittering white silver as middlemen's fee they realized that he was in earnest. Wen felt as if he were drunk or dreaming, and could not utter a word. He looked on dumbfounded until Zhang pulled at his sleeve.

"How are we to distribute this?" asked his friend. "It's for you to decide."

"Let us finish the chief business first," replied Wen.

"I want to discuss that with you," said the Persian, smiling all over his face. "The silver is in an inner chamber. It has been weighed and not a cent is missing. If one or two of you will step inside and weigh a packet, you won't have to weigh all the rest. Fifty thousand taels is a lot of money, though, and you can't move it all at once. Besides, Mr. Wen, you have no family here, and you can't take all that silver abroad. If you take so much home that will be very inconvenient."

"You are right," agreed Wen after a moment's thought. "But what do you suggest?"

"In my humble opinion," said the Persian, "you had better not go home yet. I have a silk shop here in which I have invested three thousand taels of silver. It is quite a large establishment consisting of over a hundred rooms, and the premises are worth another two thousand taels. This shop is only a few hundred yards from here; and my proposal is to reckon this shop with the land it stands on as worth five thousand taels and turn it over to Mr. Wen. Then he can stay here to carry on the business, and transfer the silver in several lots to his shop without attracting attention. Later, if Mr. Wen wants to go back to Suzhou, he can entrust the shop to some reliable assistant and travel with an easy mind. Otherwise, though it will be easy for me to hand over the silver, it will be hard for Mr. Wen to dispose of it. This is just my suggestion."

"An excellent proposal!" exclaimed Zhang and Wen, stamping their feet to express approval. "It has everything to recommend it."

"I have no wife or family at home," Wen was thinking, "and nothing left of my patrimony. If I were to take all that silver back, I should have no place to keep it in. Why shouldn't I take his advice and settle down here? Such good luck is ordained by Heaven in any case, so I had better fall in with all that is proposed. Even if the shop and the goods aren't worth five thousand taels, I shall be getting them for nothing."

"Your advice is very sound," he said to the Persian. "I agree completely."

Then the Persian asked Wen, Zhang and Chu to accompany him to an inner chamber. "There is no need to trouble the rest of you," he said to the others. "Please be seated."

When the four men had gone inside, the merchants left behind burst out in exclamations of amazement and envy.

"What an extraordinary thing!"

"What a stroke of luck!"

"If we had known," said one, "we would have gone ashore

too when we moored by that island. Maybe we should have found some other treasures."

"No, such luck is Heaven-sent," said another. "You can't make such things happen."

Presently Wen, Zhang and Chu came back.

"What is in there?" asked the merchants.

"A high pavilion where silver is stored in barrels," replied Zhang. "Just now we saw ten barrels, each containing four thousand taels; and five caskets, each containing one thousand taels. That makes forty-five thousand taels altogether. They have been sealed with paper bearing Mr. Wen's name, and after his tortoise shell is delivered they will be his."

Then the Persian came in.

"I have the deeds of the property and the accounts of the silk shop here," he said. "You will see they are worth a good fifty thousand taels. Let us go to your junk now to fetch the goods."

As they walked together to the boat, Wen warned the others: "There are too many people on the junk. I shall pay you well if you keep quiet about this."

The others also feared that if all the merchants on board knew what had happened, they would demand part of the fee; so they agreed to say nothing. Upon reaching the junk, Wen removed his luggage and bags from inside the shell, stroking it as he congratulated himself on his luck.

Then the Persian ordered two young men from his shop to carry the shell away.

"Take it straight inside," he cautioned them. "Don't leave it outside the house."

When the other men on the junk saw this shell being carried away, they remarked: "So even this rubbish has been sold. I wonder how much he got for it?"

Wen, however, kept silent as he carried his luggage ashore. Those who had accompanied him the first time also hurried ashore to examine the shell carefully, peering inside and feeling it all over. Then they exchanged mystified glances.

"What's so wonderful about this?" they demanded.

After inviting them back to his shop, the Persian proposed that they visit Mr. Wen's new property. They all went to the middle of the business quarter, where they saw a fine large building. In front was the shop, and at the side was an alley which led to a massive stone gate. Inside were a big courtyard and a great hall on which there hung a placard bearing the inscription: Hall of the Advent of Jewels. This hall was flanked by rooms lined with cupboards and shelves containing all manner of silks and brocades; and behind the main building were many other rooms and pavilions.

"A house like this is as good as a prince's mansion!" thought Wen. "And with this silk shop there should be no end to the profits I make. I may as well settle down here. Why should I want to go home?"

"This is very good," he said to the Persian. "But I am all by myself. I shall have to find some servants and assistants before I can move in."

"That should present no difficulties," said the Persian. "I can provide you with all the staff you need."

Overjoyed, Wen walked back with the others to the Persian's shop, where the dealer offered them tea.

"There is no need for you to go back to the junk tonight, Mr. Wen," said the Persian. "You may as well move straight into your new quarters. There are assistants and servants in your shop already, whose number you can gradually increase."

"Now the deal has been completed," said one of the merchants, "there is really no more to be said. But there is one thing we would like to know — what makes the shell so valuable? May we ask you to enlighten us?"

Wen joined in this request too.

"It is strange that you gentlemen have crossed the seas so many times and yet don't know this," chuckled the Persian. "Haven't you heard that the dragon has nine sons, one of whom is the Tuo Dragon? If you use its skin to make a drum, the sound can be heard dozens of miles away; and it is called a Tuo Drum. After ten thousand years a Tuo Dragon discards its shell and becomes a dragon proper. Its shell has twenty-four ribs to match the twenty-four festivals of the year, and in the joint of each rib there is a big pearl. It cannot shed its shell or become a dragon before the ribs are fully formed; and if it is caught before then, its skin alone is of any use — there is nothing inside the ribs. But when the twenty-four ribs are complete with a pearl in each one, it becomes a dragon and flies off, leaving the shell behind. This shell of Mr. Wen's was discarded in the right season and the ribs are complete, so it is much bigger than the shells of Tuo Dragons caught before their metamorphosis. Though we know that such a thing exists, who can tell when or where the dragon will discard its shell? The shell itself is worthless, but the pearls, which shine at night, are priceless. It is sheer luck that this has come into my possession today."

When the merchants heard this they were still rather incredulous; but the Persian went into an inner room for a short time, to reappear smiling.

"Gentlemen," he said, taking a wrapper of foreign cloth from his sleeve. "Look at this!"

When he undid the wrapper, in a nest of threads they saw a pearl of dazzling brightness, about one inch in diameter. The Persian put the pearl on a black lacquer tray which he set in a dark place; whereupon the pearl started rolling from side to side without stopping, and emitted rays of light a foot long. Then their host turned to the merchants, who were gaping in astonishment.

"I am very much indebted to you all for your help," he said. "In my country this single pearl will fetch what I paid for the shell just now. That means the other twenty-three are presents you have been kind enough to give me!"

They were all thunderstruck. Yet they had signed an agreement, and could not go back on their word. When the Persian saw their dismay, hastily putting the pearl away he left the room again to order his servants to fetch a box of brocades.   To all but Wen he gave two lengths of brocade each.

"I have put you to a great deal of trouble," he explained. "I would like to show my appreciation by giving you this to make a couple of gowns."

Then he took from his sleeve over a dozen strings of small pearls, and gave them a string apiece.

"This is a small present for light refreshments," he said.

To Wen the Persian gave four strings of larger pearls and eight lengths of brocade; and Wen and the merchants were pleased and thanked him.   Then the Persian and the others escorted Wen to his silk shop, where all the assistants and apprentices were called out to be introduced to their new master. After this the Persian took his leave and returned to his own shop; and presently several dozen porters arrived carrying the ten barrels and five caskets of silver marked with Wen's seal. Having seen these stowed in a safe place in his bedroom, Wen rejoined the merchants.

"I am deeply indebted to you all for taking me on this trip," he told them.   "Without your help I could never have met with this unexpected fortune."

Then going into an inner room he fetched from his baggage the silver he had received for the sale of his tangerines, and gave the merchants ten coins each, presenting an extra ten coins to Zhang and the two others who had helped him with money at the beginning of the trip.   By now these silver coins meant very little to Wen, but the merchants were delighted to have them and thanked him again and again.   Then Wen took out a few dozen more coins.

"I'll trouble you to divide these among our fellow travellers on the junk," he said.   "Give them one each from me. After I have settled down a little, I mean to come home.   But since I shan't be going with you now, I will say goodbye for the time being."

"There are still those thousand taels for the middlemen which are not yet divided," Zhang reminded him.   "You will have to distribute those, so that there will be no argument."

Wen admitted that he had forgotten this matter. After discussion with the others he allotted one hundred taels to the other men on the junk, dividing the remaining nine hundred among those present, but giving one extra share to Zhang, who had taken the lead in this affair, and to Chu, who had drawn up the contract. Then, fully satisfied, they all thanked him heartily.

"But we let that Mohammedan off too lightly," said one. "Mr. Wen should have put up the price and demanded more."

"One mustn't be too grasping," replied Wen. "I had a long run of bad luck, when, whatever I tried, I lost my capital. Now fortune has smiled on me and showered this wealth on me out of the blue. It shows that everything is ordained by fate, and it is useless to strive for more than is allotted to you by Heaven. If the Persian had not recognized the shell as a treasure, it would have been of no value to us. We are indebted to him for pointing it out. How could I be so ungrateful as to wrangle over the price with him?"

"Mr. Wen is right," agreed the others. "In fact, this fortune he has received is a reward for his virtue."

Then with profuse thanks they went back with their various gifts to the junk, to go about their business.

Thus Wen became a wealthy merchant in Fujian, where he married and settled down; and not for some years did he return to Suzhou on a visit to see his old friends. Many sons and grandsons were born to him, and his family remains wealthy to this day.

Fine gold will lose its sheen when fortune frowns,
Rough iron will shine like gold when fortune smiles;
But let not fools who hear a tale like this
Go seeking dragons' shells in distant isles!

The Story of a Braggart

'Tis not a creature's size alone
That makes it weak or strong;
A centipede can kill a snake,
Although it is not long.

Since no creature in the world is without a rival, none should boast of its size or strength. In South China there are huge pythons, hundreds of feet long, which feed on human flesh; so all the natives there keep centipedes, the largest of them over a foot in length. They shut these centipedes up within or beside their hard, hollow pillows; for when a python approaches a centipede will make a harsh, rustling sound and once let out, will arch its back and leap ten feet to grip the great snake's neck like a vice and suck its life-blood till the python dies. Thus a monster hundreds of feet long and thick as a barrel is killed by a creature one foot long and no thicker than a finger, as witness the ancient saying: A centipede can kill a python.

Or take the following story. In the third year of the Zheng He period of the Han Dynasty (90 B.C.), a king of the Massagetae in the west presented Emperor Wu with a wild beast. It had a yellow tail and was something like a two-month-old puppy, being roughly the size of a wild cat. When the envoy carried this animal in to present it, and the emperor saw how puny it looked, he laughed.

"Do you call this a wild beast?" he demanded. "Let me hear it bark."

The envoy raised one finger, whereupon the beast licked its chaps, tossed its head and let out a roar like a thunderclap, its eyes flickering lightning. The emperor fell off his golden

劉東山時挍
順城門

throne, while his attendants and imperial guards dropped to their knees, all the weapons in their hands clattering to the ground. Very much annoyed, Emperor Wu ordered the beast to be taken to the imperial park and thrown to the tigers; and the warden of the park accordingly carried it there and set it down by the tigers' den. But when the tigers saw it, they shrank back fearfully then fell on their knees before it; and when the warden reported this, the emperor became angrier than ever and swore to have the beast killed. By the next day, however, both envoy and beast had vanished.

As for men, there is no limit to their strength or skill. A strong man may always meet another stronger than himself. There was once a scholar, whose name and native place I have forgotten, who had remarkable strength, excelled in military arts, and had always championed those in distress. Going to the capital for an examination, he took no servant with him but relied on his own strength and skill, riding alone on a good steed and carrying his dagger, bow and arrows at his waist. On the way he hunted game to eat with his wine at the taverns where he rested. One day, as he was travelling through Shandong, his horse galloped so fast that he passed the usual stage; and upon reaching a village as night fell, he decided to stop there. Noticing a house with its gate ajar and lamplight shining out, he alighted and led his horse inside to a large courtyard empty but for three or four boulders from Lake Taihu, with three rooms at the far end and another on each side. An old woman was sitting in the middle spinning flax; but she stood up at the sound of a horse's hooves and asked the stranger his business.

"I've lost my way, ma'am," called the scholar. "I want to beg a lodging for the night."

"I don't think I can put you up, sir," she replied. "It's not for me to say."

A note of sadness in her voice puzzled the scholar.

"Where have the men of your house gone, ma'am?" he asked. "Why are you alone here?"

"I'm an old widow, and my only son is a travelling merchant."

"Have you no daughter-in-law?"

A shadow passed over the old woman's face.

"I have a daughter-in-law who is a match for any man and well able to manage a house," she answered. "But she's a great, strapping termagant with a fiery temper. The least little thing will make her fly into a rage, and she can knock me down with one finger. Although I hold my breath and watch my step, she is always finding fault with me and bullying me. That's why, when you asked to stay, I told you I couldn't decide."

When she had said this, her tears fell like rain.

The scholar frowned indignantly.

"Can such a thing be?" he cried. "Where is this shrew? I'll soon rid you of her."

He tethered his horse to a boulder and drew his sword.

"Don't attempt the impossible, sir," said the old woman. "My daughter-in-law is terrible once she's roused. She knows nothing of sewing, but goes out every day after the noonday meal to catch deer or rabbit in the hills with her bare hands, then cures the game she brings back and sells it for a few strings of cash. She often doesn't get home till late at night. If not for the money she brings in, we couldn't make ends meet; so I dare not offend her."

At that the scholar sheathed his sword again.

"All my life I have challenged the strong, championed the weak and helped those in distress," he declared. "A mere woman should be easy to deal with. But since you depend on her to support you, ma'am, I won't kill her. I'll just give her a sound beating to teach her to mend her ways."

"She will be back soon, sir," said the old woman. "I hope you'll be careful."

The scholar waited in great indignation till a huge shadowy form came through the gate and a heavy load was thrown down in the courtyard.

"Fetch a light, old woman!" someone shouted. "And take this in."

"What fine beast have you caught this time?" quavered the old dame.

She shone her lamp on it, then gave a start; for the dead beast was a huge tiger with beautiful stripes. When the scholar's horse saw the tiger, it reared in terror; and the young woman asked:

"Where does that horse come from?"

Dark as it was, the scholar could see that she was tall and swarthy; and she had carried a tiger home on her back.

"She seems a very powerful woman," he thought with dismay.

So he hastily led his horse to one side and tethered it again, then stepped forward.

"I am a scholar who has lost his way," he said. "After passing the usual stage, I was lucky enough to reach your honourable village; and when I saw your gate was not locked, I made bold to ask for a night's lodging."

"You must excuse my mother-in-law," said the young woman with a laugh. "How could she keep a distinguished guest standing outside so late at night?" Then she pointed to the dead tiger. "I came across this wild cat in the hills today and struggled with it for a long time before I killed it," she explained. "That's why I am late. I have been very remiss as a hostess; but I hope our honourable guest will overlook it."

She spoke so frankly and politely that he thought: "This woman must be amenable to reason."

And aloud he replied: "Not at all, not at all."

The woman went inside and brought out a chair.

"I would ask you in," she said, "but it is not fitting for men and women to mix; so I must ask you to sit in the corridor."

She set a table before him, lit a lamp and put it on the table, then picked up the dead tiger in the courtyard and carried it to the kitchen. After a short time she reappeared with a pot of warm wine, an enormous dish of steaming tiger meat, another of salted venison, and several plates of pheasant, hare and other cured game.

"Please don't take offence, sir," she requested him, "at our humble fare."

Impressed by her courtesy, the young man poured himself wine and drank; and presently, when he had finished the meal, he raised clasped hands in salutation.

"Thank you for such a feast," he said.

"You cover us with shame," she replied.

When she brought a tray to clear away the dishes, the scholar seized the opportunity to speak to her.

"How is it," he inquired, "that one as brave and intelligent as yourself is a little lacking in respect to your elders?"

When the young woman heard this, she plumped the tray down and stopped clearing the table.

"What has that old witch been saying to you?" she demanded angrily.

"Nothing, nothing!" the scholar explained hastily. "I just felt your manner to her showed a certain lack of respect, and was not quite what one would expect from a daughter-in-law towards her mother-in-law. And seeing how well you treat your guests and how able and reasonable you appear, I ventured to raise the point."

Seizing the lapel of his coat with one hand and the lamp with the other, the young woman marched him over to the boulders.

"Stand there!" she ordered. "I have something to tell you."

The scholar could not get away, but he promised himself:

"If she fails to justify her attitude, I'll give her a good beating."

Then the young woman patted the rock against which she was leaning.

"Listen to what happened the other day," she said, "and say which of us was in the right."

She described a disagreement she had had with her mother-in-law.

"That's one case," she told him.

Then, as she traced a line with her finger on the boulder, rock splinters flew up and a groove more than one inch deep appeared. She enumerated three incidents and traced three lines, each of them over an inch deep, as if carved out with a chisel. The scholar turned crimson and sweated with fright.

"You were right each time, ma'am," he stammered. "You were right each time."

His brave scheme to correct her had vanished completely. As if doused with a bucket of icy water, he scarcely dared breathe. After the young woman had had her say, she brought out a couch for the scholar and fed his horse, then went in, locked the door of the room she shared with the old woman, put out the light and slept. But the scholar could not sleep a wink all night.

"What strength!" he marvelled. "It's a good thing I didn't come to blows with her. Otherwise that would have been the end of me."

When dawn broke he saddled his horse, thanked his hostess and left without another word. And never again dared he give himself airs or meddle with other people's affairs, for fear he might be worsted by someone stronger than himself.

I shall tell you now of another man who, because he boasted of his ability, received a bad fright and made a fool of himself.

> *The tiger lords it in the woods,*
> *And savage beasts before it fall;*
> *But if a lion's roar is heard,*
> *The tiger is no use at all.*

During the Jia Qing period (1522-1566), there lived in Jiaohe County, Zhili Province a man named Liu Dongshan, a sergeant in the Beijing police force who had mastered all military arts and was a fine archer and horseman. Because his arrows always found their mark, he was famed for his bowmanship; and however fierce a bandit might be, Liu would catch him as easily as a turtle in a jar. So he gradually became a man of substance, and after he was thirty he resigned from the police service, of which he was tired, to become a horse-dealer.

Towards the end of that year, having driven a dozen donkeys and horses to the capital and sold them for more than a hundred taels of silver, Liu went to Xuanwu Gate to hire a donkey to ride home. In the hostelry attached to the stables he met a neighbour named Zhang, who had also come to the capital; and they had a meal together.

"Where are you off to?" asked Zhang.

"I've come to hire a donkey," replied Liu, after telling Zhang of his successful transaction. "I shall spend the night here and start home tomorrow."

"Travelling has been difficult recently," said Zhang. "There are highwaymen near Liangxiang and Zhengzhou who rob travellers in broad daylight; and you are carrying a good deal of silver and riding alone. You had better be careful."

When Liu heard this he smiled all over his face, clenched his fists and went through the motions of drawing a bow.

"In twenty years I have never met an archer who's a match for me," he declared with a hearty laugh. "I shan't lose any money on this trip, I promise you."

He spoke so loudly that everyone in the tavern turned to look, and some asked his name or murmured their admiration. But Zhang, conscious that he had spoken tactlessly, took his leave.

Liu slept till the fifth watch the next morning, when he washed and dressed, bound his silver tightly round his waist under his jacket, slung his bow on his back, girded on a sword, and stowed twenty arrows in his high boots. Then he picked a sturdy mule, leapt on its back, and with a flick of his whip was off. After about a dozen miles he reached Liangxiang, where he was overtaken by a rider who reined in his horse as soon as he came up with Liu. This horseman was a handsome, well-dressed youth of twenty or thereabouts.

He was armed with a sword and a bow,
Had a hat made of felt on his head,
Had a score of new shafts on his back,
While his horse wore a tassel of red.
His fine shirt was of bright yellow silk,
'Twas a handsome young horseman indeed!
And his mount pawed the ground as it neighed,
For his beast was a mettlesome steed.

As Liu gazed at him, the young man called out: "Shall we travel together, sir?"

Then he clasped his hands in salute, and added: "May I ask your name?"

"Liu Dongshan, at your service."

"I have long heard of your great fame, sir; and I am fortunate to have met you. Where are you going?"

"I am going home to Jiaohe."

"What luck for me! I come from a scholar's family in Lingzi, and studied the classics as a boy; but I was so fond of shooting and riding that I gave up book learning. Three years ago I took some capital to Beijing to set up in business, and did not do so badly; so now I am going home to get married. If I can have your company on the road, sir, I shall feel much safer; and we can travel together as far as Hejian. Fate has been kind to me."

Since this youth had a well-lined purse, and was soft of speech, handsome and slight, Liu felt that he could not be a bad character. And he was only too glad to have a companion on the road.

"I shall be delighted to accompany you," he said.

That evening they put up in the same inn, dined together, slept in one room, and felt as close to each other as brothers. As they rode side by side out of Zhuozhou the next day, the young man said:

"You have a great reputation for capturing bandits, sir.

May I ask how many you have caught, and whether you met any brave fellows?"

Liu was just waiting for an opportunity to boast of his skill, so this question proved an irresistible temptation; and, since his companion was young and green, he began to brag.

"With this bow and these two hands I have caught more bandits than I can count," he declared. "But I never met a worthy opponent. Rats like that are nothing to me. Because I'm past my youth now and prefer a quiet life, I've left my old profession; but if we come across any highwaymen on the road, I'll catch a couple to show you how to do it."

The young man gave a faint smile.

"You don't say so," he murmured.

Then leaning over from his saddle he stretched out his hand.

"May I have a look at your bow?" he asked.

When Liu passed it over from his mule, the young man took the bow in his left hand and drew it to its full extent with his right, bending it several times in succession as effortlessly as if it were soft string. Liu changed colour in amazement, then asked to look at the young man's bow. This bow weighed about twenty pounds and, though Liu tugged and strained till he was purple in the face, he could not even bend it into the shape of a crescent moon. He thrust out his tongue in dismay.

"What a strong bow!" he cried. "What amazing strength you must have! I cannot begin to compare with you."

"I am not particularly strong," replied the youth. "But your bow is too soft."

Liu was loud in his praise, while the young man modestly disclaimed his compliments.

After lodging in one inn that night they set off together again the next day; but when they were passing Xiongxian and the sun was sinking in the west, the young man suddenly spurred his steed and galloped forward as if he had wings, until Liu could see him no more. The former police sergeant, who had much experience of bandits, was naturally alarmed.

"I'm in for it now," he thought, "if this is a bad man. How can I defend myself against such wonderful strength? I shall never escape with my life."

Although his heart was going pit-a-pat, he had to press on. And after he had ridden another two stages he saw the young man some hundred yards ahead, with an arrow fitted to his bow which was bent like a full moon.

"You say you have never met your match," cried the youth. "Listen to my arrows now!"

While he was still speaking, arrows started whistling past Liu's ears like little birds skimming by. But not one of them touched him. Then the young man put another arrow to his bow and aimed at Liu's face.

"You are an intelligent man," he said with a laugh. "Hurry up and give me that money for your donkeys and horses before I shoot."

Aware that he was no match for this youth, Liu tumbled down from his saddle in a panic, untied the bag of silver at his waist and went down on his knees to offer it with both hands.

"Take my money," he said, kowtowing. "But spare my life!"

The young man reached down from his horse to take the bag.

"Who wants your life?" he shouted. "Be off with you now! I have business here; so I can't go with you, my little fellow."

He turned his horse's head and made off northwards like a streak of smoke. Yellow dust sprang up behind him and soon he was lost from sight. After standing like one stupefied for some time, Liu started beating his breast and stamping his feet.

"I don't mind losing the silver, but how can I hold up my head after this?" he raged. "My reputation will be ruined. Curse it!"

Thoroughly crestfallen, he shambled empty-handed back to his home in Jiaohe, where he told his wife what had happened and she lamented with him. Then they decided to raise enough capital to open a tavern outside the city. Liu stopped going about with bow and arrows and dared not mention his misadventure either, for fear that the story might spread and spoil his good name.

One cold winter day three years later, Liu and his wife were selling wine in their tavern when eleven horsemen stopped at the door. Mounted on fine horses richly caparisoned, they were dressed in doublets and armed with bows, arrows and swords. Alighting one after another, they unsaddled their steeds and entered the tavern, while Liu took the saddles and led the horses to his stable.

One of the horsemen, a lad of fifteen or sixteen who was over six foot tall, did not dismount.

"I shall go into the house opposite," he told the rest.

"We shall come presently to wait on you," they replied.

When the lad had left, the ten men started drinking; and Liu prepared chicken, pork, beef and mutton for them. They fell to with appetite, and soon finished nearly seventy pounds of meat and seven jars of wine, then bid Liu send wine and food to the lad in the house opposite. All this food and wine was still too little for them, however; so they opened their leather bags and took out deer trotters, pheasant, roast hare and other game.

"This is our contribution," they told Liu with a laugh. "Come and join us."

Liu declined, but sat down at their table to watch them. He was glancing at a man with a felt hat hiding his face in the left hand corner, when the fellow suddenly raised his head. Then Liu, frightened almost out of his wits, moaned in terror. For this was the young man who had robbed him at Xiongxian.

"This is the end!" he thought. "How is the little money I've got going to satisfy them? Last time one man proved more than a match for me; and now there are ten of them, no doubt all equally powerful. What can I do?"

His heart thumping, he stared wretchedly into his wine cup, not daring to say a word. But presently they all stood up and asked him to drink

"How have you been since last I saw you, Mr. Liu?" called the young man on the left, pushing back his felt hat. "I appreciated your company and help last time we met, and I have never forgotten you."

Turning pale, Liu fell on his knees.

"Spare me!" he cried.

The young man leapt from his seat, raised Liu up and took him by the hand.

"This will never do!" he said. "When we overheard you that day in the tavern by Xuanwu Gate boasting of your skill and claiming that no one was a match for you, we felt indignant; and my friends told me to play a trick on you. But I broke my promise to go to Hejian with you, and I have often remembered how we travelled together and felt grateful for your kindness. Now I must repay you tenfold."

He took one thousand taels of silver from his bag and put them on the table.

"Please accept this trifle as a token of my esteem."

Sure that he must be dreaming, Liu looked stunned for a moment.

"You are joking," he said at last. "I can't take that."

Seeing his bewilderment, the young man clapped his hands encouragingly.

"How can a gentleman lie?" he demanded. "You are a stout fellow too — why should you be so timid? Do you think we really need your money? Hurry up and take it."

Hearing this, Liu realized that he was sincere; and, like one waking from a dream, he dared no longer refuse but went in and told his wife, bidding her help him carry the silver inside. This done, he discussed with her what to do.

"These gallants have been so generous that we must treat them well," he said. "Let us slaughter some pigs, open some more jars of wine, and ask them to stay here for a few days."

When Liu returned to the outer room to express his thanks, he conveyed this wish to the young man, who told the rest.

"Since this is an old friend, why not stay?" they said. "But we must ask permission."

Then they went across the road to speak to the lad in the house opposite. Liu, who accompanied them, noticed that they treated the boy with great deference, while he for his part behaved with great dignity.

"Very well," said the boy, when they had explained that the tavern-keeper wanted to keep them for a few days. "But mind you don't sleep too soundly after feasting, and show due consideration for your host. If I hear the least brawling, the two daggers at my side will taste blood."

"We understand," they replied, although Liu was puzzled.

Returning to his tavern, they fell to drinking heartily again and sent more wine to the house opposite. The ten men did not keep the lad company, however, but left him to eat and drink alone; and he consumed five times more than any of them. Then, smiling, the lad took a silver ladle from his bag, relit the stove and made himself pancakes. After eating about a hundred pancakes he cleared the table and strode out; but where he went Liu did not know. He came back, however, that evening and lodged in the house opposite, without entering the tavern. The other men feasted and enjoyed themselves with Liu; and whenever they went across the street to see the boy, he said very little to them and carried himself haughtily. To satisfy his curiosity, Liu privately questioned the man he had met before.

"Who is your young leader?"

Instead of answering, the young man repeated the question to the others, and they laughed but did not reply. After two days they packed up, mounted their horses and cantered off, the lad riding in front and the others following behind, leaving Liu as mystified as ever.

Now that he was comfortably off, thanks to the thousand taels of silver, Liu felt insecure in his tavern and moved into the city to set up in business. Later, when he told others his story, some said that the lad was obviously the leader of the band; but judging by his behaviour he was afraid lest there might be a plot against them and therefore stayed in the house opposite where he could keep an eye on things. That he did not eat with the others simply showed that he was their superior. And when he went out at night by himself he was obviously on some secret mission; but, of course, there was no way of knowing what it was. After this, Liu, who had always boasted of his strength and skill, stopped talking about military arts and laid aside his bow and arrows to become a respectable citizen, living to a ripe old age.

And the moral of the story is that man should not set too much store by his strength or ability; for his fancied superiority means only that he has not yet met his master.

The Alchemist and His Concubine

Though their clothes are too tattered to keep out the cold,
They assure you they change all base metals to gold.
Then why don't they make gold for their own uses, pray?
Why just carry the burden for others all day?

This verse was written by Tang Yin, a Ming Dynasty scholar, to expose the many alchemists who trick and deceive the greedy and gullible, claiming that they can make a philosophers' stone out of herbs, to transmute lead into gold or mercury into silver. They call this the hermetic art. They ask for silver to work with, then seize a chance to run off with it, which they call "absconding with the pot." Once a priest offered to practise this art for Tang Yin.

"You have a saintly air, sir," he said. "For you I can do this."

"I notice you are in rags," countered Tang Yin. "If you have mastered the hermetic art, why don't you transmute gold for your own use? Why just do it for others?"

"Because I have this gift, Nature is against me," replied the priest. "I can do this only when I have found some beneficiary favoured by fortune. I myself have not the luck. Having observed that you were born under a lucky star, I am asking you to be my partner."

"Let me make a proposal," said Tang Yin. "I will not interfere with you while you practise your art, but simply help you with my luck; then when you have obtained the philosophers' stone we can divide the gold equally between us."

When the priest realized that the scholar was making fun of him, he knew that this was no patron for him and quickly

made off. Then Tang Yin wrote his poem exposing such impostors. But there are still men of first-rate intelligence who fall into such traps.

Let me tell you about a rich native of Songjiang named Pan, who was a scholar of the Imperial College. He was widely read, eloquent, and a thoroughly likable fellow; but he had a passion for alchemy. Since birds of a feather flock together, alchemists swarmed around him and in due course fleeced him of a great deal of silver. Yet even after being deceived time and again, he had no regrets, but simply said he had not been lucky enough to meet a genuine alchemist; for an ancient art like this must finally be crowned with success, and then all his former failures would seem as nothing. So his obsession grew. News of this spread until all the alchemists had heard of him, and charlatans from all around conspired to cheat him.

One autumn, when Pan rented rooms in Hangzhou, his attention was attracted by a stranger in the next house who had also come to see the West Lake. This man had plenty of servants and baggage; and Pan learned that the woman with him, who was very beautiful, was his concubine. Every day this stranger would hire the biggest boat in Hangzhou, order a feast and engage singsong girls to play music, then drink, sing and make merry with his concubine on the lake. He had many finely chased drinking vessels of gold and silver, and every evening when he returned to his lodging, escorted by dozens of lanterns, he would distribute largesse on a princely scale. Pan, watching from next door, was tremendously impressed.

"My family is considered wealthy," he thought, "but I can't spend money like that. This man must be fabulously rich."

He soon persuaded an intermediary to convey his respects, after which he and the stranger met and exchanged greetings. As soon as an opening occurred, Pan remarked:

"Your wealth surpasses anything I have ever seen, sir."

"Oh, this is nothing," protested the other politely.

"Indeed," insisted Pan, "you must have mountains of gold

and silver. Otherwise, living as you do, you would soon reach the end of your fortune."

"Mountains of gold are easy to spend," replied the stranger. "What's needed is an inexhaustible supply."

Pan's curiosity was aroused.

"What do you mean by an inexhaustible supply?" he asked.

"I cannot speak of such things when we have only just met."

"I must beg you to enlighten me."

"Even if I tell you, you may not underst.and or believe me."

When these mysterious insinuations only made Pan plead more earnestly to be told, the stranger dismissed his servants.

"I have the philosophers' stone which can transmute lead into gold," he whispered. "Gold is like earth to me."

At this reference to alchemy, which was his passion, Pan was transported with joy.

"So you are an expert in the hermetic art!" he cried. "I am devoted to alchemy, but have never been fortunate enough to meet a real master. I will gladly spend all I have if you will teach me your skill."

"This cannot be taught in a casual way," said the stranger. "But there is no harm in carrying out a few experiments by way of diversion."

He called a servant-boy to light the stove, and melted a few ounces of lead in a cauldron; then took from his pocket a package of powder and flicked some of it into the molten metal. And presently, when he emptied out the contents of the cauldron, all the lead had changed into fine glittering silver! Now, reader, there is no powder in the world that can transmute lead into silver. This was what is called the essence of silver, which this man had distilled by a chemical process from one ounce of silver; and when he melted it in the cauldron, the lead dross absorbed the essence of silver and took on a silvery colour. But there was no more silver than he had put in himself — not a speck more. Alchemists often take people in with this trick.

Pan was quite overcome with joy.

"No wonder he can spend money like water and give all his time to pleasure," he thought. "Apparently it is easy to make silver. I always lost money when I tried before; but this time I am lucky to have met a real adept. I must beg him to help me."

So he asked the stranger: "How do you make the philosophers' stone, sir?"

"This process is called the conception of the mother silver," replied the stranger. "Take any amount of silver as your base, treat it with chemicals and heat it in the cauldron. After you have heated it nine times and brought it to the right temperature, it will *citronize*, then become *silver potate*. When you open the cauldron, all you have to do is extract the philosophers' stone, a single particle of which will transform base metals into gold or silver, while the mother silver remains unchanged."

"How much silver is needed?" asked Pan.

"The more silver, the more potent the philosophers' stone," was the reply. "With half a casket of it, you will be as wealthy as an emperor."

"Though I am not rich," said Pan, "I can raise a couple of thousand taels. If you are willing to teach me and will be my guest while you make a little of this philosophers' stone, the wish of my life will come true."

"I seldom teach my art to others," replied the stranger. "Nor do I usually show others my experiments. But I was struck by your sincerity and air of saintliness, and the fact that we are neighbours here proves that our meeting was predestined. I shall do what I can for you. Let me know where your home is, and I shall call on you."

"I live in Songjiang, only two or three days journey from here. `If you will condescend to come, why not pack up and accompany me now to my humble home? If we part here, something may happen to deprive me of this privilege."

"My home is in Henan Province, where I have left my mother," answered the stranger. "I brought my concubine here to enjoy the celebrated Hangzhou scenery, and the time passed so pleasantly that I kept postponing my return; for though I came empty-handed I defrayed all my expenses by means of my cauldron. But now that I have found a kindred spirit, I shall not keep my secret to myself. After I have taken my concubine home and paid my respects to my mother, I shall come to you. That won't be too late, will it?"

"I have a country house where your lady can stay," proposed Pan. "Wouldn't you prefer to bring her with you to keep you company while you work? Though we cannot entertain you well, we shall do our best to please you and make your lady comfortable. I shall be more grateful than words can express if you will come."

The stranger nodded.

"Since you are so much in earnest," he said, "I shall speak to my concubine, then prepare to leave."

Pan was delighted. He immediately wrote a card to invite the alchemist to feast with him the following day on the lake; and the next day escorted the stranger very respectfully to a boat, where each made a parade of his scholarship. They talked on and on, regretted that they had not met earlier, and parted well pleased with each other. Pan had also sent food and wine next door for the concubine. The day after that the alchemist invited him in return to an even more magnificent feast at which, it goes without saying, all the plate was of gold and silver. Since Pan could think of nothing now but alchemy and had lost all interest in the sights, he soon completed his arrangements to travel with the alchemist to Songjiang. They hired two large junks at the harbour, moved their luggage aboard, and set sail together. The young lady in the alchemist's cabin often peeped out from behind her curtain; and Pan, stealing glances at her, saw that she was ravishingly beautiful. But, alas!

A bridgeless chasm kept them far apart;
He could not utter all that filled his heart.

Pan regretted that he had no means of sending her a message.

To cut a long story short, however, the two boats soon reached Songjiang, where Pan invited the alchemist ashore and escorted him to his house.

"This is where my family lives," he said, offering his guest tea. "But there are too many people here; so I would like to invite you and your lady to my country house which is quite near, and where I can stay too in the study in the front courtyard. We shall not be disturbed there. And it is so secluded that no one will know when you light your furnace. What do you think?"

"I must not be exposed to vulgar curiosity and noise when I practise my art," agreed the alchemist. "And since my concubine is here, there is all the more reason for living in seclusion. It will be most convenient if we can stay in your country residence."

Pan thereupon ordered the boatmen to take them to his country house; and he and the alchemist walked happily together up to its gate, which bore the inscription "Garden of Pleasure."

"This quiet, elegant spot is just right for alchemy," declared the alchemist after looking round. "It is a good place for my concubine too; so I can work with an easy mind. You are a fortunate man."

Then Pan sent maids to escort the young lady from the boat. Splendidly dressed and accompanied by her two maids, Spring Cloud and Autumn Moon, she swayed gracefully into the garden. Pan stood up to leave as she approached, but the alchemist stopped him.

"We are close friends," he said. "Let me introduce her to you."

And when Pan looked into her face he saw that she was of more than earthly loveliness. All rich men crave for money and beautiful women; so now he felt himself melting away like a snow man near fire, and forgot even alchemy for the time being.

"There are plenty of inner chambers in this house," he told the alchemist. "Your lady can take her pick of them. And if she has not enough maids, I can send for a few girls to serve her."

While the alchemist and his concubine looked over the house, Pan hurried home to fetch a pair of gold hairpins and gold ear-rings, which he gave to the alchemist.

"May I offer these trifles to your lady?" he asked. "Please don't be offended by the poorness of the gifts."

When the alchemist saw that the trinkets were of gold, however, he refused.

"You do me too much honour," he replied. "I can easily make gold, but it costs you a great deal of money; so I cannot accept these gifts."

"I know you are not interested in such trifles," said Pan, rather abashed. "But please accept them as a token of my sincere respect for your lady."

"Since you are so good to us, it would be unfriendly to refuse," replied the alchemist. "Let me accept them then. When I have made the philosophers' stone I shall repay your kindness."

He left the room with a smile to order a maid to take these gifts to his concubine and bid her come out to thank their host, while Pan reflected that to see her once more was well worth the cost of the trinkets.

"This man has not only mastered alchemy but possesses this marvellous beauty," he mused. "What more could one ask of life? Luckily he has agreed to perfect the philosophers' stone for me, and I should be able to transmute gold myself before long. I wonder if I can reach an understanding with this beauty now that she is here? To succeed there too would be wonderful. I mustn't spoil everything though by being too hasty. I had better attend to the alchemy first."

So he asked the alchemist: "When will it be agreeable for you to start?"

"We can start as soon as you provide the silver."

"How much is needed?"

"The more the better. For the more silver, the more philosophers' stone; and if you have enough you need not repeat the process."

"In that case," said Pan, "I shall provide two thousand taels of silver for the cauldron. I shall go home today to fetch it, and move over here tomorrow to work with you."

That evening he entertained the alchemist to a feast, and they were happy in each other's company. That he also sent wine and dainties to the inner chamber goes without saying.

The following day Pan brought two thousand taels of silver to his country house, besides all the apparatus: retorts, stills, pelicans, bolt-heads and so forth which he had in his home. With his long experience of alchemy he knew all that was required, and soon had the necessary lead, amalgam and other ingredients ready.

"I appreciate the pains you are taking," said the alchemist. "But you will find my method different from those you are used to."

"That is just what I beg to teach me."

"This philosophers' stone of mine is the *lapis novenarius*. Nine days complete one cycle, and when nine times nine days have passed the cauldron can be opened and the philosophers' stone will be perfected. On that day you will come into a great fortune."

"I cannot tell you how grateful I am!" cried Pan.

Then the alchemist ordered his page to light the furnace and place the silver in the cauldron little by little. This done, he showed Pan his formula, poured some strange chemicals on the metal so that fumes of different colours arose, and sealed the cauldron with a hermetic seal. Last of all, he dismissed his servants.

"I shall be staying here for about three months," he told them. "Go home and inform my mother."

Accordingly they all left except the furnace boy.

Every day after that the alchemist inspected the furnace to

see the colour of the flame, but never opened the cau'dron. In his spare time he chatted, drank or played chess with Pan, until they became the best of friends. Pan also sent many little gifts to the concubine to win her favour, and she would send back some trifles with her greetings. More than twenty days had passed like this when a man in hempen mourning garments dashed, sweating, into the country house. It was one of the servants who had been sent home, who now kowtowed to the alchemist.

"The old lady is dead!" he cried. "Please go home at once, sir, to attend to the funeral."

The alchemist looked aghast, then fell weeping to the ground.

"Since your mother had reached the end of her natural span of life, you need not grieve too much," said Pan much dismayed. "Please do not distress yourself so."

"There is no one in charge at home, sir," said the servant to the alchemist. "You had better lose no time."

Then the alchemist dried his tears and turned to Pan.

"I meant to do you a good turn to show my gratitude; but now this great misfortune has befallen me, which I shall never cease to lament. The philosophers' stone is not perfected yet, and the process must not be interrupted; so I am in a quandary. Although my concubine is only a woman, she has been with me long enough to know the right temperature for the fire; so she could remain here to watch the furnace. But since she is young and has no one to look after her, I do not like to leave her here alone."

"What scruples can you have when we are such close friends?" demanded Pan. "By all means leave your lady here. No prying busybodies will come near the laboratory, and I can send some respectable women over to keep her company. Or, if you prefer it, she can sleep with my wife while I remain here. In this way we can watch over the cauldron until you come back. What objection can there be to that?"

The alchemist hesitated for a few moments.

"The news of my mother's death has confused me," he said at last. "I know that the men of old sometimes entrusted their wives and children to friends; and since you are so kind I agree to leave her here to watch the furnace while I go to attend to my mother's funeral. I shall come back soon to open the cauldron, and in this way I shall have discharged my duty to both sides."

When Pan heard that the concubine would stay behind to watch the furnace, he was ready to agree to anything in his joy.

"If you will do that," he answered, beaming, "we can see it to a successful conclusion."

The alchemist went inside to explain matters to his concubine, then brought her out to see Pan.

"Your task is simply to watch the cauldron," he charged her. "You must on no account open it. If you do anything wrong, you will be sorry for it later."

"What if you cannot return till after the eighty-one days are up?" asked Pan.

"After the silver has been exposed to sufficient heat, a few days more in the cauldron will only produce more of the philosophers' stone," replied the alchemist. "A little delay is of no consequence."

After some words in private with his concubine, he took his leave.

Since the alchemist had left his concubine behind, Pan was not troubled by fears that he might not come back for a long time or that the philosophers' stone might not be perfected. His one thought was that now he had a splendid opportunity to seduce the young woman, which he must not let slip. He was wondering distractedly how to set about this, when Spring Cloud came in.

"My mistress would like you to have a look at the furnace in the laboratory, sir," she said.

Pan hastily spruced himself up and hurried to the young lady's door.

"Your maid told me I might escort you to the furnace, madam," he called.

"Please lead the way," she answered sweetly. "I shall follow you."

Then she emerged from her room, swaying prettily, to greet him.

"You are my guest, madam," protested Pan. "How can I precede you?"

"I am only a woman," she replied. "How dare I presume?"

Thanks to this exchange of courtesies, though neither touched the other they remained face to face for several minutes. Finally Pan prevailed on her to go first with her two maids, and the sight of her tiny feet, like golden lotuses, fired his blood as he followed her. When she reached the laboratory, she turned to her maids.

"Unauthorized persons are not allowed in here," she told them. "Wait for us outside."

Pan hurried after her into the laboratory to inspect the cauldron, but the truth is he had eyes only for the young lady, whom he wished he could swallow alive. He had lost all interest in alchemy! Unfortunately the boy who tended the fire was there; so Pan could only cast admiring glances at the beauty without paying her any compliments. Only as they were leaving did he summon up courage to say:

"Thank you for accompanying me, madam. You must be lonely in your room without your husband."

The young lady said nothing, but smiled to herself and walked off without deferring to him. By now Pan was afire with passion.

"If there were nobody else there, I might succeed with her," he thought. "What a nuisance that boy is, who stays in the laboratory! If I can get him out of the way tomorrow before I ask her to visit the furnace, I should be able to have my way."

He ordered a servant: "Prepare some food and wine tomorrow for the boy who stokes the fire, and tell him that I am

treating him because he has been working so hard.   Be sure
to get him dead drunk."

That evening he drank disconsolately alone, thinking of the
beautiful concubine in the inner chamber and of all that had
passed that day.   Then pacing restlessly up and down he
chanted:

"They transplant a magnificent, beautiful bloom
In my poor cottage garden today;
But I sigh by my plain lowly terrace in vain,
For the spring is fast hasting away."

He walked to the hall and chanted this loudly several times
in the hope that the young woman would hear him; and presently Autumn Moon came out with a cup of fragrant tea for
him.

"My mistress heard you reciting poetry, sir," she said.   "And
thinking you may be thirsty she invites you to drink some tea."

Beaming with joy, Pan thanked her profusely.   And scarcely
had the maid left when he heard chanting from the inner room
too.

"Will no one pity the blossom,
The sport of the rough spring wind?
If only you will love her,
She will not prove unkind."

Then Pan knew that the beauty was favourably disposed
towards him; but he dared not break into her room, and as
soon as he heard her door shut he went to bed to wait for the
dawn.   The next morning, his servant invited the boy who
stoked the furnace to a meal; and tired of staying every day
by the fire, the lad was only too eager to accept; he did not
set down his wine cup until he was completely fuddled, then
fell fast asleep.   As soon as Pan knew that the boy was out
of the laboratory, he went to the concubine's door to ask her
to accompany him to inspect the cauldron; and she came out
as she had on the previous day and walked ahead of him to

the door of the laboratory, where she told her maids to wait
for her. Pan alone followed her inside. When they reached
the furnace and found the boy missing, she feigned surprise.

"How is it there is no one here?" she asked. "Why did you
let the fire go out?"

"Because I am afire," replied Pan with a laugh, "I told him
to leave his fire for a while."

"You shouldn't have let the furnace go out," she protested,
pretending not to have understood him.

"Let us heat it with our own fire," said Pan.

The young woman looked grave.

"How can anyone studying alchemy speak and think of such
things?" she asked.

"Your husband shared a bed with you here," countered Pan.
"Isn't that the same thing?"

The concubine had no good answer to make.

"That was right and proper," she murmured. "But you are
suggesting something wrong."

"We were destined to love," declared Pan. "This is right
and proper too."

And clasping her in his arms he knelt before her.

"What would my husband say?" she asked, helping him to
rise. "I dare not do anything wrong. But you have been so
good to me, I find it hard to refuse you. I will meet you tonight."

"Why not now?" begged Pan. "The evening is too far away."

"But someone may come in, and that would never do."

"I have taken care to keep the boy away, and nobody else
will come. This laboratory is so secluded that no one will
know."

"But the furnace is here," she protested. "If we spoil the
work, you will be sorry. This really won't do."

By this time, however, Pan had lost all interest in the philosophers' stone. He took her in his arms.

"I don't care if it costs me my life," he swore.

He waited no longer for her consent, but felt he was in
paradise.

"Our bliss was too short," he said presently. "You must grant me a night."

He went down on his knees to her again, and she hastily raised him once more.

"I promised to receive you tonight, but you would not listen," she reproached him. "How could you act like this beside the furnace?"

"I dared not let slip such an opportunity," replied Pan. "I couldn't help it."

"Shall I come to your room tonight, or will you come to mine?"

"Just as you wish."

"I have two maids sleeping with me, so my room is not convenient. Tonight I shall slip over to you; and tomorrow I shall tell my maids about you, so that you can come to me."

That night after everyone was asleep, she came to the hall where Pan was waiting for her, and he took her to his room. From then on they enjoyed themselves without restraint in his room or hers. Pan had never had such a wonderful adventure. He did not mind if the alchemist never came back and the philosophers' stone was never perfected. They had taken pleasure in this way for more than ten nights, when one day the gateman announced that the alchemist had returned; and, much taken aback, Pan had to welcome him. Presently the alchemist went in to see his concubine, and after talking to her for some time returned to his host.

"My concubine says that the seal has remained unbroken and the cycle of time has been completed," he said. "Today I have only just arrived. Let us open the cauldron tomorrow after we have sacrificed to the gods."

Though deprived of his usual night's pleasure, Pan found some consolation in the fact that the alchemist was back and would shortly present him with the philosophers' stone. The next day, after purchasing paper charms and offering sacrifice, they walked into the laboratory. Once over the threshold, however. the alchemist's face fell.

"What has caused this strange atmosphere?" he muttered to himself.

He opened the cauldron and looked inside, then stamped his foot.

"All lost! All lost!" he exclaimed. "The philosophers' stone has vanished in smoke, and even the silver base has turned to dross! Someone has ruined this by indulging in vice and lust here."

Pan turned pale and could not reply, for he knew this was the truth. The alchemist, meantime, was grinding his teeth with rage.

"Who else has been here?" he demanded of the boy.

"Only Mr. Pan and the mistress, who came here every day. No one else dared come in."

"How was the philosophers' stone spoilt then?" shouted the alchemist. "Fetch your mistress here at once to answer me that."

The boy hastily brought her.

"What did you do here while you inspected the furnace?" demanded the alchemist fiercely. "How does the philosophers' stone come to be spoilt?"

"I came here once a day with Mr. Pan to look at the cauldron," she replied. "The hermetic seal was never tampered with. I don't know how it can have been spoilt."

"I never said the seal had been tampered with," retorted the alchemist. "You're the one who must have been tampered with!"

He asked the boy: "Did you ever leave this place when Mr. Pan and your mistress were here?"

"Only once," replied the boy. "One day, when Mr. Pan treated me to a meal because I'd worked so hard, I had a few cups too many and fell asleep outside. That's the only time they were alone here."

"So that's it," sneered the alchemist.

He ran to his baggage roll and pulled out a whip.

"I'll teach you a lesson, you bitch!" he roared.

"I said it wouldn't do!" she cried, dodging the blows. "Mr. Pan is to blame for this."

Pan, quite dumbfounded, longed to sink through the ground.

"What did you say when I entrusted her to you?" demanded the alchemist with an angry glare. "Yet in the few days that I've been away you've done this vile thing. You are worse than a beast! How could a rogue like you hope to perfect the philosophers' stone? I have been too blind. Well, I had better beat her to death; it is no use keeping such a shameless bawd!"

He charged forward to beat his concubine, who fled in terror to her chamber while her two maids, who begged him to forgive her, received a stroke apiece for their pains. Seeing what a rage the alchemist was in, Pan had to kneel to him.

"I have behaved quite inexcusably," he said. "I am willing to say nothing of my loss if you will pardon me."

"You have only yourself to blame," retorted the alchemist. "It was your wickedness that caused the philosophers' stone to disappear in smoke. But why should I give you my favourite concubine, you lecherous dog? How are you going to make amends for what you did to her? I have a good mind to kill her and make you pay for it with your life!"

"Let me atone for my sin," pleaded Pan.

He hastily ordered a servant to fetch two large ingots of silver worth one hundred taels, then begged on his knees to be forgiven. But the alchemist did not even deign to look at him.

"I can make silver easily," he scoffed. "Why should I want yours?"

Pan kowtowed again and added another two hundred taels.

"With this you can buy another concubine," he said. "It was very wrong of me. Please forgive her for old time's sake."

"I don't want your silver," growled the alchemist. "But if a scoundrel like you doesn't lose money, you will never mend your ways. I'll take this to give to some charity."

He packed the three hundred taels of silver in his case,

summoned his concubine and servants, and made them move
all their baggage to the boat on which he had arrived the
previous day.

"I've never been so insulted in my life!" he swore as he
left. "Insolent slave!"

He swore all the way to the boat, which set sail as soon
as they were aboard.

Pan had been so terrified that the alchemist might kill his
concubine, that now, in spite of all the money he had lost, he
considered he had got off lightly. He honestly believed that
it was his fault that the silver in the cauldron had gone up
in smoke.

"I was too impatient," he reflected. "If I had waited till
the philosophers' stone was ready and then kept her here a
little longer, or if we had kept clear of the laboratory, it would
probably have been all right. It was my hastiness that made
me lose my silver. What a pity to meet a genuine alchemist
yet fail to get the philosophers' stone! Still, it was a marvellous
adventure while it lasted!"

He had no idea how thoroughly he had been tricked.

The fact is that when 'this swindler heard that Pan was
coming to Hangzhou, he had posed as an alchemist to cheat
him. He stayed with him for some time to inspire him with
confidence; and when a servant announced that his mother had
died and he hurried away, taking the two thousand taels of
silver with him, he left the young woman there to allay Pan's
suspicions. The seduction was planned too, in order that all
the blame might be put on Pan, who would have to apologize
and could not demand any compensation. The wretched man
fell into this trap, convinced that this rich stranger must have
the philosophers' stone. Little did he know that what he took
to be gold and silver utensils were plated copper and lead; but,
of course, no one drinking in the lamplight would think of
testing the metal. So he was cleverly taken in.

Even after being deceived like this, however, Pan did not
lose hope. He simply blamed himself for missing a golden

opportunity, and became more addicted to alchemy than ever. One day he met another alchemist who discussed the hermetic art with him, and Pan found this stranger so congenial that he invited him home.

"The other day," said Pan, "I came across a man who could really transmute base metals into gold and showed me how he did so, then started making the philosophers' stone for me. But unfortunately I offended him, so that he left without completing it."

"I can do that too," declared the stranger.

He proceeded to give the same demonstration, adding a pinch of powder to lead to turn it to silver.

"Good!" exclaimed Pan. "Last time I failed, but this time I shall surely succeed!"

He raised another thousand taels of silver for this alchemist, who called in two or three of his men to assist him. After seeing him make silver so easily, Pan trusted him implicitly and did not watch him carefully; so one night the stranger made off with the contents of the cauldron, and the following day was nowhere to be found. These two frauds left Pan quite bankrupt, and angry and ashamed into the bargain.

"To think of all the time and effort I've wasted over this business!" he lamented. "Last time I was to blame for what happened; but this time, when I thought everything was going smoothly, they cheated me! I'll see if I can track them down, because they must be up to the same tricks somewhere else. Or I may meet a genuine alchemist who will show me how to make the philosophers' stone."

So he packed up some clothes and began to roam the country.

One day, in a crowd by the West Gate of Suzhou, he came across the same gang. But just as he was about to denounce them they greeted him cheerfully as if he were an old friend, invited him to a clean table in a big tavern, and ordered wine and food.

"The other day we took advantage of your kindness," they apologized. "But this is our way, so please don't take offence.

Now we would like to discuss how to pay back what we owe
you and settle the matter."

"What do you have in mind?" he asked.

"We spent your silver as soon as we got it, so we can't return it to you. But there is a rich man in Shandong who has
also asked us to make the philosophers' stone for him. We
have reached an agreement with him, and as soon as our master
arrives he will give us the silver. However, our master is on
a long journey and will not be back for some time. If you will
take his place, as soon as this rich man hands us the silver we
will repay you. It is very simple. But if you refuse, we can't
pay you however much you may insist. What do you say to
this?"

"What sort of man is your master?"

"He is a monk; so we will have to ask you to cut off some
of your hair. Then we will travel with you as your disciples
to Shandong."

Eager to get his silver back, Pan agreed and cut his hair.
Then they treated him with respect and took him to Shandong, where they introduced him as their master to the rich
man. The latter invited him most deferentially to sit in the
hall and discuss alchemy; and since Pan knew a good deal
about this subject and was an educated man, he discoursed
learnedly and at length till his host was much impressed. That
same night the rich man produced two thousand taels of silver,
and arranged for the work to start the following day. Then he
invited Pan to drink, and had him carried when he was drunk
to an inner chamber to sleep. At dawn the tricksters discussed
how to set up the furnace; and as Pan knew some of the routine
he joined in their discussion and gave them certain instructions.
Then the silver was put in the cauldron to be melted; and the
men who were pretending to be Pan's pupils watched the furnace while their host took Pan aside to consult him and offer
him drinks, so that he could not get away. These rogues thereupon seized the opportunity to abscond with the silver, leaving their master behind. The rich man had no misgivings,

because the monk was still there; but when he discovered the next morning that the whole gang had disappeared, he seized Pan and threatened to hale him before the magistrate in order to apprehend the others.

"I am a native of Songjiang," protested Pan tearfully. "I don't belong to their gang. But I am interested in alchemy and not long ago they cheated me of some money. I met them later on the road, and they promised to pay me back after they had made the philosophers' stone for you if I would cut my hair and pretend to be their master. I came here expecting to get back my money, little thinking they would cheat you too and leave me in the lurch."

He wept long and loud. The rich man questioned him carefully and, after discovering that Pan was indeed a wealthy citizen of Songjiang who had formerly had dealings with his family and had been tricked into this, he decided not to prosecute him, and let him go. Then Pan, who had no money for the journey and was dressed like a monk, had to start begging his way home as a mendicant friar.

When he reached Lingqing Harbour he noticed a beautiful woman peeping out from behind the curtain on a big boat. Her face was familiar, and looking more closely Pan realized that she resembled the alchemist's concubine who had been his mistress.

"Could it be she?" he wondered.

When he approached the boat and made inquiries, he learned that she was a famous courtesan, who had been engaged by a young Henanese scholar on his way to the capital for the palace examination.

"Can he really have sold his concubine?" marvelled Pan. "It may be no more than a striking resemblance."

He wandered up and down near the boat watching the woman, until a maid came out from the cabin.

"Our mistress asks whether you are a native of Songjiang?" she inquired.

"I am." said Pan.

"Is your name Pan?"

"Yes. How did you know?"

Then the woman in the cabin called out: "Ask him to come over here."

Pan walked towards the cabin, and the woman addressed him from behind the curtain.

"I am the woman that alchemist called his concubine," she told him. "Actually I am a courtesan from Henan; but he told me what to do, and I had to carry out his instructions and help him to trick you. I'm afraid I did you a bad turn. But how did you get into a state like this?"

Pan told her sadly how he had been deceived again and was now trying to beg his way home.

"I can't help feeling sorry for you," said the woman. "I'll give you some money for the road, and you had better go home as fast as you can. If you come across any more alchemists, don't let them take you in. After being their accomplice, I know their tricks well; and if you will take my advice I shall feel I've repaid you for those nights of love."

She told her maid to give him a packet containing three taels of silver, which Pan accepted thankfully. Although she had turned out to be a courtesan, he was so grateful to her for helping him to reach home that he took her advice and never trusted alchemists again. However, his hair had been cropped and he had been covered with shame; so all his friends who heard of his misadventures had a good laugh at his expense. I hope this will be a lesson to all those who are obsessed by alchemy.

A Prefectship Bought and Lost

Who can foretell if fortune will endure?
When you have wealth, why should you strive for more?
Clouds change their shape each second in the sky,
And even oceans may at last run dry.

Human pomp and glory are nothing but vanity, and must not be considered true or enduring. Yet nowadays when men have a run of luck they think it will last for ever, and onlookers think the same; whereas actually it may vanish in a twinkling like smoke or ashes, for all too often the gold mountain becomes a mountain of ice.

The proverb says: Better to start poor but end rich than to start rich and end poor. How a poor man must savour the sweet after the bitter when he suddenly finds himself rich and respected! But if the once rich and mighty fall on evil days, their followers scatter like monkeys when their tree crashes down. Such a downfall is hard to bear. Yet while they prosper the wealthy and powerful behave exactly as they please, without any qualms of conscience and without caring whether they come to a good end or a bad.

This story is about a native of Jiangling named Guo Zhilang, who also lived during the reign of Emperor Xi Zong. Guo's father was a rich merchant in Central China, and Guo often accompanied him on his journeys by boat. After his father's death, Guo became the head of the family and the master of a great fortune and thousands of acres of land. His estates were so huge that no crow could fly across them, and his gold and silver so abundant that no thief could steal all his wealth. The richest man of the Upper Yangzi River Valley, Guo lent money

467

to all the merchants there and mixed solely with wealthy men.

Guo had one weakness which was only natural: when accepting payment he weighted his scales, when lending money he used sub-standard weights; moreover, he considered his silver as the best quality and that of others as the worst. So all merchants who borrowed from him lost by the transaction. They had to put up with this unfair treatment, though, for he had the capital. While the merchants suffered all the hardships of travel, Guo could tamper with the accounts in any way he pleased; but they could make their profit only by using his capital. If they offended him and he demanded repayment of his loan, then they were out of the game; so they put up with his squeeze because it was worth their while. Thus Guo's fortune grew from day to day, for money breeds money.

A very rich merchant, who had borrowed many thousand taels of silver from Guo to do business in the capital, had remained away for several years and sent no message back. At the beginning of the Qian Fu period (874-879), Guo remembered that this debt was not yet paid; and though his debtor was such a prosperous merchant that nothing was likely to go wrong, he wished he could send someone to the capital to collect payment.

"I hear the capital is a marvellous place where a man can have a wonderful time with singsong girls," thought Guo. "I may as well take this opportunity to make a trip there. First, I shall collect the debt; secondly, I shall have some fun with singsong girls; and thirdly, I may have a chance to get an official post which will set me up for life." So he made up his mind to go.

Guo was not married but had an old mother, younger brother and sister at home, as well as many servants and retainers. He told his brother and sister to look after their mother well, appointed a chief steward to manage his household, and left the others to their various tasks; then, taking with him a few servants who were used to travelling long distances on business for him, he set out for the capital. Since boyhood Guo had been accustomed to sailing on merchant junks and was a good hand at punting and rowing, so he did not find the journey hard, and before long he reached his destination.

The rich merchant to whom Guo had lent money was Zhang Quan, otherwise known as Moneybags Zhang. He owned several pawnshops and silk shops in the capital, and lent money to officials and bigwigs. He was a good negotiator too; and if he agreed to act as middleman or buy anyone an official rank or title, he was always as good as his word. Since all the citizens of the capital knew this merchant, Guo found him at once upon asking for him.

When his creditor arrived, Zhang remembered that it was Guo's money that had enabled him to come to the capital, set up in business and prosper; so he welcomed him heartily. After the usual exchange of compliments, Zhang ordered a feast and sent sedan-chairs to fetch a few famous singsong girls to keep Guo company. Both guest and host had a good time; and after the feast Zhang kept a beautiful girl named Wang Saier to sleep with Guo in the library. Since this was a rich man entertaining another rich man, it goes without saying that the room and the furnishings were of the finest.

The next morning, before Guo had got up or had time to mention the purpose of his visit, Zhang reckoned up his debt and found that principal and interest mounted to several hundred thousand taels. This sum he gave to Guo.

"I have been too busy to leave the capital," he said. "Besides, it would hardly be safe to travel with so much money, and I could not very well entrust it to anyone else; so I am a few years behind with the payment. I am very glad that you have come now yourself, so that we can settle this matter."

Guo was pleased by Zhang's good faith.

"I have never been here before and I have no place to stay," he remarked. "You have been good enough to pay me back my principal with interest; I wonder if I may trouble you now to find me lodgings?"

"I have many empty rooms," replied Zhang, "and I often invite friends to stay. How can an old friend like you think

of going elsewhere? I must insist on your being my guest.
Whenever you want to leave, you can arrange your journey from
here. I assure you it will be no trouble."

Guo was delighted, and moved into a large guest-house next
to Zhang's own residence. That same day he gave Saier ten
taels of silver for her services the previous night; and in the
evening he invited Zhang to a feast at which he asked the girl
to accompany them. Zhang did not want his guest put to any
expense, so he gave Saier ten taels of silver, bidding her return
the other ten. Guo, however, would not agree to this. They
pushed the money back and forth and, when neither would take
it, the girl was lucky enough to pocket both shares, to the
satisfaction of both men.

That evening the two merchants played drinking games with
the girl and had a gay time, enjoying each other's company so
much that they did not part till they were tipsy. Saier was a
noted courtesan. When she saw how rich Guo was, she used
all her wiles to charm him; and after two nights with her Guo
was completely bewitched. He would not suffer her to leave his
side or go back to her quarters; but from time to time she
invited other singsong girls from her establishment to drink with
Guo and amuse him, and he gave them innumerable presents.
On top of that, the procuress devised all manner of excuses to
ask for money: birthdays that had to be celebrated, purchases
that had to be made, debts that had to be paid, and so forth.

Since Guo was open-handed and spent money like water, a
band of parasites swarmed round him and persuaded him to
visit other courtesans. These spendthrifts from rich families are
never constant in their love, but drift from flower to flower and
court each fresh beauty they meet; so, apart from Saier, Guo
saw a great deal of other girls as well. And wherever he went
he scattered money recklessly. Then his worthless companions
introduced him to some young nobles who were fond of gambling, who cheated him so that he almost invariably lost, and most
of his silver found its way into their pockets.

But though Guo was fond of pleasure, he was after all a man

of property with an eye to the main chance. At first he spent lavishly because he had received so much interest in addition to his principal; but after two or three years he felt he had squandered enough and found, upon reckoning, that he had run through more than half his money. Then he thought of his home, and decided to go back. He broached the subject to Zhang.

"Now that Wang Xianzhi has revolted in the provinces," said Zhang, "the roads are cut. You must not think of travelling with so much money: you would never reach home. I advise you to stay here a little longer until things quiet down."

So Guo stayed a few days more. Then a vagabond friend of his named Bao Da happened to mention that, because of the military emergency and lack of funds, the government was selling official posts, the rank depending on the amount paid. Guo's mouth watered when he heard this.

"For a few million cash, what sort of post could I get?" he asked.

"The government is utterly corrupt," said Bao. "If you paid in the regular way, you would get a minor post only; but if you give a few million cash secretly to the officer in charge, you should get a prefectship at the very least."

Guo was shocked.

"Do you mean to say one can buy a prefectship?" he demanded.

"What honesty can you find in the world today?" retorted Bao. "With money you can buy anything. Haven't you heard how Cui Lie bought the post of Minister of Civil Affairs for five million? A commander's title is worth only the price of a drink; and a prefectship is not difficult to get either. Provided you go through the right channels, I guarantee you will have no trouble."

As they were talking, Zhang came in, and Guo jubilantly told him what they had been discussing.

"Yes, it can be done," said Zhang. "In fact, I have done it for quite a few people. But I wouldn't advise you to do this."

"Why not?" demanded Guo.

"It's hard to be an official nowadays," explained Zhang. "To do well you have to have backers and supporters, kinsmen at court and followers on all sides. Only then can you strike roots, make money, climb higher and higher and squeeze the people as shamelessly as you like. With backing and connections you can get away with anything. But you are all on your own. Suppose you do get a good post, if you have no one to stand by you when you arrive there, things may not turn out too well. Even if you do manage all right, remember that the government is out for all it can get. Since the authorities know that you bought your post, they will wait till you've been there one or two months and are doing well, then swoop down on you and smear you with mud. You'll find you've spent all that money for nothing. If it were good to be an official, I would have become one long ago."

"That's not the way to look at it," countered Guo. "I have plenty of money at home, but no official rank; and since it wouldn't be easy to take back the sum I have with me, why not spend some of it here? If I can get a gold belt and purple gown, I shan't have lived in vain. Even if I don't make anything out of it, what does it matter? I don't need the extra money anyway. I don't care if I don't do well; I shall have been an official. And even if my term of office is short, I shall still have the glory. I've made up my mind to this, friend. Don't try to dissuade me!"

"Well, if you are determined," answered Zhang, "I shall help you."

Then and there he and Bao Da discussed what steps to take. Bao Da had plenty of experience in such work, and Zhang was a substantial citizen who was used to big deals: between them they could arrange the matter easily.

In the Tang Dynasty people used copper cash, and a thousand cash made one string. Even when silver was used, sums were reckoned in terms of cash, one string of cash being equivalent to one tael of silver. Now Zhang and Bao Da privately sent five thousand strings to the officer in charge of

ranks — the treasurer to the eunuch, Tian Lingzi, and as able
a man as you could find. As luck would have it, a man named
Guo Han, who was about to be notified of his appointment to
the prefectship of Hengzhou in Guangxi, had just fallen ill and
died; and his letters of credence were still in the office. When
the officer in charge received the five thousand strings of cash,
he changed the place of domicile on the papers and gave them
to Guo, who thus became Guo Han.

The prefectship of Hengzhou once secured, Zhang and Bao
came with great joy to congratulate Guo, felt quite light-headed
and drunk with greatness. Then Bao Da hired a company of
actors and Zhang gave a feast. Guo changed into official dress,
and all his hangers-on hearing he had become a prefect came
to congratulate him too. With trumpets and drums they feasted
for a whole month.

As the proverb says: Flies gather on filth, and ants on grease,
while pigeons fly to the homes of the rich. Since Guo had been
known for his prodigal ways in the capital, now that he was a
prefect many begged him to be their patron, and these followers
became fiercer than their master. As stewards and runners they
heralded Guo's approach wherever he went, bullied local officers, and cheated traders and country folk. Then Guo felt he
was walking on air and, anxious to parade his splendour at
home, he chose a date for his departure. Zhang gave him a
farewell feast, and his good-for-nothing friends came with the
singsong girls to say goodbye too. Guo by now was very high
and mighty. While he haughtily distributed gifts as if these
people were far beneath him, they fawned on him because he
was a prefect, and put up meekly with all his insolence. If he
but glanced at one of them or mentioned his name, the man felt
overwhelmed with honour.

When this had gone on for several days, preparations were
made for the journey and Guo set off in great style, looking
every inch a high official. On his way he was thinking: "Now
I have not only a large property at home, but am also prefect

of an important prefecture. In future, there is no knowing how far I may go!"

With the prefect so pleased that he could not resist making a parade, the servants who had accompanied him to the capital boasting to the new followers of Guo's wealth, and the new men exulting to think what a wonderful master they had found, needless to say they gave themselves airs all the way to Jiangling, whether travelling by horse or by boat.

But when Guo reached his native place, he was shocked at what he saw. For —

No smoke was there, no sign of human life,
The whole deserted countryside was dead,
With charred and gutted ruins underfoot,
And withered, dying branches overhead.
White walls were stained with blood of those cut down,
Red beams were blackened with the flames of war;
The corpses lay unburied where they fell,
For ants to tear, for crows to peck and claw.
Upon the hens and dogs left homeless now
The savage wolves and kites were free to prey.
A man of stone or iron who saw this sight
Must shed a tear before he went his way!

This region had been laid waste by rebels, and barely one out of every hundred inhabitants was left. If not for the river which formed a landmark, nobody could have recognized the locality. When Guo saw this desolation, his heart began pounding; and when he reached his home and gazed around, he could not help giving a cry of despair. For the whole place was in ruins, his great mansion had been razed to the ground, and he did not know what had become of his mother, brother and sister, or all his household.

In fear and bewilderment he searched for several days until he found a former neighbour and learned that, when the place was plundered by the rebels, his brother had been killed and his sister carried off — to what fate none could tell! His mother was living with two maids in a tiny thatched hut near an old temple; but since all the other family retainers had fled and the money was gone too, she had nothing to live on but what she and her maids earned by their sewing. When Guo heard this he was cut to the heart. He quickly led his followers to where she was, and mother and son clasped each other and wept.

"Who could foresee the disaster that happened after you left!" sobbed his mother. "Now your brother and sister are lost, and we are penniless."

Presently Guo wiped his tears.

"It is no use lamenting," he said. "Luckily I have an official post, so there will be wealth and splendour coming to us. You mustn't worry, mother."

"What official post have you got?" she asked.

"Not a bad one," he replied. "The prefectship of Hengzhou."

"How could you get such an important post?"

"Now the eunuchs are in power, you don't have to pass the examinations to become an official. When I went to collect the debt from Zhang, he paid me back with interest; so I had plenty of money there, and I paid a few million for this post. I came home in style to see the family; and now I must travel post-haste to Hengzhou."

Then he ordered his servants to fetch his official cap and belt, and having donned his official robes he asked his mother to sit down while he kowtowed to her. After this he told his old servants and the new servants from the capital to kowtow to the old lady too. His mother felt a little comforted; but still she sighed.

"While you were doing so well outside, son," she said, "you didn't know that the family was broken up and every cent we had was stolen. If you hadn't bought this post, you could have brought more money home."

"You are talking like a woman, mother," protested Guo. "Won't I have money now that I'm a prefect? All officials nowadays make millions by squeezing the people. Since we have no property left, we had better leave here and go to my post.

After a year or two, we shall easily be able to restore our family fortunes. I still have two or three thousand strings of cash with me, quite enough for our present needs; so don't worry."

Then his mother's grief turned to joy.

"How lucky that you have managed so well, son," she said, beaming. "Heaven be praised! If you hadn't come back, I wouldn't have lived much longer. Now, when can we leave?"

"I was thinking of finding a good wife to share my splendour before going to my post," said Guo. "But it doesn't look as if we should wait for that. We had better go straight to my post. I'd like you to come aboard my boat to rest today, mother. As there is nothing to keep us here, tomorrow I shall hire a big boat, choose an auspicious day and start. The earlier we get there the better."

That evening Guo escorted his mother to the boat, leaving all her broken pots and pans in the thatched hut. He then ordered his men to hire a large vessel to take them all the way to Guangxi, had his baggage carried over the following day to the new junk, burnt sacrificial papers for luck, and set sail amid sounding trumpets and drums.

Both Guo and his mother looked cheerful, prosperous and haughty now. Guo had suffered no hardships but lived well all along; so although he looked proud and complacent, this was nothing new. His mother, however, had gone through such difficulties that she now seemed like one transported from hell to heaven. She felt puffed up to twice her normal size!

They travelled past Changsha down the Xiang River to Yongzhou. North of the river was a Buddhist Monastery called Douluchan Monastery, and here the boatmen moored for the night; for on the bank was a huge banyan tree, so large that it took several men to encircle the trunk, and they made fast the mooring rope to this tree, then pegged it to the ground.

Guo went ashore with his mother to visit the monastery, accompanied by attendants carrying official umbrellas. When the monks saw that this was an official, they came out to welcome him and served tea; and upon learning after discreet inquiries that this was the new prefect of Hengzhou, they became even more respectful and showed Guo and his mother round the whole monastery, stopping before each image of Buddha so that the old lady could bow in gratitude for his protection. When dusk fell they returned to their junk.

That night a high wind lashed the trees, heaven and earth turned dark, and a great storm raged.

> *Then the wind and the rain made display of their might,*
> *Like ten thousand swift horsemen that gallop by night;*
> *While the booming of waves was like drum beats in war,*
> *And the banks fell away at the thunderbolts' roar.*
> *Then the howling of tigers affrighted the air,*
> *And the dragons shrank back in their watery lair;*
> *Though the boat was made fast to a tree's mighty trunk,*
> *Yet the tree was uptorn, and the vessel was sunk!*

When this gale sprang up the boatmen were alarmed, but they thought their junk was fastened to such a large and deeply-rooted tree that it should be safe no matter how fierce the wind. While they were sleeping, however, there came a mighty crash. For the banyan tree was old and its roots had loosened the bank which was washed day and night by the river waves: thus it was by no means firmly rooted. Then the tree was big and bore the full brunt of the wind; and, on top of this, here was this heavy boat fastened to its trunk. When the wind beat against the junk, the vessel wrenched at the banyan which was already shaken by the force of the storm; and when the roots could no longer keep their hold on the loosened rocks, the tree fell with a crash on the boat. The tree was heavy and the vessel light, so water rushed in and the junk sank, its broken cabin planks floating away, while the servants who had been sleeping were washed overboard.

In less time than it takes to tell, the panic-stricken boatmen raised a cry and Guo awoke. Since he had learned to sail a boat when young, he helped the boatmen tug the rope until they got the prow of the junk ashore; then he hastily assisted his mother on to the bank. But though his mother's life was saved, the men in the back cabin had been swallowed up with all Guo's baggage by several great waves; and when the boat broke up they were drowned.

It was then pitch dark and the monastery gates were firmly bolted, so their cries for help went unheeded in the noise of the storm. Huddled there in their wet clothes, they could only beat their breasts and stamp their feet as they lamented their fate. They waited till dawn, when at last the monastery gate opened and they hurried inside to ask for the abbot whom they had met the previous day.

"Have you been robbed?" demanded the abbot, when he saw the state Guo was in.

Guo told him how the tree had fallen and sunk their boat. Quickly going to the bank, the monks were shocked to find the battered junk half under water, with the banyan tree lying across it. They ordered the monastery attendants to help the boatmen salvage what they could from the wreckage; but, alas, everything had been washed away by the waves. Nothing was left, not even the prefect's credentials. When the abbot had given Guo a quiet room where his mother could rest, Guo decided to report this accident to the Prefect of Lingling, requesting the authorities to issue a written statement of his loss in the storm so that he could proceed to his post. Having made this decision, he asked the abbot to send to the yamen; and the abbot, who was friendly with the prefect, sent a messenger with a report of the matter.

As everyone knows, however, troubles never come singly. Guo's mother, who had only just recovered from the shock of losing her younger son and daughter in the revolt, could not stand this second shock. Now that all their servants and money were lost, her face turned waxen for grief; she would take neither food nor drink but lay weeping sadly in bed, refusing to get up. Seriously alarmed, Guo tried to console her.

"As long as the forest is left, we need fear no lack of fuel," he said. "Although we have been so unfortunate, I still have my post. Once we reach Hengzhou, all will be well."

"Son," replied his mother, sobbing, "my heart is broken. I shall never get over this fright. You needn't try to comfort me. Even if you become an official, I shan't live to see it."

Guo still hoped that his mother would recover, and that the local authorities would give him a written statement so that he could go to his prefectship in Hengzhou and live well there. But the shock had indeed been too much for the old lady, for her illness proved mortal and within two days she was dead. Guo lamented bitterly, but there was nothing he could do. After consulting with the abbot, he called himself at the yamen to beg for help. The Prefect of Lingling had read the report of the accident a few days earlier, and knew that it was true; moreover since Guo was the prefect of another district, he, as a fellow official, was bound to help him. He could not wash his hands of the matter. So he sent men to have the old lady buried, gave Guo a generous sum for his journey, and saw him out politely.

Thanks to the Prefect of Lingling, Guo's mother had received a respectable funeral; but because Guo had to observe mourning for three years, he could not proceed to his post; and when the monks saw that he had no power, they gradually grew insolent and tried to get rid of him. Having no home to turn to, Guo was reduced to staying in the house of a Yongzhou dock-master whom his father had met during his travels. He had no money beyond what the prefect had given him, and this sum dwindled daily until soon it was exhausted. But what compassion do hucksters have? The dockers began to complain, and became less and less willing to supply him with tea, food and utensils. Guo, for his part, was well aware of their resentment.

"As head of a prefecture I am equal in rank to a baron," he protested. "Though I am in mourning, my day will come. How can you treat me so badly?"

"What's a prefecture?" retorted his host. "Even an emperor

who loses power will starve or fare ill. You have not gone to
your post yet, and even if you had, we don't live in Hengzhou —
why should we look after you? Fellows like us have to work
for a living. We can't afford to support idlers."

Guo had no answer to this. Tears welled up in his eyes, but
he had to swallow his humiliation. A couple of days later, his
host deliberately picked a quarrel with him, and his situation
became even more intolerable.

"My friend," said Guo to the dock-master, "I am all alone
in a strange place with no one to turn to. I know it is wrong
to have put you to so much trouble, but I have no choice. If
you know of any way by which I can make a living, please tell
me."

"People like you with high rank and low ability are not fit
for anything," replied his host. "If you want to find a job, you
must lay aside your official airs and work like an ordinary
labourer. That's the only way out for you. But are you willing
to do that?"

The suggestion that he should work for hire made Guo angry.
"I am still a local official," he said indignantly. "How can
I stoop so low?"

Then he thought: "The prefect here treated me quite handsomely. If I tell him of my difficulty, he is sure to find me a
way out. How can he allow a prefect to starve in his district?"

He wrote a card, but since he had no attendants he had to
take it to the yamen himself; and when the runners saw how
shabby he looked, they took him for some shameless fellow come
to beg for money, and would not accept his card. Only after
he had pleaded with them, told them his whole story and
described how liberally the prefect had treated him and attended to his mother's funeral — which the runners knew to be
true — did they consent to take his card in. But when the prefect saw Guo's card he was annoyed.

"How can he be such a fool?" he exclaimed. "When I heard
that he had this accident in my district and knew that he was

a high official, I treated him very well. Why should he come and trouble me again? Quite likely the tale he told me before was false, and he is a rogue who cheats people of their money. Even if his story was true, he must be a barefaced scoundrel who will never be satisfied. I acted out of kindness, but I seem to have laid myself open to trouble. Well, I won't arrest the fellow, but I'll pay no attention to him from now on."

He ordered his attendants to return Guo's card and tell him that the prefect would not see him.

After losing face like this, Guo was unwilling to leave. He sat down in front of the yamen and waited for the prefect to emerge, then called out for all the street to hear.

"Who is making so much noise?" demanded the prefect from his sedan-chair.

"Prefect Guo of Hengzhou!" shouted Guo.

"What proof have you?"

"I had credentials, but they were lost in a great storm which capsized my boat."

"Since you can produce no proof," replied the prefect, "how do I know that you are telling the truth? And even if your tale is true, I have already given you money for the road. Why do you go on making trouble here? You are obviously a rogue. If you don't clear off quickly, I shall have you beaten."

When the attendants saw that the prefect was angry, they started beating Guo with their rods, and he had to take to his heels. He returned despondently to his lodgings, where his host already knew what had happened at the yamen.

"How did the prefect treat you?" inquired the dock-master sarcastically.

Thoroughly ashamed, Guo sighed but dared not say a word.

"Didn't I tell you to lay aside your official airs?" went on his host. "But you wouldn't listen to me, so you got snubbed. Nowadays even the title of prime minister is not worth anything. You must stop dreaming and work for your living."

"What would you advise me to do?" asked Guo.

"Just think: what are you fit for?"

"The only thing I understand is rowing or steering a boat," said Guo. "I learned that when I was travelling with my father as a boy."

"Fine!" replied his host, delighted. "Plenty of vessels put in at this dock, and they often need boatmen. If I introduce you, you'll be able to make enough money to feed yourself."

Guo had perforce to agree. Thereafter he worked on the boats which passed there, and as time went by saved up a few strings of cash. When the traders in the market came to know him and learned his story, they nicknamed him Prefect Guo the Boatman; and when he was wanted on a boat, they asked for Prefect Guo. This song was also sung about him in the market:

What kept you, Sir Prefect, from going to Hengzhou?
'Twas Fate that willed it so.
Your post was a bought one, your office a short one,
For soon Fate brought you low!
Your rudder is now all your placard of office,
Your yamens are afloat;
And this is the end of a lordly official,
For now you row a boat!

After working for two years as a boatman, Guo's period of mourning expired. But with no credentials he could not take up his post; and to obtain fresh credentials in the capital, he would again have had to spend a few thousand strings of cash. How could he raise so much money? So he resigned himself to his life as a waterman. It is undeniable that a man's way of life sets its mark on his appearance; for when Guo was a prefect he looked like an official, but now that he had worked several years on boats he looked and behaved like a boatman. It is amusing, is it not, to think of a prefect ending in this fashion? And since it seems that human wealth and splendour count as nothing, I warn you, good people all, not to set too much store by power and profit.

The poor should not bewail their fate,
Nor the rich make proud display;
It is the end of life that counts,
And not the present day!

The Merry Adventures of Lazy Dragon

Great thieves have keen intelligence and guile,
And practise many a cunning trick and wile;
Enlist these gifts, my prince, for law and order,
And they will beat the foeman on our border!

In ancient times, Lord Meng Chang is said to have kept three thousand protégés, many of whom were night-hawks and pilferers. When he was detained against his will by the King of Qin, one of the king's favourite concubines sent him a message.

"I hear that Lord Meng Chang has a white fox fur coat worth a thousand pieces of gold," she said. "If he will give it to me, I will put in a good word for him so that he is allowed to go home."

Now Lord Meng Chang had already presented the only white fox fur coat he possessed to the King of Qin, who kept it in the palace treasury. How was he to procure another? One of his light-fingered protégés made a proposal.

"I can steal like a dog," said this fellow. "I'll get it for you from the palace."

What did he mean by this? He meant that he could imitate a dog's bark; so, pretending he was a dog, he vaulted over the palace walls as easily as if he had wings and stole the fur coat for the concubine, who then pleaded successfully for his master's release. That same night Lord Meng Chang hurried to Hangu Pass and, fearing the king might change his mind and come after him, was anxious to cross the border at once. When he learned that the gate did not open till cockcrow, he was frantic. Then another of his protégés said:

"I can crow like a cock. That's what's needed now."

He gave a long crow exactly like a cock's; and when he had done this two or three times all the cocks in the neighbourhood started crowing, the porter hearing them opened the gate, and Lord Meng Chang made good his escape. This lord had many protégés; but it was these two mimics who helped him to escape from the King of Qin. So it seems that all arts, no matter how humble, have their uses. Nowadays, however, only success in the civil service examinations leads to an official career — no other accomplishments are recognized. And when men of great wit and cunning are given no scope, many of them take to evil courses. If they were employed according to their ability they could make themselves useful, and this would prevent them from becoming thieves and outlaws.

In the Song Dynasty there lived in Hangzhou a famous thief called Here-I-Come. This was not his real name, of course; but when stealing he left no trace behind him save these three words written large on the wall; and only after seeing this inscription the next day would the inmates of the house look around and discover their loss. If not for this writing not a soul would have known of his presence, so great was his skill.

The citizens of the capital were so harassed by this housebreaker that many of them appealed to the government, and the city magistrate ordered his constables to make a careful search for Here-I-Come. Since they did not know his name, they had no idea whom to arrest; but since they were given a date for the arrest, they had to redouble their efforts. And no thief, however cunning, can conceal himself for ever. Sooner or later the authorities are bound to get on his track. So by dint of searching hard the constables finally caught the man and haled him before the magistrate, reporting that they had arrested Here-I-Come. Though they did not know his name, this was undoubtedly the culprit.

"What proof have you?" demanded the magistrate.

"We have made a thorough investigation, Your Honour," replied one of the constables. "There can't be any mistake."

"I am a good citizen," protested the prisoner. "I'm not that Here-I-Come. The officers were desperate to make an arrest; so they've made me a scapegoat."

"This *is* the man," insisted the constable. "Don't listen to a thief, Your Honour."

"We had a lot of trouble finding this fellow," put in some of the others, seeing that the magistrate was still dubious. "If Your Honour is taken in by his lies and lets him off, we shan't be able to catch him again."

Although the magistrate wanted to release the prisoner, he felt there might be something in what his subordinates said; and if he let the real thief go, he could hardly order his men to arrest him again. So he sent the man to gaol, where the prisoner promptly set about wheedling his gaoler.

"I know it is the rule that a man should offer the gaoler money when he enters gaol," he said. "But all I had on me was taken by those constables. I have some silver though, under a broken brick in the shrine of the Mountain God Temple; and I'd like to give that to you, brother, to show my respect. You can pretend you are offering incense there to get it."

Not certain whether to believe him or not, the gaoler ran over to have a look; and sure enough he found a packet containing more than twenty taels of silver. Was he pleased! After that he treated his prisoner very well, and they gradually became the best of friends.

"I have nothing here with which to show how I appreciate your kindness," said the prisoner one day. "But I have another package under the bridge. I'd like you to have that as a token of my respect."

"The bridge is always thronged with passers-by," objected the gaoler. "How can I take anything with so many people watching?"

"Take a basket of clothes, brother, and pretend to wash them in the river," said the other. "When you've got the package, just put it in the basket and cover it with clothes. Isn't that easy?"

By following these instructions, the gaoler secured the

package without being seen and found that it contained more than one hundred taels of silver. His joy and gratitude knew no bounds and, beginning to look on the prisoner as his own kinsman, that evening he bought wine to drink with him.

"I would like to go home tonight for a visit," said the prisoner as they were drinking. "I promise to come back before dawn. Will you let me out?"

"I can't very well refuse him," thought the gaoler, "after accepting so much from him. But what will happen if he doesn't show up again?"

"Don't worry, brother," said the other, seeing him hesitate. "Those constables brought me here as a substitute for Here-I-Come, but the magistrate couldn't condemn me because there is no real evidence against me. I am bound to be released sooner or later, so why should I try to escape? Please set your mind at rest: in less than four hours I shall be back."

The gaoler saw that there was reason in what he said.

"It's true that he hasn't been found guilty," he thought. "Even if he disappears, it shouldn't be too serious; and I can spend some of this silver he's given me to hush the matter up. Besides, there's always the chance that he might come back." So he agreed to let the prisoner go.

Instead of leaving by the door, the prisoner vaulted up on to the roof without making a sound on the tiles and vanished. Before dawn, while the gaoler was still in a stupor from the wine they had drunk the previous night, the man leapt down again from the roof, shook the gaoler and said:

"Here I am! Here I am!"

"So you kept your word!" exclaimed the other, starting up.

"How dare I risk getting you into trouble by not coming back?" asked his friend. "I am very grateful to you for letting me out, and I've left a little token of my gratitude in your house. You might collect it now and come straight back. I shall probably be saying goodbye to you before long, because I expect to be released soon."

Although at a loss to understand him, the gaoler hurried home.

"I was just thinking of sending you a message," said his wife. "Before dawn this morning, I heard a noise on the roof and a packet dropped into the room. When I opened it, I found it was full of gold and silver plates! The gods must have sent us this!"

Realizing that this was the gift from his prisoner, the gaoler hastily signed to his wife to be quiet.

"Hush!" he said. "Put it away. We'll raise money from the plates gradually later."

Then he hurried back to thank his friend.

Presently, when the magistrate took his seat in court, many people came to report cases of theft. Six or seven families had been robbed during the night, and on the wall of each house the thief had written "Here-I-Come"! These indignant citizens begged the authorities to arrest the criminal.

"I didn't think that man we committed to prison the other day was the real thief," said the magistrate. "Apparently Here-I-Come is still at large, and we have wronged an innocent man."

He ordered the gaoler to release his prisoner immediately and the constables to arrest the genuine thief by a certain date. Although the magistrate did not realize that he was releasing the true Here-I-Come, the gaoler was well aware of the fact. But he was so impressed by the thief's extraordinary skill — and so well bribed — that he kept his mouth shut.

But say, readers, when a thief is so cunning could he not be employed for worthier ends? No more, however, of these tales of former dynasties.

During the Jia Qing period of our own dynasty there lived in Suzhou a marvellous thief called Lazy Dragon, about whom many tales are told. Although a thief, he was loyal to his friends and fond of a joke; so, many of his adventures make amusing stories.

Think you that thieves love only plunder?
This daring burglar was a wonder.
His kindliness and princely ways
Secured him high renown and praise!

Up the first lane before Xuanmiao Temple in the east quarter
of Suzhou lived this man whose real name we do not know,
but who called himself Lazy Dragon and was generally known
by this nickname. From his childhood, Lazy Dragon was small
but brave, cunning and open-handed.

His limbs were soft as if he had no bones,
His step was light as if he rode the breeze;
He leapt on roofs or rafters with one bound,
And climbed up walls and parapets with ease.
He changed his tactics as the time required,
Could plan like lightning where to hide his loot;
Could make the noise of rat or cat or cock,
And imitate the sound of drum or flute.
He gave impersonations to the life,
So all who saw them would have sworn them true.
He came and vanished like a sudden storm —
A finer thief than this you never knew!

In addition to his great skill Lazy Dragon had some remarkable abilities and habits. From childhood he could walk
up a wall in his boots and imitate the accents of thirteen provinces. He could go for several nights without rest or sleep,
for days at a stretch without food or drink. Sometimes he
would consume several pecks of rice and several gallons of wine
at a sitting, yet not feel satisfied. At other times he would go
for days without food, yet not feel hungry. With straw ashes
in the soles of his shoes, he walked without a sound. And
when he fought, he moved as swiftly as the wind. Birds of
a feather flock together, and since Lazy Dragon could not hide
his talents he naturally mixed with other young loafers and took
to stealing. In those days there were several clever thieves,

but as soon as they saw Lazy Dragon's dexterity they knew that they were outclassed.

Lazy Dragon had never owned much property, and after he became a thief he left his home to drift from place to place, so that none knew where to find him. When he wandered about by broad daylight in public or slipped into some house, his shadow only could be seen flitting past — never the man himself. He would often pass the night in a rich man's house, curling up to sleep like a hedgehog among the rafters, under the raised floor of a pavilion, behind the screen or in the painted hall, as the fancy took him. And, whenever opportunity offered, he would steal.

Lazy Dragon's constant transformations and his habit of sleeping all day won him his nickname. He was also known as Plum Blossom, however, because after stealing anything he would invariably sketch a plum blossom on the wall — in white chalk if it was a dark wall and in charcoal if the wall was white.

There was a great storm at the beginning of the Jia Qing period, when sea serpents raged among the hills near Dongting Lake and a cliff by Taihu Lake crumbled to reveal an ancient tomb and a red lacquered coffin containing many jewels, all of which were promptly stolen. When news of this reached Suzhou, Lazy Dragon happened to be sailing with some friends on the lake, so he made his way to the spot. The vines binding the coffin had been severed and nothing remained inside but a skeleton, while beside the tomb lay a broken stone tablet bearing an old, blurred inscription. Lazy Dragon realized that this must be the coffin of some ancient nobleman, and out of compassion for the dead he sealed it up again, hired some local labourers to pile up earth, and poured a libation of wine over the new grave mound. This done, he was preparing to leave when his foot touched something in the grass, and stooping down he discovered an old mirror which, unknown to all, he hastily hid in his stocking. On his return to the city, his first act was to go to a quiet spot and clean the mirror. Its glittering surface was only four or five inches across, and the knob on its back was surrounded by monsters, sea-fish, dragons and waves. The whole was encrusted with a green patina stained by cinnabar and quicksilver and gave, when tapped, a clear tinkling sound. Knowing that this was a rarity, Lazy Dragon kept the mirror on him; and when night fell he discovered that it emitted light which made all around as bright as day. After that he carried it with him wherever he went and found it a great boon, for now he no longer needed a light at night. While others dreaded the dark, he could walk about as if it were day; and this made it even easier for him to steal.

Though a thief by profession, Lazy Dragon had a number of virtues: he never ravished women, never robbed good people or those in distress, and never broke his word. In fact, he was just and generous and would give away all he stole to the poor. All his dislike was for wealthy misers and moneyed men who had got rich by unjust means, whom he loved to mock by his pranks. Thus wherever he went people flocked to him, and his fame spread.

"I have neither parents nor family to support," he would say with a laugh. "So I borrow from those with a superfluity of wealth to help the poor. It is Heaven's will that the haves should help the have-nots — this is not simply my idea of justice."

One day Lazy Dragon heard that a great merchant had deposited a thousand taels with a weaver named Zhou, and determined to lay hands on that silver; but being slightly tipsy that day he missed the place and landed by mistake in a poor man's house where almost the only furniture was a large table. Having made an entrance, however, Lazy Dragon did not want to leave at once, so he hid himself under the table. Presently the master of the house sat down to a meal with his wife; but their fare was poor, and the husband's face was worried.

"That debt has fallen due," he told his wife, "but I have no means of paying it. I see no way out but suicide."

"You mustn't take your own life!" protested his wife. "You

had better sell me, and with the money you get start a small business."

Their tears were falling like rain when they were startled to see Lazy Dragon leap out from under the table.

"Don't be afraid," said he. "I am Lazy Dragon. I am here by mistake — I was really looking for a merchant I had heard of. You seem to be in a bad way, so I shall give you two hundred taels with which to do business. Take heart, and don't do anything desperate."

The unhappy couple, who knew him by reputation, bowed.

"If you will be so kind, we shall owe our lives to you," they said.

Then Lazy Dragon went out. Two hours later there was a thud within their closed door, and when they looked they found a cloth bag containing two hundred taels of silver — money Lazy Dragon had taken from the merchant. They nearly danced for joy. And later they set up a tablet bearing Lazy Dragon's name before which they did reverence as long as they lived.

A man who had played with Lazy Dragon as a lad lost all his money when he grew up, and was in rags when he met his former friend on the street. He hid his face with his fan for shame and would have gone past, but Lazy Dragon laid hold of him.

"Don't I know you?" asked the thief.

The other admitted in embarrassment who he was.

"Have you come to this!" exclaimed Lazy Dragon. "To-morrow I shall take you to a rich man's house to get some money. But don't say a word to anyone about it."

The other knew Lazy Dragon's ability and knew, too, that he always kept his word; so the next evening he sought him out and accompanied him to the mansion of an official.

The crows were winging through the dusk,
A mist had swathed the leafy trees,

No creature moved, no sound was heard,
But all was hushed in woods and leas.

Bidding his friend wait outside, Lazy Dragon leapt on to a tree and vaulted over the wall. He was away for a long time. Crouching with bated breath outside the wall, the poor man waited until dogs started barking and rushed towards him with bared fangs. As he ran around the wall to escape, he heard a faint splash on the other side of the wall; then something like a water bird alighted from a tree, and he saw Lazy Dragon — wet through and thoroughly crestfallen!

"For you I nearly lost my life!" panted Lazy Dragon. "There are piles of gold in there — bushels of it! But no sooner did I get the gold than dogs outside started barking and woke the people inside, who came after me. So I had to throw away the gold and take to my heels. It's too bad for you."

"You usually get whatever you want," said his friend. "If things have turned out like this today, it must be owing to my bad luck." He sighed and was very sorry for himself.

"Don't worry," said Lazy Dragon. "I'll do something for you another day."

So his friend left disconsolately.

More than a month had passed when Lazy Dragon met the fellow again on the road.

"I really can't carry on any longer," lamented the poor man. "Today I had my fortune told, and received a very lucky omen. The fortune-teller said I should come into sudden wealth thanks to a friend. I think that friend must be you — who else could it be?"

"Yes," said Lazy Dragon with a laugh. "I had nearly forgotten. I filched a box of gold and silver for you that day; but I was afraid that if I gave it to you then and the official's family raised a hue and cry, you might not be able to hide it. So to be on the safe side I left the box in the pool inside his courtyard. Now over a month has passed without any trouble;

he must have given up hope of recovering it, and it should be safe to collect it.   Let's go back there tonight."

As soon as it was dark the poor man called for Lazy Dragon, and before long they reached the place.

Swift as bird upon the wing,
He darted through the flowery brake;
Bold as dragon in the waves,
He cleaved the waters of the lake.

In a flash Lazy Dragon came back with a box on his back. Hastily repairing to a quiet spot, they opened the box, illumined it with the mirror, and saw that it was crammed with gold and silver. But Lazy Dragon took nothing. Without even troubling to find out how much there was, he gave the whole box to his poor friend.

"These treasures should last you a lifetime," he said. "Make good use of them, and don't be like foolish Lazy Dragon who has never been able to keep any property."

The poor man thanked him and took his advice. He used the money to set himself up in business, and later became a wealthy man. Such generosity was typical of Lazy Dragon.

You may say: No doubt Lazy Dragon was very skilful, but did he never run into trouble?

Well, readers, it is true that sometimes luck went against him and he found himself in a tight corner; but with his ready wit he could usually extricate himself. One day, for example, when he entered a house and found a wardrobe open, he slipped inside, meaning to steal some clothes. But before the inmates of the house went to bed they locked the wardrobe with a padlock so that he was a prisoner! As soon as he found he could not get out he hit upon a plan. Wrapping some clothes tightly round himself and making a big bundle of some more garments which he set against the door, he imitated the noise of a rat gnawing clothing.

When the master of the house heard this, he called for the maid.

"Why have you shut a rat in the wardrobe?" he shouted. "Do you want to ruin all our clothes? Hurry up and open the wardrobe to drive it out!"

The maid brought a torch and unlocked the wardrobe. But the moment she opened the door the bundle of clothes fell to the ground, and swift as thought Lazy Dragon rolled out after it, knocking the torch out of the maid's hand so that she gave a shriek. Afraid that more people would gather and make it difficult for him to escape, he seized the bundle, tripped the maid up, and was off. When the master got up and stepped on the maid, thinking she was the thief he started kicking and beating her; and she screamed at the top of her voice until the rest of the household heard the noise and rushed in. But when they lighted a torch, they found the master struggling with his own servant; and by the time peace was restored Lazy Dragon was far away.

Another time there was a weaver who received advance payment for a large order of silk. He kept the silver in a box on the inner side of the bed where he and his wife slept, so that they could guard it at night; but when Lazy Dragon heard of this money he determined to get it. Entering their chamber, he set one foot on the outer edge of the bed and reached over for the box on the other side. Just then the weaver's wife woke up and realized that there was something on the edge of the bed. Groping about in the dark, she caught hold of the robber's leg and held it fast.

"Quick!" she called to her husband. "Get up! I've got a thief here by the leg!"

That same instant Lazy Dragon took hold of the weaver's leg and gave it a hard pinch.

"It's my leg! It's my leg!" The weaver shouted with pain.

Thinking she had seized her husband's leg by mistake, the woman immediately let go. And while husband and wife were arguing the matter, Lazy Dragon grabbed the box and dashed from the room.

"It *was* a thief's leg," said she. "But you made me let go."

"My leg still aches from that pinch you gave it," declared her husband. "Thief's leg? Nonsense!"

"Your leg is inside," insisted his wife, "and the one I caught was on the outside. Besides, I wasn't pinching it."

"Well then," retorted her husband, "it was the thief who pinched my leg. But in that case you shouldn't have let go."

"You confused me by shouting," she countered. "So naturally I thought I'd made a mistake and let go. That's how he got away. Well, he's tricked us properly. He must have stolen our money."

When they felt for the box on the inner side of the bed and found it gone, they fell to accusing each other again and kept at it hammer and tongs for hours.

On another occasion Lazy Dragon broke into the storeroom of a second-hand clothes shop, and since it was dark took out his mirror in order to pick the best clothes. But —

The very walls have ears! Beware
The secret watchers everywhere!

There was an amorous couple awake upstairs in the house next door, and when they saw through their window a bright flicker of light in the storeroom, their suspicions were aroused. They knocked on the window and called to the clothier:

"Watch out, neighbour! There seem to be thieves in your house!"

Then the shop people sprang up in alarm, shouting: "Thief! Thief!"

Lazy Dragon had noticed in the front courtyard a huge pickle jar covered with matting, so now he raised this cover and crept inside, pulling the matting back into place after him. When the shop people had lighted lanterns and searched the whole premises without finding him, they went to the back yard.

"This jar is the only thing they missed just now," thought Lazy Dragon. "When they don't find me in the back, they are bound to look here. I had better hide in some place which they have already searched."

Realizing that his clothes were soaked with pickles and would leave a trail wherever he went, he stripped himself and climbed out of the vat naked to make pickle stains with his feet all the way to the gate. Then, leaving the gate ajar, he came back and hid himself in the storeroom.

After the shop people had searched the back yard, they returned with their lanterns to the front; and this time, to be sure, they uncovered the jar and found a suit of clothes inside which was none of theirs.

"These must belong to the thief!" they cried.

But then they saw the footprints from the jar to the gate which was wide open.

"The thief must have taken fright and hidden in the jar," they said. "When we went to the back, he took off his clothes and fled. It's too bad we let him slip through our fingers."

"Well, we're rid of him now," said the clothier. "Let's shut the gate and go to sleep."

Confident that the thief had gone, after setting things to rights they went back to bed and fell sound asleep.

All this time, however, Lazy Dragon was reclining comfortably on the bales of fine clothes in the storeroom. Now he chose the best, wrapped them tightly round himself and slipped an old, dark coat on top. He then did up some more finery in a cloth coverlet and, as dawn approached — having spent most of the night at this work — he picked up his swag, vaulted to the roof without rousing a soul in the shop, and jumped into the street. The sun had not yet risen, and as he was walking along he met three or four men, whose suspicions were aroused at the sight of this solitary figure carrying a heavy bundle at such an early hour.

"Who are you?" they demanded, barring his way. "Where have you come from? You must account for yourself before we let you pass."

Without saying a word Lazy Dragon reached behind his

back for a round package which he tossed to the ground; and while the other men were snatching at it he proceeded on his way. The bundle was so tightly wrapped that they were sure it must contain something precious; so they gathered round to undo it. As if peeling bamboo shoots, they unfastened layer after layer, only to reveal further layers underneath, each tightly bound to the next. Even after they had undone quantities of wadding one foot thick, there still remained an object as large as a fist.

"What can it be?" they demanded, snatching at it to unwrap it, and scattering the rags and cotton they had already removed on the ground. Just then another group of men came up.

"So you stole our clothes and are dividing the loot here!" cried the newcomers.

Without waiting for an explanation, they brandished their sticks and rushed forward. The men accused tried in vain to stop them, then fled — all but one old man who was seized. It was still too dark to see his face; but they belaboured him all the way back to the clothier's shop, ignoring his protests in their rage. Soon it grew bright, however, and the shopkeeper saw that the old man was none other than his son's father-in-law, who lived in the country. Though he ordered his assistants to stay their hands at once, the old fellow had already been beaten black and blue, and all the clothier could do was apologize and offer him wine to express his regret. He told him, too, about the theft.

"I was walking with two or three friends from our village before dawn," said the old man, "when we saw a fellow with a big bag on his back come towards us. We stopped him to ask him his business; but he dropped a bundle, and while we were snatching at it he slipped away. Who could have guessed that it was nothing but layer after layer of rags and cotton! After he tricked us into letting him go your men came up and, without finding out the right and wrong of the matter, started beating us and frightened my friends into running off. By now — luckily for him — the thief must be miles away."

When the shop people heard this they reproached themselves bitterly; and when the neighbours knew that instead of catching the thief the clothier had beaten his relative, they thought it a great joke. As for the bundle, Lazy Dragon must have made it while waiting to get out of the storeroom, so that if ever he were chased he could use it to delay his pursuers. These stories show his cunning in emergencies and his skill in getting himself out of tight corners.

The fame of Lazy Dragon, the marvellous thief, spread far and wide until Commander Chang of the garrison head-quarters in Suzhou heard of him and ordered his sergeants to bring this man to him.

"Are you the chief of the thieves?" he demanded.

"I am no thief, much less their chief," replied Lazy Dragon. "I have never been convicted in court or involved in a single case of robbery. I happen to know a few tricks and sometimes play pranks on my relatives and friends; but if I have done anything wrong, I beg Your Honour to over-look it. If ever you have need of me, you may be sure I shall gladly go through fire or water to oblige you."

The commander was impressed by his nimble appearance and frank speech; he considered that with no evidence it would be difficult to convict this thief; and now Lazy Dragon had promised to work for him and might prove useful. Accord-ingly he decided not to arrest him. As they were talking, a man named Lu who lived near the West Gate presented a cockatoo with a red beak and green plumage to Commander Chang, who bade him fasten the bird's chain to the eaves.

"I have heard that you are wonderfully light-fingered," said the commander to Lazy Dragon with a smile. "Though you claim merely to have played pranks but never stolen, you must have robbed a good many people in your time. And though I mean to pardon you, I would like to see your skill.

If you can take this cockatoo of mine tonight and return it to me tomorrow, I promise to let you off."

"That should not be difficult," rejoined Lazy Dragon. "Allow me to take my leave now. I shall return you your bird tomorrow morning." He then bowed and left.

The commander ordered two night watchmen to guard the cockatoo carefully, threatening them with severe punishment if anything should happen to the bird; so the two guards stayed glued to the spot. Although their eyelids were heavy they tried hard not to sleep, dozing off to waken again at the slightest sound as the hours dragged painfully by.

At the fifth watch, just before dawn, Lazy Dragon made an opening in the roof and let himself down into the commander's study. On a clothes-hanger he saw a dark brown silk cloak, on the table a cap, and on the wall a small lantern inscribed with the title: Garrison Commander of Suzhou. At once an idea came to him. Donning the cape and cap, he took out the smouldering spill he carried, blew up the flame and lit the lantern. Then holding the lantern so that its light would not fall on his face and imitating the old commander's voice, walk and manner to the life, he opened the door of the hall and walked out under the eaves. Since there was little moonlight then it was quite dark, and the two exhausted guards were nodding at their post.

"It is growing light," said Lazy Dragon, patting them on the shoulder. "You need not watch any longer. Off with you!"

As he spoke, he raised his arm to take the cockatoo by its chain, then swaggered back into the hall. The two watchmen had been having a hard time of it trying to keep their eyes open, and this sudden dismissal was as welcome as an imperial amnesty to a condemned man. Not suspecting for a moment that anything was wrong, they were off like a streak of smoke.

Soon day dawned and the commander came out. When he saw that the cockatoo had gone, he shouted for the guards;

but they were nowhere to be seen. He ordered them to be summoned, and they arrived still half asleep.

"I told you to watch that cockatoo!" bellowed the commander. "Where is it now? Why did you leave your post?"

"At the fifth watch you came out yourself, sir," protested the guards. "You took the bird inside and told us to be off. Why do you ask *us* where it is?"

"Nonsense!" roared the commander. "When did I come out? You must have seen a ghost!"

"It really was you, sir. We were both here. How could we both see something that wasn't there?"

The commander began to be suspicious. On going back to the study he happened to look up, so he saw the hole in the roof and knew how the thief had entered; and while he was puzzling over the matter he was told that Lazy Dragon had come to return the cockatoo. Commander Chang went out smiling to ask how he had done it, and was surprised and pleased when Lazy Dragon explained how he had masqueraded in the garrison commander's cloak and cap and taken the cockatoo to the study. The commander treated Lazy Dragon well thereafter; and the thief for his part took him various presents in exchange for Commander Chang's trust and protection. It is, alas! all too common for police officers to protect thieves.

> *What makes a cat content to sleep with mice?*
> *Why, both desire the same delicious fare.*
> *If those who capture thieves are thieves themselves,*
> *No wonder thieves are rampant everywhere!*

Lazy Dragon was always up to tricks. One day a gambler who had won a thousand cash in the gaming house was on his way home when he met the thief.

"Tonight I shall put this under my pillow," he told Lazy Dragon, pointing to his money. "If you can get it, I'll treat you to wine tomorrow. If you fail, you treat me."

"Done!" replied Lazy Dragon with a laugh.

When the gambler returned home he told his wife: "I did pretty well today. I'll put the money under my pillow."

His wife was so pleased that she killed a chicken and heated some wine for a little feast. They did not finish the chicken, however, and the good woman put away what was left in the kitchen. As they went to bed her husband told her of his wager with Lazy Dragon, and each urged the other to keep awake, little knowing that Lazy Dragon was already outside the window and could hear all they said. When he realized that they would be lying awake, so that taking the money would prove difficult, he hit on a plan. Going to the kitchen, he picked up a hemp stalk and chewed it to make a noise like a cat eating chicken. The woman sat up with a start.

"There is still half a chicken left — enough for a meal tomorrow!" she said. "I'm not going to let that dratted cat run off with it!"

Jumping out of bed she ran to the kitchen. Lazy Dragon immediately bounded to the courtyard where he dropped a large stone into the well. The big splash it made startled the gambler.

"Surely she hasn't fallen into the well just for half a fowl!" he exclaimed. "That would be no joke."

As he rushed out to look, Lazy Dragon slipped into the room and took the money from under the pillow. When husband and wife had called to each other in the dark and satisfied themselves that all was well, they walked back hand in hand to their bedroom. But finding the pillow moved and the money gone, they cursed their stupidity.

"The two of us were awake and on our guard, yet we let him fool us like that! Disgraceful!"

At dawn Lazy Dragon came to return the money and to demand that the loser pay his forfeit. With a laugh the gambler put a few hundred cash of his winnings into his sleeve and invited Lazy Dragon to a nearby tavern.

While drinking they discussed the theft, clapping their hands and roaring with laughter; and when the tavern-keeper asked what the joke was, they told him.

"I have always heard of your great skill," said the tavern-keeper to Lazy Dragon, "but I never could believe it before." Then he pointed at the pewter winepot on the table. "If you can take this pot tonight I'll treat you tomorrow," he said.

"Done!" answered Lazy Dragon with a laugh. "That's easy."

"I won't have you spoiling my door and windows, mind!" said the tavern-keeper. "I shall leave it on this table, and we'll see how you get it!"

"All right, all right!" replied Lazy Dragon, then left.

That night the tavern-keeper had the door well bolted, and searched the premises with a lamp to make sure that there was no way for Lazy Dragon to enter.

"I'll put the lamp on the table and sit here watching the pot," he decided. "I'd like to see what he can do then!"

He sat there till midnight, but nothing happened; and between boredom and exhaustion he found himself dozing off. At first he struggled to keep awake, but soon he could resist no longer and leaning his head on the table he started to snore.

When Lazy Dragon heard this snoring outside, he noiselessly climbed the roof and removed a few tiles. Then he fastened a pig's bladder on to a thin, hollow bamboo, and lowered it slowly into the winepot. The winepots in these taverns are broad at the base but narrow at the neck, so when he blew through the bamboo the bladder swelled up to fill the pot; and when he stopped the end of the bamboo he was able to pull the winepot up, after which he replaced the tiles exactly as before. When the tavern-keeper awoke, the lamp on the table was still burning but the winepot had gone. And when he looked around and saw that none of the windows had been forced, he could not imagine by what magic it had been spirited away.

Another time Lazy Dragon was standing with a few cronies by a tavern at the North Gate, when a young Fujianese gentleman whose boat had moored by the river bank ordered his attendants to air his clothes and bedding on deck. The bright silks and satins dazzled all who saw them, but they marvelled most at one coverlet of a rare and seldom seen material from the West. When Lazy Dragon's friends saw how the gentleman flaunted his wealth, they said:

"If we could filch that foreign coverlet from him, it would be rather a joke. Here's a chance for you to show your skill, Lazy Dragon. What are you waiting for?"

"I don't mind getting it for you tonight," chuckled Lazy Dragon. "Tomorrow you can return it to him and ask him for money for a few drinks."

After visiting a bath-house and washing himself clean, he returned to the riverside to watch for his opportunity. He waited till ten o'clock when the Fujianese gentleman and his friends, drowsy and half drunk, spread their bedding together on the cabin floor, blew out the lamp and lay down. Then swift as lightning Lazy Dragon leapt aboard, burrowed under the quilts and, chatting in the Fujian dialect, rolled this way and that so that the others complained they could not sleep. Still mumbling sleepily in Fujianese, Lazy Dragon jostled his bedfellows and created such a disturbance that he was able to take the foreign coverlet. Rolling it up he opened the cabin door, walked out and jumped ashore without any of the passengers realizing what had happened.

When dawn came and the loss of this valuable coverlet was discovered, a hubbub broke out aboard; and the gentleman, very much upset, discussed the matter with his friends. Although it was not worth going to court over a coverlet, he did not like to do nothing; so he offered a reward of a thousand cash to anyone who would recover it for him.

Then Lazy Dragon and his friends went to the boat.

"We have found the coverlet," they said. "If you give us the reward to buy wine, we guarantee to return you your bedding."

The gentleman ordered a thousand cash to be brought immediately and promised that this should be theirs as soon as his property was brought back.

"You might send a servant with us to fetch it," suggested Lazy Dragon.

The gentleman bade his steward accompany them, and they repaired to a Huizhou pawnshop where they found the coverlet.

"This comes from our boat," said the steward. "How did it get here?"

"Someone brought it in this morning," replied the pawn-broker. "When we saw that it wasn't a local product, we smelt a rat and wouldn't give him the money. 'If you don't trust me,' he said, 'I'll find a friend to be my guarantor. You can be weighing out the silver for me while I fetch him.' When we agreed he left, and that was the last we saw of him; so we knew it must be stolen property. Since it belongs to your boat, take it. And if that fellow comes back, we shall catch him and send him over too."

They took the bedding back to the Fujianese and told him what the pawnbroker had said.

"We are strangers here," said the young gentleman. "I am quite satisfied to have recovered my property — why should we look for the thief?"

He gave the thousand cash to Lazy Dragon and his friends, who spent it in the tavern. The man who went to pawn the coverlet had, of course, received instructions from Lazy Dragon to leave it there while they went to claim the reward. This was just one more of his many tricks.

A practical joker like Lazy Dragon knew how to make things hot for anyone who annoyed him. Once a party of thieves invited him to go with them by boat to the Huqiu hills to drink and enjoy the scenery. At Shantang they moor-ed behind a rice shop and passed through the shop to buy fuel and wine; but the rice merchant, who objected to having this boat moored at his back door and these pleasure-seekers passing in and out, swore at them and tried to drive them away.

The thieves were protesting indignantly when Lazy Dragon winked at them.

"Since he doesn't want us to pass through his shop, let's move further downstream and find another landing place," he said. "Why lose your tempers?"

He bade the boatmen cast off, but the thieves were still angry.

"It's not worth arguing with such people," said Lazy Dragon. "Tonight I'll get even with them."

They asked what he proposed to do.

"Find me a boat this evening," said Lazy Dragon. "And leave me a keg of wine, a hamper of food, and a stove and fuel to heat the wine. I mean to row back to enjoy the moon all night. You'll understand my scheme tomorrow — there is no need to disclose it now."

That night after feasting at Huqiu they went their different ways, having agreed to meet Lazy Dragon early the next morning. He kept only a good drinker as his companion and an able punter, who returned with him on the small boat to the rice shop. The shop was already closed, and since there were many boats on the river that evening with passengers aboard fluting, singing and enjoying the moon, the men in the rice shop went to sleep suspecting nothing. Lazy Dragon moored his craft close by the rice shop's back door.

He had observed during the day that there was a rice bin in one corner of the shop over the water next to the back door; so now he took from his sleeve a small knife, cut out a knot in the wooden door, took from his pocket a bamboo tube, thrust the tube through the hole into the bin, and gave it a gentle shake. Immediately rice from the bin started cascading down the tube like water; but the noise Lazy Dragon made by toasting the moon and shouting and laughing as if he were tipsy drowned the swish of the rice. Passing boats had no inkling of what was happening, much less the shop people sleeping inside.

In the early hours of the morning when rice stopped flowing from the tube, Lazy Dragon knew that the bin was empty; and by then their cabin was full too, so he bade the boatman cast off and they punted slowly away. Presently they reached a quiet spot where all the thieves had gathered as arranged, and Lazy Dragon explained what he had done. They clapped and roared with laughter as he bowed.

"Divide this between you," he said, "as a token of my thanks for last night's party." He himself took nothing.

Not till the rice shop assistants opened that bin did they discover that it was empty; but they could not conceive when or how the rice had disappeared.

There was a time in Suzhou when hundred-pillar caps were all the rage, and every young man of fashion swaggered about in one. The Taoist priests of White Cloud Monastery near Nanyuan also bought such caps in secret, to wear when they went out to enjoy themselves disguised as laymen. One summer day they decided to set off for the Huqiu hills the following morning, so they booked a boat and ordered a feast. The third son of Weaver Wang was friendly with these Taoists and often joined them on their jaunts in which each paid his own way; but since he always expected others to treat him and was rowdy after drink, the priests decided not to ask him this time. Young Wang got wind of their scheme, however, and was annoyed at being left out; so he asked Lazy Dragon to help him spoil their fun. Lazy Dragon agreed, slipped into White Cloud Monastery and stole the priests' Taoist caps.

"Why didn't you take their new caps?" asked Wang. "What use are these priestly caps?"

"If they lost their new caps, they wouldn't go to the Huqiu hills tomorrow," replied Lazy Dragon. "What fun would that be? Don't you worry. Just see what trick I play on them tomorrow."

Mystified as he was, Wang had to let Lazy Dragon have his way.

The next day the priests disguised themselves as young gentlemen in light gowns and caps, and set off by boat on their pleasure trip. Dressed in black, Lazy Dragon followed them aboard and squatted at the helm, so that the Taoists took him for one of the crew, while the boatmen thought he was the gentlemen's attendant. When the boat started the priests unbuttoned their clothes and took off their caps to drink and make merry; and Lazy Dragon seized this opportunity to pick up the new caps and stow them in his sleeves, substituting for them the priestly caps which he had stolen the previous day and kept in his pocket. When they reached the bridge and moored, Lazy Dragon jumped to the bank and made off. The priests were about to put on their gowns and caps to stroll ashore when they discovered that their hundred-pillar caps had gone, while neatly folded and piled in their place were the priestly caps of gauze which they usually wore!

"How extraordinary!" they exclaimed. "Where are our caps?"

"Don't ask us," said the boatmen. "You put them there yourselves. There's no hole in the boat: they can't be lost."

The Taoists looked round once more, but still found no trace of their caps.

"There was a small fellow in black aboard, who has gone ashore now," they said to the boatmen. "Call him back, will you? He may have seen our caps."

"He isn't one of us," said the boatmen. "He came with you."

"He wasn't with us!" the priests shouted. "You must have worked in league with a thief to steal our caps. Those caps cost several taels apiece. Don't think you can get away with this!"

They seized the boatmen and would not let them go; and when the men protested indignantly and loudly a crowd gathered on the bank to watch, and a young man stepped forward and leapt aboard.

"What is all the trouble about?" he asked.

The priests and the boatmen told their different versions of the story; and since the priests knew this man they thought he would help them. But with a stern look he started reproaching them.

"You are all Taoist priests," he said. "Naturally you would come aboard in Taoist caps. Your own caps are here. What hundred-pillar caps could you have? You are obviously blackmailing these boatmen."

When the onlookers heard that these were Taoist priests who had their caps there but were accusing the boatmen of taking some other caps, they raised an indignant outcry. Some local idlers and busybodies even stepped forward shaking their fists.

"Curse these thieving priests!" they cried. "Let's beat them up and send them to the magistrate!"

"Don't beat them!" cried the young man, waving his hand to stop the bullies. "Let them go!" Then he leapt ashore.

Fearing trouble if they delayed, the priests urged the boatmen to cast off at once. Their fine caps gone and their disguise seen through, they could not roam the hills in any case; so they started glumly back, their money wasted and their pleasure spoilt.

Now who was the man that jumped aboard? It was young Wang. Lazy Dragon let him know after he changed the caps; so while the priests were raising a hubbub, Wang came forward to show them up and spoil their fun. Having reached their destination, the Taoists were still refusing to let the boatmen go when Wang sent a man to return their caps and tell them: "Next time you decide to have a feast and show off these caps, be sure to let Master Wang know."

When the priests received this message, they realized that young Wang had made fools of them and guessed that this was Lazy Dragon's work, because they had heard of his fame and knew he was Wang's friend.

At that time, in the neighbouring county of Wuxi, there lived a magistrate who was notorious for his rapacity.

"The magistrate of Wuxi has piles of gold and jewels in his yamen," someone told Lazy Dragon. "And all his treasures

are ill-gotten gains. Why don't you relieve him of some of them
to distribute among the poor?"

Lazy Dragon thought this was a good idea. He went to Wuxi
and crept stealthily one night into the magistrate's mansion,
where he was struck by the luxury that met his eyes.

> *With silk and cloth the chests were crammed,*
> *With precious stones the shelves were rammed,*
> *With silver ingots all the floors were strewn.*
> *The pots were not of earthenware,*
> *But all of gold or silver rare;*
> *Each poker was of ivory there,*
> *Of precious horn each spoon!*
> *The ruin of many homes, indeed,*
> *Was caused by this official's greed;*
> *He squeezed the whole place dry by wicked rule;*
> *But while he strained each nerve to squeeze yet more,*
> *He styled himself Protector of the Poor!*

There was more wealth here than Lazy Dragon could count.
"The gates are locked," he reflected, "and watchmen keep
sounding their clappers and bells outside. It will be difficult
to take much."

Then he saw a small cask which was so heavy that it must
contain gold or silver; and he was taking this when it occurred
to him: "Since this is the yamen, I had better make sure that
the magistrate doesn't punish innocent people tomorrow."
Taking out his brush he painted a plum blossom on the wall by
the shelf, then quietly left by way of the eaves.

Two or three days later the magistrate, looking through his
treasures, discovered the loss of a small cask containing more
than two hundred taels of gold, which was worth over a thousand
taels of silver. Then his eye fell on the plum blossom drawn
near by, which looked recently sketched. He was dumbfounded.

"This is obviously not the work of any of my men," he
thought. "But who could enter my chamber and coolly draw

this plum blossom as his sign? This is no common thief. I must catch this fellow."

He summoned some sharp-witted police officers to look at the mark left by the thief, and the constables were amazed when they saw it.

"We know who it is, Your Honour," they announced. "But he can't be caught. This is the work of Lazy Dragon, the wonder thief of Suzhou. Wherever he goes he draws a plum blossom as his mark. His is no ordinary skill, for he can come and go in the most miraculous manner; and he is so loyal to his friends that he has many devoted followers. To try to catch him would stir up worse trouble than the loss of some gold or silver. You had better let him go, Your Honour. It is not safe to offend him."

"You scoundrels!" declared the magistrate angrily. "If you know who it is, why can't you catch him? You people are in league with thieves and try to protect them. I've a good mind to have you all beaten; but I'll let you off for the time being so that you can go out and arrest him. And I warn you: if you fail to bring him to me within ten days, you will pay with your lives!"

When the police dared not answer, the magistrate ordered his secretary to draw up a warrant for two of the constables to take, and to inform the magistrates of Suzhou and Changzhou that he wanted this criminal apprehended.

Much against their will, the two constables travelled to Suzhou, and no sooner had they entered the West Gate than they saw Lazy Dragon standing there. They patted him on the shoulder.

"Friend!" they said. "We don't mind your robbing our magistrate; but why did you have to show off by drawing the plum blossom? Now he has ordered us to arrest you by a certain time. What do you say to that?"

"Don't worry, friends," replied Lazy Dragon coolly. "If you'll step into a tavern with me, we can sit down and talk."

He took them to a tavern where they chose a table and started drinking.

"This is my proposal," said Lazy Dragon. "Since your magistrate is so keen to arrest me, I certainly won't make things difficult for you. But if you will give me one day's grace, I shall send a message to him which will make him cancel the warrant and countermand his order for my arrest. How about it?"

"It's all very well to say that," rejoined the constables. "But you took rather a lot from him — all gold he said it was — so how can he just let the matter drop? If we go back without you, we'll get into trouble."

"Even if you insist that I go with you," reasoned Lazy Dragon, "I haven't got the gold any more."

"Where is it then?"

"I shared it with you as soon as I got it."

"Stop joking, old fellow!" they protested. "You'll find this no laughing matter in court."

"I've never lied in my life," retorted Lazy Dragon, "and I'm not joking. You've only to go home to see." He lowered his voice to whisper: "You'll find the gold in your gutters."

The officers knew his skill. "If he makes a statement like this in court," they reflected, "and if it's true that there are stolen goods in our homes, we shall be considered his accomplices."

"Very well," they agreed. "We dare not ask you to come with us. What do you propose to do?"

"If you go back first," said Lazy Dragon, "I'll follow immediately; and I guarantee that the magistrate won't dare press the matter. I would never do anything to land you in trouble." Then he took from his belt about two taels of gold and gave it to them. "This is for your travelling expenses," he said.

As flies to blood, so officials are drawn to money. The constables' eyes sparkled at the sight of that ruddy, glittering gold, and they pocketed it with broad grins. The suspicion that this gold probably came from the magistrate's cask made them more reluctant than ever to arrest Lazy Dragon.

When they had left, Lazy Dragon travelled by night to

Wuxi. He got there the following morning and entered the magistrate's house after dark. This magistrate had a wife and a concubine, and since he was sleeping this night with his wife, his concubine was alone in her bed. Lifting her bed curtain Lazy Dragon groped about till he found her glossy hair coiled in the shape of a dragon, and gently clipped most of it off. Then he found the magistrate's seal box, prized it open, put the coil of hair inside and closed the box again. This done, he drew another plum blossom on the wall, and slipped away without touching a single other thing.

The next morning, upon waking, the concubine was surprised to feel her hair tumbling about her neck; and when she put up her hand and found her long tresses gone, she gave a shriek which roused the whole household. Everybody came rushing to find out what had happened.

"Who played this cruel trick and cut off my hair?" sobbed the concubine.

This was reported at once to the magistrate, who hurried over. When he found her shorn like a nun in her bed, he could not imagine what had happened; but he was grieved and horrified at the loss of her lovely hair which had floated down like dark clouds.

"Last time gold was stolen, and the thief has not yet been caught," he mused. "Now another bad man has been here. Nothing else matters very much; but what if he has taken my official seal!"

He called quickly for his seal box which was brought to him, sealed and locked as usual. Upon opening it, he was relieved to find the seal still in the top compartment; but then he noticed some hair, and the removal of the top shelf revealed a thick coil of hair underneath. He examined his other treasures, but nothing was missing. Then he saw another plum blossom on the wall, making a pair with the first.

"What, again!" uttered the magistrate in consternation. "Finding me after him in earnest, he has played this trick as a warning. By cutting off my concubine's hair, he means to show that he can cut off my head! By putting the hair in the seal box, he means that he can take my seal. This man is a thoroughly dangerous character! The constables were right the other day to advise me not to offend him. If I don't stop, I shall get into great trouble! The gold is a trifle; I can make it up by squeezing a few rich men. I had better let this matter drop."

He hastily ordered the two officers sent to Suzhou to be recalled, and cancelled the warrant.

Upon leaving Lazy Dragon, the two constables had gone straight home to search their gutters as the thief had directed; and, sure enough, each found a sealed packet of gold bearing the date of the theft in the magistrate's yamen. Not knowing when Lazy Dragon had planted this money there, they could only suck their fingers in amazement.

"It's a good thing we didn't arrest him," they said. "If he confessed and they found the stolen goods here, we should never have been able to clear ourselves — not if we had a hundred tongues. But what answer are we to give the magistrate?"

They were worrying over this with their assistants when a messenger arrived from the yamen and, thinking he had brought a warrant for their arrest because they had failed to catch the thief by the time appointed, they were even more alarmed. It turned out, however, that he had brought a countermand. And when the constables asked the reason, the messenger told them what had happened in the yamen.

"The magistrate has had the fright of his life!" he said. "How dare he arrest Lazy Dragon?"

Then the two officers realized that Lazy Dragon had kept his promise by going back to the yamen to play this remarkable trick.

Towards the end of the Jia Qing period the magistrate of Wujiang was a crafty, cruel officer whose greed and corruption were notorious. One day he sent a trusted runner with presents to Suzhou to request Lazy Dragon to call on him in Wujiang County. Lazy Dragon accepted the gifts and went.

"In what way may I be of service to Your Honour?" he asked.

"I have long heard of your fame," replied the magistrate. "And I want to entrust a secret mission to you."

"I am nothing but a vagrant," replied Lazy Dragon. "Since you show such regard for me, I will go through fire and water to carry out your wishes."

Then the magistrate dismissed his attendants in order to speak freely.

"The imperial inspector has reached my county and means to find fault with me," he said. "I want you to go to his yamen and steal his official seal, for then I can make him lose his job. That would please me, I can tell you! If you succeed, I shall reward you with a hundred taels of silver."

"I shall bring you the seal without fail," promised Lazy Dragon.

He was away for half the night, coming back with the inspector's seal which he courteously presented with both hands to the magistrate.

"How clever you are!" exclaimed the magistrate, overjoyed.

Hastily rewarding Lazy Dragon with a hundred taels, he bade him leave quickly for another county.

"Thank you, Your Honour, for your gift," said Lazy Dragon. "But may I ask what you intend to do with the seal?"

"With this seal in my hands," chuckled the magistrate, "I shall stop him from taking any action against me."

"I am so grateful for your kindness," said Lazy Dragon, "that I would like to offer you some advice."

"What is it?"

"I hid myself for half a night above the rafters in the inspector's office, and I saw him going through the official reports by lamplight, writing swiftly and endorsing documents. This shows that he is a quick-witted, capable man, and no trick can fool him. I would advise Your Honour to send the seal back to him tomorrow, saying that it was found during the night by a watchman but that the thief has escaped. Even if he has his suspicions, he will be grateful to you and a little awed, and will certainly not find fault with you."

"How can I stop him from having his way if I return his seal?" demanded the magistrate. "No, no, that doesn't make sense. Be off with you now, and don't worry about me."

Then Lazy Dragon dared say no more but left quietly.

The next day when the inspector opened his seal box, he found it empty. He ordered all his household attendants to make a thorough search, but they could find nothing.

"The magistrate knows that I have a low opinion of him," he thought. "Since this is his territory, he must have his spies everywhere; so he has sent someone to take my seal. Well, I know how to deal with him."

Ordering his attendants to say nothing of his loss, he sealed the box as before; then on pretext of illness he stopped attending office, ordering all official documents to be sent to the chief of police for the time being. The magistrate knew that this was not a real illness and laughed up his sleeve; but after several days etiquette demanded that he call on his superior officer to inquire after his health. When the inspector heard that the magistrate was at the gate, he ordered his attendants to open the side door and invite his guest into the inner chamber where he lay in bed. There he chatted pleasantly about local customs, questions of administration, taxes and duties, speaking frankly and cordially and offering his visitor one cup of tea after another. Puzzled by these signs of cordiality, the magistrate was beginning to feel rather embarrassed. But as they were chatting, word was suddenly brought that the kitchen had caught fire; and attendants, runners and cooks rushed in.

"The fire is coming this way!" they shouted. "Run, Your Honour!"

The inspector's face fell. Hastily rising, he picked up his seal box, which was locked and sealed, and gave it to the magistrate.

"May I trouble you to keep this safely for me in your office for the time being?" he requested. "And will you send men to put out the fire immediately?"

The magistrate was panic-stricken, but dared not refuse: he had to leave with the empty box. By then all the local firemen had gathered, and they put out the fire. Only the two kitchens were burned; all the offices were uninjured; and the inspector ordered the gates to be closed. Everything had happened in accordance with the instructions he had given after his seal was lost.

When the magistrate reached home he thought: "The inspector has put this empty box in my hands. If I return it like this, when he opens it and finds the seal missing he will hold me responsible."

In vain he racked his brains: he could not think of a way out. Finally he had to moisten and remove the sealing paper, put the stolen seal back into the box and seal it up again. The next morning when the inspector had taken his seat in court the magistrate returned the box, and the inspector asked him to stay while he opened it and put his seal on all the documents he had left unsigned. That same day the inspector announced his departure and left Wujiang. He told the provincial governor about this theft, and together they reported the magistrate's evil deeds to the government and had him dismissed.

After Lazy Dragon became so well known, he was occasionally suspected of thefts committed by others. When a dozen silver ingots disappeared from the treasury of the Suzhou prefectural government, the officers said: "The thief has left no trace. He may be Lazy Dragon."

Lazy Dragon had, in fact, had nothing to do with this theft; but when he saw that he was considered responsible, he decided to get to the bottom of the business. Suspecting the warden of the treasury, he hid himself one night in a dark corner of the yamen, then went to eavesdrop outside the man's room.

"Since I took that silver," he heard the warden say to his wife, "everybody has started suspecting Lazy Dragon. That's a stroke of luck. But Lazy Dragon will never plead guilty; so tomorrow I'm going to write out a detailed account of his thefts and send it to the prefect. Then, you may be sure, he will be arrested and have to shoulder the blame."

"This looks bad!" thought Lazy Dragon. "I had nothing to do with this, but now the warden who stole the silver in his charge wants to clear himself by pinning the theft on me. And since all officials stick together, and my record isn't exactly spotless, I shall never be able to prove my innocence. It would be better to fly. I don't want to be tortured for something I didn't do."

He left the same night for Nanjing, where he roamed the streets as a blind fortune-teller. But some time later a man called Zhang from Suzhou Prefecture, who was very good at spotting thieves, happened to visit Nanjing and knocked into Lazy Dragon on the street.

"This blind man looks odd," thought Zhang.

A closer look satisfied him that this was Lazy Dragon in disguise. He took him aside to a quiet spot.

"There is a warrant out for your arrest," said Zhang, "because of that silver you stole from the treasury. That's why you've fled here and disguised yourself like this. But you can't deceive me."

Lazy Dragon took Zhang's hand.

"You know me," he said. "You should be able to clear this matter up for me, instead of taking the same line as the rest. That silver was stolen by the warden of the treasury himself — I heard him admit as much to his wife when they were in bed. I swear this is the truth. But he was plotting to put the blame on me and I was afraid the prefect might believe him, so I fled here. If you will go to the yamen to report the matter, you will receive the government reward and clear me at the same time; then I shall make you a present too. Don't spoil my trade here now."

Since Zhang had been commissioned by the prefectural government to investigate this theft, now that he had a reliable clue he left Lazy Dragon and went back to Suzhou to make a report. And when the warden of the treasury was examined

THE MERRY ADVENTURES OF LAZY DRAGON

and the silver found in his house, Lazy Dragon's innocence was established. After receiving a government reward for solving this case, Zhang went back to Nanjing where he found Lazy Dragon still walking the streets as a blind man. Zhang went up to him and nudged him.

"Your Suzhou trouble has been cleared up," he said. "How is it you've forgotten your promise to me the other day?"

"I didn't forget it," replied Lazy Dragon. "Look in your rubbish heap at home and you will find a little token of my gratitude."

Zhang was very pleased, for he knew that Lazy Dragon never lied. He took his leave of the thief and went straight home where he found a package of gold and silver buried in the ashes of his rubbish heap next to a glittering dagger! Then Zhang shot his tongue out in dismay.

"This man's really dangerous!" he muttered. "He's put this dagger here with his gift so that I won't dare to interfere with him another time. Heaven knows when he hid these here — his skill is amazing! I certainly won't risk offending him again."

When Lazy Dragon learned from Zhang that he had been cleared in Suzhou, he knew that he was in no immediate danger; but he feared that if he remained a thief he would be arrested in the end, so he decided to give up stealing and make an honest living as a fortune-teller. He stayed for a few years in Changgan Temple where he died eventually of old age. Although so celebrated a thief, he was never bastinadoed and never had his arm tattooed in punishment, while even today the citizens of Suzhou like to relate his endless pranks and tricks. Such a prince of thieves is infinitely superior to those men in official robes who say one thing but mean another, and will commit any injustice in their greedy search for personal gain. With his wonderful skill, if Lazy Dragon had been able to spy behind the enemy's lines or to lead a surprise attack at night, he could have achieved great deeds. Unfortunately he lived in a time of peace when literary attainments alone were highly regarded, and his escapades could merely furnish material for the gossips.

Half the world are thieves today —
True! But this we can't gainsay:
One like him — so just and brave —
Must be dubbed an honest knave!

www.ingramcontent.com/pod-product-compliance
Lightning Source LLC
Chambersburg PA
CBHW020624020726
47494CB00001B/33